THE DEVIL'S DELIGHT

Alasdair almost found the power of restraint. Almost. And then Vanessa's lower lip trembled yet again.

Restraint washed away, the undertow drowning common sense with it. Resistance channeled into another, stronger sensation. Desire, sharp enough to stab through him like a lightning bolt.

His throat tightened around a groan as he angled his head and slanted his mouth over hers. There was never a sensation to match the feel of Vanessa's lips — so incredibly soft — beneath his.

He thought a quick, simple taste would slake his curiosity as well as his desire for her. He was wrong. The second their lips met, Alasdair knew *quick* was not what he wanted. As for *simple,* well, there was naught about either the woman or the situation they now found themselves in that could be misconstrued as simple.

It was as though a drop of liquid fire had been siphoned into Vanessa's blood; it spread hotly throughout her body. Her lips parted to release a sigh. Of pleasure or surprise? Vanessa was unsure. Nor did it matter, for the sound never came. The Devil deepened the kiss to a feverish pitch, his mouth swallowing any sound she might have made.

When had this happened? Alasdair wondered as he eased the kiss, his mouth now devouring her full, honey-sweet lower lip.

When had he begun feeling desire for her at all?

REBECCA SINCLAIR

SCOTTISH ECSTASY

ZEBRA BOOKS
KENSINGTON PUBLISHING CORP.

ZEBRA BOOKS

are published by

Kensington Publishing Corp.
475 Park Avenue South
New York, NY 10016

First Printing: May, 1993

Printed in the United States of America

Prologue

English East March, on the Border
October 1585

"Hugh Forster, accuser of Alasdair Gray?"

"Aye."

"Come forward," Robert Carey ordered as, with a sigh, he glanced down at the list of grievances. As Warden of the English East Marches, the responsibility of seeing each complaint settled to the satisfaction of both parties on this October's Day of Truce fell heavily on his shoulders. 'Twas not going to be easy, he thought as he scanned the list. Not only was the tally of Alasdair Gray's crimes long, and in places vague, but both Gray and Forster looked equally hostile.

So, too, did their respective clans.

As on every Day of Truce, tension between English and Scots ran high, yet never could Robert remember the potential for violence seeming greater than it did today. He'd hoped the strain would ease as the day wore on. It hadn't. Tempers had been held firmly in check ever since the two groups had arrived with the dawn at the designated spot on English soil. But the assurances of temporary peace, given and received by both sides, had sounded unusually stilted.

Robert sucked in a steadying breath and glanced uneasily around him. The band of burly-looking Scots sat to his right, the English to his left. Animosity between the two conflicting factions, hotter than the fire separating them, crackled in the air. The very second he'd called the Gray/Forster bill, Robert noticed that both parties had openly glared at each other. Their gazes, as well as their random comments, were becoming increasingly bold, alarmingly insolent.

The uncomfortable feeling he'd awakened with that morning blossomed. The wild Border region of Scotland and England had cultivated Robert's instincts, sharpened them. Those instincts were now telling him something he didn't care to hear, that the Gray/Forster trial was not going to go as smoothly as the ones preceding it.

Unfortunately, common sense argued there was naught to be done about it. The bill had been called, and Hugh Forster now stood beside Robert, waiting impatiently for the trial he'd instigated to commence. As Warden of the English East March, and since George Humes, Warden of the Scottish East March, had declined to attend — not as uncommon a practice as it should be — Robert's work was mapped out for him. He knew what had to be done, and he set about doing it with determination.

Clearing his throat, Robert eyed the huge, darkly bearded man to his right, and repeated flatly the words he'd asked so many times he could recite them in his sleep: "Hugh Forster, for articles stolen, shall you fair price make, and truth say what your goods be worth at the time of their taking, to have been bought and sold in market all at one time? For . . . er, other matters, will you accept the decision of this court as law, abiding by its decree, even should it be against you? And will you swear you knew no other recovery or vindication but this, so help you God?"

"Aye," the big Scot grumbled. "I swear it."

Ah, Robert thought, now for the difficult part. His gaze lifted, scanning his countrymen. Could he be lucky enough to find that The Devil, as Alasdair Gray was called these days, had not graced the Day of Truce with his presence? "Alasdair Gray?"

"Aye."

Robert's hopes were dashed in that one, gravelly uttered word. He sighed. "Come forward and answer the complaints lodged against you."

A murmur sifted through both groups as the man in question stepped forward. He took his place on Robert's left, facing his accuser.

Alasdair Gray's posture was supremely confident; his shoulders proudly squared, his spine rigid. His strides were long and agile. Even when standing in a relaxed pose, as he appeared to be doing now, his stance suggested caution and acute awareness. So did the thick, battle-roughened fingers that fisted the hilt of the broadsword hanging at his hip.

Was there anything about The Devil that wasn't larger than reality itself? If so, Robert's shrewd eye couldn't detect it.

Beneath the padded leather jack and long trews — both of which were customary Border reiver attire — the young man's body looked superbly muscled; his shoulders wider than most, his chest thicker, his voice deeper and more commanding. His dark head towered a good four hands above his adversary's, making Hugh Forster look short and squat by comparison. Robert, shorter and thinner than both men, felt like a child sandwiched between two such impressive specimens.

Beneath the shaggy mane of raven-black hair, The Devil's face was harshly carved. Too harshly carved, Robert had heard some say. Too hawklike to be pleasing to the eye, others agreed, though rarely to The Devil's face. They proclaimed his brow too wide, his cheekbones too high, his jaw too hard and square. Just as many staunchly argued that the chiseled sculpture of Alasdair Gray's face was not only intriguing, but the harshness was countered by his eyes. Piercing and narrow, set deeply below low-riding brows, The Devil's eyes were of a nebulous hue that might be either cautious gray or passionate blue, depending upon his mood.

Right now those eyes were a mocking shade of gray. A hint of a cocky smile tugged at one corner of his lips as his attention strayed over Robert's head. The Devil's gaze met Hugh Forster's, and one of the younger man's inky brows tipped his old adversary a challenge.

Forster returned the insolent expression with a feral growl that might have been a curse, an insult, or, more likely, both.

A murmur sifted through the men who stood on the fringes of the gathering. Though not directly involved in the dispute, most had come today specifically to hear this trial. Wagers were inconspicuously — and illegally — placed. While both Gray and Forster men had sided in accordance with whom each pledged his allegiance to, the rest, who swore loyalty to neither, began sizing up the strengths and weaknesses of the two opponents.

It was a commonly shared opinion that Alasdair and Hugh were well matched. Hugh Forster's reputation as a Border reiver to be feared stood without question, while the younger reiver had been busy of late carving a choice reputation of his own.

Aside from the accusations he'd been called here to answer, Alasdair Gray, while only six and twenty summers, could already boast of numerous successful raids, trods both hot and cold, and imaginative defenses of his home keep, Cavnearal. His daring and skill with a broadsword was as legendary as his temper. His arrogance two summers past, when he'd boldly wrested Dunnaclard Keep out of Forster hands for a fortnight, spoke for itself.

The exploit had taken gall and skill to execute — but then, those were traits The Devil possessed in abundance. Few amongst those gathered here today would have attempted such a feat. Fewer still would have been successful.

Alasdair Gray had succeeded brilliantly. Albeit only for the short fortnight. That coup, coupled with his recent activities, had earned The Devil the reputation of a reiver to be watched; closely by all, and fearfully by those unlucky enough to live within raiding distance of Cavnearal.

The men fell silent when Robert Carey's gaze shifted warily between the two rivals. "Alasdair Gray?"

The Devil inclined his head, waiting patiently until the deafening cheers of his men, and the derogatory booing and hissing of Forster's, had faded before responding casually. "Aye?"

"Do you swear by heaven above you, hell beneath you, by your part of Paradise, by all that God made in six days and seven nights, and by God himself, that you are innocent of art, part, way, having or resetting of any of the goods, beasts and . . ." He glanced down at the paper in his hands and, his brows arching, picked out several crimes that fell under neither category. Frowning, he improvised. "And all else named in this bill, so help you God?"

"I do."

Robert nodded, then began reading the first of what was starting to look to his weary eyes like an endless list of grievances. He decided to begin with The Devil's more severe crimes. "You, Alasdair Gray, are hereby charged by Hugh Forster of Clan Forster, Keeper of Dunnaclard, with kidnapping his daughter, Vanessa Forster, on the twenty-third of October, in the year of our Lord, 1584. You are accused of . . . er, ravaging her repeatedly, then returning her, her good character and virtue besmirched, to her father at Dunnaclard."

Robert sighed and continued. "In an associated complaint, you are charged with then riding against the Clan Forster at Dunnaclard on the twenty-fourth of November, of stealing beasts amounting to fifty-seven pounds, and of kidnapping Vanessa Forster yet again. You are accused of prisonering her at Cavnearal for an unspecified number of days, besmirching her already tarnished reputation beyond repair. These, Alasdair Gray, are the first and most serious complaints filed against you." Robert glanced at The Devil, and thought the nickname apt. The young man's expression was hard as stone, his gaze guarded and unemotional. "How say you?"

After thirty very long, very tense minutes had ticked past, one Englishman leaned close to another and whispered, "He's gone daft! Listen to him! But for the first bill of kidnapping, m'lord has fouled all fifteen bills by confession. What the bloody hell is Alasdair Gray doing?!"

The second man scratched his shaggy brown head in confusion. "I don't know. What *is* he thinking of?"

"I can tell you what he's *not* thinking of," the first man huffed. "*Us.* There's not enough shillings in London and Edinburgh combined to pay the fine our young laird is acquiring. 'Twill mean Cavnearal's old and sick go hungry this winter should he even *attempt* to pay the Forster, God rot 'em." His open palm slapped the trampled dirt near his hip. " 'Tis not right, I tell you. Not right at all."

The second man scowled, and his gaze strayed questioningly to his laird. Alasdair's spine was rigid as ever. His gray eyes narrowed, his gaze rarely leaving Hugh Forster's face.

The second man shifted his attention to Forster, and noticed that the man's pudgy cheeks took on a ruddy hue when The Devil fouled yet another bill by confession. Hugh Forster's narrow green eyes flashed impotent rage; with his adversary conceding to the list of grievances, Forster was being denied the legal battle he hungered for.

The second man leaned toward the first and whispered sharply, "I'm of a mind that paying the Forster might not be what m'lord has in mind."

It was the first man's turn to scowl. "What else could he be after? Surely, he knows Cavnearal cannot meet Forster's price, in which case we'll be forced to accept . . ."

The second man nodded, and his smile came slow and easy. "A pledge," he supplied when the first man's voice trailed away. " 'Twould make sense, would it not? If the Forster's price is not met, which it most assuredly cannot be, then the Forster must accept a pledge of The Devil's choosing."

"Aye, I see your point, but . . ."

The thoughts of both men drifted back to another trial, held on a Day of Truce exactly one year prior.

Unlike now, on that unseasonably warm October day Alasdair Gray had been the accuser, Hugh Forster the accused. The fine in question had been steep. Far too steep for the Forster to pay.

A pledge—a man who would willingly surrender himself to the Grays and live with them until the fine was paid in full—had been offered, and grudgingly accepted.

The tradition of pledging was centuries old, a highly respected Border custom practiced by both English and Scot alike. What had been decidedly *un*common about that particular pledge, on that particular day, was his identity.

The pledge had been Hugh Forster.

Chapter One

"Daft, Vanessa. Our whole cursed family's gone daft and *that,* as they say, is that."

"Aye, Duncan, now hush up. And watch where ye step before ye fall."

Fall? Ooch! that was the *last* word Duncan Forster needed to hear right now. He inhaled quickly, deeply, and surrendered to an urge that had been tugging at him for a while now. He glanced down.

Way, *way* down.

His fingers clenched into trembling fists, and he winced when his knuckles scraped the cold, moist stone that made a solid wall at his back. Was it his imagination, or did the ledge he stood upon look narrower of a sudden? Nay, he admonished harshly, of course not. *Narrow* was what the stone shelf jutting out from the acres-long plateau of rock upon which Cavnearal sat had looked like twenty minutes ago . . . when he'd foolishly let his sister talk him into stepping onto it.

The ledge no longer looked narrow. That worried Duncan. What worried him more was that, at some point, the stone walkway had thinned. Now, in the

15

shimmering light of a quarter-moon, the craggy ledge looked virtually nonexistent.

Swallowing hard, Duncan sent his sister a worried glance. "We're both going to die, lass. Ye realize that, I hope?"

"Stop your exaggerating," Vanessa snapped irritably. A gust of wind blew in off the sea, tossing her shoulder-length raven curls about her face and neck. Smoothing the tangled strands away from her eyes with one hand, she leaned back against the stone wall and gestured to the precariously narrowing ledge with the other. Since her brother was in front, she couldn't continue on until he did; the walkway was too narrow for her to go around him. "Keep moving, Duncan, and soon this will all be naught but an unpleasant memory. I promise, someday we'll laugh about this night's adventure."

"I've me doubts," he replied flatly. As though drawn by a magnet whose force was too strong to resist, his gaze was once more pulled downward. Duncan gulped, and instantly assessed the distance between the shadowy edge and his booted toe. An inch, maybe two, was all that separated him from a deadly drop. One miscalculation . . .

He shuddered. The glance he sent his sister was grave. "Promises mean naught to a dead mon, lass."

The way his voice cracked made Vanessa look up sharply. Flattening her back against the rough stone wall, she squinted at her younger brother, and traced his horrified gaze down.

Down.

And then down some more.

Her green eyes widened when she focused on the vague, moonlit spot where the foamy waves of the Firth of Maryn crashed over the deadly boulders below the overhanging ledge.

Far, *far* below it.

The air left Vanessa's lungs in a rush; in much the

16

same way the color drained from her cheeks. Though it wasn't possible, she could have sworn she felt the vibration of churning whitecaps eroding the centuries-old stone.

The sea air smelled tangy; it felt chilly as it whipped at her hair and face. By comparison, her insides felt much, much colder. Trying not to let her tone reflect her nervousness, she said, "Think of Da rotting away in the Gray's dungeon, Duncan. And think of how proud he'll be when his youngest son rescues him near single-handedly. If *that* does naught to inspire ye to reach the end of this ledge, nothing will."

Duncan frowned. Did he detect a faint quiver in his sister's voice? Heaven above, he did, he realized, and in the same instant, felt his own tension mount. Unlike their three older sisters, Vanessa was not a woman who disturbed easily. In fact, it usually took quite a lot to get her nettled. If she was nervous now, that meant there was something to *be* nervous about.

'Twas a disquieting thought, that.

His gaze shifted to the ledge. God's blood, it was narrow! "Vanessa," he sighed, his gaze shifting to his sister, "who's to say Da is rotting away in any dungeon? 'Tis feasible The Devil's taken pity on him and decided to treat him fairly, as a laird of Hugh Forster's station demands he be treated. Is it not possible Da be, even now, partaking of Cavnearal's fine food and ale . . . while we, on the other hand, slip unnoticed to a watery grave?"

"Aye, Duncan," she snapped impatiently, "there's a chance of it. A very *small* one. Maun I remind ye that, while The Devil is known for many things, compassion and generosity are not rumored to be two of his virtues?"

"Ye needn't. However, I feel the need to remind *ye* that the same rumor — a Border ballad, actually — eludes to Cavnearal as an impregnable fortress. Better than ye and I have tried to breach these walls, lass,

17

only to meet with disappointment. What makes ye think we can succeed where so many others have failed?"

"I've a plan," Vanessa murmured, again nodding to the ledge.

Duncan shook his dark head and refused to budge another life-threatening inch. "Aye, I've heard it. And dare I say there's naught original about it?"

Curling her fingers into tight fists, Vanessa restrained the urge to slap the boy. She and Duncan had discussed the situation before leaving Dunnaclard. If her brother had doubts, he'd kept them to himself. And now, she thought irritably, was *not* the time to be airing them! "All right," she snapped. "Truth to tell, Duncan, I've several plans. If the first does naught to free Da, we'll simply move on to the next. And the next, if need be. One is *bound* to succeed."

"And if none do? What then, lass?"

Gritting her teeth, Vanessa recited the Ten Commandments. Backward. Feeling properly composed — if not a bit wicked, for the Reformation had been sweeping through the country — she said with rigid calmness, "Trust me, one will."

"Ooch, therein lies the problem. I'm thinking that trusting ye in this matter was not the smartest thing I've ever done."

Vanessa glanced nervously at the moonlit ledge that twisted at a slight incline around the rock. Lord, but it *was* narrow, wasn't it? "Aye, Duncan. And *I* be thinking that if ye dinna start walking, I swear by all that's holy I'll end the suspense here and now and shove ye over the edge myself."

He cocked one dark eyebrow at her and, thankfully, began to take slow, cautious steps along the cliff. "Ye could live with me death on yer conscience, lass?"

"Nay," she murmured as, her back plastered to the moist stone, she inched carefully behind him. "But I could free Da—and that is, after all, the crux of this mission. The sooner we whisk him away from The Devil the better." A shiver that had nothing to do with the coolness of the night raced down her spine. Every story of horror she'd ever heard told of The Devil, that black-hearted reiver, rushed through her mind. Her blood ran cold. "Who knows the tortures poor Da's suffered already at that mon's hand. I pray we reach him in time."

"The Devil's had Da but two days, lass."

"Aye, two days too long. Have a care, Duncan. There's a gap scarce half a foot to yer right."

Duncan, whose concentration had been more on their conversation than on what he was doing, glanced down. His heart stopped, and his green eyes widened when he saw a break in the stone. Had Vanessa not been paying such careful attention to their surroundings . . .

Sucking in an unsteady breath, he maneuvered himself over the tricky piece of ledge with painstaking care, then reached for his sister's hand. He didn't breathe easily again until they were both safely across the perilous, foot-long breach in the stone.

"Not much farther," Vanessa said encouragingly. "By my estimation, we be near the southern tip of the rock. The ledge narrows a wee bit ahead and—"

"More? It narrows *more?*"

"Aye. The walk goes up and around here for another few score yards, then we'll be finding the grooves I told ye of. The ones carved into the stone. With luck, Duncan, those notches will help us scale the top."

Her excited tone suggested that scaling the almost sheer slab of stone, leveled more than three hundred feet above churning water and rock, would be no more difficult than scrambling up a tree. Duncan swallowed hard. He cared not how calm and determined Vanessa sounded. For himself, he wasn't entirely convinced they'd live long enough to reach the supposed grooves, let alone *scale them.*

And what if they did reach the place where the grooves were surmised to be, only to discover they were a myth, not there at all? Aye, what then? To the best of Duncan's knowledge, his sister had never in her life visited Cavnearal. Hugh Forster would never have allowed it. So how did she even *know* of the grooves' existence? And why, *why* hadn't he thought to ask these questions before they'd left Dunnaclard? Why did he think of them only now . . . when it was too late to turn back?!

The moist sea wind lashed at Duncan's cheeks, tossing his dark hair about his face and neck. His legs felt shaky, every bit as liquid as the waves he could hear crashing over the deadly rocks below.

Far below.

He gulped. Not for the first time did he wish he'd a wee bit of Vanessa's courage and determination. Did her confidence never waver?

"I take it back," Duncan grumbled as, dropping her hand, he inched farther down the ledge. As she'd predicted, it was angling upward. And narrowing precariously. "The whole family's not daft. Yet. Oh, aye, Da's mental state be unstable; that he allowed himself to be pledged to The Devil when so many other men were handy proves it. And me own sanity maun be disputed, considering what I've allowed ye to convince me into doing this night. But *ye* . . ." He shook his head and sneaked a troubled glance at his sister. "Ah, lass, I worry for ye. Truly I do. This plan be not the workings of a sane mind."

" 'Tis no more irrational than the time ye dressed me up as a lad and snuck me into the Day of Truce, Duncan. As I recall, ye thought that jest quite hilarious . . . until our trick was exposed and Da punished us both."

Duncan scowled, his gaze raking his sister's slender,

20

moonlit form. "Ye be dressed as a lad now, yet I see naught rational in what we're doing. Also, I be thinking the punishment Da doled out for last year's charade will seem like bairn's play compared to what he'll do to us for this night's work. Have ye given thought to what will happen to us should something go wrong? Vanessa, if either of us falls into The Devil's hands . . ."

Vanessa felt a tingle of unease. If rumor could be trusted, The Devil was in possession of a temper to be reckoned with. There was no doubt Alasdair Gray would be furious when he discovered 'twas a mere woman and a boy of but a half score and four who'd bested him out of the most influential prisoner in Cavnearal's history: the Gray's arch rival, **Hugh Forster.**

Though she blamed the biting wind for causing the shiver that raced up her spine, Vanessa wasn't entirely convinced. "I'm aware of what *could* happen, Duncan, but I promise ye, 'twill not. If all goes according to plan, we'll be halfway to Dunnaclard before the Gray even notices Da be missing."

"And what if—? Ooch! I dinna believe it!"

Vanessa had been studying the craggy stone passing slowly beneath her feet. A quick movement from the corner of her eye, combined with Duncan's surprised exclamation, won her immediate attention. Her heart clattered in her chest, and she fully expected to see the ledge beside her empty, so convinced was she that Duncan had just fallen to his death. She knew a second of blind panic, followed by equally blind relief, in the instant it took her to pull her brother's gangly form into focus.

Breathing hard, and not trusting her voice just yet, Vanessa took a few seconds to compose herself. She doubted the frantic rhythm of her heart would ever smooth itself out.

Thankfully, Duncan gave no sign he'd noticed her

panicky reaction. In fact, he wasn't looking at her at all. Instead of standing with his back to the massive rock, he'd turned to face it. His gaze was narrow, fixed intently on the moist stone wall that his fingertips were eagerly reading. " 'Tis here," he said excitedly, shaking his dark head in amazement. "The grooves, lass. They be here. Exactly where ye said they'd be!"

Vanessa blinked hard, a scowl pinching her brow as she glared at her brother. He'd doubted her? And wasn't this a fine time to be letting her know it?! "Of course they be there, Duncan. Did I not swear they would be?"

"Aye, but I dinna believed ye. Until now." His gaze traced the carved notches up as far as the skimpy moonlight would allow him to see. He released a long, slow hiss, his head reeling at the prospect of actually climbing up there. It wasn't far—a mere three or four yards, thanks to the steady incline they'd been ascending—but in this light, at this angle, the length yet to be climbed looked more than a wee bit daunting.

So did the fall, if he wasn't successful.

" 'Tis steep," he murmured respectfully.

"Aye. And 'twill not be getting any shorter by standing there staring at it." Vanessa nudged her brother's arm to get his attention. "Would ye like me to go first?"

Duncan sent her a glare that, for all his youth, was steeped in a grown man's indignation. "Nay. What ye'll do, lass, is this. Stay put until I've breached the top." He saw her lips part to voice argument, and immediately cut her short. "Think, Vanessa. Who's to say when the last time these grooves were used? A fortnight ago? A year? A score of years? A *century or twa?* If a notch has eroded and canna hold weight, 'tis *I* who'll find it out. Not ye."

"But—"

"Nay, I'll tolerate no argument on this, lass. Ye'll

stay on the ledge, exactly where ye are, and ye'll not budge a muscle until I've called down assurances the notches be safe to climb."

Vanessa's scowl deepened. Rarely was her brother adamant about anything. Most times she found him easily dissuaded. Instinct said this was not going to be one of those times.

Sensing it would be pointless to argue, not to mention time consuming, she nodded. She might not like it, but she'd stay on the ledge as Duncan requested. In the meantime, the one thing her brother hadn't forbidden her to do was worry. She indulged in that with a vengeance as she watched him slip one booted toe into the long, rectangular notch carved into the stone at knee level. Her brother's hands located another groove inches above his head.

Vanessa's breath caught as she watched him begin to slowly, cautiously, climb.

The slapping of waves on stone sounded unusually loud. But the nervous pounding of Vanessa's heart was much louder. Her palms felt moist and clammy, her knees weak and threatening to buckle. For the first time that October eve, she wondered if perhaps this scheme of hers wasn't so sound as it had seemed when she and Duncan had been safely tucked away within Dunnaclard's walls.

What if her brother was right? What if some of the notches *had* eroded and could no longer hold weight? If Duncan lost his footing, if he misjudged a single slender groove by even a hair's breadth . . .

Vanessa swallowed hard, her fingers trembling as she hoisted the heavy, raven curls which fell to her shoulders — a length of unusual shortness for the times — up and away from her nape. The glossy strands felt sticky and damp. Were they moist from the damp sea spray, she wondered, or from nervous perspiration? A wee bit of both, most likely. Her heartbeat accelerated with each inch her brother climbed . . . and with each inch, a bit more of her throat convulsed.

The sole of Duncan's boot was six or seven inches above her head now. Glancing higher, she saw that his knees were shaking. Badly. Almost as badly as her own.

Call him back . . .

The words echoed in her mind, over and over, until she thought she would scream. Her jaw hurt from gritting her teeth, but it was the only way she knew to clamp the words back. Her gaze shifted to the ledge. Lower. Her attention riveted on the sharp stone that could shred a man's body on contact.

Call him back!

She glanced up, measuring the distance to the moonlit crest of the rock. It seemed so high, and Duncan had gained little ground. In five minutes, he'd scarcely begun to climb, yet his arms and legs were already trembling with exertion.

Call him back!

Duncan. Out of all her brothers—there were seven Forster men in all, not counting their da—Duncan had always been her favorite. They'd banded together at an early age. 'Twas Vanessa who cared for Duncan's scraped knees and soothed his boyhood fears, not their mother. And 'twas Duncan to whom she turned when problems beset her.

If Duncan fell . . .

Call him back!

She had to. She couldn't let him continue. 'Twas too dangerous. Better he descended to the ledge now while he still could than to risk him falling to his death.

Aye, she would call him back and, between them, they would retrace the ledge, find another, safer way into Cavnearal. They were clever. Surely they would find a way.

Her mouth opened. The first word had no more

formed on Vanessa's tongue when she saw the rock beneath Duncan's foot crumble and disintegrate. Gravel fell away from the groove, raining to the ledge, pelting her head and legs and the tops of her feet before falling over the dark, deadly brink to the churning sea below.

"Duncan!" Her heart lodged in her fear-tightened throat when she saw her brother's hand frantically trying, and failing, to find purchase in the shadowy grooves.

A muffled grunt of surprise — his, or her own? — echoed in Vanessa's ears as, horrified, she saw him start to fall.

Alasdair Gray stared moodily into his tankard of ale, and grimaced. The stuff looked flat, unsavory. Then again, perhaps it was the subject being discussed — Hugh Forster, the blasted Scot — that robbed him of a taste for the normally enjoyable brew.

"Did you hear me, Alasdair?" Keith Gray demanded in the same instant his fist slammed atop the table, close to his brother's mug.

Alasdair didn't startle, nor did he glance up. His spine did stiffen, however, his eyes narrowed imperceptibly, and his lips thinned. The knuckles of the fingers wrapped around his mug whitened with the sudden strain of his grip.

Had he not been so distraught, Keith would have seen those subtle signs and correctly ascertained that his brother's legendary temper was on the rise. He would have wisely taken heed.

Instead, the younger man rested his fists on the table and leaned threateningly forward, his blue eyes stabbing into Alasdair's emotionless face. Keith's tone took on a savage note. "I said that he was caught snooping in the storage chamber below, Alasdair. Before that, he was waylaid from investigating the vault. And before *that*, he was found in the upstairs corridors. The arrogant bastard was looking toward *your* bedchamber, brother. I tell you, he goes too far!"

Again, Keith's fist rose to deliver a stinging blow to the table. This time flesh and pitched wood never made contact.

Lightning fast, Alasdair's fingers uncurled from around the cold pewter tankard. In a blink he'd caught his brother's hand in a crushing grip. "Hold your tongue, fool. The man is within range of hearing. I'll *not* have a Forster eavesdropping on my private conversations, especially when that conversation concerns him."

"And I'll not stand for a bloody Scot gracing this hall," Keith growled furiously. " 'Tis not right, I tell you. Were Father alive to see it, he'd be heartily disappointed in you, brother. As am I."

An inky brow slashed high in Alasdair's forehead, and his fingers tightened painfully around his brother's impotent fist. "Think you I care?"

"Think I you should. 'Tis a disgrace to have a Scot, a *Forster* no less, at Cavnearal. 'Tis more of a disgrace that the cursed man is allowed the freedom to roam at will."

Alasdair was quickly losing what little patience he had. With a growl, he thrust his brother's hand away, not caring when Keith's knuckles rapped painfully hard on the tabletop. "And what, exactly, do you suggest I do about it? Throw Forster in the vault? Clamp him in irons? Mayhap torturing and starving him until his family pays the fine would be more to your tastes?"

Keith's jaw bunched hard. His blue eyes flashed angrily as he cradled his aching hand to his chest. " 'Twould be a passably fair start. Anything, Alasdair, *anything* would be preferable to treating that Scot as you have . . . like a coddled guest. God's teeth, the man's naught but a pledge. Little better than the lowliest of prisoners!"

26

Bench legs scraped loudly over stone as Alasdair shoved himself to his feet. It was his turn to rest tightly bunched fists atop the scarred table, his turn to lean threateningly toward his brother. "A pledge," he growled angrily, "who also happens to be laird of one of the fiercest riding families in the East Marches, brother. Do you not think the Wardens on either side of the Border would have a thing or two to say about Hugh Forster's mistreatment at my hands?"

"Why should you care what they say now," Keith challenged hotly, "when you've never cared before?"

Alasdair glared at his brother, who had the good sense to squirm. "Make no mistake, Keith, I care not what they would *say*. I care very much about what they would *do*."

"They'd do naught. They can't touch us here. They wouldn't dare."

"You think so? I disagree. Humes and Carey are known for their gall, which is why they were appointed Wardens in the first place. Make no mistake, Keith, their vengeance has a long reach. Neither Warden, be he English or Scot, will tolerate the abuse of a pledge of Hugh Forster's standing, and well you know it. Not only would such foolishness invalidate any payment we stand to collect from the Forster, but we'd no doubt *be* fined in compensation."

"Is that all you're worried about? A measly fine? If so, rest at ease. No price is too large to pay for vengeance. And if you'll not take my word for it, ask our sister. Already Marette has threatened to kill the Forster whilst he sleeps."

Alasdair shrugged the warning aside. "Marette is a woman, and as such is incapable of such an act. She'll do naught."

"Marette," Keith corrected sharply, "is a grieving widow. Or have you forgotten so soon that her husband was slain at Forster hands? If you ask me—"

"I ask you nothing. Nor do I care to hear your

opinion on the matter." Alasdair sighed, and combed his fingers through his hair. His gaze scanned the hall, and belatedly he realized the amount of attention his conversation with Keith was attracting. He shook his head and while his tone softened, it didn't lose its steely edge. "These people have pledged their loyalty and trust to me, Keith. I'll not disappoint them."

"You already have." Keith's hand swept the room. "Look around you, brother. These people you speak of crave vengeance on Hugh Forster for all the wrongs his clan has done us in the past. It's there in their faces to see, if you'd but look. I think I speak for all the people of Cavnearal when I say that no price is too steep to have our revenge."

Much too slowly, and much too calmly, Alasdair sank back onto the bench. He reached for the tankard, took a hearty sip, and wiped his mouth on the sleeve of his tunic. "Think carefully on that, brother. What you're suggesting would risk funds Cavnearal does not have."

Keith pulled himself up straighter. Though the flicker of doubt in his eyes came and went quickly, it was there long enough for Alasdair to see and interpret it.

"We've the funds," Keith said finally, able to keep all but a trace of doubt from his voice. "Somewhere. I'm sure of it."

"Are you? I'm not. And I think I'm better aware of what goes on in this keep than you. Need I remind you that the fine for abusing the Forster would be steep? And need I also remind you that winter is coming upon us fast? The Selby's raid a fortnight ago near depleted our herds. We've scarcely enough food and blankets to start the winter with as it is. We've no funds to buy the extras we badly need."

"We can launch raids of our own," Keith argued staunchly. "That should replenish our stock."

Alasdair sighed impatiently, and prayed that if he was going to die, hopefully it would be only after he'd sired an heir. What Keith would do to Cavnearal and its people was too alarming to contemplate. "Aye, Keith, and ride we shall. But we cannot count on victory, because the fact of the matter is, we might not be successful. Hate though I do to admit it, we aren't always such.

"What if the clans we raid launch a trod, which they are within their rights to do, and are successful? We'll get naught that way, and we could well lose a fair share of our possessions and men in the bargain." Hot and cold trods were common on the Border, the former being a pursuit launched immediately after a raid while the trail was still hot, the latter, one more carefully planned and organized. Both were successful, legal recourse in reclaiming stolen goods. Alasdair's gaze narrowed on his brother, who visibly fidgeted. "Would you have me risk what little we have for what riches we *might* get? Would you have the old, the infirm — my God, even the *children!* — suffer, all for a fleeting taste of vengeance, which is over and done in a blink?"

"Aye," Keith answered as he took a step backward, "I would." His gaze raked his brother, and his sigh was long and heartfelt. "And so, I think, would *you* have scarce one year ago. But no longer, eh, Alasdair? I think we both know why." He shook his head sadly. "That woman changed you, softened you, as I'd warned you she would. Pity you'd not listen to reason."

"I've warned you once this night to hold your tongue," Alasdair snarled, his mug slamming to the table. "I'll not do it again."

"Aye, and I'll abide by your wishes. I'll not mention Jenny McLeod again," Keith said as he spun stiffly on his heel. He stalked away, not bothering to look back as he added coolly, "Me thinks speaking of her once in a year is enough . . . if her memory makes you re-think the error of your ways."

"Error of my ways?" Alasdair growled under his breath, just before he lifted his tankard and drained it dry. The ale tasted as flat and unsavory as it had looked. It landed in his belly like a slab of lead, making his stomach churn, but that didn't prevent him from refilling the mug and again tipping his head back to drink the wretched stuff down.

He was looking for a relief that he somehow knew couldn't be found in the bottom of a mug. But that didn't stop him from searching. Ale, in the right quantity, could do a man good. Unfortunately, two tankards full could do naught for one who'd just been slapped in the face with the memory of the wife he'd loved above all else.

The wife he'd killed.

A fist of pain convulsed around Alasdair's heart. Though the feeling was expected, familiar even, it was nonetheless crushing. His teeth clamped hard, and his piercing gray eyes scanned the hall, restlessly seeking any distraction from the turbulence of his thoughts.

What his gaze settled upon proved more of a diversion than Alasdair had bargained for.

Hugh Forster's huge body was squeezed into one of the low-to-the-floor, wide-backed wooden chairs flanking the hearth. Though his dark, shaggy head was bent, his shrewd green eyes were never still. A hint of a grin tugged at the older man's lips, telling Alasdair better than words that Forster was acutely aware of all that went on around him. Including the argument that had just taken place between the two Grays.

The big, bearded man's presence was a stark contrast to the men who'd lingered in the hall after the evening meal. The incongruous sight of the burly, black-and-gray-haired Scot reminded Alasdair that something was going to have to be done about Hugh Forster.

* * *

Duncan twisted around as he went down, landing on his knees, close to the edge of the ledge. The collision was painful enough to make him grunt and pitch forward.

Vanessa's reaction was instantaneous. Kneeling by his side, she made a grab for him. Her fingers wrapping around his thin upper arms, she tugged hard.

For but a second, she thought his momentum was going to work against her. Her heartbeat doubled when she saw the shadowy brink of the ledge looming close. Desperation made her strong. Planting her knees firmly atop the hard, cold stone, she gave a mighty yank, and felt the resistance blessedly cease. Duncan lurched backward, the movement taking Vanessa with him.

Both their bottoms landed hard on the ledge, and both their heads whipped back on their necks, though the back of Duncan's slammed with more force against the solid stone wall than did his sister's.

"Ooch!" he yelped breathlessly, and rubbed the bruise at the base of his scalp. "Have a care, lass. Or are ye trying to kill me where the fall failed? Vanessa?" He scowled worriedly when she didn't answer.

"Vanessa!"

"If ye'd fallen, 'twould have been my fault. I . . . Sweet merciful heavens, Duncan, I almost killed ye!"

The voice sounded high and shaky, not at all recognizable as his sister's. Concerned, Duncan slipped an arm about her slender shoulders and gathered her close, smoothing the silky raven curls back from her temple with his palm. Her body was trembling. All over. And did he feel moisture against his skin where her head nuzzled his neck?

He dismissed the idea as ludicrous. To feel such would mean she was crying, and the lass never cried.

31

Even when they'd laid their dear, eldest sister to rest a scant month ago, Vanessa had stood in the kirkyard with her back stiff and her eyes dry. Surely she'd not be crying now, over what might have happened but hadn't . . . would she? There was only one way to find out.

"Be those tears, lass?" he asked softly. She made a squeaky sound in her throat, and shook her head hard. Too hard, Duncan thought as she sniffled loudly in his ear. His hand slipped over her cheek. Crooking his index finger under her chin, he lifted her gaze to his.

Intense green clashed with equally intense green.

"Aye, ye be crying," he said, while studying the dripping path of tears on her cheeks with wide-eyed amazement.

"I'm not! 'Tis . . . 'tis the sea air stinging me eyes, making them water, is all." She swiped the moisture away with her fist. It was a futile effort. When she saw the lump forming at the base of her brother's scalp, she felt still more of the warm, humiliating tears fall on the back of her knuckles, dripping over her wrists, splashing to soak into the tight-fitting trews she'd stolen from Dunnaclard's stables a mere four hours before.

"I'm not dead, lass. There's no reason to weep as if I were."

"Aye, Duncan, there is. Do ye not see? Ye almost died because of me foolish plan."

"But I *dinna* die." His fingers curled around her upper arms, and he dragged her to her knees, facing him. When her tears slowed but still continued to fall, he gave her a gentle shake. "I dinna die, and that, methinks, is what be important. As for the foolishness of yer plan . . ." He hesitated, winced, then shrugged. "Aye, 'tis absurd. But it *could* work. I'd not be here now if I thought differently."

"But—"

Momentarily thrusting aside the irony of *him* comforting *her*, Duncan continued staunchly. "Listen to me, Vanessa. Yer plan has merit. Even a fool could see that. The Devil will not be expecting a rescue so soon. We've that in our favor. Also, he'd not be expecting Da's escape to come in the form of *us*. A girl and a near bairn?" He chuckled dryly and shook his head. "Nay, 'tis not something even *he* would think to guard against. If we can just reach the top of this rock . . .

Vanessa pulled in a shaky breath and glanced upward. The moonlight made the place where the stone had given away under Duncan's foot look like a yawning pit. " 'Tis unsafe."

"*That* groove be unsafe," Duncan agreed tightly. His fingers flexed excitedly around her upper arms, though his grip was not painful. "The rest seemed sound, though. Were either of us large, I'd say it unwise to attempt it, but . . . Ah, Vanessa, sweet, my fingers actually grazed the crest of the rock! Had the notch not given away, I'd be up there now. I know it."

"Do ye mean . . . ?"

"Aye, I do." Giving her arms a reassuring squeeze, Duncan let her go and pushed to his feet. With a grin, he extended his hand to her. "Care ye to try again, lass?"

Vanessa dried her eyes on the sleeve of her baggy jack and nodded eagerly. "I promised Mother I'd have Da back home at Dunnaclard in time for her lying-in. 'Tis not a promise I wish to withdraw."

Again she glanced at the rocky cliff they'd yet to ascend. To Duncan's eternal relief, he saw a flash of determination spark like bright green fire in her eyes as she placed her hand in his.

"Aye," Vanessa said more confidently, "we'll give the monster another try."

Duncan grinned as he hauled her to her feet.

33

"Which monster be that, lass? The rock . . . or The Devil?"

"Both," she answered with a saucy grin of her own. "And beat them, we shall. Ye just wait and see, brother. Ye just wait and see."

Thirty minutes later, as they stood arm in arm atop the rock overlooking a breathtaking moonlit landscape, Duncan began to think that his sister might— just *might*—be right after all. It had taken time and care, but they'd done the impossible. They'd found a second entrance into Cavnearal when only one was known to exist.

The first monster had been beaten.

Now, they'd only to face the other.

Duncan frowned. 'Twas the conquering of that particular monster that resurrected his concern.

"What?!" Alasdair roared, making the man who stood meekly before him wince. "Who? Where? When?"

"The vault m'lord. Ten minutes ago," the guard answered. "I know not who, but I've my suspicions."

Alasdair followed the guard's gaze to Hugh Forster. The man sat in the same chair as before, his head still bent. For all appearance, he was oblivious to the conversation going on around him. But Alasdair doubted that was true. When a Gray's temper was riled, he was rarely quiet. Even now, the echo of Alasdair's voice continued to bounce off the cold stone walls of the hall.

The bloody Scots! It wasn't that Alasdair hadn't expected a rescue attempt; he had. He just hadn't expected it this soon, and definitely not on a night when the moon was so skimpy. Not that any of that mattered. Expected or not, the intruders were here, now, and must be dealt with.

Alasdair's right hand fisted the hilt of his broadsword as his gaze shifted back to the guard. "How many were sighted?"

"Two."

"Two?" Alasdair's brows rose in surprise. "That's all?"

The man nodded. "Aye, m'lord. Two . . . that we've caught. I'm thinking there must be more creeping about, though. Even the Forsters wouldn't be foolish enough to send so small a rescue party."

The man wasn't saying anything Alasdair hadn't already concluded himself. "Where are the culprits now? So help me, if you say they've gotten away . . ."

"Nay, m'lord, they haven't. We, um . . . gave them little choice in the matter." The guard grinned confidently. "The ragged-looking pair is, as we speak, locked inside the vault they were vandalizing when we caught them."

Alasdair grinned, his gaze slicing back to Hugh Forster. The big man's spine went rigid, the only indication he'd heard. "Very good." His grin broadened, and his attention shifted. His gaze locked with Keith's, who stood with apparent nonchalance across the room. But not for long.

Alasdair mouthed the words, "Detain him," and tipped his head slightly in his brother's direction.

A satisfied grin curled over Keith's lips, and he nodded in acknowledgment. Quickly, he gathered together a half dozen men. Keith's hand slid conspicuously to the hilt of his sword as he strolled purposefully across the room.

Hugh Forster paled.

It wasn't until Alasdair and the guard had reached the stairs leading to the ground floor that he heard the big Scot's voice booming through the hall.

"Have a care, lad. If ye nick me with that blade, I'll not hesitate to tell the March Wardens at the first opportunity. Ouch! Why, ye little heathen. Alasdair Gray?! Ye get back here, ye Sassenach devil. What be

35

the meaning of this? I demand to know the meaning of this!"

If Keith ever answered the Scot, the words were lost to Alasdair. Confident his brother had the Forster under control, he descended the stone stairway with a stealth and agility that more than one Border reiver — be he English or Scot — had seen in the past and envied mightily.

The guard raced to catch up with his determined laird. He breathed a mental sigh of relief that fate had not made him one of the two left to cool their heels down in the vault. The look in The Devil's eyes had been murderous; if the lads had not been Scot, the guard would have pitied them.

Chapter Two

"Any more plans, lass?"

"Aye, many," Vanessa grumbled. "But none that can be put into effect from the inside of a vault."

"I was afraid ye'd say that. Time to revert back to me own original one, then."

"What be that?"

Duncan sighed and said quite gravely, "We're going to die."

"We're not going to—!"

"Aye, we are. Not the death of being splattered atop craggy rocks, though I'm thinking 'twould be preferable to the end we now face. Alas, fate chose a more gruesome demise for us." His hesitation was long enough to raise the dark hairs curling at his sister's nape but short enough to stop shy of blatant dramatics. "Ah, Vanessa, we're to die at the hands of The Devil. A worse end, truly, is not to be imagined."

Vanessa felt rather than saw her brother shudder. Then again, perhaps the tremors originated with her? Sighing, she rested her elbows atop bent knees. The stone wall behind her ground into her spine as she cradled her head in her hands.

The vault they were locked in was musty smelling. Murky and dark, it was lit only by a few skimpy slivers of moonlight. She thought that appropriate. 'Twas fitting somehow that their surroundings were as bleak as their situation had become.

How had this happened? she wondered sourly, and not for the first time. *How?* Things had been going so well.

After breaching the rock, they'd sneaked behind the stables and smithy. The only time their presence could have been detected was when they'd trekked across the kirkyard. The expanse of grassy flatness was open all around, and though she'd doubted the wisdom of having to pass though it, it was the only way to the vault. Her heart had pounded the entire time, and she'd found her ears perked, waiting to hear the cry of warning that would mean their presence had been detected.

The alarm hadn't sounded. With unbelievable ease, they'd reached the fortress's impressive quadrangle, and skirted it to the back, where the vault their father was locked in was located.

At least, at the time Vanessa had *assumed* Hugh Forster was locked in the vault. That had been her first mistake; assuming *anything* where The Devil was concerned. Her second had been in entering and searching the vault.

That mistake had been her last.

" 'Tis a disgrace," she mumbled, more to herself than her brother. "To be caught after coming so far, and daring so maun. Aye, and to be caught so *easily.*" She shook her head and sighed with disgust. "I'd have preferred a battle, Duncan. A chase, even. 'Twould have made our apprehension more dignified, do ye not agree? But to enter this vault, only to hear the door slam shut behind us . . . and then to hear their laughter sneaking in beneath the door . . . !" She scowled. " 'Twas the laughter, methinks, that sealed me humiliation."

"And mine," Duncan agreed on a sigh. "From the sound of it, they found our easy capture quite comical."

"Quite . . . the cursed Sassenach, God rot 'em all." Her fingers curled into white-knuckled fists, one of which impotently slammed atop the cold stone beneath her. "I'd have liked to slap their arrogant faces, I would!"

Duncan laughed. "Ye tried, lass. Remember? They moved away from the door afore yer fist could make contact through the bars."

Vanessa's shoulders slumped, and she said miserably, "Aye, and the fools laughed all the harder. How many do ye think there were? Six score? Seven?"

"Well . . ."

"How many, Duncan?"

"Three, lass," he admitted reluctantly. "There were but three."

"Three?!"

"Aye," Duncan sighed. "However, if it eases yer mind a wee bit, from the scant glimpse I had of them, all were armed to the teeth."

"It does naught for my conscience, but I thank ye for trying." Three, Vanessa thought dispiritedly. And armed to the teeth or not, it was disappointing to know that the only swords pulled from their scabbards had been hers and Duncan's. Since they'd been on the far side of the vault when the door slammed shut, the blades had been a worthless defense. One would have to be able to reach one's opponent before one could skewer him . . . and the door had been shut and barred from without before either Forster could reach it.

Oh, the disgrace!

They lapsed into a tense silence. Vanessa lifted her head and glanced at her brother. She could see only a vague outline of Duncan in the moonlight cutting in through the four narrow windows on the outer wall.

The windows. No escape route there. The walls outside blended too smoothly into a sheer cliff. Vanessa knew that; 'twas the first thing she'd checked. A larger window was carved into the wall their backs leaned defeatedly against, but it was too far up to reach—even when she stood atop her brother's shoulders.

"How long do ye think we've been here?" Vanessa asked as she pushed to her feet. With leadened steps, she crossed to one of the narrow windows and glanced outside. The churning water of the Firth of Maryn and the jagged, moonlit coast extended for acres on either side. Ironic, she thought, that the view from a prison window should be so breathtaking.

"Not long."

"Long enough for The Devil to be summoned?"

"Oh, aye."

She frowned, the pad of her thumb automatically stroking the sharp stone corner of the window. "Then why is he not here, do ye think?"

"He is."

Vanessa startled. That was *not* her brother's voice. 'Twas too low, too deep, too steeped in masculine maturity. And if 'twas not Duncan, that meant it must be . . .

Her heart stopped, then throbbed to vibrant life. Her spine went rigid, and her eyes widened until they actually stung. No air was allowed into her burning lungs, and she didn't make any effort to correct that. She didn't want to draw breath; suffocation would be preferable to having to turn and face the owner of that voice.

A muffled sound behind her told Vanessa that

Duncan had pushed to his feet. She traced the click of his heels atop stone as he quickly crossed to her side.

The hiss of metal scraping metal, as Duncan unsheathed his sword, sounded loud and grating as it bounced off the rough stone walls. The noise reminded Vanessa that she should be doing the same, if only to show a feeble but united front. There was but one problem: Her fingers were shaking too badly to be trusted. To draw her sword now, only to drop it, would add insult to her already unbearable humiliation.

She swallowed hard, and felt her brother lean into her side. His warm breath whisked over her cheek when he hissed softly in her ear, "Say naught. 'Twill go better if he thinks he's captured twa boys. In this light, 'tis possible. Commoners, Vanessa. Lowly Forster septs is what we be, if I can manage to convince the beast of it."

Vanessa doubted that would be possible. From the rumors she'd heard, The Devil was not stupid, but since she'd been forbidden to speak, she couldn't tell Duncan that. With effort, she pushed the words back, then forgot all about them when her brother stepped forward and in front of her.

"Alasdair Gray?" Duncan demanded in a husky, determined tone that reminded Vanessa of their father's.

"The Devil in the flesh. And who are you?"

"No one of importance." Duncan's shoulders squared, and his chin thrust up at a proud angle that belied his words.

Alasdair chuckled. "The identity of any with enough gall to steal into Cavnearal in the dead of night is of importance. To me."

"We've come to liberate Hugh Forster," Duncan said, and his voice turned mocking. "Obviously

41

we've failed in our endeavor. 'Tis all ye need know about us."

Alasdair took a step toward them. His own voice lowered and turned gravelly. "Nay, boy, 'tis not. I need know more. Your names will do for starters."

Though he couldn't see the smaller of the two, who stood shielded behind the taller, lean one, Alasdair could at least see and study one of them. What he saw did not please him.

Boys? *Clan Forster had entrusted the rescue of their mighty laird to a pair of boys?!*

Alasdair would have laughed had he thought the situation funny. He did not. God's blood, the Scots were either an overly confident bunch of heathens, or they were moronic beyond reason. He knew not which.

They were also stubborn, he noted. The determined silence of the tall one, who refused to answer the question put to him, hinted at that. Alasdair grinned. Had the youths heard of the legendary Gray temper? he wondered. If they lived in Scotland, as the tall one's burr and mission suggested, they must have. If not, they were about to discover the force of it firsthand.

Alasdair's hand shifted to the hilt of his sword, which he'd left sheathed. He took another step forward. Another. "Your names . . . ?"

In the moonlight streaming in through the window, he saw the tall one's lips thin, his expression tighten. The boy, barely more than a child really, was brandishing his sword in such a way as to suggest he expected to be presented with an opportunity to use it.

Alasdair's grin broadened. Nothing could be further from the truth.

To Duncan's credit, he didn't flinch when The Devil stopped toe to toe with him. Of course, 'twould be a credit none knew of if Alasdair Gray slayed him—which, judging by the murderous glint in the steely eyes boring into him, Duncan thought might be a possibility. Woefully soon.

"Your names!"

The unexpected, booming voice startled Duncan into shouting, "Nay! We'll not give them, so ye may as well stop asking."

"Already done. I'll not ask again." A beat of hesitation was followed by, "That doesn't mean, of course, that I won't get my answer. I will."

"Not from me ye'll not."

"Correct. I'll get it from *him*."

The second he saw Alasdair reaching around him for Vanessa, Duncan reacted. His sword rose, and the blade glinted in the moonlight as it made a deadly arch toward The Devil's neck.

Alasdair, expecting such a move, agilely ducked the blow that ached to separate his head from his shoulders. He heard the hiss of the blade's passing, and judged it too far off its mark to be noteworthy. With a quick crouch and spin, almost too fast for the eye to track, he came up to his full, imposing height, his broadsword unsheathed and brandished.

Duncan lunged. Metal scraped deafeningly against metal as blades slid together to the hilt. Standing face-to-face, it was blatantly apparent the two were unevenly matched.

Alasdair was tall, with battle-experience and might on his side. He was able to throw off the boy with one arm and little expended effort. The boy stumbled back, and crashed hard into the corner of the window, grunting when the force of impact shoved the breath from his chest, which was lean to the point of scrawny.

Alasdair had no time to savor the sound. In a blur of motion he saw the small one rush him. The boy was charging, teeth bared, looking for all the world like a disgruntled kitten.

The kitten growled menacingly. Alasdair glimpsed a shaggy mane of dark hair billowing back from slender shoulders before his gaze dropped to the youth's shorter, lighter sword. The deadly tip was on a collision course with his belly.

Alasdair sidestepped, and easily deflected the blow with a single, chopping sweep of his wrist to a painfully thin forearm. The vibration of the impact ricocheted up to his shoulder. When he heard the boy's yelp of pain, and heard the sword clatter to the stone, he assumed the pain he'd caused was twofold to what he felt.

Good, he thought as he applied his heel to the hilt of the fallen sword and viciously kicked the weapon behind him. As far as Alasdair was concerned, the arrogant little heathens needed to learn their place. And he was in the perfect frame of mind to teach it to them.

The taller one had recovered enough to also attempt rushing him. The boy was quick, but not quick enough. Alasdair let him get close, let him think, feel, *taste,* success, and then cruelly snatched victory away from him. A sweep of Alasdair's arm locked their swords together at the hilt. Then, with a ruthless flick of his wrist, he jerked the sword from the boy's hands.

Vanessa held her breath as she watched her brother's sword make an end-over-end arc before clattering harmlessly to the floor. It skimmed over stone, crashing against the closed door, and finally came to rest beside her own expropriated weapon.

She winced, and thought the position brutally mocking. Her pride weathered another crushing blow. The worst, as yet.

If The Devil had thought to prove his ability, he'd

done it swiftly and admirably. But that he'd done it *alone,* that his confidence brought him into the vault without benefit of a single man to guard his back . . . ah, Vanessa cursed that as the worst insult of all. The curse quickly manifested into one directed at her own stupidity for allowing herself to become distracted. Alasdair Gray was of a sudden quite close. After that, it melted into a gasp when she felt strong fingers tightly encircle her upper arm.

The Devil tugged.

Vanessa stumbled a step before he allowed—she'd no doubt he *allowed*—her to plant her feet firmly atop the stone and regain her balance. He didn't tug again. Nor did his painful hold loosen from her upper arm, even when she tried to wrench away. Clawing at his fingers proved a useless effort; he'd shackled her to him quite easily and powerfully.

"Leave the lad be," Duncan ordered, stepping forward. "He can tell ye naught."

"On the contrary. I think he can tell me a great deal."

Duncan shook his head emphatically. "Nay, he canna. He's . . ." He hesitated, knowing Vanessa was not going to like this. Unfortunately, he could see no other way. He couldn't let The Devil take Vanessa away for questioning. There was a chance that might happen anyway, a chance Duncan didn't want to think on too hard. Nay, whatever it took he had to keep his sister with him. At all costs he had to guard her identity and keep it secret. Even if it meant divulging his own.

"He's what?" Alasdair prompted when the boy said nothing, but merely glanced at the smaller youth.

"Mute," Duncan blurted. He glanced quickly away from the glare his sister sent him, a glare that said he was right, she didn't like this at all. Well, neither did he! But one of them had to do something, and it was all he could think of. "The lad canna speak, canna answer ye, even if he wished to."

Vanessa startled when The Devil tipped back his head . . . and laughed heartily. The sound was deep and rich, bouncing off the confining stone. It was more pleasant to hear than she thought a hated Sassenach's laughter should be. The husky sound skated down her spine, and she felt an inexplicable shiver course through her. The raven curls at her nape prickled with awareness. Her heart thudded erratically against her ribs. Her breathing snagged and, for no apparent reason, she felt chill-bumps sprout on the suddenly too-warm flesh of her forearms.

Vanessa scowled, confused. 'Twas a strange reaction, to be sure. Yet, like The Devil's unexpected laughter, the peculiar sensations that felt warm and heavy in her stomach were oddly—nay, *alarmingly*—nice.

The Devil finally spoke, though it was clear by his tone that his mirth had not evaporated. "Mute? If this boy's mute, then I'm your young King Jamie. Methinks both are about as likely."

"Ye dinna believe me?" Duncan looked offended.

Alasdair shook his head, his grin still locked in place. "For a Scot, you're very astute, Nay, I'll not believe a word."

"Why?"

"Because I'm not mute," Vanessa said before The Devil could reply. Her gaze met her brother's, which was openly furious. "Think on it! Were we not talking whilst he stood in the doorway? Aye, we were. Even a thick-skulled Sassenach like this is not so stupid as to miss that."

Her words won her two very different reactions.

Duncan glared at her, his green eyes piercing the play of shadows and moonlight to remind her of his early warning to hold her tongue.

The Devil, on the other hand, angled his head and glanced down at her, his gaze guarded, narrow, yet openly curious.

Stunned, Vanessa realized this was the first time since he'd arrived that she'd actually *looked* at the man. It was a sight she could have died happily without ever having seen. Especially when one took into account that she had to crane her neck to look into his eyes. Lord, but he was a tall one!

Handsome was not a word Vanessa would have used to describe Alasdair Gray. His features were too hard, too harshly chiseled. *Ruthless* would have been an apt description, she thought, when she was able to think anything at all. The combination of unruly black hair, an aloof expression, and piercing gray-blue eyes was stunning. The sight had the power to knock the breath out of her!

Vanessa's knees went inexplicably weak. Her head spun, and her world tipped on its axis. In the same instant, she felt the gentle pressure of The Devil's fingers, still curled around her upper arm, as he effortlessly steadied her balance.

He didn't draw her close, and she was grateful for that. As it was, he was already too near. The heat of him, the strength of him, seeped through her padded jack and trews, heating the overly sensitive flesh beneath. Her arm felt warm and alive in the exact place his hand gripped it, and oddly cold elsewhere.

Strange, that. But not so strange as the hot, liquidy sensation she felt jolt through her. It was like being hit by a bolt of lightning. She shivered, and when she drew in a shaky breath, it was to find that her nostrils were flooded with the scent of Alasdair Gray. Leather and sweat and ale. Man. *That* was what The Devil smelled like. 'Twas a familiar aroma, one she'd smelled oft times in the past. Yet, for some reason she couldn't fathom, right now she felt as though she was smelling the scents for the very first time.

Strange, Vanessa thought again, her senses spinning as she continued to crane her neck and stare into his piercing blue-gray eyes. Very, very strange.

A frown pinched his brow, and Vanessa swallowed back a gasp when his head inched down farther. Her eyes widened, and she automatically tilted her own head back. The fingers manacling her arms made sure she didn't retreat far. Not nearly as far as she would like to have!

Was it possible to *feel* a gaze? she wondered as his eyes roamed her face. Aye, it must be. Because wherever he looked, she felt fire. It was as though his hands were touching her, caressing her, seducing her—not merely his eyes.

He raked her scattering of raven hair, shorter than most women of the time favored, her delicately winged eyebrows, the gentle curve of her cheek, her . . .

Mouth.

Alasdair's gut fisted when his gaze settled on her full, moist, slightly trembling lower lip, and settled there hard. His eyes narrowed as softly, huskily, he said, "You've a comely face, boy. And—ahem—hips and thighs that fill out a pair of trews better than any boy I've ever laid eyes on. Either you're feminine in the extreme, or . . . ?"

One raven brow arched. "I be no lad?"

"Aye."

Vanessa felt the thick fingers biting into her arm loosen, then fall away as she echoed, "Aye."

"Son-of-a—"

The Devil's curse was interrupted by Duncan's shrill voice as he stepped toward her. "Lass, think what ye be saying. *Who* ye be saying it to! Did I not tell ye—?"

"Ye did," she nodded, and sent her brother a sympathetic glance. How could she tell him, with The Devil listening keenly to every word, that she'd seen an opportunity to put one of her substitute plans into motion, and had immediately seized it? She tried to convey with her eyes and a tilt of her head that this chance might not come round again. That she'd be a fool to waste it. If Duncan saw what she was attempting to tell him, he gave no sign, so she added firmly, "I know what I be doing."

Duncan sighed in agitation and plowed his fingers through his dark, shaggy hair. "Nay, lass, ye dinna. 'Tis The Devil ye be making confessions to."

" 'Tis The Devil I be attempting to *bargain* with," she corrected impatiently. Couldn't Duncan see that she had the situation under control?

"What bargain?"

The intrusive third voice served to remind both Forsters that they were not alone in the vault. Not that either had ever forgotten. Vanessa knew she hadn't. There was something about Alasdair Gray's presence that couldn't, even in a pitch black room, be overlooked or ignored.

She glanced over her shoulder, and traced his voice to the door. When had he moved? The *when* of it, she realized belatedly, wasn't nearly as important as what he was doing.

"Duncan, yer sword!" she cried as she saw The Devil pass the weapon out through the bars, hilt first. Since she heard no clatter of metal on stone, she presumed someone was out there to receive it. Her gaze frantically searched the stone floor, but her own blade was nowhere to be seen. "Blasted, thick-skulled, Sassenach Devil! Ye canna *do* that!"

"Can't I? Since you're now standing on Cavnearal property, mistress, I feel the need to remind you that

I can do aught that I please. With weapons. Or with prisoners."

He turned away from the door, and took a step into the room. Only a single step, and a small one at that. So why, Vanessa wondered, did the room feel suddenly crowded? Why did the stony vault, capable of holding thirty men — *big* men — feel abruptly small and cramped?

"What bargain?" The Devil repeated, his steely gaze piercing her from out of the murky shadows.

"Aye," Duncan echoed in a tone that said he wasn't sure he wanted an answer, but he had to ask. "What bargain?"

While Vanessa didn't ignore her brother, the crux of her attention was focused on The Devil — with a smaller part devoted to controlling her trembling. 'Twasn't easy. Her heart was pounding so hard, each heavy beat seemed to melt right into the next without pause. And was it stuffy in here? Was that why she was finding it difficult to breathe? Difficult to think? She hoped that was the case, that all these odd physical maladies could be easily explained away . . . though she doubted it.

Nervousness wasn't a malady she suffered from often. She'd no practice with it, and even less patience. Disgusted with herself, she balled her hands into white-knuckled fists, which she planted firmly atop the slender shelf of her hips. Her chin lifted at a proud angle as she returned The Devil's gaze. It took effort — more than she'd care to admit — but her voice didn't waver as she said, "I've come to strike a trade with ye, Devil."

His grin was cold and disarming. "I've something you want?"

"Aye. Hugh Forster."

Alasdair took a second to digest that bit of information. Her answer shouldn't surprise him, and didn't really. What astounded him was that this mere slip of a girl had the backbone to try such an outrageous approach to win her laird's freedom. Many of his own countrymen wouldn't have dared. Truly, a Scot's audacity and devotion were something to behold. They'd even bred it into their women!

Alasdair's grin broadened, and he cocked one inky brow at her. "You've something *I* want?"

Ah, Vanessa thought, this was going to be the tricky part. Her chin tilted another notch as she answered confidently, "I do."

"What?" both Duncan and Alasdair asked together.

She answered only The Devil. "Me. I've come to offer meself, as pledge for fines owed, in Hugh Forster's place."

Chapter Three

"She did *what?*"

"She pledged herself," Alasdair growled irritably. "The stupid wench pledged herself in Hugh Forster's place."

Chair legs scraped against stone as Keith sank down heavily upon the bench opposite his brother. "Why?"

Alasdair snorted and shook his head. "Damned if I know. Damned if I care. *Damned if I'll take her!*" This last was punctuated by the fist he slammed atop the table. More than one abandoned tankard jostled with the force of the blow.

Keith's eyebrows lifted. He'd done much the same thing a mere hour ago. He recalled his brother's reaction to the outburst, and considered employing the same tactics. But only briefly. Since Alasdair wasn't a man who took censure in stride, he sought instead to calm his brother with words. "Where is the woman now?"

"Woman?" Alasdair sneered. "Trust me, Brother, she's not that. She's a girl. They sent a *girl*—those blasted Scots!—and not a very pretty one at that. She's young, she's impudent, and she's . . ." he made an impatient gesture with his hand, indicating she was slender, and that the top of her head barely cleared the broad shelf of his shoulders, "small and scrawny. Not much to look upon, considering what she's been sent here to offer."

Personally, Keith didn't care what the chit looked like. He was more concerned with the matter at hand—a matter that had the potential to become explosive given the correct fuel. "All right," he said tightly, "so she's not physically appealing. Fine. But you've not answered my question, Alasdair. Where is the *girl* now?"

For the first time, his brother glanced up from his tankard. It was, Keith noted, the second mug Alasdair had poured since angrily stalking into the hall a half hour before. This time the pewter container was not filled with ale, but with a brew whose potent fumes permeated the air. And Alasdair's breath, too, as he sneered, "I left her in the vault."

The mug Keith was lifting hesitated on the way to his mouth. "Excuse me?"

"I said I left her in the vault."

"You *what?*" A tension-thick pause was followed by, "Have you taken leave of your senses?! You can't leave a wench—even a Scots wench—locked in a vault!"

"I can when she attacks me."

"*She* attacked *you?* This, in your own words, 'short, scrawny *girl'* attacked *you?* Alasdair Gray? The legendary Devil?"

Alasdair nodded stiffly. "Methinks she took exception to my laughter."

"You laughed," Keith echoed flatly, as his mug collided with the scarred tabletop. His voice reflected his shock. "*You* laughed." He shook his head and glanced at his brother with open disbelief. "When?"

The rise and fall of Alasdair's shoulders looked as strained as his voice sounded. "When she offered to pledge herself. I thought 'twas funny." He sighed. "Truth to tell, Keith, I thought she was jesting."

Alasdair shook his head, his nostrils flaring when the unsavory memory flashed through his mind.

So unexpected had her attack been, she'd managed to topple them both to the stone before he'd known what she was about. Straddling his waist, she'd kicked and clawed, punched and . . . He grimaced, his gaze dropping to the hand wrapped around his tankard, and the angry red teeth marks marring the back of it.

The brazen wench had bitten him!

There and then, Alasdair had decided the little she-cat could cool her heels in the vault until he determined what to do with her. He'd also decided he was going to take his sweet time making the decision. A little worrying and agonizing over her fate would do her a world of good. 'Twas the only way to bring a hotheaded wench like that to heel.

No matter what his brother said, no matter how hot Keith's glares, Alasdair couldn't be coerced into regretting his actions. As it was, the chit should consider herself lucky that he hadn't hurt her. Lord knows, the temptation to do so had been there. It still was. And that bothered Alasdair. For all his temper and violent Border ways, he'd never lifted his hand to a woman. He'd never had the desire to, nor the need.

Until this night.

Now, the desire pumped hot and strong through his blood. What was it about this particular woman—nay, this *girl*—he wondered, that riled him so?

"Who she is?"

"Hmm?" Alasdair shook off his turbulent thoughts and glanced up sharply. "What?"

"I asked you," Keith repeated patiently as he waved over a serving wench to refill his tankard, "if 'twould not be easier to decide her fate if you knew who she is."

"I do know." Alasdair lifted his half-filled mug and drained it. The whiskey had ceased to burn his throat as it went down, and instead joined the nice warm pool gathering in his belly. He voiced no complaint when the serving wench, with a saucy smile, not only refilled his brother's mug, but his own as well. He returned her smile, albeit a tad sloppily.

"You know who she is?" Keith asked once the wench had sauntered out of hearing range.

"Aye," Alasdair grumbled.

"She finally told you then?"

"Nay, Keith. I figured it out myself." Alasdair lifted his tankard, glared at it, then set it back on the table, untouched. Beneath his breath, he mumbled, "For all my thick-skulled Sassenach ways, my reasoning remains sound." He thought of the small, dark-haired girl locked in the vault, and wondered if maybe that wasn't as true now as it had been this morn.

"Then who . . . ?"

He shrugged, and glanced at Keith. "The girl's scrawny and in her boy's attire not much to look upon, I admit, but her features are nevertheless sharp and distinct enough to make her parentage obvious." An ironic grin quirked at one corner of Alasdair's lips. " 'Twould appear Cavnearal's been overrun with Forsters, brother. The girl, and the boy as well, are our esteemed guest's offspring. Hugh Forster's middle children, from the looks of them."

Keith whistled through his teeth, and reached blindly for his tankard. Lifting it, he drank thirstily in an attempt to ease his suddenly parched throat. "Blast it," he gasped on a rush of breath. "First we're forced to take the Forster as pledge, and now this. Can the situation get worse?"

"I doubt it."

They lapsed into an edgy silence which, eventually, Keith was the first to break. "What are you going to do?"

"The only thing I *can* do."

Keith frowned, not liking his brother's tone. It was too calm, too low and smooth, too much a contrast to Alasdair's eyes, which shimmered with dark-gray fire. "And what," he asked warily, "is that?"

"Right now," Alasdair said as he pushed to his feet, and rearranged the broadsword swaying at his hip, "I'm going to send you to fetch the chit. You're to bring her directly to my chambers, with no stops on the way."

"And then . . . ?" Keith pressed. Already, he disliked the sound of this plan. Hadn't Alasdair claimed the wench had attacked him? Knocked him down? Aye, he had. No doubt she'd attack Keith in the same heathen fashion as well . . . if given the chance.

Swallowing hard, Keith wished the serving wench hadn't retreated to the kitchen so quickly. He could use another mug of ale. In fact, he could use a ration of the whiskey his brother was consuming in quantity. Keith held no illusions about himself. He knew that, at two and twenty, he wasn't nearly the fighter his brother had become. And if the girl could take Alasdair unawares, heaven only knew what she'd do to *him!*

He glanced up in time to see a cold grin curl over Alasdair's lips; the sight sent a shiver of unease icing down Keith's spine. He'd seen that smile often enough to know it denoted trouble. Big trouble. Trouble that, as his brother had told him one short hour ago, Cavnearal could not afford to indulge in at this time.

Either Alasdair had forgotten his own edict, or he was conveniently ignoring it.

56

"And then . . . ?" Keith prompted when his brother didn't reply. "What happens after I bring her to you?"

"*Then,*" Alasdair said, much too sedately for his brother's peace of mind, "I'll explain to her exactly what being a pledge—a *female* pledge . . . *my* female pledge—entails. I'll paint a gruesome picture for her, never fear. Methinks the wench won't be so eager to trade places with her father then."

"And if you're wrong? What then?"

"I'm never wrong." The comment was not spoken with conceit, just truth. The negligent lift and fall of his shoulders said that Alasdair would, however, indulge his brother and at least consider the possibility.

He did. He mulled it over briefly in his mind, then dismissed the idea as ludicrous. "She's a girl, Keith. In time you'll learn that with the proper persuasion, the softer sex—be they English or Scot—can be easily swayed and frightened. There's naught to think this one is any different than the rest of her gentle kind."

Gentle. Even as he said the word, Alasdair remembered how the kitten had bared her teeth and rushed him. She'd landed atop him, her legs open, her thighs straddling his waist. For a small girl, her legs were long and powerful enough to grip him with enough force to push the breath from his lungs. Then again, mayhap it wasn't the strength in her legs that had left him breathless? Mayhap . . . ?

Alasdair sighed heavily and diverted his thoughts. Landing him on the floor the way she did had earned her the singularly impressive title of being the only person alive—male or female, on *either* side of the Border—to ever take The Devil off guard. Alasdair's fingers curled into a fist, and he felt the bruised skin on the back of his hand ache in the

57

spot that now bore the little she-cat's mark.

A girl, Alasdair told himself. He had to remember the wench was naught but a girl, and therefore no match for him in either physical strength or mentality. And, of course, she was a *Scots* girl, which meant she should be doubly easy to dupe.

He focused on his brother, his confidence restored. "Rest easy, Keith. Your concern is unwarranted. Once her head has been filled with carefully selected threats, she'll be more than happy to return to Dunnaclard."

Vanessa glanced at the man walking briskly by her side. He was tall, ruggedly shaped, with a crop of fairly short black hair and piercing blue eyes that, on first sight, had labeled him a Gray.

His resemblance to The Devil was striking; a mirror image, right down to the scowl and fierce expression. Obviously, he was either a brother, or a very close cousin. Yet her eye detected subtle differences, too.

While this man was tall, The Devil was taller. While this man was broad, The Devil was broader. She surmised he was younger than Alasdair Gray by half a score. Something in the way he walked, the way he held himself, suggested he hadn't The Devil's toughness or experience.

He did, however, possess The Devil's determination. That much had been evident the moment he'd sauntered into the vault and informed her in no uncertain terms that she'd "been summoned posthaste."

He and his broadsword had convinced her and Duncan that their arguments would not be appreciated, or even tolerated. Since neither Forster had been armed, they'd no choice but to relent.

The man hadn't spoken a word to her since.

58

Vanessa scowled, and took note of her surroundings. While she knew roughly *who* the man was, she still hadn't a clue as to where he was taking her. They'd passed the great hall a few corridors and a wide stone staircase ago. Now, they were tromping quickly through a long, narrow, dimly lit hallway, lined with numerous doors on either side.

An uneasy feeling cooled the blood pumping fast and furious through Vanessa's veins. She quickly pushed the unwelcome sensation aside, deciding it seemed too much like panic. Panic was not something she had either the time or patience to indulge in right now. She was going to need a calm, level head in order to match wits with The Devil; she would have neither if she surrendered to the trickle of fear that iced through her blood.

Though she might not know *where* she was going, there was one thing Vanessa was positive of; she knew *why* she'd been summoned. The Devil had demanded it.

The man stopped abruptly at the last door at the end of the corridor. He administered three quick, hard raps to the thick oak panel.

A summons to enter was immediately voiced from within.

For the first time since he'd stepped into the vault, the man looked at her. A slight, mocking smile curled one corner of his lips. The gesture didn't reach his eyes, which remained cold and guarded. He cocked one dark brow, and nodded toward the door in a manner that suggested he'd every confidence she would obediently open it and scurry into the waiting chamber.

He'd overlooked but one thing; blind obedience simply wasn't in a Forster's nature. Nor did a Forster *scurry* anywhere. Ever. Her indignant gaze strayed from the man to the door, then back again. Slowly,

59

she shook her head.

Their combative gazes met and warred. Blue demanded. Green refused.

The man's lips thinned. His jaw bunched angrily, and a fierce scowl creased his brow as he reached out and unlatched the door. The hinges creaked when he swung it wide, then stood back, waiting impatiently.

Vanessa tilted her chin proudly, and refused to move.

The man sighed his aggravation and planted a big palm in the center of her back. A rough shove saw her stumbling inside.

"I see your point now, brother," he snapped as he spun on his heel. "Were it up to me, the stubborn little chit would stay in the vault indefinitely."

That said, he sent Vanessa one last, scathing glare before retreating to the corridor. He slammed the door shut with enough force to threaten to dislodge it from its hinges.

Vanessa planted her fists on her hips and glared indignantly at the closed door. "Aye, and 'tis thankful I be the decision is not up to ye!" she yelled hotly, then added a few choice Gaelic curses for good measure.

It was, of course, pointless. Not only did the thick oak door muffle her words, but she'd already heard his footsteps recede, and knew he'd moved out of range to hear her. Still, she felt better for having said it. Better, that is, until she heard a noise behind her, and she was abruptly reminded of the other occupant of the room.

Alasdair Gray.

The Devil.

Vanessa shivered, and felt her indignation channel swiftly into another emotion. A hotter, more disturbing emotion. One that both shocked and alarmed her because, truth to tell, the warm, silky current of sensation bolting down her spine wasn't all *that* distressing. Not nearly distressing as it should have been.

"I see you've charmed my brother already," a deep, rich, hatefully English, hatefully sarcastic, voice said from behind her. *Closely* behind her, Vanessa noticed when she felt a rush of warm, whiskey-scented breath brush over her neck. "Keith was . . . shall we say less than pleased, when I told him I'd left you locked in the vault. What, pray tell, did you do to make him change his mind so quickly? Or don't I want to know?"

Since her back was to him, Vanessa hoped he was oblivious to the disturbance his nearness caused her. Lord knew, she wasn't oblivious . . . to that, or anything else about him. In fact, she was all too aware of him. She felt the silky heat of him seeping through her baggy jack and tunic, and felt the skin on her back tingle at the threat of contact with his solid wedge of chest. Every ragged breath she drew in was inundated with his intriguing, spicy male scent.

She swallowed hard, and forced a shrug. "I, er . . . refused to open the door, 'twas all. For some reason he took offense."

Had The Devil moved a fraction closer? It felt as though he had. Vanessa's heart fluttered, and she swallowed back a surge of panic.

"Hmm, now I wonder why that should upset him?" Alasdair replied lazily, his gaze fixed on the top of the girl's head. Her black hair glistened and curled appealingly in the flickering sconcelight. Alasdair angled his head in such a way that his breath whispered softly against her ear when he added, "Methinks 'tis because you've forgotten a thing or two about thick-skulled Sassenach's, wench. We've a

61

tendency to resent prisoners who don't take orders in the accustomed manner. You'd do well to remember that in the future."

He saw a shiver tremble over her shoulders. Was it caused by the feel of his breath on her skin, or his words? He wasn't sure . . . didn't care. That she was responding to him in any way at all pleased him greatly.

Vanessa, on the other hand, wasn't pleased. Her body was reacting to The Devil's nearness in innocently strange ways that both frightened and . . . oh, yes, aroused her. 'Twasn't safe, that.

Deciding some distance might help clear her reeling senses, she stepped to the side, and moved around him, facing the room if not the man. It wasn't an overly large room, she noticed. Nor was it elaborately furnished. Compared to her father's rooms at Dunnaclard, this man's bedchamber looked tiny and bleak, woefully inadequate for a man of Alasdair Gray's station in life.

There was but a very large bed—Vanessa gulped and swiftly averted her gaze—a single chair near the hearth, a decrepit-looking wardrobe, and an old sea chest beneath one of the long, narrow windows. Those were the only furnishings. A few tapestries hung on the walls, but it was apparent from their sun-faded threads that the hangings were to keep out the draft, not for decoration. Other than that, the stone walls looked miserably austere.

Vanessa pursed her lips in surprise. This was it? *This* was the Gray's bedchamber? It wasn't at all what she'd expected—though, if pressed, Vanessa couldn't honestly have said exactly what it was she *had* expected to see here. That might have been because her voice had wilted the second her gaze, of its own accord, strayed back to the piece of furniture she'd been trying very hard to ignore.

Alasdair Gray's bed. Big and wide, with four posts carved of the very best walnut, the bed was the only elegant piece of furniture in the room.

There was, of course, a very plausible explanation for the liquid heat that suddenly pumped through Vanessa's veins. She was sure of it. Unfortunately, she'd no idea what that explanation could be.

A slight sound behind her told her The Devil had moved. Vanessa tracked his footsteps over to the wardrobe, and winced when she heard the hinges creak as he opened it. The next noise to reach her ears was glaringly out of place. It was the sound of glass clinking against glass, and the trickle of liquid bubbling into a goblet.

Not the sounds one expected to hear coming from a wardrobe, especially not when one was expecting— make that *dreading*—the rustle of cloth!

More footsteps followed. Vanessa stiffened when they stopped directly behind her. Potent male heat washed over her back, while a more potent male aroma flooded her senses.

A hand appeared over her shoulder, the thick fingers curled around the stem of a crystal goblet. Vanessa paid scant attention to the cup; 'twas the hand holding it that held her interest.

Her gaze traced over battle-roughened knuckles, over the soft black hair pelting the back of his hand, over a flexible wrist and a brawny forearm exposed by the rolled-back sleeves of his butter-yellow tunic. His shoulder was broad, his neck thick. Dark whiskers shadowed his chin and jaw, while more lightly dusted the sculpted hollows beneath his sharp cheekbones. His eyes, when she reached them, were bright with a tolerant blue light that said her curious stare had amused him.

"Here," he said as he pushed the goblet into her hands. His fingertips felt warm and rough as sandpaper as he coaxed her fingers around the cup, then lifted it to her mouth. The crystal felt ice-cold against her lips, the fruity scent of the wine mildly intriguing. "Drink up, pledge. You're going to need it."

Why? she wondered, but didn't dare ask. Her thoughts strayed to the bed stretching out behind her—*Alasdair Gray's* bed—and she decided instantly that she'd be better off not knowing.

"What's this? Not thirsty?" Alasdair asked when she made no attempt to drink, merely continued to stare up at him from over one slenderly turned shoulder. He noticed a delicate apricot flush staining her cheeks, but though he searched her eyes, the reason for it could not be detected. Pity. He would have liked to know what kind of thoughts a girl like this one entertained. Innocent ones, no doubt.

"I dinna want any wine," she murmured, turning her head away from the glass. "Had ye asked me before pouring it; I would have told ye as much." While the numbness the wine offered was a tempting lure, Vanessa resisted. Her tolerance to liquor had always been low; the amount of wine in that goblet, though scant, was still enough to set her head spinning . . . and her tongue wagging. That would not be wise.

She took a step toward the fire that snapped and danced in the hearth. The heat of the blaze should have warmed her. Holding her hands out to it, she wondered why it didn't.

"Very well then, I guess we should get right to it." Alasdair watched the girl's shoulders go rigid.

"Get to what, mon?"

"What do you think? The 'pledging' part, of course. I'm afraid you're going to have to convince me, in some way or another, that you'll make a . . . er, more interesting pledge than your father. 'Tis the only fair way to decide which of you I should keep, and which I should return to Dunnaclard."

She gasped.

Alasdair grinned and lifted the glass to his lips. Draining the contents of the goblet thirstily, he set it aside. The wine settled in his already liquor-warmed stomach as he crossed the floor and came up behind her.

"Me da?" she asked cautiously. Surely he didn't know who she was. How could he? "And who be that, Devil?"

"Let's forego the games, shall we?" Alasdair said as he settled his hands on the girl's shoulders—*Lord, but she was a delicately built little thing!*—and he felt his palms absorb her telltale shiver. His earlier suspicion was confirmed. She was going to be easily frightened. Ten minutes alone with the legendary Devil, at most, and he'd have her cowered. He was convinced of it. He glanced down at the top of her inky head, and said, "You'll deny it, of course, but your parentage is obvious, kitten. The only thing I've not figured out yet is which of the Forster's daughters you are, although I'm sure if I put my thick-skulled Sassenach mind to it, I can guess. He has . . . what? Three girls?"

"Four," Vanessa corrected spontaneously, then scowled. It wasn't the smartest thing to have said, since such a quick response suggested she was exactly who he suspected her to be. Her frown deepened, and she added lamely, "I think."

"Aye, four. I stand corrected. But one was recently laid to rest, was she not?" He felt the shoulders beneath his hands stiffen, and heard the breath catch in her throat. " 'Twas the eldest, according to rumor. So, of course, you cannot be her. That leaves but three."

"*If* I be one of the Forster's offspring."

65

"Aye, *if.*" Alasdair pursed his lips, and let his fingers drum thoughtfully atop her shoulders. "Let's see now. As I recall, Ursela Forster married the Douglas's brother two summers past. Since Jord would no doubt have a thing or two to say about his wife scampering about the English countryside raiding keeps, I'll assume you're not Ursela. Kayla Forster, on the other hand, is but ten and two."

Before she knew what he was about, and well before she could have stopped him, The Devil had spun her around. Vanessa felt the big, warm hands cradling her shoulders flex, then slowly stray up either side of her neck. Higher. Her heartbeat accelerated when he cupped her cheeks in his palms. Placing his calloused thumbpads beneath her jaw, he coaxed her chin upward, until she was left with no choice but to meet his eyes.

Alasdair searched the delicately molded face. Up close, he saw that she was prettier than he'd first thought—in a sweetly innocent sort of way. Her green eyes were a flattering contrast to the curly raven hair, the ends of which tickled the backs of his hands. The style, while unusually short, was oddly appealing. Also appealing was the way the pulse buried in the hollow of her throat raced against the heel of his palm.

"While you are obviously young, methinks you are not *that* young. Which means you cannot be Kayla. That leaves us with but one daughter." He grinned down at her, and felt her pulse beat quicken. "Hello, Vanessa Forster. I've heard of you."

Obviously, denying her identity now would be pointless. The gray-blue eyes boring into her said The Devil was confident he'd made the correct deduction. She suspected the widening of her own eyes had confirmed it. "Ye've heard good things, me hopes," she replied as, with a forcibly light shrug, she lifted her face from his hands.

Alasdair's grin broadened, and he recushioned his palms atop her shoulders. " 'Twould depend. Do you consider stubborn, reckless, and disobedient to be complimentary terms?"

She nodded.

"Then, aye, everything I've heard about you has been favorable. Tell me something, Vanessa Forster. Is your father aware of what you and your brother have done this night?"

Vanessa shook her head, and swallowed hard when she felt The Devil's fingers begin to massage her tense shoulder muscles. His touch was firm, insistent, soothing—her reaction to it something she dared not contemplate too hard.

"I thought not. He wouldn't approve, I take it?"

Again, she shook her head.

Alasdair sighed, his fingers continuing to work on her. His kneading touch, he noticed, was relaxing the nervously bunched muscles beneath his palms. "Ah, well, there's naught to be done about it now. Whether Hugh approves or not, you're here"—his gaze sharpened on her, and his tone lowered two husky pitches—"in my bedchamber, ready to surrender yourself up to me. Quite noble of you. I'm sure your father will appreciate the sacrifice . . . in time."

Sacrifice? *What* sacrifice? Vanessa's eyes widened, and her thoughts again strayed to Alasdair Gray's bed. She gulped, and shrugged away from him. His touch no longer felt soothing. Though she would have liked to take a step back from him, the fire crackling in the hearth prevented such a hasty retreat. Pity. Some distance from the confusion that was Alasdair Gray would have been appreciated.

She glanced up. "I think ye've misunderstood me, mon. I'm not here to—"a shudder trickled down her spine—" 'offer' meself up to anyone. Nay! I've come

67

only to pledge meself in me da's place, to stay in Cavnearal until the ransom is met. 'Tis *not* the same thing."

"Ah, but it is." Alasdair reached out and stroked her cheek with the back of his knuckles. He felt her tremble as her skin glided beneath his hand; the soft texture reminded him of a sun-warmed rose petal. "Really, kitten, don't you think it would have been smarter to weigh the consequences of my accepting you as pledge *before* you raided my keep? 'Tis too late for second thoughts now. Your offer has already been made. And I must admit, I'm seriously considering agreeing to the trade. You've the potential to make a . . . most entertaining pledge."

The implication in his words made Vanessa's cheeks drain of color. Was it possible to feel hot and cold at the same time? Aye, it must be, for that was exactly how she felt. That, and very, very nervous. "Think again, Devil. I'll not be *entertaining*, if what I think ye have in mind is . . ." She couldn't say it, couldn't *think* it.

His grin was reckless and quick; it didn't reach his eyes. "What do you think I have in mind for you?"

Of its own accord, Vanessa's panicked gaze strayed over her shoulder, and fixed on his bed. She swallowed, hard, twice. Nay, surely the man was not suggesting . . .

She glanced back at him, and the lusty glint in his devil-blue eyes said that, aye, not only was that what he was suggesting, but if he did decide to accept her as a pledge in her father's place, it was what he *expected* of her.

The hand stroking her cheek hesitated, then strayed down to cup her chin in the crook of his index finger. He tipped her gaze back to his when she would have rather looked away. "You look surprised. Why? What did you expect me to do with you?"

'Twas a good question. What *had* she expected this man to do with her? Truthfully, Vanessa didn't know. This was, after all, her substitute plan. Unlike the first one, this scheme had never gotten past the plotting stage. Certainly, it had never gotten this far in her mind!

Though she'd had a nagging suspicion of it before, Vanessa was now certain she was in a good deal of trouble. "I . . . I'll not lay with ye, not even to gain me da's freedom. Dinna even suggest it."

"I'm suggesting no such thing."

And he wasn't, Vanessa realized as she returned his piercing gaze. The Devil did not impress her as the sort of man who wasted time making idle suggestions. Nay, just the opposite. Everything about him *threatened* intimacy, not *implied* it.

The difference was not subtle.

69

Chapter Four

He had her exactly where he wanted her . . .
What's more, he knew it. The girl was struggling to
hide her apprehension, and failing. It was only a
matter of time before she cried defeat, a matter of
time before she admitted her error and begged for
the release of her and her brother. Any minute now,
any second. Alasdair was confident of it.

Through narrow eyes, he watched her gaze dart to
the bed, to him, then back to the bed . . . where it
stayed. A flush crept up her neck, splashed over her
cheeks; he could almost feel an increase of heat seep
through the skin beneath his fingertips.

The muscles in his jaw bunched when he saw the
lump in her throat slide up and down in a dry swallow. The tip of her tongue slid over her lower lip,
wetting the shell-pink flesh until it gleamed in the
muted firelight.

The gesture was unwittingly erotic.

Alasdair swallowed a groan. For one insane second
he ached to tip his head and replace her tongue with
his own. The urge, so strong it pushed the breath
from him, came and went in a beat; it took far
longer for the repercussions of it to stop shuddering
through his system.

His fingers flexed. Her chin felt fragile beneath
his touch. A scowl furrowed his brow. *Fragile?* Nay,
'twas not a word to be associated with Vanessa For-

70

ster, he thought as his gaze strayed to the back of his hand, and the teeth marks that marred his flesh an angry shade of red. The muscle and tendon beneath still smarted. Alasdair winced when he recalled the way the girl had charged him in the vault; the back of his head was still sore from its teeth-jarring collision with cold, unyielding stone.

Fragile? he thought again, and shook his head in disgust. Obviously, 'twas a misassumption born of too much wine and whiskey. Because of all the females living on either side of the Border, Alasdair would have wagered Cavnearal that, while Vanessa Forster might look the part, she was undoubtedly the *least* fragile of the lot.

His voice, when it came, sounded rougher than it had but a moment before. "Well, pledge, what say you?"

"Say me about what, Devil?"

"What else? Tell me how you plan to convince me that you'll make a better pledge than your father."

"Convince ye h-how?"

Alasdair shrugged. He was glad she wasn't looking at him right then, for the gesture was not as casual as it should, by all rights, have been. "It matters not to me, I assure you."

Until that moment, Vanessa had been too preoccupied staring at the bed to give Alasdair proper attention. She noticed him now, though, with a vengeance. Her gaze shifted to him, and she was shocked to see how close he was standing to her. A mere inch was all that separated his chest from hers.

The thought had no more crossed Vanessa's mind when she saw and felt him lean closer still. Their bodies touched; hard against soft, warmth against warmth. Her breath caught, and she started to glance away, but the fingers cradling her chin wouldn't allow it.

71

His voice lowered. "The how of it is not as important as the convincing itself. Somehow you must think of a way to prove to me that 'tis you who'd make the better pledge. I'll warn you now, wench, 'twill not be easy."

Vanessa had already guessed as much. She fidgeted, and not for the first time doubted the wisdom of her offer. Also not for the first time did she recall her vow to her mother—that Hugh Forster would be delivered hale and hearty to Dunnaclard in time for his eighth child's birth. The promise spurred her on. "And how would I be doing that, mon?"

"As I said, it matters not. I'd think the normal way would suffice."

"The normal way," she echoed flatly. Her gaze had drifted down, and fixed upon the laces crisscrossing the front of his tunic, the ones securing the pale-yellow plackets over the wide expanse of his chest. Her gaze rose slowly, locking with his. Was it her imagination, or had The Devil's eyes darkened to an unsettling shade of blue?

One thing that was *not* her imagination was the way her breathing shallowed, and her heart rate doubled. Her palms felt cold and clammy. A shiver raced down Vanessa's spine; fierce Forster pride was the only thing that kept her from succumbing to it.

Her reaction was odd. She wondered if it was a result of The Devil's innuendos . . . or, more likely, the way her mind seemed able to focus only on the places where his body touched hers? Whatever the cause, the sensations tingling through her were alarming, if only because they were also exciting—very—though they shouldn't be.

She took a deep breath and, exerting effort to keep her tone neutral and controlled, said, "What be the . . . er, *normal* way, Devil?"

Alasdair's grin was wicked and quick; it didn't

reach his eyes, which stayed narrow and guarded. "Exactly what you think it is."

"I was afraid ye'd say that."

"I know. 'Tis why I said it." He nodded toward the bed. "Let's get this over with, shall we?"

He toyed with the collar of her tunic, and his thumb dipped absently beneath the cloth; the roughened tip slid back and forth over her skin. His eyes darkened. For a scrawny girl, her skin felt uncommonly warm and soft. Appealingly so. It took effort for Alasdair to remember that, soft skin or not, scrawny girls were not his usual choice of bed partners. Nay, he much preferred his women well rounded and experienced. Of course he did.

"Remove your clothing, kitten, and be quick about it. The hour grows late, and I've still the chore of sampling you before I can rest." His sigh felt hot against her cheek; it stopped just shy of extravagant theatricality. "Do not look so shocked, kitten. 'Tis the only way to decide which Forster to keep . . . and which to return. In other words, which shall make the better pledge."

The tip of his thumb dipped; his nail traced the curve of her upper breast. She wasn't large by any means — he doubted her breasts would even fill his palms — but what there was of her felt enticingly warm and firm.

Vanessa's breath caught, and she swayed toward him. A strange liquid heat flooded through her, making her limbs feel light, yet at the same time leadened. Her skin smoldered to his touch and . . .

The snap of a log falling in the hearth jarred Vanessa back to her senses. Her spine stiffened as she slapped his offensive — *offensive? nay, 'twas anything but!* — hand away. "Nay, Devil, there'll be none of that. The only thing ye'll be doing this eve is returning me da to Dunnaclard." Her green eyes flashed with determination when she added, " 'Tis the bargain we've struck."

"Nay, mistress, 'tis the bargain you suggested. I've yet to agree to your terms, while you've yet to convince me that I should."

Like a magnet to steel, Vanessa's gaze was again drawn to the bed. The mattress looked so wide, so empty, so . . . aye, so *soft*. She gulped, and wondered if her cheeks had gone as cold and pale as they felt.

"Since the Forster canna pay the fine," Vanessa said slowly, if not a wee bit breathlessly, " 'tis the Gray's right to take a pledge. Aye, more than a right, 'tis tradition, 'tis the Law. I canna see, however, what difference it makes *whom* the pledge is. Note, Devil, I be saying *pledge, not* chattel."

Vanessa sucked in an uneven breath and closed her eyes. It helped to blot out the sight of that unnervingly large, empty bed. What didn't help was that, with her eyes closed, her other senses took over. A distinct, spicy male scent tickled her nostrils. She could feel the heat of Alasdair Gray's body warming the front of her thighs, her stomach, her breasts . . .

Her eyes snapped open, and because her head was already turned in that direction, her gaze immediately fell upon the bed. Her mouth went dry. It wasn't difficult to envision The Devil sprawled atop that mattress, his dark head denting the pillow, while the thick coverings draped his lean, naked—"I'll not lay with ye. Nay. Not tonight, not tomorrow night, not *any* night for *any* reason."

"That's your final word then?"

Vanessa did not trust the hint of arrogance she detected in his voice. Her eyes narrowed cautiously. "Aye."

"Good." He flashed her a grin before spinning on

his heel. His long, confident strides ate up the distance to the door. "Come along then, kitten. There's still time to return you and your brother to Dunnaclard before dawn if we hurry."

"Nay, Devil, ye misunderstood. I dinna say I was leaving."

His fingers flexed over the doorlatch, loosened, then flexed again. Too slowly, he lowered his arm to his side and turned to face her. "If you stay, 'twill be to warm my bed."

Her chin tipped proudly. "I'll not do that, either."

"Now, 'tis you who misunderstands, wench, for I'll not give you a choice in the matter."

"There always be choices, Devil."

"In this case, the choice has already been made. You've tendered your offer, I've stated my terms of acceptance. There will be no compromises."

"Ooch, but there will be, mon," she snapped. "Canna ye see it? Ye terms of acceptance will compromise *me*."

"Mayhap you should have thought of that *before* offering to become my pledge."

Aye, mayhap she should have . . . but she hadn't. Vanessa sorely regretted the oversight now, when it was too late to amend it. She quickly changed tactics. "Methinks the March Wardens would have a thing or twa to say about—"

"Damn the March Wardens! They aren't here to judge or to deem what's right and what's wrong. They aren't here to save you, wench. You'd do well to remember that."

"And *ye'd* do well to remember the value of the prisoners ye hold, mon. I'm no commoner to be bedded as ye please, nor will I stand being treated as such."

Alasdair's glare swept her from head to toe. No commoner? Aye, 'twas apparent at a glance. Her thick, shoulder-length raven hair and flashing emerald eyes set her apart from most of the women of his acquaintance, as did her male attire and proud, almost to the point of regal, bearing. Reluctantly, he had to admit that, while his first impression of her as short and scrawny held firm, the girl was anything but common. He had the knot at the base of his skull and the teeth marks on the back of his hand to prove it!

As for the "bedded as you please" part, Alasdair was shocked to find that, in spite of his opinion of her, his body was telling him something entirely different; that it would please him greatly to bed her here and now. Damn the March Wardens, damn her father, and damn the bloody consequences!

'Twas not a safe way to feel about a wench, any wench, but most especially one from the clan Forster. It didn't help that this particular wench was Hugh Forster's daughter. Alasdair decided he was going to have to step up his plan to scare the girl off. Drastic measures were called for if he wanted her back at Dunnaclard by morn.

"Bedded as I please," he repeated under his breath, yet the words were purposely spoken loud enough for Vanessa to hear. Scowling thoughtfully, he scratched the stubble of dark whiskers coating the underside of his chin. "The phrase has a pleasant ring to it, wouldn't you agree, pledge?"

"Nay, I dinna. Not when *I* be the one being bedded."

"I can hardly 'bed' you if you won't get in the bed, wench."

"Aye, Devil, and I won't, either. The only way ye'll see me warming ye bed is to pick me up and carry me there yerself."

The second the words were out, Vanessa wished she could bite them back. A spark of challenge lit the Devil's eyes, and a grin that was purely carnal tilted up one corner of his mouth.

The click of a boot heel hitting stone, as Alasdair Gray took his first step toward her, sounded loud and ominous. Even the snap of logs in the hearth couldn't mute it.

Vanessa's heart raced. While she controlled her first instinct—to take an immediate step backward—she had no control over the second—the apprehensive shiver that hastened up her spine.

Scaling the cliff hadn't killed him. The Devil had yet to harm him in any way. Duncan shook his head, and thought that of the two, the latter was the most impressive miracle. And then the door to the vault was thrown open . . . and Duncan suddenly had no time think at all.

He glanced up in time to see a dark-haired, burly figure being shoved into the chamber. Duncan squinted, but could not make out the intruder's features in what little moonlight sliced in through the narrow windows. In the end, he had no dire need for light; it took only a beat for him to identify his fellow prisoner.

Hugh Forster stumbled clumsily forward. His right shoulder crashed into the far wall with enough force to make him grunt. Spinning on his heel, and rubbing his bruised shoulder, he delivered a stream of Gaelic curses that left no doubt as to his opinion of the abuser's lineage.

Duncan winced as his father's voice slammed in his ears, bouncing off cold, mist-moistened stone. The sound of waves crashing over jagged rock in the Firth below was obliterated by Hugh Forster's sometimes imaginative, most times vulgar, swearing.

Duncan was sitting on the floor with his back

against the wall, his elbows braced on the top of his thighs. He now lowered his head to his hands. His throat felt dry and scratchy as he swallowed back a groan. Two miracles had been bestowed upon him tonight thus far. Dare he hope for another? Dare he *not?* The angry timbre of Hugh Forster's voice said it was going to take a miracle of colossal proportion to see his son survive the dawn.

The guard growled an indecipherable command at Hugh Forster, then, with a disgusted grunt, slammed the vault door shut. A scraping noise was followed by a loud thunk as a thick wooden bar was thrust into place. Boot heels echoed atop stone; then the sound receded quickly. A muffled cough sneaked through the iron bars in the door. The noise, no doubt, was issued by the Englishman left to stand guard over The Devil's prized captives.

If Duncan had shared in his sister's humiliation at having been bested by a mere three men before, 'twas nothing compared to the degradation he felt at having but a single man left to guard two Forsters.

The Devil's confidence was unnerving.

The Devil's confidence was also demeaningly astute.

Duncan glared at the large window, set high into the wall adjacent to where he sat. Though he didn't bother looking at the tall, narrow windows carved into the wall against which he braced his back, that didn't mean he was not aware of them. He was. *Very* aware of them. He was also aware that any exit through them would lead to certain death.

With youthful confidence, Duncan Forster rarely contemplated his own death. The few times he had, the vision was that of a proud Scot giving his life for his clan . . . never that of a coward sneaking through the night, only to fall and be shredded by wet, jagged stone. 'Twould be a disgrace for a Forster—*any* Forster—to meet his demise in such an ignoble fashion.

Duncan closed his eyes, blotting out the sight of the wide, high-set window he could never hope to reach. He sighed when he remembered the way Vanessa had, immediately upon being captured, scrutinized every stony inch of the vault. She'd not found a way out, and it was Duncan's opinion that if *she* could find no escape route from this cursed place, there was simply none to be had.

He tensed, feeling rather than seeing the hot glare his father turned upon him. Duncan thought fleetingly of the guard standing in the arched-stone corridor. He wondered if, should Hugh Forster try to strangle his tenthborn on the spot, the Englishman would rush in and offer him assistance? Probably not. More likely, the cursed Sassenach would aid Hugh Forster, not hinder him.

Duncan opened his eyes and stared at the stone floor. More precisely, he stared at one of the beams of silvery moonlight pouring over it. A boot came into view. 'Twas a very large, very familiar boot. Duncan traced the boot up over tight-fitting trews, the material of which was forced to stretch to accommodate the heavily muscled thigh beneath. Up, over lean hips and a flat, tight stomach. Though Hugh Forster's tunic was customarily baggy to aid unrestricted movement, the loose, butternut-yellow folds couldn't conceal the impressive breadth of his chest, or the broad fullness in his shoulders.

The lump in Hugh Forster's throat slid up and down in an angry swallow. Even beneath the dark beard, Duncan could see the tight bunch of muscle in his father's jaw that meant the man was gritting his teeth. There was a furious ruddy undertone to his cheeks, and a definite flash of fury in his narrow,

Forster-green eyes. The thick, dark brows that normally rode low on Hugh Forster's brow now rode lower still; they were slanted in a fierce V, making his expression take on a seething quality that set his son's already frayed nerves on edge.

In broad daylight, the Forster's expression had been known to make the most valorous of reivers take heed and give quarter. Moonlight and shadow now played over his features, sculpting and harshening the rigid planes and angles until his face looked as though it had been chiseled from granite. In the unsteady light, Hugh Forster's expression seemed all the more fierce. Murderous, even.

Duncan had the good sense to wince. The reaction earned him a savage scowl from his father.

Anger darkened the Forster's eyes to a shade of stormy green. Duncan found the sight less than comforting. The last time he'd seen that expression on his father's face was when Hugh Forster had discovered his youngest son had dressed his second youngest daughter as a lad and sneaked her into The Day of Truce.

The incident was a mere twelve months old; the punishment he'd received that day was still fresh enough in Duncan's mind to make his young heart pound and his blood flow cold. Last year's deception had been a lark, instigated, as always, by Vanessa. 'Twas a minor transgression compared to the scheme he and his sister had chanced this night. Chanced . . . and failed.

"I'll be telling ye twa things afore I beat ye to within an inch of yer miserable life, lad." The Forster's voice was so loud, so thick with fury, that Duncan could have sworn the stone beneath him quavered from the force of it. Or mayhap that was Duncan who trembled. "The first is that, were I unconvinced of it before, I ken now ye be no bairn of mine. 'Tis inconceivable a lad so foolhardy could spring from *any* Forster's loins."

Planting balled fists on thick hips, Hugh bent at the waist and leaned forward until his scowling face was eye level with his son's. Their noses grazed.

Duncan sat up straighter, pressing himself back against the stone as though trying to melt right into it. If only he *could!* If he'd doubted it before, he now was positive . . . the tremors he felt emanated from within himself. Never, *never* had Duncan seen his father this angry.

"The second," Hugh growled intimidatingly, "and maun important, is what I'll be doing to ye if the Devil touches so much as a hair on yer sister's head."

Truly, Duncan did not want to know what his father would do to him should that happen. Already he was eaten with guilt that he'd allowed Vanessa to convince him to take part in another of her idiotic schemes. Yet, as always, her reasoning had seemed sound. Deceptively so . . . when they'd been safely tucked within Dunnaclard's sturdy walls. 'Twas only once they'd reached Cavnearal—standing on the cliff walk, when it was far too late to turn back—that Duncan had begun to have doubts, begun to truly fathom the magnitude—*the insanity!*—of what he and Vanessa were doing.

A lad of but ten and four, accompanied by a lass a mere five summers his elder, attempting to breach the walls of a keep that not only belonged to the fiercest reiver on either side of the Border but was also reputed to be unbreachable. Madness! Of course, Duncan thought 'twas even more insane that the feat had been accomplished . . . even though the ultimate goal, Hugh Forster's liberation, had not been realized.

Duncan frowned thoughtfully. Wasn't infiltrating the best-guarded keep on the English side of the

Border a victory for any Scot to boast of? Aye! Unfortunately, being captured in the process was not. 'Twas for that folly alone that Duncan now found himself staring into his father's murderous glare.

"Ye'll be explaining yerself, Duncan, for I've a very real need to thrash ye for yer stupidity. Be warned, I'll not restrain meself unless ye start speaking posthaste."

Hugh Forster was nothing if not a man of his word; Duncan never doubted his father's ability or determination to do exactly as promised. Starting with his sister's visit to his bedchamber at dusk, the story tumbled from Duncan's lips as best he could remember it.

Hugh Forster didn't move a muscle the entire time his son spoke. It wasn't until Duncan had finished relating the tale that he straightened; the fluidness of the motion was too slow, too controlled to be natural.

"So, the lass pledged herself in me place," Hugh said. That his voice remained low and even was testament to his mounting fury. "And ye did not even once think to stop her?"

"Aye, I did . . . but ye know Vanessa when she's got a plan. I tried convincing her this scheme was madness, that 'twould never work, but she'd not listen to a word of it."

"Then why did ye not lock her in her room, Duncan?"

Duncan gaped at his father. Truly, he'd never considered it. He wished now that he had, for he realized that the perfect chance to lock Vanessa away until she came to her senses had come when she'd left his bedchamber to change her clothes. Her determination to free their father from The Devil's clutches had been infectious; Duncan had been so busy dwelling on ways to make Vanessa's plan work that he hadn't given stopping her a thought.

A guilty flush stained his cheeks as he tore his eyes from his father's. He averted his gaze to the big, single window at Hugh Forster's back.

" 'Tis a wild guess I be making here, lad, but I've a thought ye dinna bother to ask Dugald's opinion of yer sister's foolish plan, did ye?"

Duncan scowled at the mention of his eldest brother. At two score five, Dugald Forster had recently been appointed Clan Forster's captain, a rank second in command only to their father. "Why would I—?"

"Ooch! ye've got that backward. The question is, why would yer *not* be asking his advice! God's teeth, do ye think ye brother was elected Clan Captain because of his thoughtlessness? Nay! Had ye spared the time to talk to Dugald, mayhap ye and that hot-headed, reckless, brazen, careless, impetuous—" His eyes sparkled a stormy shade of green as, looking heavenward, Hugh growled under his breath, "That girl will be the death of me, I swear!" Then, louder, he continued. "The lass would be asleep in her bed at Dunnaclard instead of The Devil's prisoner."

A chill whisked over the nape of Duncan's neck; he rubbed it away with his palm as he pulled his father into focus. Something was not right here. Aye, something was not right at all. But what? His gaze narrowed suspiciously. Though he could not yet pinpoint it, instinct said his father was not reacting the way he should.

Frowning, Duncan replayed his father's words about speaking to Dugald over in his head, only this time he listened to his tone rather than the content. While Hugh Forster's voice had not lost its anger by any means, Duncan thought the pitch was a tad less harsh than it had been a few short minutes before. And a slight change in the man's expression—so

83

slight it was almost nonexistent — implied the edge to his father's fury had dulled. Not much, but a wee bit.

Hugh shook his head, then straightened. Stepping around his son, he rested a shoulder against the sharp stone corner of the window and glared down at the top of Duncan's head. A sigh poured from his lips; the way the noise bounced off moist stone made it sound more like a hiss. "I should have listened to yer mother and fostered ye out, lad. Mayhap without a cohort, that reckless, impulsive, temperamental . . ." He hesitated, closed his eyes for a beat, sighed deeply, *"sister* of yers would not have attempted a fraction of these ludicrous schemes of hers."

Duncan's head was down, his fingers linked behind his neck. Every muscle in his body was rigid. The beginning of a headache drummed in his temples. The inside of his eyelids felt dry and gritty when he blinked, reminding him of the six hours sleep he'd lost this night. "I've a thought Vanessa would have tried them with or without me," he said.

Hugh grunted his agreement. "Aye, ye be right. Ooch! lad, if I'd a muckle of common sense I'd have married the lass off to Henry Graham two summers past."

"Ye tried," Duncan said, wincing at the memory of that summer. "As I recall, she'd have none of it."

"As *I* recall, she ran away."

"Aye," Duncan replied with a sigh. "That, too."

"Gone for near a fortnight, she was. Not a soul knew where she was. Ye poor mother was worried to death."

Duncan rolled his lips inward and, lowering his head, cradled his chin atop his collarbone. It took effort to make his shrug look casual. What would his father do if he knew the truth? Duncan shook his head. The man would no doubt throttle his son, for,

84

while it was a fact that Vanessa had been gone from Dunnaclard for nearly a fortnight, and that their mother had worried endlessly, it wasn't true that none had knowledge of the lass's whereabouts. Duncan had known . . . and never told.

As though his father could read his mind, Duncan squirmed guiltily.

Hugh Forster pushed away from the window and strode to the middle of the vault; the click of his steps bounced ominously off stone, making the ensuing silence even more pronounced. A quick glance at his father's brooding expression and hands-on-hips stance convinced Duncan that this would *not* be the ideal time to confess past misdeeds.

With a sigh, Duncan lifted his ·head. The wall pressed against the back of his neck, the base of his skull, his shoulder blades; the stone felt as hard and as cold as the glare his father turned on him. The shadows were thick where Hugh Forster stood. Duncan had to squint to bring the man into focus. "If I'd told Dugald of Vanessa's plan," he said cautiously, "what would he have said?"

"Do ye mean after he finished laughing?" Hugh asked most seriously.

Duncan gritted his teeth and nodded. "Aye, after that."

"He'd have convinced ye not to do it. Rather, he'd have tried to convince that flighty, misguided, irresponsible . . . er, sister of yers. We both know ye had naught to do with the planning of this night's adventure, lad. Nay, it has Vanessa's mark on it."

"And if Dugald failed to convince her?"

"He'd not have failed."

"But if he *had?*"

"Then Dugald would have found another way to keep the twa of ye inside Dunnaclard's walls. If I be sure of nothing else, I be sure of that."

"Methinks even yer precious Dugald would not be able to keep Vanessa in a place she doesna want to be."

A muscle in Hugh's cheek twitched, and the corners of his green eyes narrowed. Those were his only signs of emotion. They were more than enough to make his son fidget. "The Devil has her jailed in this cursed place, does he not? What say you to that, Duncan? Or are ye trying to tell me she *wants* to be here?"

"Nay, I dinna say that."

"Then what *are* ye saying?"

"Only that Dugald would not have been able to stop Vanessa if she's of a mind to do something, and she was of a mind to free ye."

"And who told her I was of a mind to be freed? Hmm?"

The question took Duncan so off guard that at first he didn't respond. Not want to be freed from The Devil's clutches? Surely his father jested! Didn't he?

Duncan's gaze sharpened. Though his father stood cloaked in shadow, Duncan had long since grown accustomed to the vault's poor lighting. Even in a pitch-black room, he would have been able to discern the Forster's scowl. The man's expression was legendary; 'twas the only frown on either side of the Border to have a ballad written about it — a ballad that was sung to English bairns by their mothers as a warning against bad behavior . . . or so 'twas said.

Hugh huffed and shook his head. In long, angry strides, he crossed to the door, scowled fiercely through the bars at the guard who stood in the corridor without. Duncan wasn't positive, but he could have sworn he heard a scuffing sound, as though the guard had squirmed under the onslaught of that fiery green gaze.

Crossing his arms over his chest, Hugh turned his head and set the brunt of that gaze on his son. "Answer me, lad. Who told that addled, persistent . . . sister of yers that I was of a mind to be freed?"

"No one, but—"

Hugh's hand chopped the air in front of him, effectively silencing his son's words. "And did it never once cross either of yer minds that a laird like meself does not pledge himself for the minor offenses I was being accused of?"

"Aye, but—"

"And did it never occur to either of ye that, since I *did* offer meself as a pledge, that maybe I had me reasons to do it? Reasons I've not shared with ye?"

"Nay, but—"

"And did it never, in the three hours it took ye to reach Cavnearal, dawn on either of ye that ye were about to breach an unbreachable fortress, that ye—"

Beneath his breath, Duncan said, "Well, 'tis not *completely* unbreachable . . ."

"—just ye and that stubborn, reckless . . . sister of yers, or that instead of finding me, ye would find the end of the Devil's sword in ye bellies?"

Duncan swallowed hard, and tried his best not to squirm as his father's voice slammed off the stone around him. That Hugh Forster's tone was rising in volume attested to his anger . . . but not so much as the fists he clenched and unclenched at his sides, as though he gripped his son's throat in his powerful grasp.

"Last, Duncan, did ye never once stop to think that, in the last two months, the Forsters have had more successful raids than unsuccessful ones? That our coffers are *not* bare, that our herds are *not* lean and not near depleted?"

Duncan felt as though his father had just landed a solid punch to his middle. The air rushed from his lungs, and he lowered his head to his hands. His voice barely above a whisper, he said, "Nay, I'd not thought of any of that."

"Then mayhap ye should have . . . *before* ye and that tenacious, willful . . . er, *sister* of ye's raided Cavnearal!"

"Had we been successful—"

"I'd be thrashing ye to within an inch of yer miserable Forster hide. 'Tis only because ye were not successful that keeps me from doing it now. That, and knowing ye were but a pawn in all this, that yer sister be the real culprit."

Duncan lifted his head and glanced at his father. "She was trying to save ye."

The sound of Hugh Forster's fist colliding with the thick wooden door startled Duncan. The guard in the corridor no doubt had a similar reaction.

Hugh took a step toward his son. Then, as though he didn't trust himself not to harm Duncan should he get too close, he stopped short. His glare burned from out of the shadows; Duncan swore he could feel the heat of that gaze scorch him. "Are ye deaf, or merely dimwitted?! I've told ye once, lad, I'll but tell ye once more: *I-dinna-need-saving!* Had ye talked to Dugald, he would have told ye of our plan."

Duncan gulped and again lowered his head to his hands. If possible, the situation was worsening. "Plan?"

"Aye, a plan be what two or more people with a scrap of intelligence do *before* setting out on a mission. Ye and Vanessa would know naught about such drivel, but Dugald and I do. 'Twas our plan that in less than a fortnight the Gray's fine would be paid, and I would ride from Cavnearal all the wiser for gleaning it and the keep's inner workings. I stress the words 'would have,' Duncan. Only the Good Lord knows what will happen to us now that The

88

Devil has that thick-skulled impetuous, daft . . ."

A surge of despair washed over Duncan's tone. "Ye mean this night's efforts were all for naught?"

"Aye. Ye and Vanessa may have meant well — that's yet to be disproved — but the fact is, ye interference has put the Clan Forster in a most unpleasant, not to mention embarrassing, position. Now, not only does The Devil hold the clan's laird, but two of me bairns as well." Sucking in a furious breath, Hugh spun on his heel, gripped his hands tightly behind his back, and began pacing the stone directly in front of the door. "Ooch! Duncan, I've not a doubt The Devil is even now smiling and gloating over his victory."

Chapter Five

Alasdair Gray wasn't the sort of man who backed away from a challenge; it wasn't in his nature to even contemplate such a ludicrous notion, especially when the challenge in question was issued by a mere slip of a girl. While his liquor-soaked mind might have distorted the subtlety of it, there wasn't a doubt in his mind that a challenge *had* been issued . . . and accepted in the first brisk step he took toward her.

Vanessa gritted her teeth and made to sidestep him.

Alasdair shadowed the movement. Another step, and he was blocking her path to the door. "Going somewhere?"

"Aye, back to the vault," she snapped. "Methinks those accommodations be a fine muckle safer than the ones ye offer."

"I've not given you permission to leave."

"There be a reason for that, Devil. I dinna ask for permission. Now, be a good Sassenach and move out of me way."

Alasdair reached out and dragged the roughened tip of his index finger along the line of her jaw. The soft flesh beneath his fingertip quavered. It was the only physical contact between them. It was enough. "I am not, nor have I ever been, a 'good Sassenach.' Have you not figured that out yet, wench?"

Vanessa wanted to pull back from his touch. It was warm, unsettling! She swiftly countered the urge, deciding there was no need for The Devil to learn how much the feel of his skin against hers disturbed her. Wasn't it bad enough his touch disturbed her at all?

"Have you no answer?" he asked. "I must say, 'tis a pleasant first."

Vanessa suppressed a shiver when his stroking finger rounded the curve of her chin, then slid over the sensitive underside. Ooch! but 'twas difficult to think when he touched her so! It took a second before she trusted her voice to speak. It was time well spent, for her tone sounded as cool and regal as she'd hoped it would when she said, " 'Tis not that, Devil. I merely saw no reason to belabor the obvious. Ye've a fine reputation, and 'tis not that of a 'good Sassenach.' "

He smiled, pleased. "Good. The reputation you speak of was many years in the making. I'd hate to see all my fine work go to waste." He sighed and shook his head. "You know, wench, while I think 'tis an interesting diversion you've created, I'm not so easily diverted. Not for long. Sooner or later, I am going to turn the topic back to the wondrous pleasures that can be had from pledging . . ."

"Diversion?" she asked, feeling it better by far to leave the latter part of his statement untouched. He would get back to it soon, she'd no doubt. "Nay, Devil, ye misunderstand yet again. I was but making polite conversation."

"Really? I've always been of the opinion that pleasantries are best exchanged in the hall, over a trencher. 'Tis certainly not what I seek whilst I'm in my own bedchamber"—his finger dipped, trailing the line of her throat—"with a wench." She swallowed hard, and his fingertip traced the quick, up-and-down movement. "Nay, make that a *pledge*."

"I'm not ye pledge. Did ye not say so yerself?" she reminded him sharply, then swallowed back a groan. Her voice sounded husky and raw, indicating that his words, his touch, affected her greatly. Of course, neither did. She'd not allow them to!

"Aye, so I did. But then, is that not the matter up for debate, wench?"

"I'll not debate a thing with ye." She sucked in a shaky breath and pulled back from his touch. It did no good; his hand merely tracked her. His fingertip felt quite good against her skin, now that she thought about it. She tried not to think about it. Reinforcing her voice with a strength and determination she hardly felt, she added, " 'Tis quite simple, really. I'll not lay with ye. End of debate."

"Wrong."

"What?"

"You heard me. In case you've not noticed, your options are sorely limited. Either you prove you're the better pledge, or you'll be returned to Dunnaclard posthaste." One dark brow cocked challengingly high as he mirrored her words of only a second ago. "End of debate."

Again, Vanessa's thoughts lit upon the bed at her back. This time, however, her mind's eye filled the empty spread of mattress with an intimate effigy of her and Alasdair Gray sprawled atop it. A shiver curled down her spine; a shiver that had little to do with the hands The Devil had just cushioned atop her shoulders. His fingers felt strong as they curled inward, tunneling through her padded jack and tunic, digging into the tender flesh beneath, though not painfully so. Yet.

Alasdair watched a flood of apricot heat the girl's cheeks. Though her pose remained rigid and defiant, it was apparent his threats, his touch, were having the desired effect upon her. Very soon now she would be begging him to return her to Dunnaclard. A grin tugged at one corner of his mouth, but it was quickly suppressed.

When she held her silence, Alasdair said, "At this point, the only matter up for debate, wench, is whether you plan to warm my bed of your own free will, or whether I must put you there." His pause was short, but significant. "Rest assured, you've still one avenue of escape if you find both choices unappealing."

"And what be that?"

"Admit the foolishness of your ways and ask to be escorted home. Believe me, I'd be most happy to comply. In fact, I will deliver you back to Dunnaclard myself. Of course, before you leave, I'll have your method of gaining entry to my keep."

"Then prepare to be decidedly *un*happy, Devil, for I willna be leaving. As for telling ye how Duncan and I came to be here . . . well, ye'll have a long wait for that information. I willna tell ye, no matter what form of torture ye threaten me with."

This time, Alasdair made no attempt to restrain his grin. In fact, he made it — as well as the burning, head-to-toe glance he gave her — as suggestive as possible. "In that case . . ."

His gaze drifted past her shoulders, darkening when it fell upon the bed. The warm orangey glow from the hearth skimmed and danced atop the mattress, making it look warm and soft and sinfully inviting. Alasdair frowned. Surely it was the liquor in his system that made this bed, the mattress of which he'd slept upon for countless nights without ever giving it more than a passing thought, look suddenly new and alluring.

Aye, the liquor, he thought, seizing on the excuse. What other reason could there be? His gaze shifted, locking with wary green. Softly, as his thumbs stroked over her shoulders, he said, "Let the games commence."

After but a second's hesitation, Vanessa opened her mouth to deliver the tongue-lashing this man so justly deserved. Pity she had no breath to make the speech with, for the man's hands had just released her shoulders, and his big, warm, open palms were suddenly skimming down the front of her padded jack. His touch was casual and skilled, his destination alarmingly obvious.

Vanessa swallowed hard, and fought a surge of panic. If ever she needed a plan, it was *now*. Unfortunately, with Alasdair Gray's hands on her body, a plan was the last thing her mind was capable of forming. She would simply have to rely on instinct. That worried her, for her instinct had never been very good; she much preferred having the time to think things through, to plot, before taking action.

The descent of his hands assured her that time was a luxury she did not have.

Balling her hands into tight fists, Vanessa pillowed them against Alasdair's chest, and pushed. Hard. Since his hands had just breached the upper swell of her breasts—even through the thick padding she could feel the heat of his fingers scorching her skin—he was in no position to stop the momentum of her shove. Alasdair grunted—in pain or surprise?—and stumbled back a step. It was all the distance she needed.

Her movements quick and lithe, Vanessa sidestepped him and bolted for the door. The stone floor slapped at the bottom of her feet; even through the thick boots she wore, she could feel the force of each running step vibrate all the way up to her knees. Her hands unconsciously reached to hoist up her skirt. It took only a second for Vanessa to remember she wasn't wearing one. Not for the first time that night was she thankful she'd had the forethought to plan her attire. Not only did her boys' clothing make running uncomplicated, but it gave The Devil not a single inch of skirt to grab on to and yank her to a halt.

The door was mere inches away. Vanessa had no idea where she would go once she'd crossed the threshold—she hadn't an inkling of Cavnearal's twisting corridors — nor did she care. Anywhere that Alasdair Gray was not would be a haven.

Her first indication that all was not right was when she realized there was no sound of a pursuit being launched from behind. Oh, there was noise, yes, but not a lot of it and not the heavy, running footsteps she expected.

She frowned, even as her fingers closed on the cold metal doorlatch. Her heart was pounding madly, and though she'd run only a short distance, her lungs were sawing with the need for air. Her palms felt chilly and damp as, with trembling fingers, she swiftly lifted the latch. Flattening her palm against the rough oak door, she shoved so hard that her shoulder actually stung from the force she put into the motion.

The door did not budge.

Vanessa stared, stunned, at the thick, inanimate panel of wood, then shook her head and shoved again. Harder.

As though it was a boulder of intimidating size, the door remained firmly closed.

Locked in. At some point, either The Devil or his surly brother had locked the door. How had she not noticed?! Her breathing became shallow and rapid. She now knew how a falcon felt when its head was knotted beneath a thick black hood. It was a disturbing feeling. But not nearly as disturbing as the feel of hot, liquor-scented breath whisking over her neck.

Her hands clenched into tight fists at her side as she spun around and leaned back heavily against the door. The Devil was standing a mere two inches away. She was not overly surprised to find him that close; she'd heard him move, after all. She was also not pleased. *Alarmed* . . . aye, that would have been a better word.

"Check . . ." He casually placed his left palm flat against the door beside her shoulder, "mate." His right palm mirrored the motion. The Devil's heavily muscled arms caged her in place. He grinned suggestively and bowed slightly forward.

Even without making physical contact, the size and strength and position of his body crowded Vanessa against the hard wood grinding into her back. Oh how she wished she could think of a sharp verbal jab to stab him with! Unfortunately, for the first time in her life, she was speechless. She suspected that had something to do with the way the heat of his body was melting through her clothes, warming and caressing the flesh beneath until she felt like her skin had been touched by fire.

Alasdair wondered if the girl was going to melt her body right into the oak. She certainly looked as though she wanted to. While he couldn't blame her for her sudden need to escape, he would be lying if he didn't admit to a certain amount of anger over it. After all, *she'd* been the one to suggest this "trade" in the first place. It hadn't been *his* idea!

She stiffened, and Alasdair's attention sliced downward. Her green eyes were wider than usual, her cheeks flushed. She was breathing heavily, and the pulse in her throat was pounding. He swore softly when he saw that the jaunty angle of her chin and the rigid set of her shoulders was as defiant as ever. He wondered if pigheadedness was bred into Scots women from their cradling. No English woman of his acquaintance would dare look at him with such hostility, not even his sisters.

His gaze skimmed the delicate line of her jaw, the high curve of her cheekbone. Finally, he met her gaze. "Methinks 'tis time for this game to end. I'm tired and I've drunk entirely too much whiskey and ale this night. My reasoning is clouded, and my patience is running sore low."

Alasdair didn't realize he'd lifted a hand from the door and was running the tip of his index finger along her moist lower lip until he felt her skin tremble beneath his touch. Yet, even when he did realize what he was doing, he did not remove his hand, or pull back. He found he rather liked the feel of her soft pink flesh gliding under his own roughened skin.

Vanessa found that, while it wasn't easy to speak when her lips were being fondled by Alasdair Gray's fingertip, she somehow managed. Her tone only slightly breathless, she said, " 'Tis no game we play, ye thick-skulled Sassenach."

"Ah, I'm that again, am I? Methinks Hugh Forster should have taught his children to mind their tongues. Your sharp words will get you into trouble one of these days, kitten. Mark my words."

What Vanessa would rather have done was mark his body, or, barring that, slap the disturbing feel of his hand away. Unfortunately, she'd no weapon to carry through on the former, and could see no point in attempting the latter. Aye, she could slap him, and 'twas even feasible she might be able to squirm away from him, but to what end? The stairs she'd climbed earlier said this chamber was not on ground level, which made the windows carved into the far wall a dubious exit. With the door locked, there was, quite simply, no place for her to go!

Vanessa took a deep breath. Her gaze lifted, locking with his. Cautiously, she said, "Methinks it time ye explained the full duties of being a Gray's pledge. I've a sudden need to know." She bit back a groan when she felt the way her lips moved against his rough fingertip.

Alasdair shrugged as his attention dropped to the tip of his finger; it was now nuzzling the very corner of her mouth. He felt her breaths, hot and rapid, on the back of his hand. A shiver worked its way up his arm, trembling beneath the skin. His heart doubled its beat, and his tone dropped a husky pitch. " 'Tis something you'd have done well to think on *before* making your offer, kitten."

Aye, she was starting to think he was right, but there was no help for it now. The time to renege on her hastily made offer had come and gone. Truly, she'd rather die than let this man know she'd even considered the notion! 'Twould be admitting to weakness, and such admissions rubbed against a Forster's grain.

When she made no comment, Alasdair dropped his hand, balling it into a fist and planting it atop his hip. His other hand still splayed the door. Slowly, he bent his elbow, until his forearm was flush with the wood. His inner arm grazed her shoulder. He was close enough to feel the way her every inhalation brought the tips of her breast in contact with his chest.

His eyes narrowed and darkened, and again he blamed the liquor for the warm, tingling sensations that stabbed through him like a sharply honed dagger. "The full duties of a Gray's pledge are quite simple, since there's but one," he said, his voice low and husky.

She glared at him suspiciously.

"Blind obedience. In all matters. 'Tis all I require from a pledge."

Vanessa nibbled her lower lip to keep from groaning. So much for "simple." Had the man not yet figured out that blind obedience was as alien to her as renouncing her strong Forster pride? If not, he was about to learn it! Her gaze flickered past him, fixing on the bed. Skeptically, she said, "In *all* things, Devil?"

"Aye, kitten."

"And if I refuse?"

"I've told you what will happen. I'll return you to Dunnaclard at once."

Vanessa scowled. The feel of the hard wooden door grinding into her back made her feel trapped. But not nearly so much as the strong male body directly in front of her. "And if I've no wish to do either?"

Alasdair shrugged. "What you *wish* to do is not my concern. What you *will* do, is."

Vanessa swallowed hard, and quickly changed tactics. "Ye havena accepted me deal yet, Devil. What guarantee do I have that ye will after I—er—prove meself the better pledge?"

"You've none," he admitted. " 'Tis best to never count on guarantees, kitten. Life offers scarce few."

"I'm not talking about life, I be talking about pledging. I be talking about the weight of a Gray's word . . ." Beneath her breath, just loud enough for him to hear, she added, "If there be such a thing, and rumor has it there's not." Her gaze shifted, locking with his. "What be yer honor worth, Devil? If I agree to yer terms, will ye let me da and brother go free?"

Alasdair's eyes narrowed warily. The girl wasn't seriously considering going through with this, was she? Of course not! He hoped. Though he tried to assess her mood by tone and facial expression, truly he could get nowhere. Her eyes were wide and clear, and though he could see emotions playing behind their green depths, there was no deciphering them. Her expression was aloof, composed. The rapidness of her breaths was the only outward sign of her turmoil, and that could have stemmed from a variety of different sources—fear for her virtue being but one.

Alasdair raked the fingers of his left hand through his hair and, pushing away from the door—her nearness disturbed him more than he cared to admit—said, "As I recall, that was our deal."

"Ooch! mon, that be no answer. Will ye honor ye word? Aye or nay?"

He didn't respond, but instead pivoted on his heel and strode agitatedly toward the hearth. His boot heels made cold clicks atop the bare stone.

Without thinking, Vanessa pushed away from the door and dogged his heels. "I be asking ye a question. Will ye honor yer word? *Aye-or-nay?*"

Alasdair stopped abruptly. Bracing his hands atop the stone mantel, he bowed slightly forward, head down, gaze sightlessly trained on the crackling flames. His mind was elsewhere, focused on the bed a scarce ten feet behind him, and on the girl who stood much closer. A girl who, unless he was extremely careful, would soon be warming that bed.

His prolonged silence grated on Vanessa's nerves. She wanted an answer, and wanted it now. Aye, she *deserved* no less!

Scooting around him, she ducked beneath his left arm and came up standing directly in front of him. Very closely in front of him, if the shiver that worked its way up her spine meant anything. The heat of the fire, so close to her back, felt oddly brisk compared to the silky warmth Alasdair Gray's body emitted.

Alasdair's gaze sliced upward, over snug-fitting trews that encased slim but shapely legs. Over a dull yellow tunic that was not nearly baggy enough to conceal the small but alluring curves beneath. The padded jack added an unnatural breadth to her shoulders, hinting at the lad he'd originally thought her to be. Her hair was wind-tangled in short and gentle curls. The dark color emphasized her cream-and-apricot complexion, and complemented her crystal-green eyes.

He noticed that the pulse in the base of her throat was pounding hard. Exertion would not account for that. The room she'd just crossed was not so wide, the effort it took to follow him not so great. While the heat of the fire might explain the flush in her cheeks, it didn't explain her fast, shallow breaths. Or the way her gaze dipped to his mouth, then jerked guiltily away.

It was time.

His well-placed threats had done naught to deter the girl. God's teeth, even for a Scot, she was stubborn! If he hoped to get a wink of sleep this night, then it was time to augment his threats with action.

One hand came away from the mantel, and wrapped lightly around the girl's throat. Her eyes flashed with panic, but the emotion was quickly concealed. His attention dipped to her mouth as he said slowly, precisely, "Get in the bed, wench."

Vanessa pulled back, but not far. With the fire so close behind her, there was nowhere for her to retreat. Of course, the powerful fingers coiled around her throat also ensured close proximity. She tilted her chin proudly, and tried to ignore the way the heat of his gaze scorched over her lips as she answered him. "Nay, not until ye've answered me question."

"I'll not answer your question until you're in my bed."

"And I willna get in yer bed until ye answer me question."

His gaze narrowed and darkened, never leaving her mouth. "Aye, kitten, you will."

The tip of Vanessa's tongue dragged over her suddenly parched lips. It did no good. The heat of his gaze burned away any moisture she'd added. How she managed to keep her tone calm and firm, she'd never know. "Nay, Devil, I willna."

One dark brow cocked mockingly high. "Does that mean you're ready to be escorted home?"

"Nay!"

"Then it's to bed with you," Alasdair announced as he took a quick step back. Bending at the waist, he hoisted the shocked into temporary immobility girl into his arms . . . then, with a grin, roughly tossed her over his shoulder. She was slim and light, the burden of her weight no greater than that of one of the dogs chained up in the hall below. Much like those dogs, Alasdair fully expected the girl to regain her sense and start kicking and struggling long before he reached the bed.

The breath rushed from Vanessa's lungs in a strangled "Ooof!" when her stomach made a teeth-jarring collision with his shoulder. Sweet Saint Andrews, the man was firm! She felt as though she'd been carelessly tossed over a boulder. It took a second for her to catch her breath, and another for her to realize where Alasdair Gray was carrying her.

The bed!

Pummeling his back with her fists seemed a natural inclination; it was an inclination Vanessa made no attempt to suppress. She whacked him hard on the base of the spine—the man didn't even have the decency to grunt. "Ooch! ye brute! Put me down! This show of brutality will do naught to change me mind!"

Alasdair grinned. Obviously, he disagreed. He winced when she delivered a sharp punch to his kidney. He felt her shift to strike again, but this time he was ready for her. "Cease!" he snapped over his shoulder.

"And if I willna?"

"Then I'll do it for you."

Another blow to his kidneys told Alasdair the lass needed convincing. And who was he to deny her?! One hand was wrapped around her upper thighs, holding her securely in place. He grinned as his free hand lifted . . . and made such a powerful collision with her squirming bottom that his palm actually stung from the blow.

Vanessa yelped, and instantly stilled. Her trews were not so thick that the material could protect her from his slap. Her bottom smarted. She had to grit her teeth to swallow back a curse. She'd a feeling that venting the harsh words swimming in her head right now would not better her situation.

Her ribs ached and her temples throbbed from the blood that had rushed to her head. Her hands dangled limply at Alasdair's back, and her fingers felt icy and slightly numb.

Alasdair stopped beside the bed. While the girl

slung haphazardly over his shoulder had been still since he'd swatted her, there seemed to be an underlying tension in her. He could feel the stomach muscles pressing into his shoulder harden. The thighs beneath his fingers did the same. Was she getting ready to bolt the instant he laid her down? Could be. However, even if she tried, she'd not get far. The locked door, combined with his own determination to see her returned to Dunnaclard before sunrise, would see to that.

"Manhandling women isna a way to endear yerself to them, ye thick-skulled Sassenach."

"I've no wish to endear myself to you, so do not trouble yourself about it."

Ooch! did the man not know his admission was more troubling to her than had he agreed? "I'll ask ye to put me down now, Devil. I can scarcely breathe!"

"You have only to ask, kitten," Alasdair said as he shifted her weight on his shoulder. Her response was a muffled grunt as the air pushed from her lungs. He felt her arms flail for a second, and then her fingers fisted around the hem of his tunic. Her fingernails scratched the sensitive flesh beneath. Her grip was tight, as though she feared he might accidentally drop her on her head atop the cold stone floor. Alasdair thought it a pity his nature wasn't so cruel. Not that he hadn't considered the idea a time or two.

"Well?" Vanessa asked a bit breathlessly. Her diaphragm was pressed firmly to the hard shelf of his shoulder now, which made breathing a laborious chore. The prolonged, upside-down position was making her feel light-headed and dizzy. "Are ye going to set me down afore I faint from all this blood rushing to me head?"

"Of course. An unconscious wench would do me no good." As though he was handling nothing heavier or more important than a sack of grain, Alasdair effortlessly dragged her off his shoulder and tossed her onto the bed. While his movements weren't rough, neither could they be misconstrued as gentle. Truly, the chit would try the patience of a saint!

The mattress crunched when Vanessa's body landed roughly atop it. She bounced twice before settling. Her vision blurred, and her head swam with the abrupt drain of circulation. She could actually hear the blood rushing through the veins in her temples.

It took a second to regain her equilibrium. Her head had missed the pillows, and she'd landed catty-corner on the bed. It was from that angle that Vanessa glared angrily up at Alasdair Gray, who stood, fists on hips, towering over the side of the bed, close to her booted feet. She frowned. "Maun ye be so barbaric?"

"Aye, I must. At the rate you're going, you'll not have time to prove what a fine pledge you would make. I sought only to aid you in your endeavor." Was it Alasdair's imagination, or did the blood that had drained from her cheeks when he'd thrown her onto his bed suddenly come rushing back? Her breathing was still rapid and choppy, though she'd had ample time to regulate it. His gaze lifted, meeting hers. He watched her eyes widen, as though she'd just now realized exactly whose bed she was in . . . and why.

Vanessa muttered a Gaelic curse, and levered herself up on her elbows. Her intent was to scramble off the bed. But the way The Devil's eyes narrowed and darkened told her that mayhap an alternate plan might be in order.

A plan, Vanessa thought. A plan that would see her not only safely out of The Devil's bedchamber, but out of Cavnearal, as well—with her father and Duncan in tow, of course.

Her mind churned, but then a movement snagged her attention, and her eyes fixed on Alasdair Gray . . . and all cohesive thought fled her mind. She swallowed dryly. "Wh-what be ye doing, mon?"

"Isn't it obvious? I'm removing my tunic."

And so he was. Sweet, merciful heavens!

She watched, mesmerized, as in one fluid motion he gripped the frayed hems of his tunic in both hands and dragged it upward. Slowly. Over his hard, flat belly. Over his broad, muscular shoulders. Over his head. The glow of the fire cast his skin an appealing shade of bronze, highlighted the thick patch of black hair coating his chest in warm shades of orange. Her gaze followed that patch of hair down to where it thinned and arrowed beneath the waist of his trews. Her heart stammered.

With his back to the fire, his face was cast in shadows. But that was all right. Vanessa didn't need to see the challenging glint in his eyes to know it was there. She *felt* it. Her breath took a ragged turn as she pushed herself further up on the bed, until she was sitting on one of his pillows, her rigid back plastered against the carved wooden headboard. "Wait!" she ordered when his hand dipped, reaching for the fasteners on his trews.

Alasdair hesitated. "Wait for what?"

Eternity was what she wanted to say. But didn't. She couldn't help wondering why, the one time in her life when she most needed a plausible plan, she could not think of a single one. Nay, that was not completely true, she amended. There *was* one plan tumbling through her mind, but she'd already deemed it ridiculous; 'twas doubtful a man as shrewd as Alasdair Gray would fall for it. Still, if the situation turned dire, she just might become desperate enough to set such a scheme into motion.

Her gaze focused on The Devil's hands. His wrists were thick, his forearms thicker. His biceps were thicker still, tapering off to a most impressive breadth of shoulders. His pitch-black hair hugged the cord of his neck and the hard line of his jaw. The inky strands fell to a point just past his shoulders, and the dark ends curled slightly where they rested against the very top of his chest.

His chest.

Oh, God!

"Well?" he said when she made no reply, but continued to stare nervously up at him. He was surprised she hadn't become a very real part of the headboard, so hard was she pressing herself against it. "What would you have me wait for, wench?"

Judgment Day, mayhap? Nay, Vanessa deemed that an unsuitable reply as well. Her attention darted to the door, to The Devil, then back again. Vividly, she recalled the inflexibility of that portal when she'd pushed so hard against it. Locked. No escape route there, and she'd already judged the windows useless for anything beyond fresh air and viewing the landscape. There was but one way out of this room, and that was agreeing to let this man return her to Dunnaclard.

'Twas a problem, that. Because, as much as she wanted to, Vanessa could not go home. Not yet. Not whilst she still had a promise to uphold. Her mother's time was drawing near, less than a fortnight now, and Vanessa had sworn she'd return her father to Dunnaclard before the birthing. The last two bairns had been stillborn, and the second death had devastated her mother.

Wasn't it natural for Hannah Forster to crave her husband at her side when her time came, if only for the reassurance Hugh's presence could offer? Aye, 'twas. Just as it was also natural for Vanessa to feel honor-bound to uphold her vow to her mother. After all, 'twas common knowledge a Forster *never* welshed on a promise, unless death interceded.

Chapter Six

The pull of Alasdair Gray's gaze was like a magnet; Vanessa's attention was unwillingly drawn back to him. Her heart skipped a beat when she noticed his hands were poised on the fasteners at the waist of his trews.

"Why so quiet, kitten?" Alasdair's gaze dipped to the small, angry red teeth marks marring the back of his hand. He flexed the fingers of that hand as, slowly, meaningfully, his gaze lifted and locked with hers. "I'd have thought you to be hissing and spitting by now."

"The night isna over, Devil."

One corner of his mouth lifted in a suggestive grin. "Aye. And well I know it."

His fingers began fiddling with the fasteners, and Vanessa felt her heart lodge in the vicinity of her suddenly dry, suddenly tight throat. She pressed harder against the headboard. The pressure of wood grinding into her spine and the base of her skull was a welcome distraction. It helped her to think more clearly. Something had to be done. *Immediately!* But what?

She needed a plan.

The one she'd formulated and cast aside too many times to count came rushing back to the fore. The plan itself was flawed; even if executed perfectly, it could easily explode in her face. Unfortunately, the cursed Sassenach, who was even now stripping away his clothes, gave her little choice in the matter!

Vanessa sucked in a deep, steadying breath. She

didn't realize she was fisting the hem of her padded jack until she felt her knuckles throb, her grip was that nervous and tight. A rustle of cloth near her feet told her The Devil had rid himself of his trews. She refused to peer in that direction to confirm this, however; seeing Alasdair Gray naked would do naught to augment her courage!

The mattress dipped and crunched, as though a knee had just been braced atop it. A blast of heat emanated from a spot close to her outer calf, the warmth seeping through her trews, stroking and caressing the sensitive flesh beneath.

The room, she noticed, had become much too hot. Vanessa wished she could attribute the unnatural heat to the flames dancing in the hearth, but she knew full well that the fire had little to do with her discomfort. Alasdair Gray—his heat, his scent, his nearness—had everything to do with it.

"You know," he said casually as he braced both knees atop the mattress so he was kneeling beside her feet, "if you hold your tongue much longer, I'll think you've changed your mind and agreed to my terms."

"Mayhap I be considering it, mon. Did ye ever think of that?"

No, as a matter of fact, he hadn't. And he wasn't about to now. His goal was to see this girl back at Dunnaclard, where she belonged, come daybreak, and that was exactly what Alasdair intended to do. Whatever it took. A Gray never admitted defeat, even when the defeat in question was surrendered to a scrawny Scots lass. Aye, *especially* then.

Why, he wondered sourly, *why* hadn't she scared off and begged him to bring her home when he'd first suggested she warm his bed? 'Twould have gone far better for them both if she'd reacted in the accustomed manner, the way any normal girl who found herself in the same situation would have.

His gaze narrowed and sharpened, raking her from head to toe. This was no ordinary girl. When it came right down to it, what this girl was, was a Scot to the core. To his way of thinking, both her flaws made her of inferior intelligence, and therefore easily duped. She was, after all, female and a Scot . . . not an exemplary combination.

He noticed the way her knees were bent and drawn up, the soles of her boots planted flat atop the bed. Chips of dry mud scattered the bed linen near her feet.

His attention dipped. The trews that clung to what appeared to be slender, shapely calves and thighs were torn in spots. He saw that the jack she clutched closely to her chest was worn and thin; the padding beneath poked through the leather in several places. That, combined with her wind-tangled black hair and the smudges of dirt on her delicately carved jaw and forehead, gave her a shabby appearance.

He took a hesitant sniff of the air. And grimaced. "You're filthy, and you smell none too appealing," Alasdair announced as he moved to straddle her thighs. Her gaze was trained on the fire, but he saw the way her eyes widened when she felt the weight of him on her legs. Or maybe 'twas his words that stirred her reaction? "You need a bath."

Vanessa's voice cracked, but only a wee bit. "Dinna waste ye flattery on me, Devil. I'll be warning ye now, sweet words willna turn me head, nor do ye a bit of good."

He glared down at her. " 'Twas no compliment, that."

"Aye, and well I ken it. But 'twas either thank ye, or slug ye. I'll admit," she added with a dramatic sigh, "both options held equal appeal."

His tone lowered a derisive pitch. "In your present condition, you hold no appeal whatsoever."

His legs were vising her knees. She felt the muscles in his calves and thighs pull taut. Ooch! but he was a solid one. And powerful, if the discomfort of his legs gripping hers had anything to say about it.

Alasdair bowed forward, flattening his palms atop the pillows on either side of her hips. He scowled darkly.

God's teeth, the brat was sitting on his pillows! If the back of her trews were as ripped and stained as the front . . . Truly, her impudence knew no bounds. He sighed inwardly. 'Twas no more than he should expect from a female. A *Scots* female. "I think I've just been insulted," he said tightly.

Beneath her breath, Vanessa muttered, "Ooch! and they say Sassenach's be addle-witted . . ."

He glared down at her. "Your tongue is too sharp by far. An English wench would know better than to speak to me so."

"Aye, well, ye be too heavy by far. And yer compliment says naught for an Englishwoman's intelligence, don't ye know? 'Tis surprised I am to hear they'd admit to speaking to the likes of ye at all."

He started to move closer to her, but Vanessa placed a balled fist atop each of his shoulders and gave a light shove. She put very little force behind the gesture. Why bother? Had she not tried moving this man only moments ago? She had, and in the process she'd learned that when Alasdair Gray did not wish to be moved, he *did not* move. She squirmed beneath him, to no avail.

Ignoring her hands, Alasdair slowly lowered a little more of his weight atop her.

The curve of her hip brushed his inner forearm. The inside of his thighs gloved the outer stretch of hers. " 'Twould seem more than your body is in need of washing, wench," he said softly, menacingly. "Your tongue could use a good scrubbing as well. Aye, mayhap *more* than the rest of you."

Vanessa made no reply, but merely glared rebelliously up at him.

Alasdair was tired as holy hell, and more than a little irritated by this stubborn little scrap of a wench who seemed determined to thwart him at every turn. It didn't help that most of the liquor had drained from his body, leaving him with the foggy pounding of a headache stirring behind his eyes and in his temples, and a bitter, cottony taste in his mouth.

Games. They'd been baiting each other, doing naught but exchanging pointed barbs, from the moment Keith had escorted the girl to Alasdair's bedchamber. Dueling with words instead of swords. Nothing but frustration had come of it. It was time, Alasdair decided abruptly, to call an end to this foolishness. He wanted this girl gone from Cavnearal. *Now!*

But first, of course, he would have to get off her. Then, according to his plan, he must convince her she *wanted* to leave.

Alasdair gritted his teeth, and winced at the pain that throbbed through his temples. He thought 'twas the latter chore that would prove the most troublesome.

Ignoring the way her legs wedged so perfectly between his naked knees, Alasdair pushed himself up, rolled to the side, and rose from the bed. He glanced down at the girl, and saw that she was watching him warily. Was it his state of undress that put patches of apricot color in her cheeks? 'Twas doubtful. She'd yet to look at him fully to discern just how undressed he truly was. Twice he'd caught her attention starting to descend curiously from his face, only to have her green eyes widen, and her gaze jerk back up again.

"Get up," Alasdair commanded, even as he spun on his heel and stalked to the door. He snatched his trews up off the floor without breaking stride, tugging them roughly up his legs and over his hips only once he was standing in front of the door.

The thick panel of wood threatened to splinter when Alasdair pounded his fist against it. Immediately, there was a scrape of wood as the bar on the outer side was lifted.

The air in the corridor was cold; it blasted over Alasdair's half-clothed body when the door was swung open. Was it his imagination, or did the guard who stood framed in the portal have an amused expression on his face? If so, it took but a second for Alasdair to glare the man into somberness. "Fetch a tub and at least half a dozen buckets of hot . . ." He hesitated, scowling when

111

he remembered the girl's torn trews and dirt-smudged face, "*very* hot water. And be quick about it!"

"Aye, m'lord!"

The man's words were barely out of his mouth when Alasdair slammed the door shut. A chuckle wafted in through the quarter-inch slat of space beneath the door. The sound was followed by the scrape of wood as the bar was lowered, then the thud of footsteps as the guard hastened to do his lord's bidding.

Vanessa gulped. "What be ye doing now, mon?"

"I've ordered you a bath," he growled, not bothering to turn around as he spoke.

" 'Tis written nowhere that a pledge must be clean."

"An oversight. One I'll do my best to see corrected on the next Day of Truce. Meanwhile, I suggest you strip before the water arrives."

"I dinna want to strip!"

Alasdair's voice rose, mimicking her thick Scots burr. "I dinna ask what ye wanted. Now, be a good little pledge and take off your clothes and be done with it."

"Nay!"

Alasdair turned around slowly, and leaned his back against the door. He crossed his arms over his chest, and one dark brow cocked menacingly high. After three deep breaths, he felt he had his temper in sufficient control to speak calmly. "Would you rather I took those rags off you myself?"

Vanessa's chin lifted, and she came very close to daring him to do just that. But 'twas a dare she knew a man like this one wouldn't think twice about meeting. Still, her intense Forster pride shunned open compliance. Meeting Alasdair's gaze with a determined glare of her own, she said, "Ye could try. But I'll warn ye now . . . I willna give ye an easy time of it."

"Remember what I said earlier about expecting blind obedience, wench?"

"Aye. Remember also, Devil, that I never agreed to it."

"Methinks it's past time I persuaded you otherwise."

He grinned slowly, arrogantly, and was rewarded by the way her cheeks drained of color, then just as swiftly filled with an abundance of it. Still leaning negligently against the door, he lifted one hand and wriggled his index finger at her. "Come here."

Vanessa shook her head. She'd have voiced a hearty protest . . . had her pounding heart not just lodged in her tightly constricted throat. Truly, the man was insane! 'Twas bad enough he stood half naked and proud across the room from her—it was growing increasingly difficult to not let her curious gaze stray over him!—but to *obey* him, to cross the room and *willingly* stand near such raw strength . . . well, 'twas unthinkable. Especially when the unclothed man in question was threatening to disrobe and wash her!

Feeling too vulnerable huddled up against the headboard, Vanessa shifted position and came up on her knees, facing him. She clutched the soft leather plackets of her jack protectively over her breasts, and shook a few unruly strands of hair from her eyes with a quick toss of her head.

Their gazes warred as each silently dared the other to look away first. The air crackled with tension.

A shiver iced down Vanessa's spine when he pushed away from the door and took a step toward her.

Her mind raced. It was difficult to think straight when her gaze was being held prisoner by Alasdair Gray's sharp eyes. The skin covering his cheeks was tight, and his lips were thinned with determination. Even at this distance, she could see the pulse hammering in the base of his sunbronzed neck.

Vanessa swallowed hard. Another step and he'd be beside the bed, beside *her*. She was aware that she would have nowhere to go once her feet hit the floor, yet she couldn't suppress the urge to bolt.

The mattress crunched as she sat back on her calves and spun around, quickly slipping her legs over the opposite side of the bed. The panic she'd been fighting ever since entering this man's bedchamber bubbled free.

Vanessa had no more started to push herself to her feet when the mattress behind her dipped, tipping her off balance. She was in the process of fighting the momentum when powerful fingers coiled around her upper arms.

With an effortless tug, The Devil hauled her backward.

Vanessa's breath caught in her throat when she felt her back come up hard against Alasdair Gray's naked chest. Even her thick jack wasn't thick enough to obscure the heat of him from seeping through the bulky barrier.

Panic clawed through Vanessa. Her heart was pounding so fast and hard she wondered if it might not tire itself out and stop on the spot. Her sleeves provided inadequate protection from The Devil's grip; even through the thick leather and padding, she felt his fingers bite into her tender skin.

He was kneeling on the bed, and when he shifted, his knees vised her hips. Tightly. The back of her head had slammed against his breastbone when he'd yanked her backward; now she could feel the wash of his breath scalding over the top of her head. His breathing was equally as erratic as her own.

"Unhand me," she ordered breathlessly. She tried to squirm from his grip, but it held firm. She was not surprised.

"Only if you agree to go home, wench."

"I've already told ye, I'm here to stay. At least until the ransom be paid."

He angled his head, and Vanessa now felt his breath wash over her ear and the tense line of her jaw. The fingers gripping her arms flexed. "Then I'll not be letting go of you anytime soon. I will, however, be helping you out of those rags. Your bath will be here momentarily."

Alasdair expected the girl to fight him. He wasn't disappointed. He'd no more spoken the last word when she started struggling, wriggling and trying to free herself from his grip. As her feet came up, her boots wedged against the side of the wooden bedframe, and her legs straightened as she strained to topple him backward.

He'd already been toppled by this wench once tonight. 'Twas one time too many. He sat back on his heels, dragging her with him, her back still plastered to his chest. One hand released her arm to circle her waist, holding her tightly. God's teeth, she was small! The leather of her jack felt cold against his chest and arm, but it quickly warmed to the heat of his body. Her unfashionably short black hair tickled the underside of his jaw and his bare shoulders when she lowered her chin, then sent her head careening backward. Alasdair, correctly sensing her intent, tensed, making the collision of the back of her head and his shoulder not as painful as it might have been.

Not, that is, painful to *Alasdair*.

Vanessa grunted when the back of her head came up teeth-jarringly hard against a shoulder that had the consistency of stone.

She stilled, but only temporarily.

One by one, Alasdair uncurled his fingers from around her arm, then lowered his hand to his thigh. The tip of his thumb grazed the curve of her hip, which was nestled between his legs. He tensed, and wondered how such a simple touch could send a blaze of liquid fire searing up his arm?

Angling his head, he whispered huskily in her ear. "I'll give you but one more chance to undress yourself. If you refuse, I *will* do it for you."

To Vanessa's way of thinking, a choice was comprised of two or more workable options. There was no choice in this matter; The Devil had seen to that. Her only selections were to undress herself, or have him do it for her. Either way, the result would be the same. She shivered.

Alasdair's chest absorbed the minuscule tremor, and he grinned. "Well?"

"Hush up, Devil, I be thinking on it!"

"The time to think has come and gone." His pause was short and tense. "But, being the generous, thick-skulled Sassenach that I am, I'll allow you to the count of five to make your decision. After that . . ."

His shrug finished the sentence. Vanessa wished he'd used words. Her imagination was too sharp; it quickly filled in the gaps his trailing words had left out. And . . .

Wait a moment. Had this man just called himself *generous?* Aye! She frowned. The tales—and ballads, and poems—she'd heard told about this particular Border reiver argued his self-compliment. The "thick-skulled Sassenach" part, however, stood firm. 'Twas the only thing he'd gotten right.

"One."

Did the arm curled around her waist just tighten?

"Two."

His voice sounded closer to her ear. So close, in fact, that his breaths disturbed the hair curling against her cheek and jaw. It disturbed the creamy skin beneath still more, but Vanessa tried to ignore that.

"Three."

The muscles in the legs flanking her hips went rigid. The chest pressing against her back felt hard and hot and . . .

Sweet Saint Andrews, was Duncan right? *Had* she gone daft?! 'Twould seem so, for Vanessa knew she *should* be concentrating on concocting a plan to get herself out of this mess. Searching for a weapon would not be a waste of time. Better still, she could resume her struggles to free herself. Anything, *anything at all,* would be smarter than wasting precious time by taking a mental inventory the numerous spots where The Devil's body touched hers.

"Four."

She scanned the room, but saw nothing within reach that might be used as a weapon. Oh, how she longed for her broadsword! A weapon like that would shift the balance of power quite nicely. She cursed under her breath, remembering how bairnishly simple it had been for The Devil to disarm her in the vault. The humiliation had been—still was!—great. She refused to add to it by allowing this crude beast to undress her. Nay, she would *not!*

"Fi—"

The elbows Vanessa rammed into The Devil's gut stole the rest of his word, not to mention a good deal of his breath. Alasdair hadn't been prepared for that and . . . bloody hell, it hurt! Her elbows were sharp, her jabs stronger than a girl her size should be able to carry through on. The breath whooshed from his lungs, even as his grip on her loosened.

That was exactly what Vanessa had been waiting for. The second she felt his grip slacken, she lurched for the edge of the bed. He was quick, immediately lunging after her, but not quick enough. Vanessa had the advantage of surprise on her side.

She hit the floor running. To where she didn't know, nor did she waste time thinking about it; liberating herself from The Devil's bed had been a large accomplishment in itself. Aye, and a surprisingly simple one at that!

Indeed, now that she thought on it, her escape seemed *too* simple. 'Twas almost as though he'd *let* her. . . .

Reaching the center of the room, and with nowhere really to go, Vanessa hesitated. In the tense silence that ensued, The Devil's laughter sounded loud and grating. She spun around and glared at him. "Ye think this funny, do ye?"

His wicked grin and condescending gaze spoke for itself.

Her eyes narrowed. "Ye be a sore lot worse in the arrogance department than most thick-skulled Sassenachs, mon."

Alasdair ignored the jibe. While his grin never slipped, the laughter faded from his eyes. His gaze

117

sharpened on her. "Are you ready to go home, wench?"

"I've told ye nay time after time. Do ye have a problem with yer ears?"

"At present, the only problem I have is being in the unsavory position of housing three too many Forsters under my roof." And mayhap of drinking a tad too much whiskey, he thought but didn't add.

" 'Tis a problem easily remedied, Devil. Ye need only accept me as pledge, and let me da and Duncan go home to Dunnaclard. Where they belong." She raised her hand and snapped her fingers. "The problem is solved. Come dawn, Cavnearal will house two less Forsters.

Alasdair shrugged, and leaned back lazily on the bed, propping his shoulders against the headboard. Lacing the fingers of both hands together, he used his palms as a pillow on which to rest the back of his head. As though protesting his negligent pose, the muscles in his arms and chest looked bunched and tight, like he was prepared to pounce on a second's notice. "Unfortunately, problems such as this are not so easily remedied." He sighed. "More's the pity."

Vanessa gritted her teeth to keep from saying something she'd regret. But, oh, she was tempted!

Alasdair shifted on the bed and said blandly, "Now, about those clothes . . ."

Her glare turned into a scowl. "Back to that, are we?"

"Aye. So long as you remain dressed, we'll keep coming back to it, wench. And I guarantee you, one way or another, those filthy rags will be coming off you. Soon."

"So ye've said. The threat is getting old, Devil." The second the words were out, she recognized them for the mistake they were. Drat it all!

The change in Alasdair was subtle, yet undeniable. It was in the way his steely eyes narrowed, his jaw hardened, his lips thinned. In the way he very slowly, very precisely, slipped his legs over the side of the bed and stood.

Vanessa swallowed hard. At this distance—which

wasn't so great; certainly not as great as she would have liked for it to be! — he looked taller, broader, more powerful and imposing.

And determined. Aye, he looked most determined!

The firelight was at his back, glistening over his shoulders and casting the skin there an appealing shade of bronze. His dark hair shadowed his face, making his expression impossible to discern accurately. But Vanessa's senses filled in the gaps, and her senses told her that she might well have pushed this man a wee bit too far.

She took a step backward. He grinned, and she saw a flash of his teeth against the shadows masking his face. A peculiar, warm-cold chill washed through her. "I — I think ye may have misunderstood me, Devil."

"I know a challenge when I hear one, Vanessa."

"Challenge? Nay, 'twas not what I meant!"

"Then what *did* you mean?"

Ah, 'twas a good question, that. The problem was, Vanessa had meant every word she'd said. What she *hadn't* meant was to voice the sentiment aloud. Nor had she meant for her tone to be so sarcastic. "I meant only that, um . . ."

Their gazes met and held; hard blue, nervous green.

" 'Tis the funny thing about challenges," Alasdair said as he took slow steps toward her. "Pride goads us into issuing them, just as it goads us into accepting them." He paused for a tormenting second, a frown furrowing his brow as he angled his head to one side. "Tell me something, Vanessa. Whose pride do you think is stronger in this instance? Yours or mine?"

He stopped a hand's breadth in front of her. His wide chest and shoulders shaded her from the heat of the fire . . . and replaced it with the heat of his body. Vanessa gulped.

Her chin had lowered; Vanessa noticed this fact only when she felt the tip of his index finger beneath her chin, tilting her head back up again. His skin felt rough and warm as it abraded hers. *Rough and warm.* Aye, 'twas

119

an accurate summary of the man's scent — of the *man himself*. Rough and warm. Woodsy. Appealing. Disturbing beyond reason.

"The clothes . . ." he coaxed, and the words served to jar her back to the topic at hand. Her clothes. Or, rather, Alasdair Gray's eagerness to rid her of them.

She gripped the plackets of the jack protectively beneath her chin. The leather crinkled in her fists, the sound was obliterated by the ragged give and take of her breaths. She no longer needed to have her chin held up at a lofty angle; she was able to do that of her own accord.

Alasdair could tell the girl was gritting her teeth by the way the muscles in her jaw bunched. Her eyes were narrow, the irises now a dark, fiery shade of green. The color in her cheeks had not been put there by modesty; raw fury had inspired it. While he no longer touched her, his hand was poised a fraction from her jaw. She shook her head, and the ends of her hair whispered over his knuckles; the strands felt like silk.

He pulled back quickly, and only when he realized his gaze was trained on her mouth — for a scrawny, unappealing girl, her lips were kissably soft, dewy moist, a mouth-watering shade of pink — did Alasdair's attention lower. He frowned, forcing his thoughts onto a more direct path. Was the faded yellow tunic he'd glimpsed but briefly beneath the padded leather jack as dirty and frayed as the trews encasing her legs?

There was but one way to find out.

Crossing his arms over his chest, and leaning forward until he'd crowded her back a step, Alasdair growled, "Five!"

The girl startled at his bellow. She moved to sidestep him, but his hands shot out, grabbing her around her upper arms and hauling her roughly against his chest. The top of her head barely cleared his chin; he could feel her soft hair whisk the sensitive underside of his jaw when her head shot up.

Alasdair glanced down, and was instantly arrested by

her furious glare. He didn't notice her lift her foot . . . until she brought the heel of it down in a crushing collision with the top of his bare foot.

"Why you little so and so—that bloody well *hurts!*" Without letting her go completely, he loosened his grasp and adjusted his balance to accommodate his throbbing right foot. His hand lifted to deliver a resounding slap; 'twas an automatic response.

Vanessa gasped, but refused to flinch.

Alasdair scowled down at her. The temptation to hit her was so strong he could taste it.

Holding his anger in check took every ounce of concentration he possessed. With strained movements, he lowered his hand, let her go, then reached out and brushed her hands away from where she'd fisted the jack beneath her chin. One by one, he curled his fingers around the worn leather plackets, which were still warm and slightly moist from her grasp. His fingers flexed inwardly at the observation, and the leather crinkled in response. His grip was tight enough to make his knuckles sting.

He tugged and lifted at the same time, bringing her up on her toes until they were nose-to-nose. Her ragged breathing washed in heated waves over Alasdair's skin. As far as he could tell, that was her only sign of agitation.

"That," he said much too softly, much too calmly for Vanessa's liking, "does it. Strip now, or I'll do the chore for you. Beware, 'tis no empty threat I make this time."

Vanessa could see that. Determination was etched in the granite-hard lines of The Devil's face. This time, she'd no doubt he'd carry through on the promise. Aye, 'twas a promise, not a threat; she could read the conviction in his eyes.

"I can do naught whilst ye be holding me in this position, Devil," she said, and cringed inwardly when she heard the high, breathless timbre of her voice ringing in her ears.

"Knowing you, wench, you'd do naught if I let you

121

go. Except try to bolt again. Where you thought to be going is still a mystery to me. One I'll not lay awake nights wondering about, I assure you." As he spoke, his grip on her jack loosened but didn't fall away. Instead, he spread the plackets and nudged the coat over her shoulders. She stiffened, but didn't pull back. Perhaps she sensed it was useless? Her glare of protest would have heated all of Cavnearal in the dead of winter.

Her arms were stiff at her sides as he slid the sleeves down, then released the jack and let it fall to the floor. The padding and layer of protective metal made the garment heavy; it hit the stone with a dull thud. The tunic beneath was in as bad a shape as her trews. That was no surprise. What *was,* however, was the body that the thickly padded coat had concealed.

While her shirt was baggy, it wasn't baggy enough for Alasdair's piece of mind. Linen could only hide so much, and that watery yellow cloth didn't stand a chance of obscuring the sensuous curves that lay beneath; curves that the jack had hidden from view. Until now.

She's young, she's impudent, and she's . . . small and scrawny. Not much to look upon, considering what she's been sent here to offer.

The words he'd spoken to Keith scarcely an hour before clogged in Alasdair's throat. It took effort to work his voice around them. "Shall you finish the chore, pledge, or shall I?"

"Since I've told ye repeatedly I willna do it," she said tightly, "I guess ye will have to."

Alasdair was afraid she'd say that. His fingers paused on the laces of her tunic. He glanced at her, one dark brow tipped in askance.

She glared insolently back at him.

He sighed and began picking at the knot. Bloody hell, the thing was tied tightly! While he tried to convince himself that he was doing nothing more complicated than preparing Kirsta for bed—a chore he'd done rarely—Alasdair could only fool himself for so long.

Truly, his fingertips had never stung and smoldered when they'd brushed against his young sister's throat!

Vanessa's heart was beating fast and furious; she felt the tempo of the pulse in her throat drum against The Devil's fingertips.

He seemed to be having trouble untying the laces of her tunic. Vanessa offered no help. Indeed, she couldn't even if she'd wanted to — the harsh realization that this man was about to strip her bare had frozen her in place — and she most assuredly did *not* want to. Nay, what she wanted to do, what she *should* be doing, was fighting this man. Tooth and nail. Now!

And that was exactly what Vanessa did.

The stomp of her heel on his foot had been a lover's caress compared to the impact of her booted toe smashing into The Devil's shin. She gave him no time to react before drawing back her fist and planting it solidly in his middle, making the air whoosh from his lungs. While she might be small of stature, her brothers had taught her how to pack power in her punch. 'Twas one of the rare lessons of theirs that Vanessa actually learned to put into practice.

It was as she was lifting her hands to box his ears that Alasdair recovered. With lightning speed, he ensnared her wrists, stopping her fists from a painful collision with either side of his head. What foggy aftereffects that were left from the whiskey burned off to fury.

Robert Carey be damned! Hugh Forster be damned! This girl needed to learn a lesson, and needed to learn it badly. Alasdair was in the perfect mood to teach her.

He forced her arms down by her side, ignoring her feeble struggles. When she shifted her weight, lifting a foot for another blow to his shin, Alasdair glared her into submission. Well, all right, perhaps not *submission* exactly, she was far too spirited for that, but at least she hesitated.

Before she could plan her next move — which would undoubtedly be to render him more pain — he curled an arm around her waist and, turning, lifted her off her feet. Her back pressed firmly against his side, her bottom balanced atop his hipbone. She cursed in Gaelic, her fingers clawing at his restraining arm. The nip of her nails on his flesh stung; the feeling did little to improve his mood.

"Settle down," he growled in her ear.

"Let me be," she snapped, "and I'll consider it."

"I'd sooner set a wolf loose on a pack of winter-fat sheep. Surely it would do less damage than you."

Vanessa struggled to free herself, but to no avail. The arm banded around her middle was thick and muscular; it wouldn't be budged. "I've yet to *start* damaging ye, mon. Let me down this instant or I swear to ye, I'll . . ."

"What?" he prodded, and his arm tightened around her still more when she tried to wriggle from his grip. "What will you do, Vanessa? Summon the March Wardens? Robert Carey won't hear you from here, and George Humes isn't interested enough in Border disputes on either side to be bothered aiding you. And even if he did, I've no intention of sending a messenger to the man on your behalf. You could tell your father, but I fear he'd be no use to you at the moment. He's a bit . . . indisposed. You could yell for a guard, but my men are too loyal to show you more than a passing interest." She went completely still in his arms as he angled his head, his lips brushing her ear when he added, "So tell me . . . what will you do?"

Vanessa refused to answer; truly, there *was* no answer. She had no weapon to defend herself or back up her words. The man whose rock-solid side was pressing into her back was strong enough, angry enough, to gain her compliance in any way he chose. Speaking her mind now would not aid in her release, 'twould *delay* it. She was smart enough to know that.

It took effort, but she closed her eyes and forced herself to remain still even when she felt his free hand stray over her shoulder, and once again pick at the laces of her tunic. His fingertips chaffed her skin as he worked on the knot; 'twas not nearly the repulsive feeling it should have been.

The laces came undone. Cool air sneaked between the now-gaping plackets. Vanessa shivered. The Devil's cheek was nestled against the side of her head, and she felt the muscles there pull taut in a grin.

His free hand strayed to the waistband of her trews. He curled his fingers around a fistful of the threadworn material of her tunic. One tug, and he had the front hem of her tunic free of restriction. Two more tugs, one on either side of her waist, had it freed entirely.

More cool air rushed over her. This time Vanessa repressed her shiver, knowing it wasn't the brisk air that caused it so much as the male heat that instantly countered it.

She opened her eyes when he coaxed the baggy hem up over her stomach, working in harmony with the steel band of his arm around her waist. It wasn't until she felt his arm press against her bare stomach—his flesh was hot, the light dusting of black hair there tickled slightly—that she wrapped the fingers of both her hands tightly around his wrist. She might not have bothered. Her grip was no restriction to him; the hem of her tunic continued to rise, clearing the crest of her breasts, higher.

Alasdair whipped the garment over Vanessa's head and tossed it aside. He wasn't surprised to find she wore nothing beneath the tunic. There was not much this girl could say, do, or wear that would surprise him at this point. He was, however, more than a bit shocked by the feel of her bare skin against his. The heat and softness of her melted into his chest and inner forearm, into his *blood*.

He reached for the fasteners of her trews, and felt her stiffen in his arms.

While he could feel the delicate indentation of her ribs, there was enough feminine padding to her waist and hips to make the word "scrawny" scatter from his mind. *Slender* would have been a more apt description. In a word she was . . . ah, bloody hell, she was anything

125

but scrawny!

Heels sounded atop the stone in the corridor. The sharp click click slinked beneath the door, echoing unnaturally loud against the snap of flames in the hearth.

Vanessa's breath caught.

Footsteps.

The tub.

Sweet Saint Andrews, she was half naked!

She resumed her struggles with force. The arm around her waist tightened, pushing the air from her lungs, but she didn't care. She continued to fight wildly, kicking and scratching where she could.

The sound of wood against wood as the bar was lifted was loud and grating. There was no warning knock; Vanessa noticed the absence of it at the same time she heard the door swish open.

Alasdair also noticed the absence . . . a second too late. The instant the girl had started fighting, his glare had sliced down over her shoulder. The sight of her bare breasts — aye, the girl was *not* scrawny! — had temporarily stunned him.

His head turned, and he stiffened when the door slammed open with enough force to make it threaten to come free of its hinges.

"Alasdair!" Marette Gray yelled furiously. "Good God, Brother, what are you doing?!"

Alasdair's gaze locked with eyes that were the same blue-gray shade as his own. Only Marette's eyes were narrowed with an anger that was echoed in the harshness of her tone, and the tight set of her mouth. Her cheeks were stained a furious shade of red as her gaze left his, settling on the woman who'd suddenly grown very quiet in his arms.

If looks could kill, Vanessa Forster would be a dead woman; the look in his sister's eyes was that murderous.

Chapter Seven

Yesterday morn, Alasdair's biggest concern was re-covering the horses, sheep, and household goods Cav-nearal had lost in the Armstrong's latest raid. Two days ago, word had arrived that the Douglas was preparing to ride, no doubt to recover the stolen goods that Alasdair and his men had pilfered from Douglas soil a fortnight ago — so there was that to be prepared for as well. Of the two dozen cottages that Rory Elliot had burned during his last "visit," only seven had, as yet, been rebuilt. Win-ter was swiftly approaching; the Forster's fine was *sup-posed* to pay for enough supplies to see Cavnearal through what promised to be a very harsh season.

Family matters fared no better. Keith had recently been caught casting an appreciative eye toward Jenna Ferguson — the youngest daughter of the laird of a rival clan. Although it had been over a year, Marette still mourned her husband, and took no pains to hide it; her long face and continuous sobbing already had half the keep's occupants groaning . . . while the other half weighed the merits of strangling her in her sleep. The last time he'd seen Kirsta, his youngest sister had, in a rare display of temper, thrown a half-finished tapestry at his head. Alasdair supposed 'twas what he deserved for laughing at her disastrous domestic effort, then admit-ting he hoped 'twas not his room chosen to be gifted with her fine "rug."

Aye, yesterday morn, Alasdair would have sworn things could get no worse. That was twenty-fours hours

before his keep had been inundated with unwanted Forsters, twenty-four hours before Hugh Forster's daughter
had taken it upon herself to play the martyr and pledge
herself in her father's place.

Now, as he split his attention between his sister and
the half-clothed woman — who was again struggling
fiercely — in his arms, Alasdair concluded that not only
could things get worse, they had.

The chamber door was of solid oak, three inches thick,
yet the way Marette effortlessly sent the door careening
shut, it might as well have been no heavier than an insub-
stantial panel of pine. While Alasdair had prepared himself for the resounding slam, the woman in his arms
hadn't. Vanessa gasped, startled, then, after shielding
her breasts with her arms, went ominously still.

"There have been times I've doubted your sanity,
brother," Marette said, her voice too low, too controlled
for her to be anything but furious, "but never more so
than now. Have you gone mad?!" She glared at Alasdair.
A curtain of loose, inky-black hair swayed at her slender
waist as she shook her head and gestured impatiently to
Vanessa. "Nay, Alasdair, no answer is necessary. 'Twas a
question that called for no answer. Obviously, you have,
for a sane man wouldn't dare bring this . . . this *girl* . . .
this *Forster,* into his keep. Into his *bed!*"

The headache throbbed anew in Alasdair's temples.
His eyes sharpened on his sister. "I warn you, hold your
tongue. 'Tis none of your affair."

Marette's laughter was harsh and insincere. Her blue-
gray eyes flashed fire as her gaze shifted to the girl. It
didn't matter that she'd never met Vanessa, didn't know
her. The girl was a Forster — Marette shuddered inwardly — one of the clan that had taken her beloved
Robert from her. 'Twas reason enough for the chit to deserve Marette's hatred. Her glare shifted to her brother.
"None of my affair?" she sneered. *"None of my affair?!* I beg
to differ, Alasdair. When you start cavorting with a" —
she grimaced — *"Forster,* you *make* it my affair."

Vanessa winced. The way the woman spit the word

128

"cavorting" made it sound dirty, cheap. Exactly the way Vanessa felt at the moment, being half undressed and pinned to the muscled side of a man equally as undressed as she. Had The Devil's steely arm not secured her position, she would have broken free and grabbed her tunic. Even with half her clothing on, she'd never felt more exposed and vulnerable in her life; 'twas an unfamiliar, unsettling feeling—one she disliked intensely. Her only salvation was that, in this position, she was turned away from prying eyes, not toward them. Unfortunately, that eased her discomfort only slightly.

The arm coiled around her waist tensed, making it difficult for Vanessa to breathe. She didn't complain. To do so would be to draw more attention to herself than she thought she could endure right now. For once, she wished her hair was long enough to cover her nakedness.

Marette's voice broke the tension-riddled silence. "Keith says you intend to keep . . . *her* as pledge in the Forster's place. I hope our brother was mistaken about that, Alasdair."

The muscle in Alasdair's jaw bunched in aggravation. "I've told you, 'tis none of your concern."

"I'm making it my concern."

"Don't," Alasdair growled, wondering just how much worse this situation could become? He instantly decided he did not want to know. "I've not made up my mind whether to keep the wench or not. When I do make the decision, you can rest assured I'll not be consulting you about it. 'Tis Cavnearal business, and as such, no concern of yours." He nodded briskly to the door. "Go back to teaching Kirsta how to weave a tapestry, sister, and leave the running of this keep to the men."

His tone left no room for argument. Apparently, Marette was unaware of that fact, for argue she most certainly did. "Why? So you can 'run' Cavnearal into the ground?"

Gritting his teeth only made the pounding in Alasdair's temples worse. His voice rose to the typically loud roar that all of Phillip Gray's children, save Kirsta, had inherited. "I've warned you once, Marette, I'll not do it again. Hold your tongue, or I'll have you locked in the tower room where none need deflect the sharpness of it!"

Marette's tone rose in equal proportion to her brother's. "You'd not dare!"

"You think not?" The grin that turned up only one corner of Alasdair's mouth had, in the past, made more than one Border reiver think better of their mission and retreat. Smart men took heed of that grin, and the frosty gray gaze that accompanied it. Of course, since Marette was a mere woman — her being English, not Scot, elevated her to an only slightly higher level than Vanessa in his mind — Alasdair doubted she possessed the intelligence to acknowledge just how thin the icy terrain she tread upon was. She would soon find out, for, while he often shouted up a storm, as was his way, the fact was, Alasdair Gray rarely became angry. But he was growing angry now. It had been a difficult day, and his patience was frayed. If his sister continued to defy him . . .

A flash of uncertainty flickered in Marette's eyes. It was gone as quickly as it came. "Aye, brother," she said finally, challengingly, "I think not."

This time, Alasdair's grin was half genuine. 'Twas was what he'd hoped she would say. "Think again, Marette. I've no time for your childish antics this night." His attention shifted to the door. Even though it was closed, his booming voice could be heard well down the drafty stone corridor as he bellowed for the guard who was rarely far from Alasdair's side.

There was a commotion in the hallway as Harrington, in his haste to answer his lord's summons, collided with the two men carrying the tub. The resounding crash of wood hitting stone was followed by more than one succinct male oath.

"Aye, m'lord?" Harrington said a bit breathlessly from where he stood framed in the now-open doorway.

Alasdair was only vaguely aware of Vanessa's muffled groan — a sound she tried to trap in her throat and couldn't. He paid her no mind. Not only didn't he know

130

why the girl was keeping her silence and no longer struggling, but he didn't care. He was only glad that she was. He'd enough problems at the moment; thankfully, for the first time since he'd set eyes on the wench, she was not one of them.

He gestured impatiently to Marette, who, judging by the flush in her cheeks and the indignation in her gaze, was fuming silently. "Escort my sister to the tower room, Harrington. And see that the door is locked securely behind you when you leave. Deliver the key to me."

Harrington, tall and lean and light of color, shifted uncomfortably. Curiosity—not to mention a goodly portion of disbelief—swam in his dark green eyes. "M-m'lord?" he stammered, sure he'd heard wrong.

The men carrying the tub stopped behind Harrington. They could not enter until the man moved, and Harrington looked too shocked to be doing that anytime soon. The men's impatient curses were not lost on Alasdair . . . they meshed with those of the others following closely behind them; the men who were toting heavy buckets of steamy bathwater.

As quiet and still as she was, apparently the Forster wench wasn't oblivious to the crowd of people now clogging the doorway. Again, softly, she groaned. Alasdair could have sworn he felt a blush heat the bare skin on her stomach and back — the warmth of which seeped into the arm he'd curled around her waist, into the naked flesh of his chest.

He felt a sudden, as strange as it was strong, compulsion to rid the room of prying eyes — most of which were straining to catch a glimpse of the half naked woman in his arms. Without considering what he was doing—let alone *why*—Alasdair shifted, using his body to shield Vanessa from their curious glances. "I believe I've just given you an order, Harrington."

The man nodded, and for the first time ever, looked hesitant to carry out Alasdair's bidding. "Aye, m'lord, but—"

"Bloody hell, man! Don't just stand there, *do it!*"

131

"Aye, m'lord!" Harrington gulped, then nodded briskly. Masking his confusion, he turned his attention on Marette. "After you, m'lady," he said calmly, emotionlessly, as he waved to the doorway—which couldn't possibly be passed through with so many people gathered in it.

It was just as well, for Marette apparently had no intention of leaving. Her gaze never left her brother. "I warn you, Alasdair. Do not do this."

"Warning duly noted. Now, dear sister, there's a chamber above beckoning for your company." His attention shifted meaningfully to the guard.

Harrington stepped forward, and grasped Marette by her upper arm. He tugged gently, but the woman didn't budge. The speculative voices in the corridor grew louder.

Marette looked past her brother's shoulder. Though she could no longer see Vanessa, it was clear her enraged glare was intended for the girl. As was the furious jabbing of her finger in Vanessa's general direction. " 'Tis not *I* who should be locked in the tower, 'tis *her!* A Forster should not sleep in a warm, soft bed whilst a Gray sleeps in a cold, dark room on a narrow, lumpy cot!"

" 'Tis something you should have thought on before storming in here," Alasdair replied, his tone much too calm for his sister's peace of mind. "And now, Harrington, if you do not—"

"Aye, m'lord!" This time the tug Harrington gave Marette was not gentle. Marette, caught off balance, stumbled back a step. The men in the doorway hushed, then, as one, parted to let the two pass.

"You'll regret this, Alasdair!" Marette yelled as she was forcefully dragged toward the door. "Dearly. I'll see to that!"

"Aye, Marette, no doubt. And in the next few hours you'll have plenty of time to decide exactly how I shall regret it."

"Hours?" she shrieked. "You'd leave me up there for *hours?!*"

132

"Mayhap even days," Alasdair assured her dryly. "You'll stay in the tower until you come to your senses and calm down, sister. I'll not unlock the door before then."

"And if I don't?" Marette challenged hotly. Harrington had her almost to the door now. Though she reached out to catch the frame, no doubt hoping to stall and give Alasdair a few much needed seconds to come to his senses, the guard was too quick for her; Harrington slapped Marette's hand away before she could curl her fingers around the wood.

Alasdair shrugged. His sister was around the corner now, out of sight. He had to raise his voice to be heard; the bellow echoed familiarly off the cold stone walls. "Then I suggest you grow accustomed to your new surroundings, Marette, for you'll not be leaving them until you do!"

Marette yelled a response, but she was too far away for most of her words to be deciphered clearly. All Alasdair could make out was: "You'll pay for this, damn you!" While he'd no doubt she would try to make good on her threat, he wasn't concerned. Marette was only a woman, after all. What could she do?

Stooping down, Alasdair retrieved the tattered yellow tunic from the floor. It wasn't until he'd set Vanessa on her feet and roughly dragged the filthy garment over her head that he realized the crowd of men in the corridor had grown silent. He then moved away from her, glad to put some distance between them.

He glanced over his shoulder, his gaze narrowing one openly curious face after the next. Impatiently, he growled, "What are you waiting for? The water is growing cold."

His words brought about a rush of commotion. The large wooden tub was lugged into the room, and set in the middle of the floor. Half a dozen men rushed in with buckets of water of varying degrees of temperature to fill it.

The entire process took less than two minutes.

That was all the time Vanessa needed. Embarrassment, impotence, fury . . . all those emotions and more had been churning inside her during the last five minutes. She'd let them simmer, too humiliated to act upon any of them while she'd been undressed and pinned, like the helpless kitten he'd likened her to, to The Devil's warm, rock-solid side.

She wasn't undressed now—thank the Lord!—nor was she being restrained. Deep down, Vanessa felt the dam she'd constructed to hold back her emotions disintegrate. Mortification melted away; fury—white hot and blinding—rushed to the fore.

After casting a quick glance at the door—there were too many men coming and going with buckets of water for her to slip through undetected—Vanessa stomped across the room. With each step, her anger increased.

The Devil had his back to her. Hands on hips, he looked to be overseeing the bath's preparation as though it was a cherished ceremony.

Vanessa's physically active life had toned her body to a firmness and strength her size contradicted. When she grabbed The Devil's arm, it was with a sure, firm grip. And when she yanked him around to face her, there was a surprising amount of force behind the gesture.

His eyes darkened as his gaze met hers.

"Ye insensitive, thick-skulled Sassenach clod," she sneered. "I'll not stand being manhandled by the likes of ye! I'll not allow ye to expose me to ye men at whim! And I'll *not-take-a-frigging-bath!*"

The sound of her open palm hitting his cheek was loud against the room's abrupt silence. Alasdair's head snapped to the side from the force of the blow. The whiskers shadowing his jaw scratched Vanessa's skin as the heat of the slap warmed her palm.

One of the men—all of whom had grown oddly hushed and still as she'd approached Alasdair—gasped. The sound was loud against the backdrop of flames crackling in the hearth.

And speaking of crackling . . . the tension that perme-

134

ated the room was palpable. Vanessa traced the source to The Devil's abruptly stiff body.

His head came back around slowly. Against his sun-bronzed skin, the imprint of her slap burned a rebellious shade of red. His gaze, when it met hers, was so narrow that Vanessa could not see his eyes between the thick, inky lashes. Unfortunately, she'd no need to see them; she could *feel* the fury in his gaze wash over her in uncomfortably warm waves.

Boot heels scratched against stone as some of the men shifted uneasily. More than one leery gaze strayed to the door, yet no one moved toward it. The only time most of the men had seen that angry tick in Alasdair's jaw, the furious narrowing of his blue-gray eyes, the rigidly controlled stiffness in his body, was during a raid or trod against rivaling neighbors. To see it here, in his keep, brought on by a *wench*, was unheard of.

While some men did slip away unnoticed, most stayed to see what Alasdair would do to the foolish girl. Since she was a hated Scot, they were more curious than concerned. Surely she deserved a whipping for what she'd just done! The question was . . . would Alasdair give her one?

Whipping the chit was not on Alasdair's mind. Oh, no. Turning her over his knee and delivering a sound spanking *was*. It was hard to believe the girl had slapped him in the first place. It was bloody well *impossible* to believe she'd been stupid enough to do it in front of his men. Even Marette, no matter how badly she'd wanted to, had thought better of doing such a thing! No doubt his sister had known that slapping him in front of witnesses would force him into immediate retribution.

His cheek still stinging from her slap, Alasdair glared at the girl — who glared defiantly back at him — and wondered if this impudent little Scot was aware of the danger she'd just put herself in. If not, she was about to find out.

"No bath?" Alasdair said, and his tone was so calm, so precise, that it made his men uneasy. His bellows, they were used to, but this furious calmness was so unusual, it

135

set their nerves on edge.

"No bath," Vanessa snapped. Had she not been so angry, she might have heeded the signs of The Devil's anger. She might also have thought better of her next words, for her furious tone of voice delivered them as a challenge. "If ye wish to bed me, I canna stop ye. We both know it. But ye'll have to bed me 'filthy and smelly,' for I willna get into that tub willingly."

If possible, his eyes narrowed still more. The throbbing of the muscle in his jaw was more pronounced as he tightly clenched and unclenched his hands at his side. "Then prepare yourself for more manhandling, pledge," he growled.

A single step of space was between them. Alasdair cleared the minuscule distance in a heartbeat, and scooped the infuriating wench into his arms in two.

Vanessa wasn't surprised; she'd expected this, or something similar. She instantly set to struggling. Her fists pounded his muscled shoulders and arms. Her feet flailed, and one of the men grunted when the toe of her boot inadvertently collided painfully with his ear as Alasdair carried her toward the tub.

Vanessa cursed loudly, vehemently, in Gaelic, but her swears fell on deaf ears. If The Devil understood so much as a word of what she called him, he gave no sign.

Alasdair stopped beside the tub. Her struggles made her feel heavy in his arms, but not too heavy. Or unmanageable. There was never a question in his mind that his superior size and strength could control her. At least physically.

Vanessa's lips were parted, but the vulgarity she was about to utter must have melted on her tongue, for she grew unusually quiet. "Aye, wench, your body is in dire need of washing, but your tongue needs it even more."

The words might have been an observation. The way they fell off The Devil's tongue made them sound like a threat.

"And I suppose next ye will tell me ye are just the man to do that?" she snapped.

136

"Aye, I am."

A shiver of alarm curled down Vanessa's spine. 'Twould have been nice had the emotion reared itself a few minutes earlier, *before* blind fury had goaded her into pushing The Devil too far.

The men had backed warily away from the tub when Alasdair approached it. All except one had slipped silently out the door. That last straggler sent a curious gaze over his shoulder as he, too, quietly retreated to the hallway.

Vanessa and Alasdair's eyes met and locked; both shimmered mute challenge. Neither noticed the creak of hinges as the door was closed, or the grating scrape of wood when the bar was lowered into place.

A tense moment ticked past. The time was marked by the snapping of flames in the hearth, and the soughing of matching breaths.

Vanessa had no more convinced herself that Alasdair had changed his mind and was not going to strip her bare and fling her in the waiting water when she felt the arms supporting her loosen . . . then, without a hint of warning, fall away.

Had she curled her arms around his neck, she would have had something to hang on to when her only support was empty air. She hadn't. Instead, she'd held her arms stiffly in front of her, her hands curled in impotent fists atop her lap.

'Twas an oversight she noticed and regretted a wee second too late. Her back hit a blanket of steamy water. She tried to grab the sides of the tub, but her hands were too slippery to find purchase.

Vanessa gasped, and water filled her mouth as the force of her fall immediately dragged her down to the bottom of the large wooden tub. Steamy water covered her face as her head went under . . . and *stayed* under, thanks to the large hand The Devil settled atop the crown of her now-saturated head.

Chapter Eight

A mere half-score and two summers, Kirsta Gray had the grace and bearing of one who had lived many more years. She was a quiet girl, given to long periods of introspect, usually followed by shorter spurts of tempered gaiety. Such mood shifts were a recent development; she was, after all, teetering on the brink of womanhood. There were changes, both physical and emotional, going on inside her that seemed to alter constantly, and for the most part she was at a loss as to how to deal with them.

There were some in Cavnearal who speculated upon whether or not she was truly Phillip Gray's daughter. Oh, the physical resemblance couldn't be denied, yet her nature was such a contrast to her siblings'. Certainly, she'd not inherited the disposition of her older brothers and sister. In fact, 'twas rare for the familiar Gray temper to flare in her — Kirsta had learned long ago how to control it — but it did happen now and again.

This was one of those rare occasions.

The tankard was halfway to Keith's mouth when Kirsta grabbed it from her brother's hands and slammed it atop the table. Ale frothed over the sides, splashing over Kirsta's hand and pooling in the nooks and crannies that years of hard use had chipped into the wooden tabletop.

One of the dogs, chained near the hearth at the opposite end of the hall, barked, as though it had sensed Kirsta's unusually foul mood and was unnerved by it. Only a handful of men lingered in the hall; they were seated at

138

another table, fifty feet away. Keith's brooding scowl had convinced them to keep their distance.

Keith sighed. "I suppose you've reason for doing that, Kirsta?" he asked, and though his tone was calm, there was an underlying edge to it.

"Aye," Kirsta replied tightly, "a very good reason. There's rumors flying about this keep, and as farfetched as they sound, I've reason to believe there may be a grain of truth to some of them."

"Which rumors?" Keith asked neutrally, reaching for his tankard. He grumbled beneath his breath when his sister slapped his hand away, then slid the mug down the table, out of his reach. If that had been done by anyone but Kirsta, Keith would have bellowed his displeasure. "Well?" he asked when she said nothing.

Kirsta scooted onto the bench opposite him and, placing her elbows on the table, supported her chin atop her fists. A frown furrowed her dark brow as she studied her brother carefully. Her voice was still tight, still strained. "The first, of course, I know is true. That would be Alasdair having accepted Hugh Forster as his pledge."

" 'Tis no rumor; 'tis fact. You saw the cursed Scot with your own two eyes at the evening meal."

She had. And she'd hated seeing a Scot—a *Forster*—gracing *any* room of Cavneal. 'Twas a sacrilege. Kirsta shared her family's opinion there—especially after the latest casualty of the centuries-long blood feud: Marette's husband. She nodded stiltedly. "Aye. I did. 'Tis why I said I knew that one to be true. 'Tis the rest I'm unsure of."

And unsure she would remain, if Keith had his way. He'd no intention of confirming or denying any rumors until he'd heard them out. While he could well imagine the tales that had been carried to his younger sister's ears, he wasn't foolish enough to admit to things she might not know about. Let her learn the rest from someone else; right now, he was in too sour a mood to enlighten her any more than was absolutely necessary.

Kirsta's frown deepened when her brother made no reply. Her voice lowered suspiciously as she counted off each rumor on her long, thin fingers. "The others concern Alasdair, a bath, a bed, an insolent Scots wench — who may or may not be a cursed Forster; that part remains unclear — and our sister. More precisely, Marette being locked in the tower room which, of course, cannot possibly be true." Dismissing the ludicrous notion with a wave of her hand, she said confidently, "Alasdair would never . . ."

Her voice trailed away when Keith swore openly, and abruptly strained forward to recapture his tankard. Kirsta had no idea how much ale was left in the mug when he lifted it to his lips, but she *was* sure that, when he slammed it down again, the tankard had been drained.

For a girl who prided herself on calmness and patience, Kirsta was surprised by how swiftly her self-composure shattered.

She stood quickly. Mayhap a bit *too* quickly. The backs of her knees banged into the seat of the bench; the bench, in turn, tottered, threatening to crash to the floor.

Hands on hips, and in a bellow that would have done Phillip Gray proud, she roared, *"That does it!* 'Tis bad enough Alasdair accepted that wretched Hugh Forster as pledge. 'Twas ten times worse that he welcomed the arrogant, murdering Scot into our home as though he was a guest." She shook her head, which made the thick, dark rope of her braid swing against her nubile, lean hips. "But *this!* I swear, Keith, locking Marette in the tower room is the last straw. Alasdair cannot be allowed to do such a thing. He can*not!*"

Keith shrugged and looked wistfully down at his now-empty tankard. While his sister's anger would normally have shocked him, tonight it didn't. In fact, he found he wasn't even overly concerned by it; he'd drunk far too much ale for that, and the effects of the brew tempered his emotions.

Scowling, Keith sent his sister a corner glance. Kirsta was pacing beside the head of the table, behind the large, carved chair where their brother usually sat. Her arms

140

were crossed rigidly over her chest, her steps rhythmic and hard. While he was used to seeing that blossom of pink in his sister's cheeks, 'twas usually put there by the sun.

As though she'd come to a decision, Kirsta stopped abruptly and spun to face her brother, her cream-colored skirt whipping about her ankles. Her eyes—also more blue than gray, like Keith's—fired with anger. "Something must be done about this, and done *now*, before it goes too far."

Keith nodded stiffly. She wasn't telling him anything he didn't already know. "I agree. But what? Nay, better still, *who* is going to do the doing, Kirsta?"

She glared at him imperiously, and Keith had to remind himself that the girl was a mere half-score and two. There were so many times—like now—when she seemed much older. "I will, of course. Who did you think would do it?"

"You?" He cocked one dark eyebrow, his assessive gaze raking her from head to toe. If he'd been in a better mood, Keith might have laughed. The sparkle in his sister's eyes said 'twas a good thing his spirits were sour, for she'd not have appreciated his good humor.

"Aye, *me*," she snapped. "Alasdair has always listened to me."

"Mayhap, but only about trivial matters, Kirsta."

"Mayhap, but listen he *has*."

"Not this time, he won't. Believe me, Sister, I know. I've already tried talking to him, and he'd not listen to a word. You know Alasdair, when he's got something in his head, talking sense to him is like talking to a sheep. Both are equally futile."

Kirsta pursed her lips, and again slid onto the bench across from her brother. The sound of wood scraping stone as she pushed the bench in was loud and grating in the hall's sudden silence.

Silence? Keith's gaze scanned the room. As he'd suspected, the men who'd been lazing at the other table were gone. No doubt, they'd left the instant

Kirsta had started yelling.

"Well?" Kirsta said, staring at her brother, who'd been quiet for a full minute.

His gaze now trained on the flames that were beginning to dim in the hearth, he replied distractedly, "Well what?"

"Well . . ." she repeated tightly. "You said you spoke to Alasdair. What did he say?"

Kirsta glared at him.

Keith resigned himself to doing what he'd previously told himself he wouldn't. Unfortunately, he knew his sister. If he didn't tell Kirsta what she wanted to know, she would hound him all night. The hour was growing late, and the ale had made him sleepy. If she badgered him, he was bound to loose his temper. He didn't want to do that. Not with Kirsta. Loud noises, especially those of angry voices, upset her.

There was only one serving wench left in the hall. She was standing with her shoulder braced against the stone archway of the corridor that led to the outdoor kitchen. She looked tired, as though the only thing keeping her erect was the wall she leaned against. Keith waved her over to refill his tankard, and waited until she was out of earshot before recounting an abbreviated version of what had transpired in Cavneal since the dinner hour.

He wouldn't have been able to say exactly how he expected Kirsta to react. She was in a strange mood tonight. She'd even yelled at him! Still, what she did when the tale was told *did* surprise him.

Her posture had grown stiff with each fact he'd reluctantly divulged. By the time he was done, her spine was so stiff, Keith thought a strong wind might snap it. Her eyes were narrow, glistening a churning shade of blue. The muscle in her jaw worked as she gritted her teeth.

Keith sat back and waited for his sister's questions. They didn't come. He waited for her anger. Except for her brooding frown, that didn't come, either. Something. He was waiting for her to do something. *Anything.*

Finally, she did.

Very slowly, very calmly, Kirsta stood. The bench legs made nary a sound, and somehow, that seemed more unnerving to Keith than had they scraped.

Without sending her brother so much as a backward glance, she walked stiffly from the hall.

Keith watched her until she'd disappeared around the corner. He didn't know where she was going and, to be honest, he didn't care. He had other things on his mind — like how to talk some sense into his brother's thick-skulled head!

Alasdair had promised to scare the Forster chit senseless, then send her and her brother on their way. That was over three hours ago. The chit was still here . . . as was her father and brother, who'd both — thank heavens! — been locked in the vault; exactly where they deserved to be, in Keith's opinion.

Keith was starting to get worried. Hearing of the bath Alasdair ordered to his chambers had both surprised and alarmed him. He had a suspicion he knew what it was for. And, oh but that boded no good at all.

Bloody hell, Kirsta was right! Something had to be done and done soon. But what? And by whom? Damned if he knew!

Keith's fingers tightened around the handle of the tankard. His grip was hot and tight, threatening to dent the metal. He lifted the mug and downed the ale in one long swallow, then slammed the tankard on the table with force.

He'd regret consuming so much liquor . . . in the morning. For now, it was the only thing that kept him calm enough to think and not — as he'd done so often in the past, and which aggravated Alasdair no end — react on impulse alone.

Chapter Nine

The blanket that Vanessa had been given—no, more precisely, the blanket The Devil had *flung* at her while cursing beneath his breath—to wrap around herself was dark blue and yellow, the once-bright colors faded from many stone washings. The scent of lye soap clung to the fabric, assailing her nostrils. The blanket was thin and coarse; the rough material chaffed her skin and made her itchy. She did not complain. Her teeth were chattering too much for that.

The blanket did scarce little to warm her. Beneath the cloth her skin was still damp in spots. Chill bumps prickled on her arms, legs, and the nape of her neck. While she'd briskly toweled as much moisture from her hair as she could, the strands were still wet, hanging in dark, water-heavy waves down to her shivering shoulders.

She was sitting in a squat, fat chair to the left of the hearth. At that moment, the only thing warm about her was her gaze; in fact, it was hot as sin as she glared at Alasdair Gray's broad, naked back. Ooch! but if looks could maim . . .

He was hunched over in front of the hearth, tossing in split quarter-cuts of logs, feeding the fire, coaxing it into a blaze. It didn't take long. The fire was soon crackling and snapping, the tongues of flames greedily licking at the fresh fuel.

The room got warmer—not much, but a bit. Then

again, mayhap it wasn't the room that was cold. Mayhap 'twas the emotions churning inside Vanessa that only made her surroundings *seem* frosty.

The instant her head had gone under the steamy bathwater that first time — quite a few more times had followed — she'd felt icy waves of fury wash through her. While she was relatively dry now — and, thanks to the fire The Devil had rekindled, a wee bit warmer — that chill hadn't dissipated. It wasn't the sort of cold that a blanket and a blazing fire could banish. Because the cold, rather than coming from the outside, derived from somewhere deep within her.

A log in the hearth toppled off the pile Alasdair had carefully stacked. It crashed to the hot stone, split on contact, and hissed like frying meat as it spit up a cloud of orange sparks.

The sound and sight was lost on Vanessa, for The Devil had seized that particular second to turn his head and glance at her from over one heavily muscled shoulder. His inky hair was long enough for the ends to whisk the top of his back and shoulders, the curtain of it almost entirely concealing his neck. Almost.

His steely eyes narrowed, his gaze locking with hers. Vanessa's heart skipped. A muscle in The Devil's cheek began to tick; drawing her attention there. She swallowed hard. A thin, angry red cut ribboned from the corner of his left eye down to the center of his cheek. The slash wasn't deep; the blood clinging to it had already dried.

She shifted awkwardly, fisting the scratchy blanket beneath her chin. The cut had come from her own fingernail. It had been her way of thanking him for allowing her head up out of the water that first time — *after* she'd pulled great gulps of air into her air-hungry lungs, of course! As a reward her head had immediately been dunked again.

To the best of Vanessa's knowledge, that cut and the fading teethmarks on the back of The Devil's right hand were the only two signs that at least some of her struggles

145

had had an effect, no matter how minor. Frowning, she wondered why neither was the satisfying sight they should by all rights be.

Alasdair stood and crossed to the opposite side of the hearth. Vanessa noticed that he was as far away as he could get without losing heat from the fire. He turned, leaned his shoulder negligently against the craggy stone, and nodded briskly to the hearth. "Pull your chair closer to the fire, wench. Your hair is thick. Even so wretchedly short, it will take forever to dry. And I'll not have you wetting my pillow with it."

Ye'll not have me warming yer bed either, ye conceited oaf, Vanessa thought, but wisely didn't say. The muscle in his cheek jerked when she continued with great difficulty to return his stare with a level one of her own, and made no attempt to obey his dictate.

His lips thinned. "Will you disobey me in everything?" he asked, almost casually. Almost.

Vanessa recognized the icy edge to his tone, and took heed. She replied just as casually, "Have I not already said as much, many times?"

"I'd hoped the bath would teach you a much needed lesson, wench. Apparently, I was mistaken."

She shook her head stiffly. "Ye werena wrong at all. Ye 'lesson' taught me something most valuable. I now know I can hold me breath a sore deal longer than I'd thought." Her smile was cool; it did not reach her eyes, which flashed with silent green challenge. "Was that the lesson ye were aiming for?"

His tone lowered a husky pitch. "I was thinking more along the lines of obedience. As you well know."

"Aye, I do," Vanessa agreed, and her smile broadened until it was almost, *almost,* genuine.

A smile curving this woman's lips was not what Alasdair wanted to see right now. Not when he'd yet to recover from giving her a bath! His head still reeled with the discovery that the cumbersome jack and baggy tunic weren't the only things obscuring soft, womanly curves. Her snug-fitting trews had hinted at strong, shapely legs;

the reality of seeing this theory proved out, in the flesh, had hit Alasdair like a punch to the belly.

He'd seen her wearing nothing but a fierce blush now — bloody hell, but his blood *still* flowed hot with the memory! — and the sight had shattered any assumptions he'd clung to regarding "scrawny." Or "girl" for that matter!

Vanessa Forster was neither. Unfortunately. Alasdair knew that for sure now, and the knowledge was not greeted fondly. The vision — a full-blown, gut-wretchingly detailed memory, actually — of her standing naked and wet in front of the tub, the firelight stroking her naked flesh with warm, orangey fingers of light, her dark hair dripping wet and curling with wild rebellion about her face and neck and shoulders, refused to leave him.

Again, Alasdair wished to God the girl — nay, blast it all, the *woman!* — had done what any other female in her place would have. Hightailed it home, where she belonged!

He crossed his arms over his chest, and his fingers flexed into tight, white-knuckled fists. His jaw bunched when he realized that 'twas not the feel of his own palm, his own skin, beneath his fingertips that he felt right now, but hers. Hot and wet and naked, that's how he remembered the feel of her flesh skimming beneath his soapy palm as he'd washed her . . .

"Truth be known, Devil, I maun admit that yer bath did teach me one other wee lesson," Vanessa said finally, wondering what had put that fierce, brooding expression on his face. His eyes sharpened on her, commanding her to continue. Since she would have done so anyway, Vanessa did not consider finishing her thought as obeying his order. That, she would never do. "Ye've taught me ye are most strong and determined. Not a surprise, that, I'll admit. I now know that fighting ye in any way would be a waste of me precious time and energy."

A suspicious scowl etched Alasdair's brow. "Meaning?"

147

"Meaning exactly what I said, mon. I'll not fight ye anymore. It gets me nowhere." The words were spoken with a composure Vanessa was struggling to maintain. Beneath the blanket, where he could not see, she crossed her middle finger over her index finger. While it had been easy to think up the plan whilst her head was being held underwater, her lungs screaming for air, actually putting it into motion was something else entirely. What if he did not fall for it? Worse, what if he took her at her word and . . .

Nay, it did not bear thinking upon!

The beginnings of a victorious grin tugged at one corner of Alasdair's mouth. His blue-gray eyes shimmered, reflecting the firelight, and his sudden, slightly improved mood. "You're ready to go home, then?"

" 'Twas not what I said."

" 'Twas the impression I got."

"I beg ye pardon, for 'twas not the impression I sought to give."

"What impression *did* you wish to give, wench?" His mood darkened once more, as was reflected in his gritty tone.

"Ooch! mon, 'tis obvious, is it not? I said I'll not fight ye any longer, nor will I. 'Tis what I meant. Naught more, naught less."

The craggy stone bit into Alasdair's shoulder as he shifted impatiently. He plowed the fingers of one hand through his hair. The black strands felt damp against his palm; he'd become almost equally as wet as Vanessa during her enforced bath. "Spit it out, wench," he said tightly. "I'm in no mood to play childish guessing games with you."

Childish. The word conjured up an illusion of "scrawny" and "girl" in his mind. 'Twas an illusion that instantly splintered, replaced by the vivid memory of firelight flickering over creamy white, naked skin . . . skin that felt hot and wet and enticing beyond reason beneath his soapy hands. He groaned inwardly, his fingers curling into a fist around his hair.

148

" 'Tis no game I speak of, Devil. This situation is maun too serious for bairn's play."

"Ah, so you've finally figured that out, have you?"

Vanessa shook her head, and the dark, damp strands of her hair whisked her cheeks and brow, her neck and shoulders. "Nay. I've always kenned it."

Alasdair inhaled deeply, releasing the breath from his lungs slowly through his teeth. "You speak in riddles, wench. Tell me what you mean."

Vanessa's heartbeat doubled, and her breathing shallowed. Luckily, she was able to mask the sudden panic that skittered through her so it wasn't visible . . . she hoped. Of all the plans she'd ever come up with in her life — and there'd been a fine muckle lot of them! — this one was, without a doubt, the most ludicrous. The odds were against it succeeding, and more heavily against her actually being able to carry it through to the end. Vanessa knew that. Still, 'twas the only plan with even a shred of merit that she'd been able to think up. And she had to try, had to do *something!*

She felt her palms go cold and clammy. Her fists were so tightly bunched around the blanket she fisted beneath her chin that her knuckles smarted. Her gaze had strayed to the mark she'd left on The Devil's cheek. Her attention now swerved and, steeling herself for what she was about to do, she met his gaze unflinchingly.

"I'll do better than that," she said, and was surprised to hear her voice ring with calm resolve. Strange, since she did not *feel* calm on the inside. Inside, she was trembling like the last hale leaf caught in the first gusty winter storm. "I'll not tell ye, Devil, I'll *show* ye."

After a second's hesitation — during which she gathered around her the very last of her courage — Vanessa poked her feet from beneath the frayed hem of blanket, and stood. The stone felt cold and hard beneath her bare feet; the chill seeped up her legs, settling deep inside the bones of her already wobbly-feeling knees. Her heart was beating furiously, and if she was breathing at all, she wasn't aware of it. It took supreme effort to convince her legs not to buckle as she walked slowly toward the bed.

Vanessa was not the only one having difficulty breathing. Alasdair also found it impossible to pull air into his lungs. His blood flowed cold . . . then, just as quickly, very, very hot; it felt like molten fire pounding through his veins.

He had a feeling he knew what the wench was about to do. Alasdair prayed to God he was wrong . . . for he'd already voiced his threat to her, and a Gray did not, *could not*, renege. It wasn't in their nature to even consider it.

Vanessa felt The Devil's gaze warming her back. Her shoulders stiffened, her spine went ramrod straight. She stopped next to the bed, and for a heartbeat merely stood there clutching the blanket close beneath her chin. The hem fell only to her knees. The warmth of the fire caressed her calves, countering the cold of the flagstones beneath her feet.

She closed her eyes to the sight of that big, empty bed. *Think of yer mother, lass,* she ordered herself. *Of the babe. Dinna think of The Devil and what ye offer, but instead of doing yer clan proud.*

Those thoughts in mind, Vanessa released the blanket, and let it drop.

The scratchy cloth skimmed her spine and legs and bottom before pooling to the floor at her feet. She felt hot and cold at the same time. The cold stemmed from her abrupt nakedness. The heat, oddly enough, didn't originate from the fire, as she thought it should, but from the shocked speechless warmth of Alasdair Gray's gaze. That heat spread through Vanessa's body like wildfire.

Her heart clamoring beneath her breasts, she opened her eyes and knelt on the very edge of the mattress. The straw filling crunched beneath her knees and shins as she scooted — as gracefully as she could — toward the middle. Summoning up the very last of her courage, she lay back on the mattress, the pillow cupping her head.

I'll not have you wetting my pillow with it, The Devil had said. Vanessa smiled grimly. Petty though it was, she found a certain satisfaction in doing exactly that.

Alasdair's fingers curled into tight, knuckle-straining fists. If he'd been able to move, he would have punched the wall; he had a sudden, intense urge to do . . . something. Though he hated to admit it, he was also having the devil's own time keeping his gaze from straying to soft, inviting curves . . . a place his gaze had no right to be. His voice lowered, and went oddly husky. "What do you think you're doing?"

"Isn't it obvious?"

She'd said that to him before. Alasdair found the question-for-a-question as grating now as he had then. "If it were, do you think I'd be asking, wench?"

Vanessa found that if she focused her concentration on the timber-and-stone ceiling, she could almost forget that she was lying completely naked, like a sacrificial lamb, on The Devil's bed. Almost. She sighed, and outwardly the sound seemed calm and composed, resigned; it was only inwardly that the breath seared her lungs, inwardly that her stomach muscles trembled and her heart raced. The skin on the left side of her body felt warm. If she'd looked, Vanessa knew she'd have found The Devil's gaze on her there. She swallowed hard, and did not look.

Her voice, when it came, was equally as composed as her sigh had been. Only the nervous thickening of her accent she could not seem to control. "I've heard maun rumors about ye, Devil. The kind mothers tell their bairns tae make them behave. They say ye be braver than most, crafty, strong. A reiver to be feared and watched. Yet, nae once did they say ye also be addle-brained." She hesitated for the length of a heartbeat, her eyes boring resolutely into the ceiling which, from this position, looked very far above. "What I be doing, mon, is agreeing tae ye terms," she added in the most reasonable tone she could manage, under the circumstances. "I'd think that obvious."

He said nothing, did nothing—except stare at her, hard, she could feel him doing that.

"Well?" she asked when a long, tense moment had slipped past. "What be ye waiting for? Bed me and get the

151

cursed deed done with, aye?"

It wasn't her words that struck Alasdair like a blow — if he'd time to think on it, he would have realized that was a curiosity in itself — but the monotonous way she uttered them. Her tone had been flat and cold as slate. Bored, as though she'd been talking about nothing more consequential than inviting him to tea instead of inviting him into her — *his!* — bed!

Inviting? Nay, this wasn't similar to any invitation he'd had in the past . . . especially not one leading to a woman's bed! Of course, the women of his memory had always been hot and ready and more than willing.

This one, obviously, was not.

Even though a good deal of the bed was covered in shadows, he couldn't help but see the flush that was warming her cheeks. Her arms were down by her sides, her elbows stiffly locked. Her shoulders and neck looked like they'd been made of iron, so stiffly were they set. He didn't check her breathing — he didn't dare — but he'd a feeling it was shallow and as rapid as he guessed her heartbeat to be. Her legs, of course, were closed — no invitation there! — her knees pressed together so tightly they shook.

He gritted his teeth. *Invitation,* he thought sourly. Nay. He'd seen more entreaty in a chicken putting its head over a chopping block!

"If ye hesitation is meant to torture me, mon, I warn ye now, 'twon't work. I'm prepared to wait all night — what there be left of it — so long as me da is back at Dunnaclard come morn."

She shouldn't have spoken. The sight of her naked, stiff body had precious little effect on Alasdair — from the second the blanket had hit stone, he'd felt mostly shock. The sight of her trembling lower lip, on the other hand did.

As he pushed away from the wall and slowly approached the bed, her pink, moist mouth snagged his attention. Her lip trembled only slightly when she spoke, but it was enough. He'd seen the weakness, small though it was, and read it clearly. She was about to find out that The Devil was not as addle-brained as she'd thought!

The mattress dipped under the pressure of his right knee. The straw crunched. Her lower lip trembled again before she caught it between her teeth. Alasdair's gaze still rested there; the sight of her small white teeth nibbling that tempting flesh knocked the wind out of him. He was struck with an instant, intense urge to replace her teeth with his, to taste the skin to see if the flavor of her mouth was as pleasant as it suggested. He wanted to . . .

Get control of himself, *that's* what Alasdair wanted, *needed* to do. Contemplating the potential delights of her mouth as it moved beneath his was not going to accomplish that.

He kneeled fully on the side of the bed, and his attention strayed upward. Her green eyes were big and round, glistening in what little firelight reached this far, and she was staring at the ceiling as though it offered the answers to thousands of untold mysteries . . . or the answers to her prayers. He thought 'twas most likely the latter.

Aye, scaring this woman was going to be easy. Mayhap not as easy as he'd initially thought, but easier than the last two hours with her had led him to believe it would be. "Tell me, pledge," he said evenly as, for the second time that night, he tugged at the waistband of his trews, "do you prefer the top or the bottom?"

Vanessa swallowed dryly when the mattress shook as he rearranged his weight. She needn't look at him to know what he was doing. Her voice lifted a scant, panicky decibel. "The top or the bottom . . . what?"

"What do you think?" he said, repeating her own aggravating words back to her as he pushed the trews past his hips, down his thighs. He came very close to smiling when he heard and saw the way her breath rushed quickly in, then just as quickly out, of her lungs. The color in her cheeks burned twice as brightly. Alasdair sat down on the mattress and pushed the trews over his knees, his shins. Although he didn't look at her, from over his shoulder he added, "No worries, wench. I assure you, it makes no difference to me. Top or bottom, it's the ride that counts. And I've a suspicion that, once tamed, you'll give a man the ride of his life."

Vanessa's voice retained only a sliver of its initial calmness when she said, "I suppose 'tis no more than I should expect from such a Sassenach, but ye be a lewd mon, Devil."

"Nay, just an honest one. Now, come here."

It wasn't a request, it was a command. She bristled at that, until she felt the mattress shift yet again, and then she was beyond feeling anything as paltry as indignation. His weight was now distributed more evenly, alerting her to the fact he'd just spread himself out beside her. He wasn't close enough for their bodies to touch, yet he was close enough for her to feel his virile nearness; his presence washed over her in oddly enticing waves of sensations.

It was chilly on this side of the room, yet the left side of Vanessa's body felt not the least bit cold; her bare skin tingled with the heat of Alasdair Gray's body. His spicy male scent mingled with the more subtle essence of soap — an irritating reminder of her bath — and hung heavily in the air, teasing her senses. Her head spun, her heartbeat thundered in her ears.

Alasdair sighed wearily. He should have known better than to think the wench would obey even his simplest command. The mattress crunched as he rolled onto his side. Only a sliver of space now separated his bare flesh from hers.

Levering himself up on his elbow, his free hand snaked out and wrapped around Vanessa's waist. The skin beneath his hand felt hot and incredibly smooth, the muscles underneath fluttered against his fingertips as he hauled her roughly to his chest.

Vanessa gulped. Her plan had backfired. She'd intended to catch The Devil so offguard by agreeing — as untemptingly as she possibly could! — to his deal, that he would immediately retract it. The hot, hard feel of his chest pressing against her left shoulder and arm and hip said he was not retracting a thing, he was accepting.

Oh, Lord.

She needed a new plan, and she needed it now. It need not even be a reasonable plan; she'd settle for a ludicrous but *possible* one at this point. 'Twas a pity her mind was too numbed to think of a thing.

Well, nay, that wasn't entirely true. She *was* thinking . . . of the way the soft, dark hairs on The Devil's chest felt as they tickled the ultra-sensitive skin on her shoulders and arm with his every breath . . . of the way his roughened palm seared its liquid heat imprint into the side of her waist . . . and, last, of the way her body unthinkingly, yet oh so naturally, molded to the solid strength of his. Traitorous though the thoughts were, they, and the warm, tingling sensations the feelings themselves evoked, refused to be banished.

Vanessa wasn't the only one affected by the contact. Alasdair was suffering his share of powerful sensations as well. Had he ever thought this girl—nay, *woman,* damn it!—scrawny? He had, which only went to prove how much liquor he'd drunk. Liquor. 'Twas the only reason Alasdair could find for such blindness. Vanessa Forster was not scrawny. Her breasts, straining into his chest, were not large, but they were temptingly firm, round, warm beyond reason; he imagined they would nestle into his open hands flawlessly, the fit nerve-shatteringly perfect. Her nipples were large and pink; his flesh smarted when he wondered how they would feel beading against his open palms.

The bath, he realized belatedly, had been a grand mistake. Dirt no longer smudged her cheeks and forehead and chin; the skin there was creamy and white, with a slight red undertone from his brisk scrubbing. Her inky hair was no longer wind-tangled and dirty but, even still damp, naturally wavy, with enticing, glossy blue highlights. A few moist strands feathered the underside of his chin; they felt softer than down. The scent of soap clung to her, clung to him, again bringing back the teasing, torturous, unwanted memory of how her wet skin had felt

155

beneath his soapy hands.

The hand on her waist slipped upward, cupping her ribs. Higher. His palm was open, and his thumb nestled beneath the warm, soft underside of her right breast.

His voice came low and rough. "Well, pledge, which shall it be? The choice is yours."

Vanessa frowned. Choice? He was giving her a choice in . . . what? It took but a second for her stunned mind to comprehend his meaning.

Do you prefer the top or the bottom?

"I"—her voice squeaked; she cleared her throat—"care not, Devil. 'Tis ye speed I be more concerned with."

Alasdair gritted his teeth when she stiffened in his arms and her breasts came into even firmer contact with his chest. A sizzling warmth developed there, seeping through his skin and into his blood, pumping quickly to the rest of his body. His heart was pounding hard, and it took supreme concentration to maintain his slow, even breaths; his lungs burned for air he refused to furnish for fear of letting the wench know exactly how great holding her in his arms affected him. She must never know that, never know that a Gray was even superficially attracted to a Forster. Such could spell ruin for Cavnearal, if his men found out and branded him a weakling and a traitor.

Her accent thickened, as it always did when she was upset. "Ooch! mon, think what ye be aboot! The March Wardens willna be happy tae hear it when I tell them how ye forced me tae—"

"Enough." His sighs dripped exasperation. "We've discussed that point already. Discussed it to death, as a matter of fact. Methinks you need devise another ploy to distract me."

"But—"

"Top or bottom?" he repeated, and though Alasdair had meant for his voice to sound firm, and it did, his tone was edged with an anticipatory huskiness. He didn't mention her use of the word "forced," at least not aloud, yet the way his eyes narrowed, shimmering a sharp shade of blue from out of the shadows, said he was of a mind that little, if any, coercion would be called for.

It was a shameful thing to admit, but Vanessa suspected he might be right about that.

While her hands had balled into fists when he'd yanked her close, and were even riding the hard wall of his shoulders, she'd yet to try shoving him away, for the strength had drained out of her arms the second the outer curve of her palm had touched his warm, unyielding flesh. She was much too aware of the way her breasts flattened against his chest, of the way her hips ground against his. The front of their thighs molded together, and the dark, coarse hairs pelting his legs tickled her bare skin. His thighs were heavily muscled; a hard, powerful contrast to her slender, softer ones.

Top or bottom?

The words rang in her ears, reverberating like the ripples made by a stone being tossed in a glossy-calm lake. Vanessa swallowed hard, and it wasn't until she felt her bottom lip sting and tasted a warm drop of blood on her tongue that she realized she'd been nibbling hard on her bottom lip.

This plan of yers be no' the workings of a sane mind. Duncan's words came back to haunt her. While he'd been saying similar things for years, never before had the sentiment rang more true.

It was time to change plans. Again. Quickly. The hint of a scowl furrowed Vanessa's brow. Praise the Lord, she only hoped there was still time to do it!

Her fists, pressing against The Devil's shoulders, flexed. After an instant of hesitation, she pooled a smidgen of strength into her arms. And shoved. To no avail. Alasdair Gray did not budge, never mind outwardly acknowledge her protest. Had she not been feeling so desperate, so *trapped*, Vanessa might have cried out in frustration.

Alasdair felt her puny shove in the way the heels of her hands pinched his rigid muscles. He schooled himself to give her no reaction. 'Twas not at all difficult. His gaze had just fastened on her mouth, and the delicate lip she continued to worry between her teeth, and his stomach muscles tightened almost painfully.

Rational thought abandoned him. For just a second, even his duties to Cavnearal seemed far and distant and inconsequential.

The urge to replace her teeth with his own grew stronger. Unfightable. Alasdair thought it just as well that he didn't struggle too hard against it. Beneath his thumb — nestled so perfectly in the warm, firm crook beneath her breast — he felt her heart hammer and her breaths rush raggedly in and out. He tried to look away, thinking only an insane man would continue to torture himself so, but he couldn't. The sight of that mouth enticed him unreasonably. Any lingering thoughts of scaring her melted away, replaced by a need so intense, so urgent, it astounded him.

Her attention had been trained on the hard line of his jaw. Her gaze lifted slowly. Her eyes looked wide, the green depths shimmering with equal parts fright and confusion.

Alasdair almost found the power of restraint. Almost. And then her lower lip trembled yet again.

Restraint washed away, the undertow drowning common sense right along with it. Resistance channeled into another, stronger sensation. Desire, sharp enough to stab through him like a lightning bolt. For one heart-stopping second, a need so strong it was staggering shot through him, heating his blood until it burned in his veins, and melted all rational thought from his mind.

Unfortunately for Alasdair, one second was all it took.

His throat tightened around a groan as he angled his head and slanted his mouth over hers. There was never a sensation to match the feel of Vanessa Forster's lips — so incredibly soft — beneath his.

He'd thought a quick, simple taste of her would slake his curiosity as well as his desire for her. He was wrong. The second their lips met, Alasdair knew that *quick* was not what he wanted. Aye, and as for *simple* . . . well, there was naught about either the woman or the situation they

158

now found themselves in that could be misconstrued as simple. Complicated. Dangerous. Traitorous, even. Those words were more suitable. 'Twas a pity his mind and body cared not to acknowledge a single one.

It was as though a drop of liquid fire had been siphoned into Vanessa's blood; it spread hotly throughout the rest of her body at a mind-boggling rate. Her breath caught. Her senses tunneled until she was capable of thinking, *feeling,* but one thing, the way Alasdair Gray's mouth moved hungrily over her own.

His arm convulsed, his hand slipping over her ribs, around to her back until his fingers were splayed over her spine. With a muffled groan, he hauled her so close that not even a sliver of air separated them. They met thigh to thigh, hip to hip, stomach to stomach. Her breasts were crushed to his hard chest, and Vanessa's heart raced when she felt the heat of his skin seep into her flesh, then seep deeper still, warming the very core of her. Was it her imagination, or was she actually able to feel the frantic hammering of his heart against her sensitive nipples?

Her lips parted to release a sigh. Of pleasure or surprise? Vanessa was unsure. Nor did it matter, for the sound never came. The Devil angled his head and deepened the kiss to a feverish pitch, his mouth swallowing up any sound she might have made.

His tongue dragged over her lips in fiery, skilled strokes that made her nerve endings tingle, her head spin. The rapid give and take of his breaths puffed hotly against her cheek. Her own breathing was shallow. Her every swallow of air was thick with the scent of Alasdair Gray. His was a disturbing aroma . . . in that it wasn't disturbing at all. Nay, quite the opposite. The man's intriguing scent — underscored by vague traces of strong lye soap and whiskey — was alarmingly pleasant!

His teeth nibbled her lower lip, causing a peculiar combination of pleasure and pain there. 'Twas a most disquieting sensation; aye, a peculiar, intriguing one!

She shivered.

His arm tightened around her. If possible, he pulled

her closer still.

When had this happened? Alasdair wondered as he eased the kiss, his mouth and tongue now devouring her full, honey-sweet lower lip. *When?* he wondered again. When had his desire for this woman become so strong, so overwhelming? Better still, *when had he begun feeling desire for her at all?!*

But, of course, he already knew. Passion had erupted — hot and quick, like a fire in his veins — the instant he'd slipped his soapy hands beneath the steamy bathwater, the instant his burning palms had caressed her wet, warm skin.

For a man who prided himself on restraint, it was an unwelcome acknowledgment to Alasdair that he'd not the strength to stop this madness. He tried to remind himself he'd sought only to frighten her into going home, but when her lips parted, and she began kissing him back, the thought melted away, like fog being vaporized by a strong summer sun.

His attentions slipped lower, and his lips grazed the gentle slope of her chin. He trapped a groan in his throat as his tongue laved her warm, soft, tempting flesh. A tang of lye clung to her skin, stung his tongue; the taste was counterbalanced by her naturally sweet scent.

"Madness," he whispered raggedly, even as he nuzzled the soft underside of her jaw. "Stop me, wench. If you've any common sense at all, you'll stop me now."

His breath misted warmly over her skin. Vanessa's own breath caught somewhere in the region of her pounding heart, then pushed itself out in a sigh that was half pleasure, half confusion. His words came to her as though muffled by a fog of the most exquisite sensations; while her mind absorbed his words, the warm feelings his moist lips and tongue had set to tingling throughout her body ignored them entirely.

Stop him? Aye, she knew she should. If she wanted to. It came as no little surprise for Vanessa to realize that stopping this man was not what she wanted. Nay, not at all!

160

Truth be known, she was as absorbed in these strange but pleasurable feelings equally as much as he was. And she'd no desire to have them cease. The feel of his muscled body pressing against her naked skin, of his hand splaying the flesh of her back and leaving its warm imprint burning right into her, of his kisses feathering raggedly over her . . . all of it had sparked a curiosity deep down inside Vanessa; a curiosity she hadn't known existed. Until their lips met, and the curiosity flourished into something stronger — into a desire so powerful it tore her resistance to shreds.

Vanessa would have liked to think her reluctance to stop what The Devil had quite accurately termed "madness" was due in no small part to her need to free her father . . . to her stubborn clan loyalty . . . to pride . . . to, well, *anything at all,* even something as simple as upholding her word — which a Forster *always* did, even when it was given to a cursed, thick-skulled Sassenach. But, unfortunately, she couldn't. She'd be deceiving no one but herself if she said that any of those reasons had a bearing on why she did not shove Alasdair Gray away, as she knew she should, by all rights, have done by now.

She felt his nose nuzzle beneath her jaw. The inky fringe of his hair fell forward against his cheeks, grazing her sensitive flesh, igniting a ticklish-burn in all the places it touched. His tongue darted out, dragging over the pulse hammering frantically in her throat. His breaths felt hot and misty against her skin. They felt good. Alarmingly so.

Stop me, wench. If you've any common sense at all, you'll stop me now . . .

Aye, she was in complete agreement on that score. So much so, in fact, that Vanessa did shove weakly at his shoulders. 'Twas like trying to move God; contrary to The Devil's husky plea, he did not budge an inch.

Had her struggles been genuine and forceful, Alasdair would have stopped. Aye, without question, he would have. But they weren't. Instead, the weak and uncertain way she shoved at his shoulders was proof that whatever

161

madness was thundering through him, it was thundering equally as strongly through her.

There was no time for him to wonder whether or not to be pleased by that, for the second he began nibbling on the creamy taper of her neck, her back arched, molding her breasts and stomach more fully to his front. The hardness of his hips ground against the soft firmness of hers. Her lips parted, issuing the barest trace of a husky groan.

The sound whispered through Alasdair, fired through his blood, making the muscles in his stomach fist uncomfortably. His breath caught as all rational thought swept from his mind like snow scattered by a strong gale wind.

Alasdair knew for sure that leaving Cavnearal was no longer what he wanted from this woman.

Nay, right or wrong, what he wanted right now — dear Lord, *right this very second!* — was to roll Vanessa Forster onto her back and blanket her body with his. He wanted to plunge himself so deeply inside her that all thought of pledges and clan feuds and, aye, even Cavnearal and his responsibilities to it paled into insignificance. He wanted to feel her firm, shapely legs wrapped tightly around his hips, pulling him in deeper, and deeper still. He wanted to drown himself in the soap-and-honey smell of her, to feel her warm, tight wetness surrounding him, milking him into what he had a feeling would be a breath-stealing release . . . and he wanted to hear her husky sighs of pleasure as he brought her skillfully to that same end.

Never in Alasdair's life had he wanted a woman with this same crushing need. Never. Not even Jenny.

His wife's name, the haunting memory of her face, echoed through Alasdair's mind. Neither was the reason he stiffened and abruptly pulled his head back, glaring down at the woman in his arms. Nay, the knowledge that he was too close to losing his self-control caused that. He could not do that, especially not with Hugh Forster's daughter.

Her damp hair was scattered over his pillow, a stark contrast to the linen casing's crisp whiteness. Her eyes were closed. The color in her cheeks was high. Her lips, slightly swollen from his kiss, were parted; the lower glistened with moisture in what little firelight permeated this section of the room. It also trembled.

Strength was a quality Alasdair respected. He'd never lacked his share of it. Until now. He was surprised by how much stamina it took to slip his arm from around her, to put a scant sliver of sanity-saving space between them. He shifted, his right elbow dimpling the mattress, making the straw filling crunch as he levered himself up.

Her lashes flickered up hesitantly. Her green eyes looked dazed, puzzled.

"Ye stopped," Vanessa murmured huskily, her dark brows knitting in a frown.

"Aye."

"But why?" Her frown deepened. A better question would have been why had *she* not been the one to stop him? 'Twas a question Vanessa wasn't at all sure she wanted an answer to.

Likewise, there were questions that Alasdair also wanted left unanswered. It wouldn't do to search himself too deeply for the reason he'd halted this madness; in doing so, there was a chance he might come up with stronger reasons to continue it. That was a chance he was unwilling to take. He'd found his self-control—finally, somehow—and he'd not lose it again. Not this night. Not *any* night. Not with her. His voice edged with steely restraint, he said, "Don't look so disappointed, wench. Consider it a temporary postponement, nothing more. I've learned what I needed to know."

Until she felt the muscles beneath his hot, sleek skin bunch tight she didn't realize that her hands were still splayed in the sculpted hollow between The Devil's chest and shoulders. She pulled her hands back, stiffened, not liking his tone at all. It took effort to make her voice sound as composed as his, but she managed it. "Have ye? And what be that, mon?"

His grin was wicked and quick; it didn't reach his eyes. "Why, that you'd make a most amusing pledge, of course.

What else?"

Aye, what else indeed? Vanessa didn't know, didn't *want* to know. At the moment, she was torn between a bright yellow pang of hope, and an equally strong, murky gray pang of dread. Cautiously, she said, "Ye've accepted me offer, then?"

Alasdair's grin never faltered. "What do you think?"

And that, Vanessa realized with a start, was exactly the problem. She *couldn't* think with this man's hard, naked body so close. At least she couldn't think sensibly. The scent of him still fogged her senses. On her tongue, she still tasted his enticing flavor; hot and whiskey-sweet. "What I think"—her voice cracked, she cleared her throat—"is that 'tis time ye be letting me da and Duncan out of yer dreary vault, Devil. *That's* what I be thinking."

If his thoughtful hesitation was meant to torment, it did so admirably. It irked Vanessa to think that, with his next words, The Devil could easily make her last few, humiliating hours in his care all for naught. There was a chance he'd still scorn her offer, that his evasiveness now was meant only to torture her by raising her hopes, only to dash them again in his next breath.

"And I," he said finally, slowly, his gaze never leaving hers, "think you are right. Your father and brother will be released at dawn."

Vanessa felt a moment of relief, followed closely by an agonizingly long moment of raw panic. With her father and Duncan's imminent release came her own imprisonment. Their liberation was, of course, exactly what she'd bargained for—aye, and well she knew it—but to have the reality of it staring her in the face was disquieting. So was the way The Devil's voice mulled huskily in her mind.

Consider it a temporary postponement . . .

She swallowed dryly, and shook her head. "Now," she said, and felt a pang of satisfaction to hear that her voice sounded composed and decisive, while inwardly, she felt neither.

"Now?" he echoed, and the way one dark brow slanted

high on his sun-kissed forehead suggested that the release of two Forsters was not what Alasdair Gray was referring to.

"Aye," she said, and added meaningfully, "ye'll release me da and Duncan now."

His expression sobered. "And if I refuse?"

"Then I shall also refuse to be yer pledge."

His chuckle was gratingly soft and scornful. "Beware of the threats you make, kitten, lest they come back to claw at you. Tell me, you don't really think I'd argue with you on that score, do you? Especially since we've both known from the start that I don't want you here." And that, Alasdair realized uncomfortably, was one of the biggest lies he'd ever told. While it was true he didn't want her here, inside Cavnearal, the fact remained that he *did* want her. *Here.* In his bed. He wanted that badly.

"Now," he continued when a tense moment, marked only by the snap and pop of logs roasting in the hearth, had slipped past, "as I've said, your father and brother will be released come dawn. Not a second earlier. If you feel that violates our bargain, then by all means, feel free to leave this keep."

Her eyes were no longer languid and dazed, Alasdair noted, but narrow and shimmering with resentment. Her lips—he tried very hard not to look at them too long—moved tightly over her next words. "As ye well know, mon, I've no choice but to agree."

"There are always choices, wench."

Vanessa thought of her mother, of the baby, of her own obligation and promises to both. Trapping a sigh in her throat, she shook her head. "In this case, there be none."

It was Alasdair's last attempt to coerce her into leaving. Unlike the last time, he wasn't surprised by her stubborn refusal. He also was not overly pleased by it. "Good. Then the matter is settled."

"Aye," she agreed, and thought the "matter" was anything but. *Consider it a temporary postponement* . . . Her throat went dry; the muscles there felt tighter than an iron shackle. She averted her gaze to the ceiling, but saw not an inch of the shadowy orange glow of firelight glinting off timber and stone.

Although outwardly she didn't show it — a grand challenge, that! — she was still aware of the man who reclined lazily by her side. Very aware of him. His heat warmed her bare flesh, the threat of contact between them made her tingle all over. She felt the pull of gravity from where his body dented the mattress. The taste of him still lingered provocatively on her tongue, the smell of him still teased her nostrils and made her senses spin. If she closed her eyes, Vanessa was certain she'd still be able to feel the soft beat of his breaths rasping over her cheek and jaw and ear, still feel the pressure of his mouth covering hers.

She gritted her teeth against such traitorous thoughts . . . and did *not* close her eyes. She didn't dare.

How long they lay like that — her staring sightlessly up at the ceiling, him staring pensively down at her — she couldn't have said. Mayhap it only felt like forever?

Prudence. That was the word Alasdair would have chosen to explain why he tore his gaze away from her sweetly turned face and, after a short, reluctant pause, pushed himself up and off of the bed. Her closeness — her nakedness! — was wreaking havoc on his already tattered senses. His eyes had unwisely dipped to her mouth, and as he'd watched her tongue slide over her full lower lip he'd felt his throat close and his gut clench and a desire unlike any he'd ever known tear through him.

He needed distance. If he'd stayed on the bed a second longer — with her warm, soft body within much too easy reach — he might have . . . well, he might have surrendered to temptation.

That he was leaving was obvious. The way he tugged on his trews, then yanked the tunic over his head, punching his arms through the sleeves with enough force to rend the seams, told Vanessa that. The reason behind her sudden pang of regret, however, was not so clear.

She shivered and tugged at the sheet behind her, wrapping the cloth around herself. It didn't cover all of her — it draped in crisp white folds over her upper thighs, the top

166

hem barely covering her breasts — but it concealed enough. While she still felt naked, exposed, it was more of an emotional sort now, not the physical vulnerability that had been plaguing her since she'd dropped the blanket to the floor a dozen lifetimes ago.

She almost asked him where he was going and why, but bit the words back. It was a good thing, too; Vanessa wasn't entirely sure her voice could be trusted at that moment. Her attention had just focused on The Devil's back — broad and firm, even beneath the baggy cloth of his shirt, the play of muscles in his shoulders and arms could not be hidden. She traced the line of his spine upward.

The back of a man's neck was not a new sight to her; she must have seen hundreds in all her nineteen years. Yet it was a feature she'd never had cause to notice. Until now.

There was something about the way Alasdair Gray's neck curved down to meld into impressively broad shoulders . . . something about the way the inky fringe of his hair, scantily curled at the ends, whisked that sun-kissed part of him . . . something about the odd softness of his skin there that . . .

Vanessa startled, and blinked hard. The Devil was talking to her, she realized abruptly, and she'd had no idea what he had said. The barest hint of color stained her cheeks.

He turned his head and regarded her from over his shoulder. A frown pinched his inky brows. The barest trace of a grin tugged at one corner of his mouth. As always, it didn't reach his eyes. "Don't look so disappointed, kitten. I promise you, I will be back. Soon."

Disappointed? Should she be? About what? Vanessa's mind whirled, and now it was her turn to scowl. If he was referring to his leaving, which she'd already surmised for herself, then The Devil could think again. Disappointment was the very *last* thing she felt about that. Wasn't it? Sweet Saint Andrews, she hoped so!

He must have guessed that she'd not heard him before,

for he repeated the words her mind had been too distracted a second ago to register. "I'll give the order to release your father at dawn, and have a handful of my best men ready themselves to escort him."

"Dinna be silly, Devil. Me da needs no escort. Hugh Forster knows these Borders as well as ye. Nay, better," she added proudly. "He can find his way back to Dunnaclard unguided."

"He can," Alasdair said, and nodded tightly, "but he won't. I'll not risk him turning back the second he's out of sight to return and aid in your escape. 'Tis a pastime you Forsters seem to take most seriously."

"He canna do that. Cavnearal's walls be unbreachable, don't ye know?"

"Aye, so 'tis rumored." His eyes narrowed to scrutinize her. "And so 'twas true . . . until tonight. If a scrawny girl and a boy not yet old enough to grow his first whiskers can slip unnoticed into my keep, I've no doubt 'tis only a matter of time before others garner the secret as well. And, rest assured, wench, *I* will be the first amongst those 'others.' Before I'm done with you, I *will* have your method for obtaining unwelcome entrance to Cavnearal, as well as your source. Never doubt it."

It was on the tip of Vanessa tongue's to tell The Devil she'd rather die than divulge such information. But, as luck would have it, by the time the words had formed, the man gave her no chance to utter them.

Alasdair sent the wench one last, penetrating glare, then spun on his bare heel and stalked to the door. A single, sharp rap on the thick wooden panel had the outer bar sliding out of place. The door swung inward, and a cool breeze tunneled into the room, making the flames in the hearth dance a protest.

Vanessa shivered, and hugged the sheet more tightly about her when she saw the round, ruddy face of a portly guard peer curiously into the room. She didn't like the lecherous grin the man gave her, and was relieved when Alasdair shifted, putting his body between the guard's curious gaze and herself. His

168

broadness was a most welcome shield.

Alasdair took a step forward, forcing the guard to take two steps back. Without looking at her, The Devil reached back and slammed the door closed.

Muffled voices floated in through the slat beneath the door, but they were too soft for Vanessa to make out what was being said. Their words could have rung with crystal clarity, but she'd not have heard them over the pounding of her heart in her ears.

Alasdair Gray's voice swirled around in her mind, like a misty fog. A drop of warmth melted, then seeped swiftly throughout her body, making her feel uncomfortably hot and tingly. Her shiver did not stem from cold, for she most assuredly was not that.

Consider it a temporary postponement . . .

"I swear to ye, Da," she said aloud, her voice soft and shaky, " 'Tis my last plan. Ever. And if I'd not promised me mother . . ."

Alas, she *had* made the promise, as well as taken the only steps she could think of at the time to fulfill it. Forster pride forbade her to renege on her word. No matter how much she might have liked to!

A good quarter hour slipped past before Vanessa finally slipped from the bed and rummaged through The Devil's wardrobe. She found one of his tunics in the bottom drawer and tugged it on. The shirt was laughably large on her small, slender frame, but, of course, there was no help for that; under The Devil's orders, one of the men who'd brought her bath had been instructed to take her clothes and burn them. Now all that remained of the garments she'd worn into Cavnearal were her worn leather boots, which would not cover much of her.

With a resigned sigh, Vanessa swiped the dark, damp hair from her brow, and set about searching for a way out of this chamber. Her chance of finding one was scant, she knew . . . just as she also knew she'd not respect herself come dawn if she didn't at least try.

Chapter Ten

In the week that followed, Vanessa saw little of Alasdair during the day. Mayhap a quick glimpse of him entering or leaving the hall, or a snatched glance of him through one of the tall, narrow bedchamber — *his* bedchamber! — windows.

He'd curtly informed her upon her awakening on her first morning in Cavnearal that, as agreed upon, her father and brother had taken their leave at daybreak. He'd offered no details, and Vanessa had wisely asked for none. The Devil's stony expression and colder-than-ice gaze had warned her of his foul mood. And, of course, there were the dark smudges beneath his eyes that bespoke of a night ill spent. At the time, she'd reasoned that details would do her no good. Her father and Duncan had gained their freedom, at the expense of her own; both should have been safely home at Dunnaclard days ago.

Since such had been Vanessa's intent from the start, she saw no need to argue or debate the issue. She did, however, wonder often and hard about how her mother fared. While the birthing was a mere fortnight away, bairns were notorious for holding no schedule. 'Twas possible the delivery had already taken place.

Vanessa felt a squeezing sensation in her chest at the thought. How well she remembered Duncan's birth; the fright and the excitement, and even more of it with Kayla's. Equally well, she remembered the two stillborns that had followed; the sadness and the pain. Oh, how she longed to be home! Never had she felt so homesick. Never had she—

Vanessa had been standing beside the window, her shoulder resting heavily against the hard, rough corner of stone. Her gaze had been fixed unseeingly on the craggy rock and swirling waters of the Firth of Maryn.

Until a second ago.

When she'd unwittingly averted her attention to the bed.

Alasdair Gray's bed.

The mattress looked wide, empty, and though she knew the sheets must be cold by now—they'd both been up for hours—the rumpled bedding looked appealingly soft and warm. There was a small depression in one of the pillows from where her head had rested. There was a larger depression in the one beside it. Vanessa's mouth went dry, her throat tight, when her mind flashed her a starkly vivid picture of Alasdair Gray's devil-black head cushioned atop the pillow's softness.

She'd watched him sleep last night. Vanessa remembered that only now, when the sight of that pillow and the dent in it swirled the memory back to her in jarring detail. Aye, she thought, and her heartbeat doubled, she really had.

Something had awakened her—she couldn't recall exactly what. She'd rolled onto her side, her eyes taking a few seconds to adjust to the shadowy darkness.

And there he was.

Fast asleep.

His hard male body a mere fraction away.

She hadn't heard him enter. Not unusual, that; in the week she'd been at Cavnearal, The Devil had never awakened her when he invaded the bedchamber they now shared. In fact, Vanessa could have sworn he took great pains at night to assure himself she was always asleep before he retired.

His head had been turned toward her, as though he'd

fallen asleep watching her. His dark hair was a striking contrast to the stark white pillow casing; one strand had curled forward on his brow, and she remembered the way her fingers had itched to brush it back into place. His features had been sleep-softened, and sleep had also ironed the lines that usually creased the space between his eyebrows smooth. His inky lashes fluttered against his deeply tanned cheeks.

Asleep, he didn't look so much like the fierce Border reiver Vanessa had heard so many deplorable tales about. Nay, asleep he simply looked like . . . a man. And a very handsome, vulnerable man, at that.

Thinking back on it now, she assumed it must have been a trick of shadows and moonlight that had made him appear so . . . well, *normal*. Mayhap even a trick of her own tired mind?

One thing that she was positive had *not* been a trick of any sort was the way her palms had gone cold and moist, her blood steamy hot, as she'd gazed in sleepy confusion upon The Devil's face. Even now, hours later, her body suffered the same, untoward reaction. Her heart pumped, her body tingled and awoke to unheard of awareness, her breathing shallowed and quickened.

Consider it a temporary postponement . . .

Vanessa closed her eyes and sucked in a ragged breath. The words had haunted her every waking hour for the last week. They even manifested themselves in hot, vivid dreams that made her blush when she remembered them in the morn — and she very rarely allowed herself to remember them, at any time of the day or night. Each day was worse than the last. Each *night!* While The Devil had yet to make a move toward her — even when they slept so closely beside each other in the dark — she knew, had always known, it was only a matter of time before he upheld the promise.

She was, in his words, to be "a most entertaining pledge." So why, Vanessa wondered, had she not yet been called upon to "entertain"? Was The Devil's nerve-shattering patience in this matter a coldly devised plan to draw out her curiosity? Her agony? Mayhap to make her wonder about it—would this be the night? would *this?*—until the questions that chased circles in her mind drove her mad?

If so, 'twas an admirable strategy, for his method was working all too well!

Vanessa opened her eyes and pushed away from the window. Her arm was tender from where the stone had bitten into her sensitive flesh. The sleeve of the frock she now wore—borrowed, really . . . oh, the shame!—was too thin to have provided much protection. The hem of the skirt stopped just above her ankles. Were she in a laughing mood, she would have found the sight of the worn toes of her boots peeking out from beneath it most humorous.

Her gaze skipped to the door. Closed and barred from without, as always.

What she needed, she decided in a flash, was a distraction. She'd been caged in this keep—mostly in this one chamber . . . *Alasdair Gray's bedchamber!*—for days, and she was bored. She knew exactly how many stones had been laid to make the hearth, because in the tediousness she'd counted them thrice. She knew also the amount and length of each timber that crisscrossed the ceiling, knew precisely how many steps it took to reach the bed from the door, the fireplace, the window.

The enforced solitude had given her far too many hours to think; and she liked not a bit the path her thoughts had been straying down lately. A path with The Devil's name, the image of his sleeping face, carved upon it.

She only left the room for brief strolls through Cavnearal's twisting, turning corridors. She took one of these walks daily, mostly because her body craved exercise. She was to the point now where she could get to almost anywhere inside the keep, except the upper floor, for she wasn't allowed there. The layout of the keep had long since been put to memory.

Always, she was accompanied by a tall, muscular guard who spoke not a word. His silence was deafening, accusatory; it grated on her nerves. It was that man's stony countenance she encountered when she crossed the room and rapped briskly upon the door.

The bar was slid up, and the thick oak panel swung inward. Vanessa took a quick step back, and barely missed being smacked on the shoulder by the door's sharp wooden edge.

The guard was tall, broad, and dark. A scraggly, coarse growth of beard — one he'd obviously been cultivating for years — obscured his chin, jaw, neck, and a goodly portion of his upper chest. His eyes were mere slits in his face, the irises a frigid shade of blue. His stare was intimidating.

But then, so was Vanessa's.

Her chin tipped up proudly, and she returned the guard's glare measure for icy measure. The barest hint of a smile tugged at one corner of her mouth as she looked him up and down. Twice.

The man hated her walks, and she knew it. 'Twas one of the reasons Vanessa enjoyed them so much. Often, they were stopped amongst the corridors by another of The Devil's men, and her guard bore the jests that his most important duty these days was playing nanny to a tiny slip of a Scots woman. Oh, how he'd slipped in the ranks, they'd say. Always, the tormentors would recall some important errand that needed completing once they noticed the guard's massive hands hook into limb-rending claws.

Vanessa's smile broadened a bit. "Be ye ready, mon?" she asked, her tone light and teasing. The way his expression clouded made her want to laugh. Of course, she didn't. Well, mayhap she did . . . but only a bit, and only on the *inside*.

He grunted in response, and nodded that she should leave the bedchamber.

Vanessa did so without hesitation. Behind her, she felt the empty bed's disturbing presence, and though she knew full well the bed was an inanimate object, she could have sworn the mattress was laughing at her cowardly retreat.

The door slammed shut.

Vanessa startled at the booming sound of wood smashing against wood.

The guard smiled. A little. Coldly.

Vanessa's green eyes narrowed, and her lips thinned. She glared at the man, and her skirt rustled when she hoisted it in tight fists and swept past him. Her heels clicked smartly atop the stone as she walked, and inwardly, each footstep seemed to remind her that the boots on her feet were the only things she truly owned. The rest had been borrowed. From Marette Gray's wardrobe, Vanessa had no doubt.

The fit of the daffodil-yellow frock she wore was tight. For once in her life, Vanessa had found someone smaller than herself. The Devil's sister. Pity 'twas that woman's clothes she'd been loaned! The bodice stretched uncomfortably across her breasts. The waist nipped at her flat, firm belly. The hem of the skirt barely grazed her ankles, leaving her masculine boots in full view of any who cared to look. And it seemed that all who passed her during her daily walks did exactly that.

They reached the stairs that The Devil's brother had escorted her up what felt like years ago. After but a second's internal debate, Vanessa turned left and, hoisting her skirt still higher, descended the stone stairway. The heavy thump of her guard's footsteps echoed not too far behind her.

The foyer was empty. Eerily so. Its vacancy seemed to make the voices floating out from the hall that much more pronounced.

Two people were in the midst of an argument. She could tell by their husky tones that both were men. One

175

voice, however, was deeper, rougher than the other. It was that voice which skittered down Vanessa's spine like a drop of sun-warmed honey. The voice belonged to Alasdair Gray and, if she'd had to guess, she would have said the other belonged to his brother, Keith.

Her steps faltered, became leadened. In contrast, the voices, as she drew nearer to the hall's stone archway, became sharper, distinguishable.

"How long?" This voice was obviously Keith's . . . and it was just as obviously furious. "How long do you think it will take? She's a Scot, aye, and she's a woman. There's two strikes against her. I'll not argue either point, because we both know I can't. But, bloody hell, Alasdair, the girl is not, I repeat, *not* as stupid as you seem to think. I'd stake my life on it!"

"You worry needlessly, Keith." Alasdair's voice was low and tight. Vanessa had heard that tone enough times by now to have no trouble imagining a deep scowl furrowing Alasdair Gray's inky brow. His eyes, she knew, would be slate gray, his stare cold and intimidating. "Everything is under control."

"I think not, Brother. If she ever finds out you lied about—"

"She won't."

"How do you know that?!"

"I just do! Like I said, *everything-is-under-control!*" The Devil replied in his customary Gray bellow.

The tension-riddled silence that ensued said Keith did not believe his brother for a second . . . and that Alasdair had quickly lost patience with trying to reassure the younger man that all would go favorably.

"All right, let's change this subject for a moment, shall we?" Keith said, and his voice was too calm and frosty for Vanessa's liking. "Tell me what you plan to do about Carey and Humes . . . ?"

The guard, who was standing to the side and behind Vanessa, grunted his disapproval at her eavesdropping.

His beefy fingers wrapped around her slender arm and he gave a tug, trying to drag her away from the doorway.

Vanessa, however, was not of a mind to leave just yet. Not, at least, until she'd heard Alasdair's answer to his brother's question. The guard's grip was insistent but not tight; she had no trouble locking her knees to keep her place, and shrugging away from him. She took a step closer to the arched-stone entranceway.

The guard's fingers again wrapped around her arm. This time his grasp was not so lenient.

After a thoughtful silence, Alasdair said, "I plan to do nothing about either one of them. Why should I?"

"Because methinks you'll have no choice. Sooner or later, the two are going to hear rumors about what's been transpiring here in Cavnearal; need I remind you that you've kept it no secret? Tell me, just how long do you think it will take the Forsters to summon their Warden? *If* they've not done so already, which would be my guess. 'Tis no less than what I would do in a similar situation."

Again the guard tugged, and this time Vanessa stumbled back two steps. Her feet soon found purchase, however, and, with effort, she managed to stand her ground.

The wooden legs of a bench scraped harshly against stone. Footsteps clicked, retreated, then stopped abruptly. "And what if the Forsters *do* summon Humes, Keith? So what? The man couldn't be bothered to show his ugly mug at the last Day of Truce. What makes you think he'll tax himself to check out naught but a pack of rumors? Need *I* remind *you* that rumors about the Grays were being bandied about for generations before you and I were born? Few listen, and even fewer put stock in any of them."

Vanessa's cheeks went pale, and an icy shiver curled down her spine. The hairs at her nape pricked. The Devil's words reminded her of a childhood threat that one of her older brothers, Angus, had once used to get her to eat the morning meal. "If ye'll not eat yer porridge, it's dumping ye on The Devil's doorstoop I'll be doing," he'd bellowed at her, proving that a Forster's bellow could be equally as intimidating as a Gray's, it merely came less frequently. "Ye'd not like him, Vanessa. He has fangs this long"—Angus had pointed to the crest of his scraggly bearded chin—"and 'tis rumored he eats little girls for dinner. It be only a rumor, mind ye. Totally unsubstantiated . . . mayhap because the Gray be maun too clever to be caught doing it. Do ye want to hear what he does with the bones, lass? He picks at them with his long, razor-sharp teeth and sucks them clean of—"

Vanessa never heard the rest of that particular rumor; she'd already fled from the room, tears of fright wetting her cheeks. She hadn't eaten the meal. In fact, she'd eaten naught for two days afterward.

The guard grunted again; he was now standing closely enough for his hot breath to ravish her left cheek and neck. She gasped when his fingers tightened painfully around her arm. An icy chill seeped into her hand and fingers as the flow of blood was abruptly cut off.

"Rumors need start somewhere," Keith said, in the same instant that Vanessa picked up her foot and sent the hard heel of her boot careening into the guard's shin. The guard grunted and stumbled back a step, hauling Vanessa with him.

"If 'tis all you wanted to discuss with me, Keith . . ." Alasdair's sigh was long and impatient; it masked the rustle of Vanessa's skirt as it tangled about her legs and pitched her off balance. Dratted skirt! There was a reason she preferred not to wear one, and this was it!

She toppled clumsily backward, her shoulder blades colliding with the guard's hard chest, pushing the breath from her lungs. Momentum made her head snap back, the crown of which slammed into the guard's darkly bearded chin. A teeth-jarring bolt of pain sliced down Vanessa's neck, and white sparks danced before her eyes. Alasdair said something, but the voice came as though from a great distance and she couldn't decipher more than his general tone over the buzzing noise that was droning in her ears.

She shook her head to clear it and winced, her green eyes watering when the pain in the back of her head flared to life. Her scalp burned—even the roots of her hair tingled and ached. There was no doubt she'd have a good-sized knot back there come nightfall, if not sooner. The valley between her shoulder blades was sore. Her arm throbbed mightily. The guard had yet to release her—if anything, his grip had tightened—and her left palm now felt icy and numb, her fingers reflexively loosened and curled inward.

Her head cleared a wee bit, and a portion of her mind noticed that the conversation in the hall had switched to Marette. According to Keith, the girl had been released from the tower room days ago . . . and she was still nursing her fury at having been locked up there at all.

In the same instant, a larger portion of Vanessa's mind registered an alarming cessation of pain in her left arm, from elbow to fingertips. The guard's grip was like a tourniquet, tight and unmerciful. She glanced down, and her eyes widened when she saw that her fingers were no longer pallid blue, but swiftly turning a worrisome shade of purple.

Either the man was unaware of his own strength, or he was purposely trying to snap her arm off! Vanessa cared not which it was. At the moment, her concern focused solely on forcing him to release her before he caused permanent damage.

She had to push her words out around shallow, rapid breaths, which gave her voice a panicked edge. "If ye dinna release me this second, ye clumsy oaf, I'll scream for ye laird. Me thinks The Devil willna be pleased to see the way ye be bruising his guest."

179

The muscles in the hard chest behind her pulled taut as the guard gave his customary grunt of disapproval. His grip did not loosen a with.

Vanessa shook her head — and inwardly reminded herself not to do that again, for it *hurt!* — and wondered if all Sassenachs were so stubborn and hostile. She'd yet to find one who wasn't. Well, there was naught to be done about it now. She'd voiced a threat, and a Forster always carried through.

She opened her mouth to scream.

The cold voice that came from her right wilted the sound in her throat. "Such stupidity is no more than I'd expect from a Scot," the voice said, and the woman's chilly tone dripped recrimination. "Has it not occurred to you that Alasdair gave this man *orders* to hurt you? Nay, I can see from your expression it has not. Again, 'tis no surprise."

Vanessa's attention, which had been focused on the doorway, shifted. Her gaze clashed with eyes the same steely shade as Alasdair's, yet degrees colder and many years harder.

Marette smiled. The gesture was stiff and didn't reach her eyes, which continued to drill harshly into Vanessa. "You've a lot to learn about we Grays, little girl. Just because my brother has not hurt you yet doesn't mean he has no intention of doing so in the future."

"Mayhap," Vanessa replied tightly. "But the fact remains, the only one who be hurting me now is this burly guard."

"Tsk, tsk, tsk. You poor dear. The man is simply carrying out orders," Marette said with a shrug.

"Aye? And his 'orders' be to rip me arm off, in other words?"

"I've no idea what instructions my brother gave this man. But, aye, methinks it a strong possibility 'tis exactly what Alasdair told him to do." Marette's eyes narrowed, her gaze slicing through Vanessa like a sharply honed dagger. "You seem to be mistaken. Contrary to what you said earlier, you are *not* a guest in this keep. No Scot could ever be that, and most assuredly not a Forster." Her gaze raked Vanessa head to toe, and the slight crease at the bridge of the woman's nose spoke her condemnation. "You'd do well to remember that, you little heathen."

A chuckle rumbled in the chest pressing against Vanessa's back. It was the first time she'd heard the guard laugh; it was, she decided instantly, a sound she could have lived without ever having heard; harsh and grating, it poured down Vanessa's spine like melting snowflakes.

No help would be forthcoming from this woman. That much was obvious. In fact, from the hard glint in Marette Gray's eyes, the woman would be more likely to gleefully *help* the guard cause her more pain.

Vanessa swerved her thoughts back to her more immediate goal. Freeing herself. To that end, she did the only thing left to do. Brute strength would not gain her freedom; she knew, she'd already tried. So, instead, she opened her mouth and, in a bellow that would have done either feuding clan proud, yelled, "Alasdair Gray! If ye dinna come out here and stop this cursed Sassenach, ye'll have a pledge who's missing a limb come dusk! 'Twould make for a most unsightly pledge, Devil!"

A tense moment ticked past.

Vanessa glanced to the side and saw Marette's expression turn stony, her gaze hot and condemning. The hard male chest grinding into Vanessa's back stiffened perceptibly. The guard's fingers automatically loosened around her arm, and she felt the first warm, prickly surge of returning circulation.

On the opposite side of the two-foot-thick stone wall, Alasdair had also opened his mouth to bellow . . . but the hauntingly familiar voice that rang like thunder in his ears—bouncing repeatedly off the walls of the nearly vacant hall — wilted the words on his tongue.

Vanessa? Aye, who else could it be? *And what the devil was she shouting about?!*

His gaze met Keith's. The younger man shrugged stiffly, and looked equally as confused. Swearing beneath his breath, Alasdair spun on his heel and stalked from the hall.

The sight that greeted him froze Alasdair in his tracks.

Oric Kramer, the man he'd assigned to guard Vanessa, was standing with his burly back pressed flat against the stone wall. Two fingernail scratches traced bloody ribbons from the crest of the man's cheek downward, the jagged ends melting into his dark-brown beard. They mirrored the ones on Alasdair's own cheek, now almost fully healed. The man's gaze was slitted, and his muddy brown eyes sparkled with a murderous glint as he glared at the woman who stood facing him.

That woman was Vanessa.

And she was wearing a murderous glare of her own. Aye, a very *familiar* one at that!

She stood facing Oric, a mere yard away. The guard's body — big and tall and solid as a rock — dwarfed her slender frame, yet she didn't look the least bit daunted. After his own altercations with the woman, Alasdair wasn't surprised; tenacious was but one of several words he'd use to describe Vanessa Forster. Her left arm was wrapped limply around her middle, her right hand alternately pinching and rubbing the forearm. His attention shifted to the tips of her fingers. They were an unnatural shade of blue.

A surge of . . . well, something he'd rather not acknowledge, pumped like fire through Alasdair's veins. A glint of sunlight hitting metal snared his gaze; his eyes narrowed as his attention shifted to Marette. Nay, rather, to her right hand, which was slipping something back into the side pocket of her skirt.

" 'Tis aboot time ye showed ye ugly mug, Devil," Vanessa snapped, her accent thickening in direct proportion to her anger. "Another minute and this . . . this . . ."—she jerked her chin in Oric's direction—"massive oaf would ha' torn me arm off!"

Alasdair didn't miss Oric's antagonistic grunt, or the shimmer of amusement sparkling in his sister's eyes. He focused the brunt of his attention on the former. The glare that was rumored to put even the mightiest of Border reivers in their place shot forth. 'Twas not rumor, 'twas fact. Oric Kramer was no exception.

A flush stained the big man's cheeks as his eyes met Alasdair's, then quickly, *guiltily,* moved away. A low growl as he shook his head was all Oric offered by way of explanation. His cheeks reddened still more when Alasdair's brows furrowed in a most foreboding scowl, signifying to Oric that his explanation, heartfelt though it was, was not going to be so easily accepted. Still, Oric had his pride, and the Scots chit had, after all, been eavesdropping. Surely he was justified in what he'd done!

"Alasdair, the little bitc—er, the *girl* deserved what she got. Deserved that and more. The wench was—"

"Doing nothing to deserve such brutal treatment," Alasdair finished the sentence for Marette, and his tone was so cold and tight and low that both she and Oric stiffened cautiously.

"Brother," Marette said, as she took a step—a very *small* step—toward Alasdair, "hear what I say. You'd not have assigned Oric to guard . . ." again, her nose wrinkled as though she smelled something foul, "that filthy little hoyden if you did not trust him implicitly. Is that not true? Think, Alasdair! Oric is no liar. He never has been. If he hurt the chit, he hurt her because she forced him to do it!"

Alasdair turned to Oric. He didn't see the way Marette's eyes narrowed, or the glare of triumph she shot to Vanessa.

But Vanessa saw. The vengeful glint in Marette's eyes sent icy needles prickling at her nape, and an even colder surge of mistrust rushing through her veins.

"Well, wench," Alasdair asked, "what have you to say? Is that true? *Did* you force Oric to hurt you?"

The Devil's accusing glare settled on her, and Vanessa tilted her chin, her green eyes flashing with pride. Her voice oozing contempt, she replied, "Oh, aye, Devil. I near had to beg the mon to cause me pain. He was, of course, reluctant at first . . . but he soon changed his mind. 'Tis why I shouted for ye; I thought ye maun want to watch."

"Vanessa—" Alasdair began tersely, but was interrupted by his sister.

"Listen to her, Alasdair," Marette said, "for 'twill most likely be the only time you'll hear a Scot speaking the truth. While the chit did not beg for such treatment in words, nay, she did truly beg for it by deed. The girl was spying on you, Brother. Eavesdropping on every word you and Keith said. Surely you didn't expect Oric to allow that?!"

Alasdair's eyes pinned Vanessa to the spot. "Is that true?"

Lying would be pointless, since both Marette and Oric looked most eager to challenge everything she said. Instead, Vanessa nodded, and though she shrugged, the gesture looked stiff and tense. "Aye, 'tis. Would ye not have done the same thing in me place?"

"Nay, wench. And for good reason. I'm not so foolish as to ever find myself in your place." Alasdair noted that the color was returning to her hand; the pallid blue was now tinged with splotches of healthy pink. "How much did you hear?"

"Enough," she lied, because she'd actually heard naught of consequence, merely the suggestion of something that tickled her curiosity. She saw no reason The Devil need know that. Vanessa's gaze shifted to the young man standing a few feet behind Alasdair. Keith was glaring at her assessively. Whether his brother believed her or not, it was obvious from his expression that this younger Gray did not. The sight of Keith did, however, spur her to add, "I've discovered ye've lied to me, Devil. I dinna like that."

I think not, Brother. If she ever finds out you lied about— What? Vanessa wondered. Ah, that was the question that burned inside her. What had The Devil lied about? She didn't know, but she had every intention of finding out.

Alasdair's gaze was shrewd, his expression cold. There were no visible signs of the feelings churning inside him. Years of practice made it so. He nodded briskly to Oric. "You're dismissed. I'll guard the wench this aft, and find another to do the chore hence."

Oric gave his customary grunt. It was clear from his shrug and the slight curve of one side of his mouth that he wasn't at all displeased to be released from such an unpleasant, demeaning duty. Vanessa watched the big man push away from the wall and, after casting first her, then Marette, a sharp glare, swagger down the corridor.

Alasdair's attention shifted to his sister. "Have you business with me?"

"Aye, but none I'll discuss with"—she shuddered and nodded briskly to Vanessa—"that *thing* present."

"Then don't feel you need tarry here, Sister," Alasdair said, and his tone was low and terse.

Marette's lips thinned. "I assure you, I'll not. Heaven forbid I give you another reason to lock me in the tower." With a tilt of her chin, she hoisted her skirt and made to sweep past Vanessa. Very *closely* past her.

The women's shoulders brushed.

Vanessa stiffened, preparing herself for . . . well, she was unsure of what, but caution bade her be ready for anything. Her arm still ached, but she was ready to use it to defend herself if she must. As it turned out, there was no need.

Marette stumbled from their contact. Or so it seemed. She reached out and grabbed Vanessa's shoulders to steady her faulty balance. The woman's grip was as tight as death.

Loud enough for only Vanessa to hear, Marette hissed, "I know my brother's secret. Be in the stables at midnight if you wish to learn it. I'll see your door is unlocked and unguarded."

That said, Marette pushed free, bestowed upon Vanessa a most disparaging glare, then spun on her heel and left.

Keith's gaze volleyed between his brother and sister. After only a heartbeat's hesitation, he shook his head, sighed, and set out at a trot after the latter . . .

Leaving Alasdair and Vanessa alone in the hall.

Vanessa frowned, her mind turning over what Marette Gray had just said. Was it a trap? Or did the woman truly know the lies Alasdair had told her? Better still, did she dare risk meeting Marette alone, in the dark of night, and finding out? Her frown deepened to a scowl. Then her attention strayed, and her gaze locked with Alasdair's, and Vanessa felt her heart stutter beneath her breasts as all rational thought fled her mind.

The foyer had seemed quite large when she'd entered it a scarce quarter hour ago. Yet The Devil's body seemed somehow to shrink the stone walls in around her, until she felt as though she was trapped in a very small box — with a very large, very virile man. 'Twas a distressing feeling, in that it was both claustrophobic and pleasant at the same time. The few feet of space that separated them felt oddly diminutive. It was not enough distance for her body to ignore The Devil's warmth and presence. Indeed, she had a feeling the entire Border country separating them would not be distance enough for that!

"We need to talk, wench."

The smooth sound of Alasdair's voice cut down her

spine like a knife through butter. "Aye," she said, her own voice shaking only slightly, "I think we do."

He nodded toward the door leading outside. "Shall we?"

Vanessa had been too long without the comforting feel of sunlight and a cool autumn breeze on her cheek, fingering through her hair, to refuse. That did not, however, mean she wasn't a wee bit leery about The Devil's motives as she turned and walked stiffly toward the door.

The hinges creaked when Alasdair pushed the door open, allowing her to pass over the threshold first. It was a gallant gesture she'd not expected from this Sassenach.

The air in the bailey was crisp and cool, laced with the tangy scent of dry leaves and grass. How these people managed to grow grass upon a rock Vanessa dared not guess. While the swiftly approaching winter and nightly frosts had browned most of it, it was evident that in summer, from the outer bailey walls all the way up to the keep's main entrance, the land would be flat and green and lush.

Well-worn paths crisscrossed to and from the many outside buildings—the bakery, the stables, the vault, the smithies, to name but a few. Alasdair took her arm—'twas her left one; she winced when his fingers grazed the bruises the brutish guard had left there—and 'twas down one of those trodden dirt walkways, the one leading toward the kirkyard, that he now guided her.

" 'Tis a passably fair day, would you not say?" Alasdair inquired casually as they strolled onward. His gait was long and even, slow, seemingly aimless, as though he'd nowhere else on earth to be but right here. With her.

Vanessa frowned, wondering what the man was planning to do now. She would, no doubt, learn soon enough. That he was toying with her was obvious.

Why, and to what end, was not so apparent.

She shrugged stiffly and glanced up at the sky. It was gray and cloudy, albeit not with water-darkened storm clouds. In the distance she heard the waves of the Firth slapping against the jagged rocks hugging the base of the large boulder Cavnearal sat upon. "There be a bite in the air," she said agreeably, and her congenial tone was laced with wariness. "Methinks winter will come early this year."

"Methinks you be right." He stopped at the outer ring of the kirkyard. "A very early, very harsh winter."

His fingers loosened around her arm, then dropped away. Until that very second, Vanessa had been unaware of the heat of The Devil's hand burning into the flesh beneath her sleeve . . . until it was gone, and she felt a reciprocal rush of coldness seep into her in the exact spot where his palm and thick, strong fingers had so recently been.

A soft, cool breeze gusted, fingering Vanessa's hair back from her face and shoulders. One inky strand slipped over her brow, blotting her vision.

She reached up to push it back . . . only to have The Devil do it for her. His fingertips felt hot and rough against her skin. They felt . . . Ooch! but, truth be known, they felt quite nice!

Her breath caught in her throat and her eyes lifted to Alasdair's face. The same breeze scattered The Devil's hair; the ebony strands tossed around his chiseled cheeks and jaw, puffing over his brow. His lashes swept down, the thick fringe half hooding his gaze as it dipped to her mouth, lingered, then traced itself back up to her eyes.

He angled his head and leaned slightly forward. His lips parted. As though tugged by a magnetic force, Vanessa leaned forward, also. The Devil was going to kiss her and, God help her . . . aye, she was going to let him. 'Twas the only thought her mind was capable of entertaining at that moment.

"The drawbridge," he whispered huskily, his mouth drawing closer. Closer. "Do you see it?"

Her vision was sharp; although she didn't focus on the drawbridge — her gaze was still ensnared by his — she could see the blurred outline of it from the corner of her eye. She nodded mutely, her throat suddenly too dry and tight to push words through. Her pulse hammered in her ears.

He leaned closer still. His mouth was a scant inch from hers. Her blood pumped like molten fire through her veins, throbbing in her ears. "Tell me," he said softly, seductively, "how difficult was it for you and your brother to cross my bridge undetected?"

" 'Twas not —" Both her mind and body froze. It took all her concentration not to let her open palm swing at The Devil's cheek, the way it wanted so badly to do. Ah, but there were better ways to handle a man like Alasdair Gray.

Vanessa went up on tiptoe and, placing her hands atop his hard, broad shoulders, she leaned forward and, with provocative slowness, closed the sliver of space between them. The tips of her breasts brushed the wide expanse of his chest. She craned her neck. The breeze ruffled through her hair and caressed her cheeks as, softly, softly, she pressed her lips to his and whispered raggedly against them, " 'Twas not near as difficult as ye may think, Devil. Ye need new guards."

A bolt of shock stabbed through Alasdair. It wasn't caused by her words, for those had yet to register in his abruptly numb mind. Nay, the cause lay entirely with the feel of her lips feathering over his own as she spoke; lips that felt softer, moister, than a dewy rose petal at dawn. Her breaths washed like misty fire over his mouth, his cheek, his jaw. Her breasts firm and wonderful as they strained lightly against him. The rhythm of his heart took an unexpectedly erratic turn.

Only a portion of his mind — a very *small* portion — was able to think with enough clarity for her words to register. The impact of her statement, however, was lost on him. Her body felt too soft and sweet, her lips too tantalizingly moist and warm, for his concentration to be sidetracked for long. His voice low and husky, he said, "Mayhap you should tell me how you accomplished it then, so I can better prepare my men."

"Aye," she breathed softly. "Mayhap I should."

But she wouldn't, hadn't any intention to, and they both knew it.

His right palm settled on the upper curve of her left hip. Vanessa felt the heat of his hand steam past the paltry covering of scratchy cloth, until it felt as though his battle-roughened fingers were caressing her bare flesh with no hindrance of fabric to obstruct them.

Her mind flashed her an image of wet skin and soap. Her breath snagged and her body and scalp tingled, remembering all too well the feel of his hands scrubbing the dirt from her body, from her hair. Her heart-pounding reaction then, as now, couldn't be attributed to the remembered sting of harsh lye soap. Ooch! if only that were so! But, nay, 'twas more the sensual burn of The Devil's hands — so big and strong — skimming over her body, setting her blood aflame, which made her knees go suddenly weak and watery. His free hand cupped her chin, tilting it higher so their lips were now lightly fused together. It was not a complete kiss; the pressure of his mouth merely hinted that it might be soon.

Vanessa's reaction was as shocking as it was devastating. For a fraction of a second, she came very close to telling this man anything he cared to know — and even that which he did not — if only he would ease this torment of wondering and kiss her more fully as a reward! While it was a shockingly traitorous thought, it also felt quite natural and right. Oddly so, in fact.

"I suppose," Alasdair said as he oh so gently tasted her full, trembling lower lip with his tongue and teeth, "that 'tis possible you didn't come over the bridge at all." One of them shivered, and he hoped to God it hadn't been him.

Vanessa sighed, and the sound was high and shaky. Were it not for the support of his hand and arm, which now slipped with provocative slowness from her hip to curl around her waist, she would have humiliated herself by stumbling weakly against him. Her hands were still splayed atop his shoulders. Her fingers curled inward convulsively, fisting the soft yellow folds of his tunic, the tips of them digging into the solid bands of sinew beneath.

The hot tip of his tongue made a moist pass over the crease of her lips.

Anything Vanessa might have said—and she wasn't entirely sure that, at this point, she was capable of uttering a single word—wilted in her throat. Her lashes swept down. A mistake, that, she realized an instant too late.

With her eyes closed, her senses sharpened by alarmingly seductive degrees. The pressure of his mouth against hers, the provocative, spicy male scent of him, even the blazing heat and sensuous firmness of his body, lightly pressed to hers . . . all of it culminated to batter what little clearheadedness she'd managed to retain, prickling her senses to awareness like the stab of a thousand sharply pointed needles.

Her lips parted of their own accord.

His tongue sneaked between them, stroking the vulnerable inner recesses of her upper lip until Vanessa could have sworn her blood turned to molten fire as it pumped hot and fast through her veins and pounded in her ears.

It was getting difficult to speak. Alasdair realized that only after he'd slipped his tongue from her honey-sweet mouth and opened his mouth to try. Words circled in his mind, but he was unable to push any of them past his dry, tight throat.

191

He wanted to kiss this woman. Fully and completely. The need to do that rocked through his body, clenching in his gut like a leadened fist. He wanted to wrap this woman in his arms, to feel the entire length of her body pressed hungrily to his. He wanted to hold her incredibly close as he stripped her of that ugly dress. He wanted to . . .

Nay, damn it! She was a Forster. A Scot. What he wanted to do simply could not be done, no matter how badly he wished it, desired it, *craved* it! Vanessa Forster was the enemy. The daughter of his most fierce rival. Yet . . . bloody hell, why was he having such a devil of a time remembering that?!

But, of course, Alasdair already knew the answer. It just was not possible to think logically—to think *at all!*—while holding this woman in his arms; while feeling her soft, hellishly sweet curves pressed against him; while feeling the hesitant pressure of her lips against his, pummeling his normally good sense and reason.

That he needed to let her go was obvious. Whether or not he had the strength to do it was not so clear. Truth be known, he did not *want* to release her. Not now. Mayhap not ever.

That realization had a sobering effect on Alasdair. It gave him the extra ounce of willpower he needed to pull back from her—slowly, reluctantly—like nothing else could have.

After a second, Vanessa's lashes swept up. Her green eyes were wide, dazed, confused.

He pressed his forehead to hers—even that innocent contact was not as uncomplicated as it should, by all rights, have been—and returned her gaze levelly. His voice low and gritty, he said, "You must be an excellent swimmer, wench."

"Nay, Devil, I am not," she whispered breathlessly. Odd, but Vanessa found it difficult to move her lips around the words. Mayhap because her mouth was leadened down with the fiery feel of his mouth on hers?

"And climber."

She shook her head vaguely. It was difficult to think beyond the way his breaths washed over her mouth and chin. "Nor that."

"In fact," Alasdair continued as though she'd not spoken, "methinks you'd need be a phenomenal climber to have scaled"—he nodded vaguely behind her—"that sheer sheet of rock. For centuries, men have tried, and failed."

The allusion in his voice was clear. For centuries strong, proud, intelligent *men* had endeavored to breach Cavnearal's mighty cliffs and intimidatingly high battlements. None had met with success. 'Twas easy to imagine The Devil's resentment to find that, the deed finally accomplished, it had been executed at the hands of a small Scots girl and her brother, a boy not yet old enough to sprout his first whisker.

He would want to know how she'd accomplished such a feat. Were the situation reversed, Vanessa would demand to know the same. Unfortunately, such was a secret she'd no intention of sharing. Not with him. No matter what. Only when she was returned safely home to Dunnaclard would she then gleefully share the information with any who cared to listen. 'Twas, she reasoned, no more than any Forster worth his clan name and loyalty would do.

Home. Dunnaclard. The words echoed in her ears, her mind, meshing with the ones Marette Gray had so recently spoken to her. *I know my brother's secret. Be in the stables at midnight if you wish to learn it. I'll see your door is unlocked and unguarded.* Vanessa frowned. Mayhap she would be leaving Cavnearal sooner than she'd thought?!

"You're a stubborn wench," Alasdair said, shocking Vanessa out of her reverie. "Even for a Scot."

Vanessa chose to take his words as a compliment. She smiled, and wondered inwardly why The Devil's gaze suddenly narrowed, and his lips thinned. "Aye,

Devil, and 'tis grateful I be that ye noticed."

Alasdair pulled back, and a gust of breeze whisked the dark hair back from his face. The ends scattered around the broad expanse of his shoulders, tickling her knuckles as it feathered over them. His sun-kissed bronze skin was now further enhanced by a ruddy undertone that could only be misconstrued for happiness if one were blind.

His voice was low and grittily harsh. "I'll get the information I require from you, wench. Eventually. In any way I can. You know that, do you not?"

"I know only that ye will try."

"And succeed."

She shrugged stiffly. "That has yet to be determined."

A confident grin turned up one corner of Alasdair's mouth . . . even as the tip of his index finger traced the smooth, flowing line of her jaw.

Embarrassing though it was to admit, Vanessa trembled at the feel of his fingertip stroking her flesh. His path turned inward, cresting her jaw with tantalizing slowness. Then, finally, upward. The edge of his fingernail scratched lightly against her full lower lip.

His head angled to the side and his eyes darkened to smoldering blue as his gaze dipped, fastening on her gently parted lips.

Was he recalling the feel of their mouths pressed lightly together with as much vivid clarity as she? Vanessa couldn't tell. It was difficult to think; her mind was spinning, her senses spiraling. She found it impossible to concentrate past the feel of Alasdair Gray's hand stroking her face, the promise of his lips as they inched with agonizingly slow precision closer to her own.

"Dinna kiss me, Devil," she breathed raggedly. "Dinna dare."

"Why?" he asked huskily, seductively. His lips feathered hers as he added, "Who is there to stop me, Vanessa Forster? You?"

"Aye," she answered softly, and wished that her voice sounded much firmer than the high, shaky, uncertain tone that rang in her ears.

She was looking deeply into his eyes, and therefore didn't see his challenging smile. But she sensed it all the same.

"Then do it, wench. If you feel you must."

Vanessa intended to do exactly that. Until he shifted, and his lips pressed more urgently against hers. Her breath snagged, when his arms slipped about her slender waist, tightened, capturing her small, lean body tightly to his firm, hard length. There was no need for her to stand on tiptoe this time; his grip hauled her roughly upward along the enticingly rock-solid length of his body.

Like night and day, this kiss was a stark contrast to the first. His mouth felt hard and firm and warm as it devoured hers. His kiss was ravenous. Demanding. He ate at her lips as though he was a starving man and her mouth was an incomparable banquet to his famished senses.

Stop him! a voice deep inside Vanessa uttered harshly. *Ye promised ye would, did ye not? And a Forster always upholds his word!*

Her fingers curled inward, clutching fistfuls of the shoulders of his shirt. The cloth felt hot and damp in her hands . . . undoubtedly from the heat and tightness of her grip. There was no question in Vanessa's mind that she would push him away. Now. Hard.

Just as there was no question in Alasdair's mind that he'd not allow it. For a week he'd slept closely beside this woman, watched her sleep, stroked her silky raven hair while she dreamed, all the time wondering how her sweet pink lips would feel and taste. Aye, and how the soft, slender length of her body would feel writhing hungrily beneath his. For a week — seven long days and seven even hellishly longer nights — he'd denied himself those answers.

Pledge or not, he couldn't dishonor her. No matter what he'd told Vanessa while trying to get her to vacate his keep, Alasdair was very much aware of how the March Wardens on both sides of the Border would look upon such an action. They would, to put it mildly, not look upon it fondly. Alasdair's fine would be steep. More than Cavnearal could afford to pay right now as they stood poised on the precipice of what promised to be a most severe winter.

And yet . . .

Sweet God, the feel of this woman's mouth moving shyly, hesitantly, beneath his own, the feel of her body flattened to his from thigh to chest, all of it combined and somehow managed to strip the consequence bare, until it seemed trivial and insignificant. Alasdair's heart thudded loud and fast in his chest, in his ears. At the moment he could think of nothing beyond the clawing need in his gut, the blaze of desire that pumped hot and swift through his blood, the ache inside him that demanded he take her, possessing her in every sense of the word. He wanted—nay, *needed!*—to brand her as his own in a way that was as old and as elementary as time itself. The fact that doing such would lead to a good deal more trouble than he cared to deal with right now mattered not at all. The feel of this woman's body and lips, however, mattered greatly, as did his unquenchable desire to explore both more thoroughly. With his hands, his mouth, his body . . .

Vanessa moaned softly. His mouth opened over hers, swallowing the husky whisper of sound. His tongue stroked her lower lips, her upper, coaxing them apart. The tip caressed her moist, pearly teeth, which were still closed. Her fingers loosened around his shirt, her hands opened, splaying over his wide, hard shoulders. Inch by inch, her hands crept upward. Dazed, she wrapped her arms around his neck and tunneled her fingers in his hair. Her breath caught, and her heart raced, pounding like thunder in her ears.

Sun-warmed satin, that was how the long, inky strands felt as they slipped through her fingers, tickling her palms and wrists.

It was with the greatest effort that Alasdair allowed his senses to slip past the woman he held so tightly in his embrace. Other sounds and sensations intruded gradually in his mind. The whicker of a horse. The distant screech of playing children. The foamy crash of waves breaking over craggy rocks. The heat of the sun on his hair and scalp. The tang of sea mist lacing the cool autumn breeze.

They were outside, standing on the edge of the kirk-yard. Anyone could see them. The knowledge was sobering.

Alasdair's arms loosened, even as he eased the intimacy of their kiss. He allowed Vanessa's soft, sweet body to slip slowly down the hard length of his until her feet were again planted atop the ground.

Vanessa's knees buckled. Were it not for The Devil's grip—loosened, but still undeniably there—she might have collapsed. A humiliating thing to acknowledge, but true all the same. She leaned weakly against him, her forehead braced lightly against the hollow beneath his shoulder.

Alasdair pulled in a ragged breath and rested his chin atop her head. Grudgingly, he noticed how soft her hair felt as it scraped the sensitive underside of his jaw. A faint trace of lye soap still clung to the silky strands; the scent wisped in his nostrils, and coursed like molten heat through his blood.

"Tonight," he whispered raggedly, and his voice sounded eerily high and unfamiliar, even to his own ears.

The word echoed in Vanessa's mind. *Tonight.* For some reason, the implication did not threaten so much as impart untold promises. The waiting, finally, was at an end. Almost.

Vanessa's mind and senses were still foggy from The

Devil's kiss; she was unsure if she should feel happy about that, or scared senseless. In the end, she decided 'twould be best to feel nothing at all. If she could.

Tonight . . .

She drew in a shaky breath. Between Marette's promise and Alasdair's, the coming of moonlight and darkness hinted at being most interesting indeed.

Chapter Eleven

The darkness was complete.

If there'd been a fire blazing in the hearth, there was no longer any sign of it; the wood there was now nothing more than dozens of charred cinders, which radiated only a minimal amount of heat—and even then, only if one stood extremely close.

Outside, in the distance, coming from the direction of the village, a bagpipe wailed. Its hauntingly shrill tune rolled with the night over moonswept hills and valleys. Every so often the tune would pause, then resume with vigor. Once in a while, the melody simply changed in mid-chord, according to the musician's whim.

The man playing the pipes was one named Fenn. Whether that was his first name or last, Alasdair had never learned. The man was simply, to one and all, known only as Fenn. The bagpipe had been . . . er, *acquired* on a raid against the Douglas near half a score ago. Fenn had considered the instrument a grand trophy, to the point where he even withstood the other men's ribald teasing with his normal good humor.

It had taken Fenn six months to learn how to coax the simplest tune from the bagpipe—and even that was of so sour a quality that it could hardly be recognized as music. Another six months had him squeezing out childish songs that the village children begged for him to play time and again. Six months after *that*—and extensive hours of sometimes ear-shattering practice—Fenn had taught himself how to play some fine, on-key tunes.

Now, the man played the pipes with the skill of one born to them.

The villagers, who'd once complained mightily about the repulsive racket, had at some point grown accustomed to it. They no longer griped when Fenn pulled out his pipes. Indeed, quite a few had grown to *enjoy* hearing the mournful wail of the pipes, wafting like a lover's whisper over the hilly land and moonlit Firth as they lay in their beds at night, drifting off to sleep—although 'twas doubtful any would admit as much to Fenn.

The song being played tonight was soft, lulling. While Alasdair was unfamiliar with the name of the piece, he recognized it as one of Fenn's favorites, usually played when the big, lumbering, red-haired man was in one of his introspective moods. Over the years the tune had grown to be one of Alasdair's favorites, too. It was an English song; Fenn refused to play any melody that sounded remotely Scots . . . even if he did know any, which was doubtful.

A muffled noise—the scuff of a booted heel on stone?—dragged Alasdair's attention back to the seemingly deserted room. Only it wasn't deserted. Vanessa Forster was in here somewhere. Not only did the guard who stood outside the barred door assure her presence, but Alasdair could *feel* the woman's nearness. The sensation was akin to a surge of lightning burning through his blood.

He inhaled deeply, and caught a wisp of her soapy scent. 'Twas a stark contrast to her kinsmen, Alasdair thought as he stepped into the room. Most Scots of his acquaintance bathed only when necessary, and even then, reluctantly. But not so Vanessa

Forster. Nay, after the woman's first enforced bath, she'd had made it a practice to wash daily. Such was a pleasant surprise to Alasdair, if not a most confusing one.

Except for the pipes that continued to play in the distance, and the steady give and take of his own breaths, the room was oddly silent.

Three more steps brought him dead center of the eerily dark room. In a corner of his mind, Alasdair registered the lack of steel slapping against his outer thigh. He'd left his broadsword outside with the guard—a new guard, not Oric. And for good reason. Too well he remembered the way Vanessa had tackled him to the floor in the vault, the way her teeth had sunk into the back of his hand, the way she'd fought like a furious kitten until he'd finally dumped her into the tub. Nay, 'twas best not to take unnecessary chances where this woman was concerned.

If she were to somehow wrestle his sword away from him . . .

The thought was, of course, ludicrous. Yet, he admitted reluctantly, not as ludicrous as it would have been a scant half a fortnight ago. Alasdair felt more comfortable for having taken the precaution.

His heart picked up speed. His right hand tightened into a fist around what would have been his sword hilt had he been wearing his sword, but was instead naught but cool evening air.

His eyes were adjusting to the darkness. If he squinted, he could make out vague details. The hulking rectangle of the bed to his right. The squat shadow of a chair in front of him. The dim shape of the cold hearth behind that. And, finally, the vaguely feminine shape leaning against the stone wall beside the tall, narrow left-hand window.

The room echoed with the harsh click of his boot

heel atop stone when he took a step toward the window. Toward the shape. Toward Vanessa.

He heard a soft inrush of breath, and then the shape beside the window shifted, melted back, blurring with the shadows that clung to the room like a black velvet blanket.

Vanessa.

While he knew exactly when he'd shattered the illusion of this woman being a "scrawny girl" — *bloody hell, was he ever going to forget giving her that bath?!* — when, he wondered, had he stopped thinking of her as "wench"? As "pledge"? When had he begun referring to her by her given name?

He didn't know, didn't want to. For whatever reason, her name tripped easily over his tongue, and tasted like a sweet drop of nectar. Frowning, Alasdair realized that he'd said her name aloud.

"Go away," she whispered hoarsely. The compact shape of her moved back another step, melding as though one with the shadows. He could barely make her out now; if not for the direction her voice came in, Alasdair might have lost sight of her entirely. "Go away afore ye do something we'll both be living to regret come morn."

"I?" he countered huskily as he took another, smaller step toward her, "or *we?* There's a difference."

"Ooch! does it matter which? The end will be the same, regardless."

"Nay, 'twill not. You see, kitten, I intend to have no regrets when this night is over. And, be it in my power, I shall see to it you have no regrets, either."

"Too late, Devil. Me regrets already be many." And foremost amongst them, Vanessa thought with a weary sigh, was her foolhardy short-sightedness in pledging herself in her father's place. Oh, she'd had ample reason, aye — a Forster maun keep his promise at all cost . . . and, truly, what else was she to do?! — but all the same, she thought this not to be her smartest scheme.

Vanessa's lips thinned. Damn her asinine plans to hell and back! Duncan was forever saying they'd get her into trouble one day. Ooch! but she doubted either of them could have guessed how *maun* trouble! Why, oh, *why* had she not listened to her youngest brother?! Why had she — ?

"Are we having second thoughts, kitten?"

"Nay, 'we' arena," she lied sharply. It wouldn't do for The Devil to know she was doubting herself, although it was obvious he already suspected as much. She would not, however, confirm his suspicions. Too easily he could use such information against her. "Should 'we' be?"

"I don't know. Why don't you tell me?"

"I just" — Vanessa swallowed dryly, and her voice cracked when she realized The Devil had at some point cleared the last few steps between them — "did."

He was standing behind her. *Closely* behind her. The heat of his body seeped through the coarse gray cloth of her borrowed servant's blouse; the warmth tingled over her back, making her skin burn. The dark hairs at her nape prickled with awareness. Alasdair Gray's spicy scent wafted around her, made her senses reel.

In the distance, the wail of the pipes grew louder, as though the hauntingly shrill notes were trying to mask the loud, erratic pounding of her heart.

In a quick, nervous gesture, she moistened her suddenly parched lips. "I'm telling ye, Devil, ye dinna want to do this." Her tone lacked conviction. They both knew it. Still, Vanessa refused to admit that, even to herself, as she added, "Think of the consequences!"

"Damn the consequences!"

"Ye say that now, but when Humes and Carey hear about—"

"Damn the bloody Wardens as well!" he cut her off sharply. His hands settled atop her shoulders. He exerted no pressure, yet the possessiveness of his grip was obvious to them both. "Pledge or no pledge, I want you in my bed, woman. Now."

The words, so sincerely spoken, cut through Vanessa like a dagger. Truth be known, it was what she wanted, too. Ever since she'd first felt his big, soapy hands skimming her body that first night. She remembered with vivid clarity how it felt to have his naked body spread out beside her. How it felt to have his strong arms wrapped around her. How it felt to have his mouth, hot and demanding, working its magic on her own.

Aye, she wanted him. The warmth that pooled in her belly and seeped lower in slow, throbbing waves told her that. His hands were still splayed atop her shoulders, unmoving, and yet her breasts tingled, the nipples pearled and strained against the coarse gray cloth as though begging for his attention to slip lower. She wanted—needed, *craved!*—to feel his hands—*his* hands!—on her body. Everywhere. Now.

Never in her life had Vanessa felt desire for a man. Such had always been a mystery; overheard, but never experienced.

Until now.

Desire crashed over her in a wave of white heat that was impossible to ignore or deny, threatening to drown her in its violent undertow. Hot and sharp, sensations unlike any she'd ever felt before, whipped through her, snatching her breath away, making her heart slam wildly beneath her breasts, thunder in her ears.

Her surroundings blurred, faded, tunneled down until all she could think about, all she could *feel,* was the man standing so closely behind her. From the first moment she'd seen him, he'd lit a fire in her blood; his words — *I want you in my bed* — had fanned the flames. Instinctively, Vanessa knew that only this man, only Alasdair Gray, only The Devil, could extinguish this sweet, throbbing blaze of desire . . . because only he had been able to spark it.

His fingers flexed, digging past the cloth and into her shoulders. Again, his grip was not painful, merely insistent.

Angling his head, Alasdair brought his lips close to her ear and whispered raggedly, "Now, Vanessa. I want you in my bed now . . . more than I've ever wanted anything, *anyone,* in my life."

His breath washed hotly over her scalp and ear and cheek. Vanessa shivered. Her mind was a tumultuous whirlwind of thought and sensation; both battled each other for prominence. She couldn't let this man take her the way her body ached to be taken by him. And yet, at the same time, she'd no strength to push him away. Indeed, she'd no desire to do it. She wanted to be possessed by this man in ways she'd never dared dream about.

Could she refuse him?

A better question would be, could she refuse herself?

Vanessa closed her eyes and pulled in a shaky breath. The answer that bolted through her mind and body was alarmingly spontaneous and sincere. It was also strong — too strong to fight or deny. Indeed, she realized abruptly that she wanted to do neither.

In the end, the unusual, yearning sensations The Devil had sparked within her, the sensation that throbbed warmly between her legs and made her breasts strain against the coarse gray fabric of her blouse, won out . . . as she'd an uneasy feeling they'd both known it would.

Alasdair was aware of the exact second her reluctance melted away and was replaced with compliance. It was when he felt the muscles beneath his fingertips slacken and the rigid line of her spine relax. It was when her chin lost its haughty tilt. Her soft sigh of surrender was more musical to his ears than the distant wailing of the pipes.

" 'Tis wrong, this," she whispered, even as she leaned weakly back against him.

"Aye," he agreed huskily. "Very."

"The Wardens will have ye head for it," she added, even as she nestled the crown of her head against the sculpted hollow beneath his right shoulder. She could feel the erratic drumming of his heartbeat against the nape of her neck.

"No doubt." His hands massaged her shoulders, then ran slow, sensuous paths down to her elbows, trailed back up, then down once more.

"And mine as well, when they learn I dinna fight ye." Her knees felt weak beneath the coarse gray skirt. The Devil's chest, so wide and hard, made a perfect brace for her back. Were it not for that, and his large, strong hands cupping her elbows, Vanessa was unsure of how long she'd have managed to stay on her feet.

His cheek rested against her hair. The soapy, vaguely flowery scent clinging to each dark, glossy strand teased his nostrils and his senses. His voice came low and ragged as he nuzzled the tip of his nose against the delicate curl of her ear. "Then don't tell them. There's no reason they need know."

"I'll"—her voice cracked when the tip of his tongue dragged over the back of her earlobe, and she shivered—"not lie about such a thing."

He hesitated, nibbling her earlobe thoughtfully.

"Why not? 'Tis what any wench in your position would do."

"Ah, but I be not 'any' wench, Devil." While she strove to make her tone sharp and indignant, Vanessa was only moderately successful. With The Devil's tongue laving the nape of her neck, logical thought was simply too complex to indulge in!

"Aye, and well I know it." With one hand, Alasdair swept her hair to the side, exposing the vulnerable taper of her neck. Her skin shimmered like cream in the silvery moonlight, a heady contrast to the pitch-blackness of her hair.

"I—I'll not grieve when they h-hang ye for this, Devil," she stammered, and her breath clogged in her throat when his teeth nibbled her upper spine, from her hairline to her shoulders.

"Then I suggest you stop me now, kitten. Before I do something worth hanging for."

"I canna," she replied softly, raggedly . . . truthfully.

The hand not holding her hair slipped from her elbow to wrap loosely around her waist. His fingers opened, splaying her abdomen. The imprint of his hand felt though it had burned through the rough gray barrier of cloth and branded itself right into her skin.

"Cannot," he asked huskily, "or *will* not?"

"Both," she sighed.

Alasdair's heart was pounding so loudly in his ears that he could barely make out her answer. Her waist felt small and fragile. The skin and muscle beneath the rough gray cloth trembled to his touch. Or, mayhap that was the touch that trembled? If so, Alasdair did not want to know of it. He was no hot-blooded youth indulging in his first sight and feel and taste of a wench—those days were long past—and he refused to act like one. Yet . . . bloody hell if that wasn't exactly the way he felt!

He nibbled his way over the side of her neck, stopping to lave her earlobe with the tip of his tongue before slowly burning his way toward that fragile place where cheek and jaw met. His fingers tunneled in her hair as he gently eased her chin up, her head back. He opened his legs, sandwiching her hips between his rock-hard thighs. Bending his knees slightly, he slid his chest with provocative slowness down her spine, until he was hunkered low enough so the back of her head and neck was pillowed atop the hard cushion of his shoulder.

"Dinna worry about the Wardens," she breathed raggedly. "Me da and brothers will kill ye 'long afore Humes and Carey ever hear rumors about what ye've done." Vanessa hesitated. Was it her imagination, or did the solid chest grinding into her back stiffen? She was unsure, nor was there time to dwell on it . . . The Devil's lips were feathering over the corner of her eye, and rational thought was suddenly beyond her.

"I'm not concerned," he replied.

"Ye should be."

"I'm not," Alasdair insisted firmly. The hand splaying her stomach rose in tantalizingly slow degrees. His palm cupped her rib cage; the calloused pad of his thumb stroked back and forth over each individual rib. Higher. Higher still. The skin beneath the cloth seared into his palm. "At present, I've more pressing matters on my mind."

"Aye," she sighed, and wondered if she'd responded to his words, or the warm, pleasurable sensations his stroking thumb had sparked within her?

The web between his thumb and index finger came to rest against the rounded firmness of the underside of her breast.

Vanessa's breath caught, and it felt like every

208

ounce of her concentration was focused intently on that one spot. Gritting her teeth, she bit back the words that would command his hand to ascend, to cup her fully, the way she hungered for him to do.

Her body ached for his touch. She burned for his full possession. Yet staunch Forster pride ran deep and strong; it forbade her to ask for either.

Tonight.

The word spiraled through her in a dizzying surge, setting her blood on fire. In a shadowy corner of her mind, she recalled Marette's promise, but vaguely. Midnight was too far off to worry about just yet. Besides, right now *everything* seemed distant, unimportant. Everything except Alasdair Gray's hand . . . and the sinfully exciting way his touch — *his nearness, the furnacelike heat of his body, the intoxicating, spicy male scent of him!* — made her feel.

Time stood still. Her world narrowed sharply, until she felt like she and Alasdair were the only two people left in it. Her life stopped and started right here. Right now. In this man's embrace.

The chest grinding against her back rose and fell with a ragged sigh. His hand lifted, lightly crested her breast, hesitated. For the length of a single, throbbing heartbeat, neither of them moved nor breathed. Then, slowly, one by one, Alasdair's fingers curled inward, until her rounded firmness was nestled in the very center of his burning palm. The fit was as exciting as it was flawless.

In the distance, the cry of the pipes faded, then swelled to a crescendo. The sound was obliterated by Vanessa's husky moan.

Stop him! a tiny voice of sanity screamed in her mind, yet she found it bairnishly simple to not heed the warning. Truly, she did not *want* to stop him. Not now. Mayhap not ever.

Of its own accord, her back arched, her breasts

straining against the confining cloth, straining toward the magic of Alasdair's touch. The crown of her head pressed hard against his chest. The hand that had swept her hair away from her neck melted away, only to reappear encircling her waist. His other hand began to knead her breast, gently at first, and then more urgently.

He hauled her roughly against him. His chest was an unyielding brick wall against her back, his hips lean and solid, pressing into the soft curve of her bottom in vague, rhythmic thrusts. She could feel the long, hard need of him sear like fire through the cloth that separated her warm, hungry flesh from his.

Her head swam and her body ached as a swirl of desire washed through her veins. The muscles in her stomach tightened beneath his hand, trembled, knotted with a sharp pang of yearning. The sensation seeped higher, curling like the fingers of a warm mist around her heart, even as it trickled rapidly lower. Passion flamed, and like a wave of liquid heat, pooled in that secret place between her legs.

She moaned low and deep when, through the cloth, he rolled her nipple between his thumb and index finger. She felt as though she'd been struck by lightning. Her blood tingled in her veins as sensation upon sensation, unlike any she'd ever felt before—indeed, never knew *existed!*—exploded inside her.

" 'Twill be worth the cost," Alasdair murmured huskily, even as he angled his head and nuzzled her earlobe through the silky curtain of her hair. "Well worth it, methinks."

Vanessa's body and, aye, even her mind, echoed agreement. Consequences be damned, at this moment she knew she would pay any price if it meant the magic of Alasdair Gray's touch would not be removed. Not now. Not, at least, until she'd unearthed the answers her breathless, hungering body craved.

Touching this woman, Alasdair discovered, was an experience comparable to none. There was something about the feel of her slender back braced against his chest — hard to soft — something about the way her hair tickled the underside of his jaw — silk to sandpaper — when he cushioned his chin atop her head. He felt her stomach muscles tense and flutter beneath his touch.

The breeze outside had fingered through her hair, and left a faint, fragrant trace of heather clinging to each silky strand. Pushing her hair aside with his nose, he nibbled the side of her neck. With effort, he trapped a groan in his throat. Her skin tasted like an intoxicating mixture of whiskey and cream. Both sharp and smooth at the same time.

He stroked the tip of his tongue up from the slope of her shoulders all the way to the base of her ear, savoring the tangy underflavor of salt mist that still clung to her skin. She shivered, moaned, arched back into him. His arm tightened around her waist, holding her close.

If ever he'd wanted a woman more than he wanted this one — right here, right *now* — he couldn't remember it. Not even his Jenny. Indeed, Alasdair was surprised to find that at that moment, he couldn't even remember the face of the pallid, frail creature he'd married five years ago. Nor any of the women before or since Jenny. He couldn't remember ever *being* with any woman before this one. Couldn't remember ever touching one the way he was now touching this one. Ever wanting to touch a woman the way he wanted, needed, *had* to touch this one.

Everywhere.

Slowly.

Until she was driven as wild with need as he was.

He wanted to carry her to the bed—his bed—and lay her out there. He wanted to slowly strip her bare. To worship every beautiful inch of her naked body with his hands and mouth in the way a man was meant to worship the woman he was about to make love to.

And he might have done just that. Had he thought he could stall his possession of her long enough to make it to the bed.

He did not.

This was not right. He should not want a woman—not *this* woman, not a *Forster!*—so badly. But he did.

Desire fisted in his gut, tightened in lower, more urgent regions. His need was driving him hard, clawing him up on the inside, shredding reason and consequence until all he could think about, was possessing her. He wanted—*craved!*—to feel her writhing beneath him, to feel her firm, slender legs wrapped around his hips, moving in frantic time with him, pulling the very core of him deeper into the very core of her. He wanted to brand her body with his own.

He shouldn't. Alasdair knew that as surely as he knew Hugh Forster would demand his head on a platter if Alasdair dared to dishonor the man's daughter. Yet, more surely, he also knew that, damn the bloody consequences, he was going to have this woman.

Her breast felt oh so very good in his hand. The need to see and taste and touch without the scratchy barrier of cloth was simply too urgent to cast aside or deny.

The pulse in her throat throbbed against his fingertips as he angled her head up. He licked and tasted and teased the sensitive taper of her throat, even as the tip of his fingernail skated down the opposite side of her neck and sneaked beneath the stiff white tatted collar of her bodice.

Her skin was hot to the touch.

Burning.

For him.

There was no sense in denying it; Vanessa ceased trying. This man was not taking advantage of her, though it would have been a soothing balm for her pride had that been the case. The arm encircling her waist was firm, but not painfully tight—his grip was breakable. While his touch was urgent, it was not unnaturally demanding. She could pull away from him now if she wanted, and she had a feeling he would release her. She could call a halt to this madness now, if she wanted, and that same instinct told her that he would let her.

There was only one problem.

She did not want to.

"Your blouse," Alasdair whispered huskily in her ear, and the feel of his breath misting warmly on her skin sent a shiver of excitement skating down Vanessa's spine. "Take it off. I want to see you"—his thumb rasped the sensitive peak of her nipple through the cloth—"feel you"—his tongue laved her neck, his teeth nibbled, creating the most wonderful combination of pleasure and pain—"taste you. All of you. Now."

Sweet Saint Andrews, may the devil take her eternally damned soul—er, so to speak—but that was exactly what Vanessa wanted, too. Badly. It was what every nerve in her body cried out for, what every throbbing beat of her heart demanded!

Skin to skin. She'd once overheard her father say that to her mother. Hannah Forster had blushed fiercely. Vanessa had always wondered why. Until now. Now she knew. Because that was exactly how she wanted to feel The Devil.

Skin to skin.

Mouth to mouth.

Heart to heart.

Ooch! How she wanted that!

Her arms had been down by her side, her elbows locked and rigid . . . she realized that only now when she lifted her right hand, her fingers poised over the narrow laces that crisscrossed the plain gray placket. She hesitated for the length of a heartbeat before grasping the laces and tugging. The knot fell away, and the strain of her breasts beneath the cloth widened the placket. Cool night air rushed in through the gape; it was quickly heated to the unnatural warmth of her skin.

The tip of his index finger traced the line of her collar. Around. Lower. Lower still. His skin was rough; it rasped against her smooth flesh as he stroked a path from the dimple in the center of her collarbone, downward. With a mere nudge of his knuckle, the laces loosened, the span between cloth and cloth widened, as though inviting the intimate intrusion of his finger.

Vanessa swallowed hard as he stroked the upper swell of her breast; dipped and nuzzled the tight, shadowy cleft in between; then turned his silky attention to the other. Her skin burned to his touch, her desire smoldered.

There was a tightness in her stomach. Nay, that was wrong. Not her stomach. Lower. In a place she'd allowed no man to ever see or touch. In a place she now very badly needed a man—*this* man!—to see and touch and—she blushed deeply—aye, even taste.

She felt hot there. Moist. Every time he tugged on her nipples, the muscles between her thighs pulsated with a yearning she didn't understand, wasn't sure she wanted to, so long as she could continue to *feel*. The thought of Alasdair touching her there was almost embarrassing. Almost. For at the same time it was also very, *very* exciting.

Her breathing shallowed. His shoulder made a hard cushion for the back of her head; 'twas the most wonderful pillow Vanessa had ever felt. His ragged breaths were echoed in the rise and fall of his chest against her back. His hips, lean and hard, pressed into hers as though demanding she acknowledge the long, hard, aching length of his need.

And she did. Indeed, her entire body seemed aware of it. Aware also of the way his hand urgently tugged free the laces of her bodice and, after tossing them carelessly to the cold stone floor, parted the material wide.

The bagpipe in the distance had grown silent. She thought. Then again, mayhap 'twas the thundering of her heart in her ears that prohibited her from hearing it. Vanessa didn't know, didn't care. At that moment, his hand settled over her breast.

Her nipple beaded to instant, aching life; it felt like a pinprick of fire burning into the very center of Alasdair's palm. His fingers curled inward slowly, almost reverently, savoring the feel of her. Silky smooth, her skin was softer than velvet. "Ah, wench," he rasped between the quick, warm kisses he distributed over the curve of her cheek, the line of her jaw, the very corner of her mouth, "what you do to me."

"And ye to me," she whispered, just as hoarsely.

"Aye," he murmured without conceit, "I do." His thumbnail flicked her nipple to signify he'd understood what she meant.

Her sigh was pure yearning as she arched back against him and smiled. 'Twas a ridiculous thing to do, smile, but she could not help it. His skilled kisses, his hot caresses . . . both made her feel most unlike herself. Oddly enough, she cared about that not at all. It felt good to be in this man's arms. *Right.* Whether it truly was or not no longer mattered. It had ceased to matter the instant his mouth had sealed over hers that afternoon in the kirkyard, the very second his silky voice had promised "tonight" . . . and his smoldering gaze had promised oh, so much more.

Vanessa Forster had heretofore doubted she could act brazen if someone put the pointed arrow of a crossbow to her temple and demanded it. Therefore, it was with more than a little surprise that she heard her own voice, low and sensuously husky, echo in her ears when she said, "The bed be over there, mon. I suggest we retire to it, unless ye've a penchant for cold, hard stone."

"The only thing I've a penchant for right now is you," he replied. An undertone of urgency gave his voice an appealing, scratchy quality. Her breath caught sharply in her throat when he began slowly to knead her breast. His other hand, splayed over her belly, inched downward. "Now. In my arms. Naked. I care not where. Here or in my bed, it matters' not to me."

Had he purposely stressed the word "now," or had she only imagined it because her own thoughts were tarrying in that direction? And did it matter? Nay, it did not! That Alasdair continue to touch her, that he touch her more intimately . . . soon . . . *everywhere* . . .

Ah, now *that* mattered a great deal!

His open palm skimmed down over her stomach, paused at the junction of her thighs—he released a shaky breath—then drifted lower. He fisted a handful of rough gray cloth and dragged her skirt, and the thin white rail beneath it, up. The night air sifted beneath the hem, momentarily cooling Vanessa's passion-heated flesh.

The scratch of his rough fingertips against the smooth, bare front of her thigh was a pleasure matched by none. Hard to soft, virile power to feminine fragility.

Vanessa frowned. Fragile? Had she just thought of herself as fragile?! Aye, she had. 'Twas odd but, now that she thought on it, fragile was how she felt when wrapped in this man's strong embrace. Fragile. Protected. And . . . aye, *special.* While it made no sense—Alasdair Gray had no doubt bedded dozens of women, surely she was nothing special?—it was, nonetheless, how she felt. How his kisses and caresses *made* her feel.

His hand opened, splaying over her thigh. Her skirt pooled around his wrist in dark-gray folds as he stroked his way up her leg. Higher. Higher still. A path of white-hot sensation tingled in his fingers' wake. His thumb trailed over the slender indentation of her waist before his hand slipped inward, toward her stomach, then plummeted downward.

Vanessa expelled the breath she only now realized she'd been holding until her lungs burned, and quickly gulped in another. There seemed to be a sudden shortage of air in the bedchamber. Either that, or she'd stopped breathing. It was difficult to tell. Her head was swimming, but she thought that might have been because Alasdair had just caressed—indeed, was *continuing to caress!*—that warm, moist, secret place between her legs.

She tensed.

So did he. His hands—both the one beneath her bodice, and the one under her skirt—stilled. They did not, however, pull away. "What is it?" he asked, his lips moving against the side of her neck. "What's wrong?"

"I . . ."

"Aye?"

"I . . ." Her tongue darted out to moisten parched lips. It didn't help. The sliver of sanity that had made her speak out was fading quickly. She tried hard to hang on to it, but the way her voice cracked made it obvious 'twas a losing battle. "I . . . we c-canna *do* this!"

His sigh was a hot blast of hair against her neck. "We can't?"

"Nay!"

"Why not?"

"Because . . ." Vanessa's mouth snapped shut. She had no answer. At least, none that would sound logical at a moment like this.

"Because . . . ?" he prodded.

"Because, er, weeell, because—ooch! mon, stop that! I canna think when ye . . . !"

"Touch you like this?" he asked far too innocently for Vanessa's liking as his thumb and index finger lightly pinched her nipple, rolling it gently back and forth until she drew in a noticeably shaky breath. "Or like this?" he added as the fingers of his other hand combed through the nest of tight, dark curls between her legs.

The long, slow, intimate stroke of his fingers was electric. A charged current shuddered through Vanessa, stealing anything else she might have said. If her knees had felt watery before, 'twas nothing compared to how they felt now. Were it not for the strong support of his body, she would have embarrassed herself by collapsing to the stone floor at his feet.

"I don't want you to think, woman," Alasdair whispered hotly in her ear. "Right now, I want you only to *feel*."

"Y-yer wish be my command then, Devil." And indeed it was. Vanessa knew she couldn't have stopped feeling if she tried . . . and *trying* hadn't been a consideration for quite some time now.

"Open your legs for me, Vanessa. Let me touch you."

She did. Not until much later would Vanessa wonder if she'd been obeying his request, or simply responding to the sound of her name on his lips. Until now she'd been "wench," "pledge," or something equally as impersonal. The way his tongue curled around her name was more musical than the melodic wail of pipes, which were once again echoing in the distance.

Warm.

Wet.

Wonderful.

That was how she felt as Alasdair stroked and caressed her intimately. She moaned. Her back arched, pressing her breast more fully into his palm, even as her hips thrust forward of their own accord, searching for more of his touch.

Her eager response fed Alasdair's own need. She felt better than any woman had ever felt before, yet it wasn't enough. He wanted more. *Needed* more. Desire hummed through his blood, pounded in his temples, clenched like an iron fist in his gut.

Now. Damn it, he had to have her *now!*

Patience had always been one of Alasdair's many fine qualities. He wasn't thrilled to discover his supply of it was oddly depleted. Despite the room's chilly temperature, beads of perspiration dotted his brow and upper lip. More moistened his shirt to his chest and back. The muscles in his arms and legs were tight with tension, with a need that was almost overpowering, as he forcibly restrained himself from doing that which he most wanted at that moment to do: toss this dark-haired spitfire to the floor and have at her.

'Twas but a momentary lapse.

219

He wouldn't do that. Of course not! The mere thought was repulsive, not to mention barbaric.

Alasdair drew in a long, slow, deep breath. He released it calmly, precisely, then repeated the process thrice, until he felt a smattering of his self-control return. A very *small* smattering. He was still very much aware of the woman in his arms, very much aware of the way her soft body pressed against his, complementing his hard curves and angles to bittersweet perfection. The moist, velvet area between her thighs was an enticement unto itself as he slowly, slowly, slipped one finger inside her.

Vanessa's spine went rigid, and a gasp of shock whispered past her lips. The back of her head ground into the hard wall of Alasdair's shoulder. She didn't realize she'd been nibbling her lower lip until she felt a sting there, and tasted a salty drop of blood on her tongue. Yet even that sensation came at her as though from a great distance, for the center of her being was unable to focus on anything but this man's warm, gentle intrusion.

While one hand continued to knead her breast, the other stroked her ever so slowly, fanning the fire that his smoldering kisses and caresses had already kindled in her blood. It never occurred to Vanessa to ask Alasdair to stop; as far as she was concerned, she'd made her decision when she'd first accepted the intimacy of his touch, and a Forster's mind rarely wavered from a given path once it was set. She wanted this man, and *only* this man. To say otherwise, even if only to herself, would have been a monumental untruth.

"The bed," Alasdair murmured huskily, almost regretfully, in her ear as his hand left her to tug the hem of her bodice from the waistband of her skirt, "is no longer a possibility, kitten. I want you too badly to wait that long."

"Aye," Vanessa sighed breathlessly, both her mind and body in agreement. She needed him as badly as the shaky undertone of his voice said he needed her. Her body ached for his touch, until she felt as though her life had culminated to bring her to this one beautiful moment in Alasdair Gray's arms. Her breaths rushed shallowly through her lungs. Her heart was pounding, and every frantic beat cried out that if she did not become one with this man right now, this very second, her reason for living would cease to exist.

She lifted her arms, allowing Alasdair to yank the blouse up her arms, over her head. He tossed it aside carelessly.

His palms hungered to feel her naked flesh skimming beneath his open palms, with no barrier of cloth to impede what he hoped would be a long, slow, thorough investigation of her alluring body. He remembered vividly the feel of her skin, moist and slippery from soap, sliding like wet velvet beneath his scouring palms. The muscles in his stomach clenched. It took an extraordinary amount of effort for Alasdair to summon a gossamer sliver of what seemed to be his rapidly dwindling supply of patience.

After but a second's hesitation, he placed his hands on the gentle curve of her shoulders. A frown creased his dark brow. She felt small beneath his big, calloused palms. Indeed, it was hard to believe this was the same little spitfire who'd tumbled him to the floor of the vault a mere week ago, and bitten his hand.

Ah, but she *was* the same woman, Alasdair reminded himself, and he'd do well not to forget that fact. Even now, when she appeared naught but slight and feminine and vulnerable, her previous actions proved clearly that appearances were deceiving.

221

His hands still on her shoulders, he took a small step backward. The room seemed unnaturally cold, but only in the places where her body had pressed warmly against him. Alasdair tried to ignore that as his hands drifted slowly down the slender taper of her back. The skin beneath the rail shivered at his touch when his hands stopped at her waist. Or mayhap it was his touch that shivered.

Her skirt was anchored about her waist by a pair of tiny closures. Alasdair couldn't begin to count the number of closures like this one that he'd skillfully undone in the past. Yet, for some reason, experience with such a garment — and the stripping thereof — did naught to help him loosen this one. It was frustrating to find that his fingers felt oddly big and clumsy as he fumbled, his hand refusing to undo the garment in the smooth, casual way he'd intended.

Alasdair cursed hotly beneath his breath.

Vanessa grinned, and glanced seductively back at him from over her shoulder. "Do ye need help, mon?"

"None." His fingers continued to pick awkwardly at the fastening; it remained stubbornly closed.

"Be ye sure of that?"

"Quite," he snapped.

Vanessa shrugged and, with a sigh, faced forward once more, her grin broadening when she felt him continue to work on the closure . . . without success.

"Bloody hell, did you weld the thing shut, woman?!"

She shook her head, and the dark fringe of her hair whisked her shoulders. "That's not to say I wasna tempted to, though."

He hesitated. "Then why did you not?"

"Lack of the proper tools, for one thing." She shrugged, and her grin broadened. "That, plus I dinna think such a wee resistance would stop ye."

"You're right, it won't." The statement was punctuated by the loud rending of cloth as Alasdair grasped the waistband in his fists and proceeded to rend the garment down the middle. One by one, his fingers opened, and the cloth sifted over her hips, down her legs, puddling finally on the floor around her feet.

It was Alasdair's turn to grin.

She was standing in front of the window, a mere hand's breadth away, backlit by the pale glow of moonlight pouring in through the long stone rectangle. Her hair glistened an appealing shade of glossy silver-black.

While he'd first been appalled by the shortness of her thick, dark hair—no decent woman, English *or* Scot, would be seen with such a masculine cut— Alasdair was now more than a little pleased by it. On another woman, a long, flowing curtain of hair would have concealed the tempting view he was now treating himself to. And oh, what a mistake that would have been!

"Come here," he said finally, his voice low and gritty as the need to touch her—everywhere, now!— reasserted itself with nerve-shattering force.

The need to *be* touched—everywhere, now! heated her blood, made her head spin.

She turned around slowly, almost shyly. Her eyes, which had been fixed on the cold stone floor, ascended. She scanned the thick firmness of his legs, outlined beneath his snug-fitting trews. Her attention strayed over his lean hips and tight stomach, over the broad expanse of his chest and sinewy arms, hidden beneath his dark-green doublet and saffron-colored shirt.

His jaw was tight, his lips thinned as though in anger. But Vanessa knew better. It wasn't anger that was driving The Devil this time, and driving him

223

hard, 'twas lust, raw and carnal, of the same strength as that which now flowed hotly through her own veins. It was evident in the muscle ticking beneath his left cheekbone, and in the smoldering blue-gray gaze that burned out of the moonlight and shadows . . . burned into her.

A step of space separated them. In inches, the stretch was small. Not so small was the significance of her closing that distance. To do so would be to obey The Devil's dictate; her parentage, as well as a centuries-old blood feud, decreed that a Forster must never do that. To take that single small, yet at the same time monumental, step would also be admitting to Alasdair that from that moment onward, whatever happened between them happened with her willing consent.

There was still time to change her mind. That Alasdair had not reached out and hauled her to him told Vanessa that. Though he was silent, his smoldering gaze pensive, he was giving her one last chance to change her mind.

After a beat of hesitation, she lifted her chin and took one purposeful step forward, putting them in close enough proximity for the tips of her breasts to brush The Devil's wide, hard chest.

Alasdair's reaction was instantaneous. His sigh was one part pleasure, one part tortured frustration as he encircled her waist with one hand. The fingers of the other opened, tunneling through her thick, silky black hair. He angled his head to the side, and their gazes locked as his mouth crashed down on hers.

Unlike the first kiss that afternoon in the kirkyard, this one was wild and hard and demanding. He ate at her lips until they parted. The tip of his tongue stroked upper and lower, the pearly line of her teeth and, finally, teased the warm, moist tip of her own when it shyly met his persistent thrusts and parries.

Alasdair's head spun, and he became drunk on the taste of her. Her breasts strained against his chest, and his hands itched to touch them. The arm around her waist slid lower; his hand opened, cupping the curve of her bottom. The linen felt cool against his palm, the skin beneath furnace-hot as he curled his fingers around fistfuls of the fabric and pulled her closer, grinding her hips against the long, achingly hard length of him.

Madness.

Desire this strong could be naught but madness. Yet, even though his rational mind knew that, the extent to which he wanted this woman battled logic. The taste of her mouth, the feel of her soft, voluptuous body arching hungrily into his . . . all of it combined to drive Alasdair insane with desire, until white-hot need clawed him up inside, demanding the release that he instinctively sensed only this woman could provide.

Never, *never* had it been like this for him before! And if he wasn't so crazy with need right now, that realization would have stopped him cold. As it was, no power on heaven or earth could stop him from having this woman. Right here. Right now.

His tongue speared into her mouth, swirling and mating with hers as, still holding her closely, Alasdair maneuvered her back a step. The stone wall pressed against her back, and against the knuckles of his hand, splayed over her bottom.

Vanessa's hands crept up over Alasdair's shoulders. Higher. Her fingers opened, plunging into his hair. The inky strands felt like hot silk as she cupped his head and pulled him closer still. She returned his kiss with a boldness that shocked them both, putting into sensuous practice everything his skilled lips and tongue had so recently taught her.

The stone wall pressed at her back, while Alasdair's equally solid chest blanketed her front. The former offered much-needed support—her knees were far too watery to be trusted—the latter set her blood on fire.

Her heart thundered in her ears when she felt the arm around her waist dip; the chilly night air cooled the passion-heated skin of her legs when he fisted the skirt of her rail and dragged it up. Up. Over her thighs, her hips, her stomach. Higher. His mouth left hers only long enough to whip the garment over her head.

The stone wall felt hard and cold against her back, although not uncomfortably so. That feeling was bland compared to the tidal wave of raw, carnal sensation that washed through her to feel Alasdair's still-clothed body pressing against her naked front.

His mouth moved hungrily from her lips to her cheeks, downward. He kissed the line of her jaw, the curve of her chin. His mouth worshipped the taper of her neck, his tongue licked and teased the pulse that hammered in the base of her throat.

She swallowed hard when his attention moved lower still. His breaths felt hot and misty against her skin as he dragged his tongue over the upper swell of first one breast, then the other.

"Sweet," Alasdair murmured as his free hand cupped the underside of her breast. While she heard the rest of his words, she felt them more . . . in the way his lips moved against her rigid nipple when he spoke. "Ah, Vanessa, you taste so very sweet."

No words could adequately describe the sensations that bolted through her when Alasdair suckled her nipple. Her shaky sigh spoke for itself. It was pleasure in its rawest form, the sweetest kind of torture imaginable—in that it made her throb and ache for his touch in another, more intimate, place as well.

226

She moaned softly, and her back arched. Her fingers held his head steady, as though she was afraid he would pull back at any second and she would forfeit the magic of his mouth. Under no circumstances would she allow that to happen. This felt much too good!

His tongue stroked and tasted, his teeth nibbled and teased until she burned. She was breathing hard, and her head was spinning. There was a demanding tightness in her stomach, her thighs, and that most sensitive place in between. An unfamiliar urgency was building inside her, throbbing through her blood, making her tremble with the need for . . .

What?

Vanessa didn't know. Yet. But she would. Soon now, she was sure of it. Because Alasdair's skilled kisses and caress promised to teach her what that "something" was.

The need to touch his bare skin had been eating at her; it was too strong now to deny. Her fingers loosened around his hair, and her open palms ran over the wide, hard shelf of his shoulders. Lower. She was familiar with men's garments, having worn some herself at times. And since Alasdair put up no resistance, it took her only seconds to strip him of his doublet and tunic.

His chest was pelted with dark, thick hair that tickled her fingertips and palms as she ran her hands worshipfully over him. His skin felt hot and smooth to the touch. Wonderful. The muscles beneath trembled under her stroking hands.

She paused at the waistband of his trews, and felt him hesitate, then stiffen. A stab of disappointment shot through her when his mouth left her breast, and he straightened.

"Allow me," he said as he brushed her hands aside.

227

Vanessa watched boldly, breathlessly as he toed off his boots, then slid the snug-fitting trews down his hips, over his heavily muscled thighs . . . lower. She felt a twinge of panic when she saw the proof of his desire, but it quickly faded. This was what she wanted, there was no turning back now. Indeed, she did not want to.

A few seconds later, Alasdair was standing before her, naked and proud in the silvery glow of moonlight. His eyes darkened to a smoldering shade of midnight blue as his gaze met and ensnared hers. He studied her carefully, his gaze sweeping her from dark head to bare toes, missing nothing. For but a second, she thought he was going to give her the chance to change her mind.

He didn't. Instead, he reached out and, placing his hands atop her bare shoulders, drew her against him. This time his kiss was long and slow and deep, evoking a response from her that seemed to come from a place deep within her soul.

Vanessa wrapped her arms around him, clinging to him tightly. She felt not an ounce of fear when he pressed her back against the wall and, his hands now cupping the back of her thighs, lifted her legs and guided them around his waist. Her ankles crossed and locked at the small of his back as her hips arched imploring against him. She could feel the blazing, hard tip of him pressing intimately against her, and she thought she might die on the spot if he did not put a swift end to the explosion that was building up inside her.

She turned her head and, her lips moving against his hair and ear, whispered breathlessly, "Dinna torture me so. If ye will be taking me, then take me now."

"Trust me, woman, I torture us both," he replied, just as breathlessly. Passion-dazed green eyes meshed with lusty blue. "But not for long."

His lips slanted over hers. He kissed her deeply, hungrily, even as his hips thrust forward, and, in one clean stroke, he penetrated the warm, velvety sheath of her. His mouth swallowed her gasp as he broke the barrier that separated girl from woman.

She felt hot and wet and deliciously tight. If perfection had a feeling, this was it.

It was all Alasdair could do to remain still, giving her time to adjust to the sensual intrusion of his body, when what he really wanted was to drive himself into her, fill her completely, over and over again, quick and hard, until they were both crying out for release.

His need for her raged through him, taunting him until his desire was barely leashed. Sweat beaded his brow and upper lip. Every muscle in his body was taut with the effort it took for him to hold his desire in check, until she gave the sign that her body had accepted the intimate invasion of his, and craved more.

The sharp pain of his possession came and went so quickly that Vanessa wondered if she'd truly felt it at all. And even if it had been real, the feel of Alasdair hard and full inside her caused a bevy of sensations to wash over her, rinsing away anything and everything that had come before it.

In mere seconds, the pressure inside her body had begun building again, reasserting itself with force. She tightened her legs around his waist and moved her hips inquisitively against his.

Their groans were simultaneous and long.

"Now who is torturing whom?" Alasdair asked huskily against her mouth as, placing his hands on either side of her hips, he slowly, slowly guided himself more deeply inside her. He could feel her body stretching to accommodate him, hugging him tightly until he thought he would go insane from this slow pace he'd deliberately set.

"Ye be" — she sucked in a shaky breath when he almost withdrew from her, then arched forward once more, plunging deeper still — "torturing me" — and yet again — "from the feel of it."

Right now, I want you only to feel . . .

His previous words echoed through Vanessa's mind, through her body. Oh, aye, she was definitely doing that, no question about it! In fact, she was at that moment feeling sensations she'd no idea existed.

Until now.

Until Alasdair Gray had shown her.

Need, smoldering and demanding, pooled in her stomach and trembled lower, swirling in the place where their bodies strained together, apart, then together once more. His strokes became longer, deeper; the friction kindled the most wonderful sort of fire in her blood and between her legs.

More. She need more of him, all of him, right now. Her hips arched forward, accepting the long, hard length of him, straining for more, and still more. He filled her completely, time and time again, each thrust and retreat more breathtaking than the last.

She felt the muscles that intimately gloved him pulsate, hugging him tightly, drawing him deeper still. Vanessa was unaware of the grinding pressure of the wall against her back, yet *very* aware of the hard male chest that pressed against her tender breasts, the hairs there tickling her nipples, as his lean hips pumped against hers.

A ripple of satisfaction shivered warmly down her spine, but she stubbornly pushed it aside. She didn't want to feel that yet, for it would mean an end to this pleasure. And she didn't want this pleasure to end. Not now. Mayhap not ever.

Unfortunately, she had no choice. Much as her mind wanted her body to hold back, it refused. His every thrust drove her closer and closer to the brink of the most wonderful madness she'd ever known until, finally, she could no longer stop the spasms of rapture that exploded inside her.

The climax rocked through her body. Her fingers dug into his bare shoulders as she tipped her chin up, her head pressing against the wall as she moaned her pleasure.

Alasdair's rhythm never broke. From the second he'd entered her, he'd had the devil's own time not drowning in the feel of her. Now, her shudders of completion milked a like response from him . . . a response that shook him to the core with its intensity.

It wasn't until the very last spasms rocked through him that Alasdair realized that nothing had ever felt this good in his life. He'd an uneasy feeling nothing — *no one!* — would *ever* feel as good as this woman felt to him right now.

Chapter Twelve

" 'Tis not possible, I tell ye!" Duncan cried. His eyes were wide with horror, his gaze volleying between the squat, narrow window—that, if he held his breath, he just *might* be able to squeeze through—and his father.

Moonlight and shadow played over Hugh Forster's face, carving his expression to one of grim determination. "Yer brother would never say such a thing, lad. Indeed, Dugald would not think twice, he would simply *do* it."

Duncan tapped his temple with his index finger, and at the same time tried not to notice the way his finger—nay, his entire hand!—shook. "Then Dugald be not well, Da. What ye ask of me is death!"

Hugh Forster's beefy shoulders rose and fell in a careless shrug. "Mayhap. But to die whilst trying to escape a Gray's keep be an honorable death."

"Honorable or not, 'tis still death!"

"Ooch! Fer once stop thinking o' yerself and start thinking o' that impetuous, hotheaded, disobedient . . . er, *sister* o' yers! God only knows what The Devil's done to her by now." Hugh's gaze sharpened on his son. "We've tried all else, yet the fact remains that the only way out o' here aside from that door"—Hugh nodded briskly to the door, which was locked and guarded from without—"be this window. Would that I were smaller, lad, and 'twould be *I*

232

going out this way. Dinna doubt it."

Duncan *didn't* doubt his father for a minute. And it went without saying that he also wished Hugh Forster was of smaller stature. The thought of wriggling out that tiny window and clinging with naught but his fingers and bare toes to the crevices of a rock that looked, from this vantage point, to be almost sheer, was terrifying. Worse, at the end of the more-than-fifty-foot-drop lay the jagged rocks and foamy surf of the Firth of Maryn.

Of course, the alternative was equally as unpalatable: staying with his father in this musty, smelly dungeon that The Devil had moved them to on their second day of captivity.

Duncan swallowed hard, his attention straying from the window to his father. The former promised almost certain death . . . but then, so did the latter. Hugh Forster looked like he was ready to snatch his son up by the scruff of his neck and pitch the lad out the window in question if Duncan did not do as he was told, and do it posthaste.

Truly, he had no choice.

"Well?" Hugh prodded, when Duncan did naught but lick his lips and shrug indecisively.

"Ye'll not reconsider?"

"I'll not." His father scowled; it was a frown that, in the past, had made more than one stalwart Border reiver tremble in his boots and hastily turn for home. Duncan, of course, was already doing that, although for an entirely different reason.

Duncan nodded vaguely and sighed. "Are ye sure ye can live with me death on ye conscience?" He felt an odd sense of familiarity, not so very long ago he'd asked Vanessa the same question. Her answer then was eerily similar to their father's.

"Ye'll not die if ye take yer time and do the job right." That said, Hugh squatted down and, lacing

233

the fingers of both hands together, offered Duncan his cupped palms as a boost up to the window. He glanced up at his son and snapped, "Now would be a good time, lad."

Duncan smiled weakly. "Aye, as good a time as any to die, I imagine." His legs felt watery as he bent his right knee and placed his foot atop the "step" of his father's hands. Outside the window he heard waves pounding against the rock. The sound was distant yet inordinately loud, and almost masked by the erratic throbbing of his heart in his ears.

The soft sound of grinding wood upon wood did not awaken Vanessa, but simply melded itself smoothly into the dream world floating in the velvety blackness behind her closed eyelids.

In her dream, she was at Dunnaclard. Yet, oddly enough, she was not happy to find herself safely home and out of The Devil's clutches. Just the opposite, in fact. She felt extremely agitated as she briskly paced the sconce-lit corridor in front of her mother's bedchamber. She was alone, and that in itself was peculiar, while at the same time strangely right, as dreams so often are.

Sounds floated from beneath the thick oak door, echoing in the cold, stony corridor.

A groan was followed by a high-pitched, agonizing scream.

The latter twisted like an icy fist around Vanessa's heart. She spun on her heel and reached for the doorlatch . . . only to find it was not there. In its place was a thick slab of wood which crossed the door completely, trapping the occupants inside the bedchamber.

Another scream split the chilly night air. The sound curled down Vanessa's spine like splinters of broken glass.

"Mother!" she cried. The single word sounded foggy, seeming to come at her as though from a great distance, and even when it reached her ears, the voice sounded not at all like her own.

"Vanessa?" a small, shaky voice, muffled by the thickness of the door until it was almost indecipherable, called back. "Oh, thank God! Yer da. Where is yer da, lass? Ye promised to bring him home in time for the birth. Ye *promised.*"

"Aye, Mother, and I did! Is he not in there with ye?"

"No one is here, lass. I be alone!"

"Sweet Saint Andrews," Vanessa murmured as she reached out and gripped the slab of wood that barred the door. A splinter sliced into the heel of her palm; she winced, but ignored the twinge as she struggled to unbar the door. Cursed thing! No matter how hard she shoved, the slab of wood would not budge. Indeed, the obstruction felt as though it had been somehow welded permanently to the door.

"Bloody hell!" Vanessa wasted not a second wondering at the fluency with which The Devil's curse had slipped over her tongue. Her concentration was focused solely on the door. She struggled with all her might to lift the bar. For all her effort, it shifted but a fraction.

The sound of wood scraping wood was magnified by the empty corridor; it sounded unnaturally loud against the heavy backdrop of silence.

Wood against wood . . .

Vanessa awoke with a start.

A gasp whispered past her lips, even as she sat bolt-upright in the bed. Her heart hammered beneath her breasts, thundered in her ears. Her right hand splayed over her chest, as though trying to

235

muffle her heart's frantic rhythm. Her green eyes were opened wide, yet she could see nothing save the vague shifting of moonlight and shadow. She blinked hard, forcing her gaze to adjust to the darkness. It did not take long.

Unexpectedly, the mattress beneath her shifted and crunched. She placed a hand atop the covers near her hip to steady her balance. At the same time, she glanced to the left, and her gaze fell upon the man who lay next to her in the large bed.

Alasdair Gray.

Oh, dear Lord!

The memory of the last few hours—*spent in wild abandon in this man's arms!*—washed over her like a tidal wave. She felt her cheeks heat to a vivid shade of crimson. 'Twas a color that deepened when she felt an odd coolness steal over her neck and shoulders and bare breasts.

Bare breasts?

Aye! Oh, sweet merciful heavens, she was still naked!

Vanessa fumbled with the bedding. Gripping the sheet in tight, trembling fists, she dragged the thin covering up beneath her chin. 'Twas foolish, she knew, for The Devil's deep, even breaths told her he slept on. Yet she felt suddenly small and vulnerable to awaken and find herself naked in this man's bed . . . her skin still smoldering with the memory of his touch.

What have I done?! Vanessa screamed inwardly as she combed her short, thick hair back from her face with the fingers of her free hand. Those fingers shook. She was not surprised. The possible repercussions of what had transpired between herself and Alasdair Gray had seemed minor and inconsequential at the time she'd consented to lay with him—and, aye, hate though she did to admit it, *consent*

236

she most certainly had—yet they now hit her with all the force of a stone wall tumbling down atop her head.

'Twas bad enough The Devil was a hated *Sassenach,* but he was also, and more importantly, her father's arch rival! Since the days of their great-great-grandparents, the Grays and Forsters were destined to feud. And feud they had, most vehemently, although if pressed, Vanessa doubted any man on either side would be able to recall the exact transgression that had given birth to the feud all those many generations ago. It had something to do with a horse, that was all she knew.

And now, Vanessa had committed a most unpardonable sin. She had allowed herself to be bedded by the enemy. By The Devil—a man 'twas rumored would as soon slit your throat as look at you.

Not so long ago, Duncan had questioned her sanity. Vanessa now questioned it herself. Truly, she'd need to be insane to have done what she did this night. The disgrace it would wreak on her family should word of tonight's events reach them . . .

Nay, she could not think on it. There would be time enough for recriminations later—a fine muckle lot of time for it! For right now, she'd do well to take her leave of this cursed keep whilst there was still the opportunity to do it.

The cause of the grinding sound that had awakened her was obvious. She'd only to recall Marette's words that afternoon to know 'twas The Devil's own sister who'd unbarred the door from without. The trick now would be in dressing quickly and silently, and taking her leave of this bedchamber—indeed, of Cavnearal!—before The Devil awoke.

The thought of leaving, of—with luck—never having to set eyes on Alasdair Gray again, bolstered her courage somewhat. It also created an odd, empty ache inside her chest, and a clawing need that fisted around her heart, but those were things she forced herself to ignore. She had to. There was much work to be done this night.

Slowly, silently, she released the sheet and folded it to the side. The evening air was a chilly slap to her naked flesh as she eased her legs over the side of the bed.

The Devil murmured in his sleep.

Vanessa froze, her breath catching in her throat. She dared not glance back at him for fear any movement on her part would awaken him fully . . . if he was not already, of course.

A tense moment ticked past. Another.

When no other movement came from his side of the bed, Vanessa gradually began to relax a wee bit. Alasdair's slow, rhythmic breaths assured her that he was still asleep. For now.

She rose from the bed, her bare feet making nary a sound as she padded across the room. Her clothing was naught but vague, shadowy lumps, scattered indiscriminately over the floor near the window.

Vanessa frowned, thinking of the dingy gray skirt, and herself, riding astride while she wore it. The image was laughable. Nay, the garment would never do. She would need freedom of movement when riding—for, once she found a mount, she intended to fly like the wind back to Dunnaclard—and it had been her experience that a woman's trappings could never provide that.

Instead of retrieving the ugly servant's frock, she quickly and silently relieved Alasdair's wardrobe of one saffron tunic and a pair of ginger-brown trews. Both were comically big on her. The sleeves of the tunic needed to be rolled up half a dozen times, while the hem of the trews had to be folded up even more, until they made a thick cuff at mid-shin; the waistband had enough room to spare that she was actually able to tie a small knot with the excess material. Where the trews were nerve-shatteringly tight when encasing Alasdair Gray's heavily muscled thighs and calves, they sagged in baggy folds around her own slender hips and legs.

Vanessa was not concerned. Her appearance was the least of her worries right now. Extricating herself from Cavnearal before this night's mistake could be repeated, on the other hand, was of primary importance.

She sat down on the floor to pull on her boots. Her eyes, of their own accord, shifted to the bed.

A slice of moonlight cut through the window, and poured over the bed. At this angle, she could see only the top of Alasdair's head. His hair was sleep-tousled; the inky color made a vibrant contrast against the backdrop of a white linen pillowslip. He was lying on his side, facing the spot she had so recently vacated. His left arm was bent, his hand splayed limply over the dimple her head had made in the other pillow.

Sleeping, he did not look so much like the man about whom dark rumors abounded. His brow was bairnishly smooth and uncreased. His lashes, thick and dark and long, fluttered against his sunbronzed cheek. His lips were not pinched tight with anger, the way Vanessa had grown accustomed to seeing them, but rather sensuously thin and relaxed. Her own lips burned as she remembered only too well the feel of his mouth moving hungrily over hers. His kisses had been long and deep and draining. Intense. Consuming. Like the man himself.

Dragging her attention away from Alasdair took more effort than Vanessa would ever admit. On tiptoe, she crept toward the door and very slowly, very

239

quietly, opened the portal just far enough to peek through the crack. The sconce-lit corridor was empty, as was the chair that had been dragged up against the wall to the right-hand side of the door.

A sigh whispered past Vanessa's lips as she opened the door wider and slipped through the opening. She didn't notice how badly her fingers were trembling until she turned and closed the door behind her. Indeed, her entire body quivered; half from relief, half from worry that, while she'd escaped The Devil's bedchamber undetected, she'd in reality accomplished very little. She'd still to reach the stables.

And standing in a corridor that would not remain empty for long was not going to help get her there. That in mind, Vanessa hurried quickly down the corridor, stopping only once she reached the stair landing.

Though she listened carefully, she could detect no noise from below. Vanessa was not, however, about to let that lull her into what could very well be a false sense of security. Caution was of extreme importance. She'd no doubt that, were she caught, there would be no second chance for escape. The Devil would see to that. Were the situation reversed, she would do the same.

Her heart in her throat, she swiftly descended the narrow, shadowy stone staircase.

Unlike the corridor and stairs, the foyer was not empty.

Vanessa did not realize this fact until, her hand on the latch of the door that led out of the keep, she heard the soft but distinct sound of a throat clearing behind her.

Very *closely* behind her.

Even the soft sound of the door closing would have awakened Alasdair. *If* he was asleep. He wasn't. From the second Vanessa had removed herself from his bed, he had been fully awake and alert.

He'd heard her footfalls as she'd padded across the cold stone floor, and also heard her softly hissed curses when she regarded the dingy servant's frock as though it were a leper's. The sound of her rummaging through his wardrobe was louder still, and was followed by the enticing rustle of cloth.

'Twas then Alasdair had opened his eyes but a crack, and peered at her through the shield of his thick, dark lashes.

No fire crackled in the hearth, which made the room bitter cold. Since he'd never been affected by the cold, the chill was a mere inconvenience; certainly nothing to trouble his thoroughly sated body into moving to light a fire.

No glow of flames caressed Vanessa's body . . . only the enticing glow of silver-washed moonlight, which made her skin shimmer an appealing shade of cream. She turned her back on him to dress, and awarded him an unobstructed view of her slender back and wonderfully curved bottom. For a small woman, her legs seemed to go on forever; hips, thighs, shins . . . all of her was firm and deliciously shaped.

His slitted gaze devoured her. No more than an hour had passed since he'd made love to this woman, and yet already Alasdair could feel his body quickening with renewed hunger.

The force of his desire was staggering; had he been standing, it surely would have knocked him to his knees. Passion that strong—especially when directed at a cursed Forster, no matter how comely she was—was frightening to him. For a man unused

241

to feeling such a base emotion as fear, the knowledge that the emotion coursing through him now was none other did not sit well.

As though the movement was made in his sleep, he rested his forearm over his eyes to blot out the deliciously disturbing sight of her. As he'd feared, the tactic didn't work. Even in the blackness behind his eyelids he saw Vanessa Forster's tempting body, and remembered all too vividly the feel of her unusually short black hair sifting like silk through his fingers, and the satiny feel of her naked flesh pressing against his chest and hips as he pumped his life into her, claiming her body in a way no other man ever had.

If he'd cared to think on it, he might have realized that 'twas exactly that, the claiming of her body and nothing more, that caused an unsettling fist to clench in his gut. As it was, the thought had no more entered Alasdair's mind before it was instantly escorted back out.

That the wench was fixing to escape, Alasdair had no doubt. He'd also heard the grinding of wood as the bar without was removed, and he had a feeling he knew whose hands had removed it, although that was a matter to be dealt with later. That he'd absolutely no intention of stopping Vanessa, however, Alasdair realized only now.

The mere sight of this woman's naked body stirred the responses of his own in a way that Alasdair could not accustom himself to. Even Jenny, as much as he'd loved his wife, had never affected him to such a degree! His desire for this woman, the daughter of his fiercest rival, was hot and strong and . . . aye, 'twas dangerous.

If for no other reason save that, he had to let her go.

Alasdair was no fool. He knew his strengths as

242

well as his limitations. He knew that if the woman stayed in his keep, he would repeat the mistake he'd made this night before another sun could set. However, if he removed the temptation that was Vanessa Forster—now, *tonight!*—he could turn his attention back to more pressing matters; chiefly, the running of this keep and the preparations for winter. With Vanessa gone, he would not have to concern himself with weakening, or with letting his lust rule his good sense by surrendering and doing that which his body wanted most to do.

Take her.

Make her his.

Over and over.

Until she *knew* she was his.

Nay, he would not stop her from escaping. Indeed, if he could do it inconspicuously, he would *aid* her in her attempt! He'd no real need to keep her. He'd known that for days, although he only now admitted as much to himself. He had her brother and father locked in his dungeon; the two men served as security that the fine owed him would eventually be paid. And once he'd collected his purse from the Clan Forster, Alasdair could then turn his energy to preparing his people for the fierce winter months ahead.

See? He'd no need for Vanessa Forster at all.

So why, he wondered as he heard her open the thick oak door and slip out into the dimly lit corridor, did the closing of that door sound like the shutting of the door to a dungeon cell? Why did the coldness of the room, which hadn't bothered him in the least but five short minutes ago, suddenly invade his skin and settle right into his bones? Why, when he moved his arm and opened his eyes, did his heart skip a beat when his attention immediately fixed on the small dimple in the pillow beside him,

243

and his gaze fastened on the single strand of short black hair that curled atop the linen casing?

And did he truly want an answer to a single one of those questions? Nay, he did not! While he was honest enough to admit that the thought of perhaps never seeing Vanessa Forster again did not exactly sit well with him, that was *all* Alasdair was willing to admit.

With a muffled grunt, he rolled onto his side. Yet his gaze refused to waver from that dimple Vanessa's head had made in a pillow that now seemed disturbingly unused.

With a hissed curse that would have made any of his more hearty men-at-arms blush, Alasdair swept the pillow on which Vanessa's head had rested just a short time ago off the bed and onto the floor.

Bloody hell, what was wrong with him to be entertaining such thoughts — such longings — for a cursed woman?! Aye, and a cursed *Scots* woman, to boot?! Not for the first time that day did Alasdair question his sanity . . . and like not at all the answers he found.

If there was a God, and he'd no doubt that there was, then with Vanessa Forster's leaving, he could finally regain control over his keep as well as his emotions!

Or so he fervently hoped.

A bead of sweat rivered down his forehead and trickled into his eye, momentarily blurring his vision. His fingers tightened reflexively on the scanty crevice of rock he was precariously clinging to. The stony gap his bare toes were nestled in was no wider than his little finger.

That he'd managed to somehow creep — very, *very* slowly — halfway to the top was of no little amazement to Duncan. Truly, he'd thought to fall to his death long before now. That he hadn't was encouraging. In a way. He still had much ground to gain yet—he was merely halfway, after all—and the roar of surf beneath him was a constant reminder that falling was still a very real possibility.

The sea mist lent the chilly night air a salty tang; it also made the rock moist and slippery, making the steep climb all the more treacherous. Duncan was careful to make sure he had a firm grip on the scanty crevices of rock before trusting even a small portion of his weight to it. The memory of his near fall a half fortnight ago was still fresh in his mind. 'Twas an experience he'd rather not repeat. Of course, Vanessa was not here to haul him back this time . . . and falling onto the wet, deadly rocks below held no appeal for him, either.

Vanessa.

His sister was not far from his thoughts. Long into the night he had agonized over what her fate had been at The Devil's hands. That fearsome reiver's dislike for all things Scots, and most especially Forster, was known far and wide.

It was his concern for Vanessa that made Duncan blink the sweat from his eyes and keep climbing. Slowly. Carefully.

For the past seven days he'd sat impotently in The Devil's dungeon. The wondering and not knowing what had become of Vanessa had near driven Duncan mad. At least his precarious climb up the base rock of Cavnearal provided him with a chance, no matter how small, of finding out . . . and, if luck was with him, coming to her aid.

That was, of course, providing he reached the top intact.

In Duncan's estimation, his chances of doing that, then sneaking into the keep—which was now no doubt heavily guarded—and finding his sister, were comparable to him someday lairding the Clan Forster. In other words, with his five elder brothers in line to inherit before him, 'twas well nigh impossible.

"Going somewhere?"

The voice, small and high and undeniably feminine, stopped Vanessa in her tracks. Her breath clogged in her throat as she stiffened and spun on her heel. A frown creased her brow when she saw no one. Had the voice been in her head? Nay! "Who's there?" she called out, then, when there was no response, added sharply, "Dinna be a coward. Come forward and show yerself."

There was a movement in the shadows clinging to the side of the stairs. Another, smaller shadow disengaged itself and slowly emerged.

The speaker, Vanessa was surprised to see, was a lass of no more than fourteen summers; indeed, the girl's sweetly innocent face and slight stature suggested she might even be a few summers younger than that. The dag—a small, snub-nosed pistol that was known to be quite unreliable—aimed skillfully at Vanessa's chest suggested something else entirely.

Vanessa's attention volleyed between the dag and the girl's wide blue eyes. "Be ye planning to shoot me?"

"If need be."

"Ooch! If ye plan to stop me from leaving, then, aye, there *will* be a need. Dinna doubt it, Kirsta Gray."

If the girl was surprised at Vanessa's use of her name, it didn't show in either her gaze or her equally determined expression. But then, Vanessa doubted the girl was surprised. While the Grays

246

and Forsters had fought hard for centuries, both families made it their business to be familiar with the other's doings. Mayhap they knew more of each other *because* of the bloodfeud rather than in spite of it.

Kirsta's dispassionate gaze raked Vanessa from head to toe. "I'll not ask if my brother knows of your intent. 'Tis obvious he does not."

Vanessa's gaze narrowed shrewdly. "And do ye plan on waking him to tell him, lass?"

"Of course not." The girl's chuckle was soft and merciless, an echo of Alasdair's. "Your kind is not wanted here. No one will be sorry to find you gone come morning. Least of all Alasdair."

The girl's words cut deep, deeper than Vanessa would ever admit. Deeper still, because she knew they were true. Alasdair would be angry to learn she'd escaped Cavnearal—providing this girl did not shoot her instead, of course—but not sorry. Nay, 'twas more likely he'd be relieved to have her gone. And why, Vanessa wondered, did that knowledge hurt so very much?

Vanessa cleared her throat and shrugged; the gesture was not as casual as she would have liked for it to be. "Then ye have no reason to shoot me, do ye, lass?"

"On the contrary," the girl corrected, her young voice ringing with a maturity that belied her years, "I've every reason. 'Twas a Forster who killed my sister's husband, was it not? Therefore, it seems only fitting that a Gray take the life of a Forster in compensation. And since you are the only Forster within sight . . .

"Nay, Kirsta, that won't be necessary," another voice, this one years more mature and seductively feminine, said from behind the girl. A skirt rustled in the darkness as Marette stepped to her sister's side. The woman's gaze, cat-narrow and shrewd, locked with Vanessa's. "The wench will be leaving Cavnearal tonight, and she won't be returning. Isn't that so?"

"Aye," Vanessa agreed, even as her gaze strayed toward the shadowy staircase. How long before Alasdair awoke and found her gone? Minutes? Hours? She didn't know . . . nor did she care to stand here conversing with his sisters when her chance for escape was so near at hand!

Marette smiled coldly, her attention shifting to her sister. She stroked the girl's golden hair fondly with the back of her knuckles, and her tone thawed noticeably when she spoke to her. "Go back to bed, sister. I'll see to our"—her lips pinched over the word—"*guest.*"

"You are going to help her escape?" Kirsta asked, incredulous.

Marette nodded. "Aye, someone must, don't you think? Father would be turning over in his grave if he knew we'd not one Forster in our midst but . . ." The woman hesitated only a fraction before swiftly modifying what she'd been about to say. "Well, three Forsters inside Cavnearal's walls in less than half a fortnight is three too many. I want them gone, Kirsta. And if helping this"—a tremor shook her shoulders—"*Scot* escape is what it takes, then do it I most certainly shall!"

The hand holding the gun lowered to Kirsta's side as her blue eyes rounded on her sister. "Alasdair will be angry. Methinks he'll have you locked in the tower again if he ever finds out 'twas you who helped this Forster escape."

Marette's laughter was as cold and as merciless as her tone. "Let him try."

"But—"

"Hush, sister, you worry needlessly. Alasdair will

248

never find out how the wench escaped unless *you* tell him." Marette glanced at her sister sharply. "And you'd not breathe a word of it . . ." She paused, one dark brow rising accusingly high, "would you?"

"Nay, never!" Kirsta swore with a vehemence that Vanessa found oddly endearing.

Marette smiled. "I thought not. Now, be a good girl and do as you're told, Kirsta. And, please, for heaven's sake, do make sure you put Alasdair's gun back in his desk before you seek your chambers."

"Aye, Marette. I will." Kirsta looked down at the dag in surprise, as though she'd forgotten she still held it. While the girl had pointed the gun skillfully enough before, the repugnance with which she now regarded the weapon bespoke her aversion to it.

A tense moment ticked past, during which Marette kissed the top of her sister's golden head, then hugged her close and whispered something in her ear that made Kirsta laugh nervously and nod. After one last, anxious glance at Vanessa, Kirsta gathered the skirt of her white linen nightrail around her legs, and hurried up the stairs.

Marette waited until her sister was out of earshot before spinning on her heel and glaring at Vanessa. "See what you've done to my family, heathen?" she snapped furiously. "Kirsta has never in her life *touched* a dag before, let alone pointed one at someone with the intent to kill." Her steely gaze narrowed furiously. "*You* brought her to that. 'Tis something else I can never forgive you for."

Vanessa's eyes narrowed angrily. It was on the tip of her tongue to curtly inform this woman that she did not require her forgiveness about anything. Luckily, common sense intervened and she bit the words back. Marette Gray could, at any time, sound the alarm that would alert the keep—alert *Alasdair*—to Vanessa's imminent escape. Antagonizing the woman would not be wise.

Not trusting herself to speak, Vanessa instead
nodded and turned briskly toward the door. The
frosty night air felt sharp against her cheek as she
opened the door and stepped outside. Her breath
misted in front of her face, and she hugged her
arms around herself for warmth. Ooch! how she
longed for the heavy, quilted jack that The Devil
had burned.

Vanessa quickly descended the three wide stone
steps, not once bothering to glance behind her to
see if Marette followed. The quiet closing of the
door and soft footsteps that kept time with her own
told Vanessa that she had.

As soon as her feet were on solid ground,
Vanessa edged her way over to the front wall of the
keep. Alasdair's clothing might indeed look ludicrous on her, but the drab coloring made it simple
for her blend in with the shadows clinging to the
stone wall.

She walked swiftly and silently to the corner of
the keep and hesitated, waiting for Marette to catch
up to her. She peeked warily around the corner, but
saw naught but moonlight and thick shadows.
Ooch! but for once it would seem luck was with
her.

Vanessa frowned, eyeing the kirkyard. She hoped
the stinginess of moonlight concealed the blush that
heated her cheeks when she remembered the last
time she'd set foot in that place. Her lips still smoldered with the memory of Alasdair's kiss, while her
body still burned from his recent possession.

"What is it?" Marette hissed from closely behind
her.

"I was checking around the corner," Vanessa lied,
when what she'd truly been doing was leaning her
shoulder against the rough stone wall and giving

herself a second to catch her breath . . . and her equilibrium. Thoughts of Alasdair Gray tended to knock both severely out of kilter. Over her shoulder, she whispered sharply, "Be there another way out of this cursed place, or maun we stroll through the kirkyard for all to see?"

"Through the kirkyard is the only way out. Cavnearal was purposely designed that way. In case the fortress walls were ever breached, we'd be able to pick our enemy off from the battlement as they tried to gain entrance to the keep."

What the woman did not say, but Vanessa heard clearly in her derisive tone, was that such a precaution had never, in all of Cavnearal's history, been necessary. Until Vanessa and Duncan had done what many before them had tried and could not: trespass into a keep that 'twas rumored was unbreachable.

Vanessa's gaze volleyed between the flat, moonlit expanse of the kirkyard, and the craggy battlements of the keep's far curtain wall. She saw no movement, could detect no guards walking the battlements. But just because she could not see them didn't mean they weren't there. For the time being, she would presume they were. To do otherwise would be foolish in the extreme.

Crossing the kirkyard without detection was not going to be easy. Caution was essential. It mattered not that a Gray was her cohort; were they caught, Marette would undoubtedly claim she was attempting to *abort* Vanessa's escape, not *aid* it. In that case, what would most likely be Vanessa's only chance at freedom would then be forfeited.

"Sweet Saint Andrews," Duncan whispered in awe as, with a hearty shove, and an equally hearty

251

grunt, he catapulted himself up and over the top of the stone wall he'd spent the better part of an hour alternately clinging to for his very life and precariously climbing.

Sweat plastered his dark hair to his scalp, as well his dirty, ripped shirt to his chest, and his equally filthy and torn trews to his thighs and calves. His breathing was as hard and as ragged as the stone he most gratefully rested his sweat-slickened cheek atop. In all three centuries of Cavnearal's turbulent history never had a Forster been so delighted to touch these cold stone walls.

He closed his eyes, savoring the moment, and his grin was giddy with relief. If he didn't know better, he'd have sworn he was starting to believe in miracles. Naught else explained how he'd managed to shimmy up this wall like a spider, hovering at all times a mere fifty feet above certain death. That he was still alive was a blessing he cherished. That he'd actually accomplished what he'd set out to do — a most unusual feat in itself . . . well, victory was a heady feeling! Unfortunately, in this case, it was also extremely short-lived.

He'd no more had time to catch his breath when Duncan heard the crunch of gravel grinding beneath a boot heel, and a distant — but not *too* distant — murmur of male voices.

His eyes snapped open. In a blink, he assessed his surroundings.

He was lying at the edge of a long, narrow parapet walk. The walkway, he noticed, was straight, branching into a T at both ends. It was the end from which he'd heard the voices that gained Duncan's full attention. Squinting, he saw a disturbance of moonlight and shadow play against the solid stone wall.

Duncan was on his feet in a heartbeat, and at the

other end of the walkway in two. He was thankful he'd moved so fast, for he'd no more had time to press his back and shoulders up hard against the wall when the speakers emerged at the other end of the walkway.

He peeked around the corner, and trapped a groan in his throat. There were only two guards; there might as well have been an army. Both were light-haired, tall, wide-shouldered, and barrel-chested. The broadswords hanging in scabbards at their waists looked long and thick and heavy; the muscles in Duncan's arms ached just thinking about trying to lift one.

A pewter tankard was passed good-naturedly between them. It took only a few exchanges before the contents were gone and the mug set aside atop the shelf of the curtain wall.

The hiss of metal scraping metal as one of the guards drew his sword was loud and grating. "See this, Rory? 'Tis my pride and joy, this sword. Made by the most expert craftsman in all England." The man—middle-aged, if his voice was anything to judge by—paused meaningfully. " 'Tis this I'll be wagering that the young laird did that which young laird's are wont to do with such eye-catching prisoners."

The voice that answered was at least a score younger. "Aye, and 'tis thanking you for winning that pride and joy of yours that I'll be doing. Mark my words, Garth, The Devil does not fancy heathens like that one. And why should he? Many a comely *English* lass has set her sights on him. There's skirts aplenty to chase, if he's of a mind to play. No need to look across the Border for that which he can get right here . . . in a more civilized manner."

The older man glared at his companion. "I'll be

253

thinking 'tis your tender age that distorts your thinking so."

"One score four is *not* so young!"

"Nor is it so old that you cannot see the obvious. A woman is a woman, boy. In the dark, one is as good as the next. They scratch a man's itch, which is why the good Lord put them on this earth to begin with. You'll learn as much . . . when you get older. Trust me."

"Trust you?" the younger man scoffed. "Trust *you?* Nay, I think not."

"Thinking's got naught to do with what goes on between a man and a woman. And if you be of a different mind, then you're younger and more foolish than I thought."

"Why you—!"

There was a scuffling sound, then silence.

Duncan peered cautiously around the corner and, even though the older man's back was to him, he could easily see that the older one was now fisting the younger man's collar. Their faces were very close together.

"Settle down," the one called Garth snapped. "I meant no offense."

"Mayhap not, but offense *was* taken. You give m'lord credit for having not a scrap of common sense by accusing him of bedding the heathen."

"I give m'lord credit for having the same lusty drives as any man, boy. Naught more, naught less." The older man's curt tone of voice indicated the conversation was at an end. "Blast it all, where'd I put that bloody tankard? If I didn't know better, I'd swear it sprouted legs and keeps walking away."

Duncan ducked and, pressing his back hard against the wall, sent up a desperate prayer that these men would be about their business soon. His prayer, to his dismay, was not readily answered.

"You old fool, are you blind as well as stupid? 'Tis on the ledge," the younger man reminded his companion testily, and nodded in the mug's direction. It was obvious from his clipped timbre that he was still angry, and just as obvious he also planned to keep their previous topic of discussion closed.

Garth mumbled something under his breath that was uncomplimentary by tone, and snatched up the tankard. He tipped the mug to his lips, then sneered grumpily. " 'Tis dry. You drank it all."

The younger man looked offended. "I took naught but sips. 'Twas *you* who—"

"Oh, hush. I'll go fetch more. 'Twon't take me but a moment."

The older man started to stride away, and Duncan's breath caught when he heard the crunch of heels grinding crushed stone draw closer to where he stood.

After a beat of hesitation, Duncan glanced first to the left, then the right. The former ended the corridor only a few short feet away in a solid stone wall; the latter branched off yet again, with one shadowy passage no doubt leading to a stairway. There was only one problem; Duncan would have to pass the doorway to get to the stairway, and he could not do that.

The guard's footsteps neared.

Duncan's heart was pounding so loud and fast that he was surprised the racket hadn't alerted the two men to his presence.

"If The Devil finds out you've been drinking while on watch, he'll have your head," the younger man called out.

The footsteps stopped abruptly. "And who, do you think, would carry such a tale to his ears, boy?"

"Not I, I assure you. And methinks 'tis not to his ears that the tale will carry, but to his *nose*. That brew you drink is potent enough to be smelled for miles."

The older man found this statement amusing enough to chuckle over. Duncan was too panic-stricken to care why. "Aye. 'Tis the best whiskey to be found on either side of this cursed Border, boy. Know it. If naught else, those heathens *can* brew the finest whiskey. A man's got to admire them for that, if naught else." He chuckled again, this time coldly. "No doubt the brew's strength is the reason you took only baby sips, eh, boy?"

Two more footsteps brought the older guard so close to the doorway near which Duncan hid that he could see a burly silhouette of the man cast upon the wall not two feet from his face. The shadow looked large and menacing. Lethal. He swallowed dry, and held his breath, afraid even that slight sound would give his presence away.

"Aye," the one called Rory replied dryly, "no doubt. 'Tis lucky you are we've been assigned the sea wall to guard, for if one of the guards at the entrance tower were found enjoying the drink as much as you do, he'd be drawn and quartered before dawn."

The older one agreed, good-naturedly. "But since no one in centuries has even tried to invade Cavnearal by sea attack, and since there is but one entrance into this keep . . .

"Until now."

"Eh?"

The young guard's voice dripped exasperation. "I said 'until now.' Or did you forget so soon that the heathen acquired access to the fortress in a way that's yet to be discovered?"

The one called Garth grunted his opinion on the

matter. His good humor had suddenly evaporated. "More whiskey," he muttered as he took another step toward the doorway.

Where Duncan's heartbeat had been thundering before, it now started skipping beats. What was he going to do? He had no weapons, and even if he had, he'd be no match for the size and strength of those two. Should he plead mercy when that impressively large guard stepped through that doorway and discovered him pressed against the shadows and rock? And he would be discovered, Duncan knew; 'twas the way his luck had always run.

Duncan frowned, and brought his thoughts up short. *Plead mercy?!* Sweet Saint Andrews, he couldn't believe he'd thought such a thing, never mind actually entertained the idea, even if only for a second. Dugald, if caught in the same situation, would die before he would beg mercy of a Gray. 'Twas what any good Forster would do . . . Vanessa included. It was, Duncan decided, what he would do as well.

"Mayhap," the older one grumbled as he took one more step toward the door, "I'll find that wench you fancy and send her up here to improve your disposition, boy. An hour with Deirdre and you'll be of a different opinion about how strong and illogical a man's lusts can sometimes be."

The young guard perked at his companion's suggestion, although his too calm tone indicated he'd rather his companion not have noticed. "Go get your whiskey, old man. I'll not stop you, nor breathe a word of it to m'lord. I will, however, suggest you take the stairs leading toward the hall, not the ones to the upper chambers. Unless, of course, you've a longing to listen at m'lord's bedchamber door, and prove your convictions wrong."

Duncan filed away the curse the older guard muttered for future reference, and breathed a heartfelt sigh of relief when, after a nerve-grinding pause, he heard the man spin on his heel.

Footsteps briskly retreated.

Duncan's heart commenced beating again . . . with an erratic vengeance. Mayhap his luck was changing after all?

The thought no more had time to enter Duncan's mind when the younger guard called out a warning to the older one.

"Garth. Garth! Come here, man. Quickly!"

Frowning, Duncan peered around the corner, and watched as the younger guard pointed to something in the keep's courtyard.

"Do you see what I see? Two women, right there, crouching beside the quadrangle's corner wall."

"Methinks you've drunk too much whiskey," the older man replied gruffly. "I see only—"

"There!"

A tense pause was followed by Garth's growled, "Aye. Aye! Good Lord, boy, 'tis the heathen. I'd recognize those dark, short locks anywhere."

"Aye, as would I. But who is that with her?"

The older man scowled, following the direction the younger one was pointing. "Don't know. She clings to the shadows—I can barely make her out."

Duncan felt a stab of pleasure at the mention of his sister—truly, he'd wondered at times if The Devil had not eaten her, as was rumored he did to any Scot he encountered, especially those weaker and feminine—but his pleasure was woefully short-lived.

Vanessa was alive and well or she'd not be in the courtyard, and he'd not a doubt that she was attempting an escape. That was the good news. The bad news—and 'twas very bad at that!—was that she'd been spotted by these two burly guards. Any second now, they would sound the alarm, and his sister would once again be captured. If The Devil had not set to torturing her yet, the man most assuredly would when he found out Vanessa had been trying to escape him.

Unless Duncan somehow managed to render these two guards impotent to sound the alarm, that is. How he could do that was not readily apparent. He was unarmed, the two guards were not. He was a mere half the size and strength of both. Even if he'd had a weapon, the odds of an encounter with those two prime Sassenach specimens ending in his favor was rather doubtful.

Still, that was his sister down there. His *favorite* sister! If it was within his power to help her, even if all he was able to do was purchase her a wee amount of time, he must do it. He must at least try!

"You're insane."

"I've been called worse by better," Vanessa snapped, and ignored Marette's sharply indrawn breath. "Ye said yerself there be no other way out but across the kirkyard."

"You'll be seen!"

Vanessa shrugged. " 'Tis the chance we maun take."

"Nay, heathen, not we. *You*. I've gotten you thus far . . . the rest you must accomplish on your own. I'll not risk being killed by my own men to save you."

Vanessa glared at the woman from over her shoulder. Even though her gaze was in shadow, her green eyes shimmered with disgust. Were the woman Scot, Vanessa would have slapped her hard for such cowardice. Since she was not, Vanessa instead dismissed the woman's reticence as typical Sassenach weakness—one flaw amongst many. "Then go back inside where ye'll be safe, woman. I've no further need of ye."

The words had no sooner fallen from Vanessa's lips than Marette was hoisting her skirt and preparing to swiftly retrace her steps back into the keep.

Vanessa's next words froze the woman in her tracks. "Before ye go, I'll be hearing that secret about yer brother."

"And what secret is that?" Marette asked, her voice tauntingly casual.

"Dinna play daft with me. 'Tis the secret ye alluded to this aft that I be referring to."

"Oh," Marette replied, and the corners of her lips turned up in a secretive smile, "*that* secret." Her eyes narrowed and the steely depths, so much like Alasdair's, shimmered in catlike amusement. "Mayhap I've changed my mind about sharing it."

"And mayhap I'll need take it upon meself to change yer mind yet again," Vanessa said, her voice low and tinged with anger. She'd been crouched beside the corner wall of the keep. She now stood and, spinning on her heel, advanced menacingly toward Alasdair's sister.

Marette gulped. The chit was unarmed, yes, but the fury in her green eyes burned from out of the shadows, and burned into Marette. The heathen's expression said that Vanessa Forster would not hesitate to reach down Marette's throat and tear the words out, if need be.

Marette pulled in a shaky breath and took a nervous step backward. She did not miss the smile of victory that tugged at the corners of Vanessa's mouth. Her voice cracked noticeably when she spoke. "Since you'll be leaving tonight either way"— her steely gaze shifted meaningfully between the parapet walk and Vanessa—"I suppose there's no reason for you not to know."

"Know what?" Vanessa prodded when the woman said naught more.

Marette's smile was icy. "Why, that your father and brother were never released, of course. What else?"

Vanessa staggered back a step, as though she'd been physically struck. "You lie!"

"Do I? Are you sure?"

The implication in Marette's words—for she'd an uneasy feeling Alasdair's sister was indeed speaking the truth—hit Vanessa like a physical blow. The air pushed from her lungs, and she had to fight another, much stronger, urge to slap this woman. "I don't believe you," she said finally, and very, very weakly.

Marette's grin broadened. "Yes, you do. I can see it in your eyes, hear it in your voice. Whether you care to admit it or not, you know full well that I speak the truth."

Vanessa shook her head hard, as though trying to clear it of the barrage of confusing thoughts that were abruptly spinning frantic circles inside her mind. "Nay," she said, then forced herself to repeat the word with a self-assurance she did not feel. "Nay, 'tis not true! Alasdair said—"

"What?" Marette snapped, cutting Vanessa short. "What, *exactly*, did my brother tell you?"

Vanessa felt a searing stab of betrayal arrow through her heart. Alasdair had lied to her. In that instant, she was positive of it. Oh, how that hurt!

Marette, on the other hand, had not lied. When she'd said Hugh and Duncan had never been released, as Vanessa had until now believed, she could tell Marette was not lying; the truth was in the woman's stony expression and frosty, challenging

261

gaze.

Your father and brother took their leave of the vault at dawn. Or so Alasdair had informed her that first morning, over a week prior. She didn't doubt that was true. However, what Alasdair had neglected to mention was *where* her da and Duncan had gone after they'd left the vault. Vanessa, taking Alasdair at his word, had not asked. She regretted that oversight now. Ooch! how she regretted it!

The pain of betrayal was a tangible thing, clawing her up on the inside. It took effort for her to tamp it down and look past it. She could not, under any circumstances, let her emotions get the better of her. Nay, not now. Time enough for that later . . . for now, she'd more important matters to attend.

"Where?" Vanessa asked finally, her voice much too low and calm for her to be anything but furious. "Where are they?"

Marette shrugged. "I've no idea. The dungeon, I would imagine."

"And where be that?"

This time, a sly grin was Marette's only answer.

Vanessa advanced on the woman a step. Another. Marette, in turn, retreated two steps for every one of her adversary's.

"Dinna try it. Ye canna run from me," Vanessa spat, reading correctly the emotion she saw flicker in the other woman's eyes. "I'll have the location of Cavnearal's dungeon, and I'll have it now, or so help me, I'll—"

The threat remained unfinished, as two things happened at once.

Marette gathered up her skirt, spun on her heel, and made a dash back toward the keep's door. Vanessa was in the process of chasing after her when a movement on the parapet walk snagged her attention. She glanced there only briefly, but it was enough . . . for at the same time, a hauntingly familiar voice called out to her from that direction.

She stopped in mid-run, and the blood pumping fast through her veins turned ice-cold. If she'd harbored even a sliver of doubt that Marette had been speaking the truth, that sliver was effectively dashed.

The voice that called out to her was Duncan's.

"Run!" Duncan yelled breathlessly. "Get . . . Dugald! Get help, lass!"

Vanessa assessed the situation in a blink, and reacted to it in two. Even from this distance, she could see that her brother was not alone on the parapet walk; two big, strong guards were even now struggling to subdue him. To Duncan's credit, he was giving them the devil's own time.

Marette had already fled; there was no chance for Vanessa to catch up to the woman and force the location of the dungeon out of her now. Duncan's yell had undoubtedly alerted the rest of Alasdair's guards to her presence; soon they would be chasing after her.

That left Vanessa with only one course of action. Faster than she thought possible, she dashed through the kirkyard, her destination, the place where the hidden grooves in the rock had first admitted her into Cavnearal.

Chapter Thirteen

The door to Alasdair's bedchamber was thrown open without so much as a knock of warning. The thick oak door crashed noisily into the stone wall behind it, and Rory MacPhearson barged into the room. "M'lord, come quick. The cursed wench is trying to escape!"

Alasdair bit back a groan. When he'd decided to let Vanessa go, he'd taken into account that she would try to exit Cavneral by the same means she'd entered it; a means that still remained a mystery to him. It was a strong testament to how much the woman affected him that Alasdair had still been willing to allow her escape, even knowing she'd bring the information back to her kin, and that Cavnearal, from that night onward, would need be guarded doubly until her method of entrance had been ascertained. And blocked.

Cursing beneath his breath, Alasdair flipped back the covers and pushed from the bed. The cold night air was like a slap against his naked flesh, but he paid the discomfort no mind as he snatched up his trews from the floor and tugged them on. His tunic was quick to follow; he did not bother tucking the long tails into his trews, but instead let the garment fall in wrinkled saffron folds from his shoulders to mid-thigh.

He reached for his sword, which was usually on the stand beside the bed, forgetting he'd taken the precaution of leaving the weapon beneath the guard's chair in the corridor before entering his bedchamber.

Bloody hell!

His angry gaze pierced Rory MacPhearson, who had the good sense to squirm. "Where is she?" he asked the young guard curtly. "The vault again?"

Rory shook his head. "Nay, m'lord, we've not caught her. Yet," the man was quick to add. "The last glimpse of her, she was streaking across the kirkyard. And running at a most impressive speed, I might add. Garth set out in pursuit of her, whilst I was dispatched to alert you of her intended escape."

Alasdair sighed, then nodded. The occupants of Cavnearal were already less than thrilled to have three Forsters housed within its walls; were any to discover that Alasdair not only knew of the wench's plans to escape, but had *allowed* it . . .!

Long, powerful strides carried Alasdair across the room. When Rory did not move, but simply stood where he was in the doorway, staring at his angry lord, Alasdair simply pushed the man aside and strode over the threshold.

The hiss of metal against metal was loud when Alasdair bent at the waist and slipped his sword from its scabbard. The scabbard remained beneath the chair; unnecessary baggage, since he'd nothing to hang it on.

Rory snapped to his senses and, spinning on his heel, entered the corridor in time to see his lord turning the dimly lit corner leading toward the stairs. A sigh that was half relief, half nervousness hissed through the young guard's teeth as he quickly set out after Alasdair. He was ever so thankful he was not the impudent little heathen toward which all of The Devil's anger was now directed.

That Alasdair had been naked when Rory barged

into the room did not even occur to the young man until quite some time later.

Climbing up the notches carved into the huge boulder upon which Cavnearal sat had not been easy. Indeed, Vanessa's breathing still shallowed and her heart still palpitated when she recalled how Duncan had almost fallen to his death when the rock had given away.

However, Vanessa was quick to learn that, if she'd thought climbing *up* had been difficult, climbing *down* was more arduous still. The black velvet sky had sported a full moon just half a fortnight ago. Now, the moon was only three quarters full, and with the boulder shadowing everything on the seaside, she found the lack of light more than an inconvenience.

It took her ten minutes to find the place where she and Duncan had found the notches, and another five for her to lower herself down far enough so her head could not be seen by any who passed by. None did. Yet. However, the male voices she heard shouting from the bailey indicated the grounds would be thoroughly searched soon.

Vanessa intended to be gone long before that happened.

Her dart across the kirkyard had left her breathless. Try though she might, her breathing refused to regulate, especially when her searching foot encountered the breach that had once been a grove, and that was now nothing more than a treacherous, gaping hole.

Like most of her countrymen, her religion had switched from Catholicism to Presbyterianism when it was clear that the Old Church in Scotland was destined to fall. Still, she felt not the least bit traitorous to mumble every papist prayer and verse she could remember from her childhood. She doubted God

266

would care about such a triviality were she to fall to her death now.

Her breath caught as she looked down.

Down.

Then down some more . . . to where the foamy waves of the firth crashed against the rocks.

She swallowed dryly. From this angle, the ledge which was her goal looked frighteningly narrow and far off. Dying in an attempt to reach it seemed to be a very real possibility.

The voices in the keep grew louder. A dog barked, and the distant whicker of a horse carried to her on the misty sea air.

Vanessa descended the rock slowly, cautiously. She tried not to think about what she was doing—and certainly tried not to look down again! As she picked her way carefully downward, of their own accord, her thoughts strayed to Duncan, then wrapped around the information Marette had callously supplied her.

Your father and brother were never released . . .

The words cut through Vanessa like a sharply honed dagger, piercing her heart and twisting cruelly.

The Devil had lied to her. The bastard! Worse, she'd believed him, had actually *trusted* him. His betrayal cut deep. Deeper than it by all rights should have . . . deeper than she would have liked.

The only thing that hurt more was knowing her promise to her mother had not been honored. Oh, how that stung! Nay, 'twas through no fault of her own, Vanessa knew, knew also that she'd tried her best to get her father home as she'd sworn she would.

The Devil had thwarted her.

The Devil had *lied* to her! And then . . .

Aye, and then The Devil had bedded her.

His latter crime was the one that pinched the most. Even worse than his lies.

The toe of her boot touched the ledge. Her heart skipped a beat, and she felt a giddy surge of triumph wash over her when she at last felt solid rock beneath her.

She'd made it to the ledge! She still had far to go yet before reaching Dunnaclard, aye, but at least she'd survived the most lethal part of her escape. Now, if she could inch her way over the ledge and reach the spot where it melded smoothly into solid ground in a place that was adeptly concealed behind a set of thick, solid birch trunks and equally thick rocks . . .

The sounds in the bailey magnified. Vanessa's back was pressed hard against the rock, and she could hear hoofbeats thundering in her ears even as she felt the vibration of them against her suddenly rigid spine.

Alasdair was searching for her, and he was accompanied by the majority of his men, from the sounds. While they could not find her here on the ledge, once she left this shelter his odds of hunting her down increased sharply.

Vanessa sighed. There was no help for it. Her only course of action now, to ensure her concealment, was to remain on the ledge until the search was either called off or lengthened to encompass the grounds outside the immediate area.

Slowly, wearily, she slid down the cold stone wall until she was sitting on the equally cold, precariously narrow ledge. Her legs were bent, her feet flat atop the ledge. Curling her arms around her shins for warmth, she rested her cheek atop her bent knees and set about to wait.

Ooch! but she hated waiting!

Keith reined his horse in next to his brother's. The younger Gray was quick to notice that he was the only one amongst the fifty or so mounted men who dared to approach Alasdair. He wasn't surprised by that. Most of these men had been in his brother's charge long enough to know that when The Devil's eyes lightened to chips of steely ice, as they had now, it was in their best interest to give Alasdair a very wide berth. Unless, of course, they were of a mind to give up their lifelong practice of breathing . . .

"Let me see if I have this right, brother," Keith said as, leaning forward, he rested his forearm atop the saddle's pummel and regarded Alasdair. "The wench escaped whilst you slept — an accomplishment in itself, I might add, since you've always been a very light sleeper — and then," he clicked his fingers, and the sound carried unnaturally loud on the cold night air, "vanished. Is that correct?"

Alasdair glared an affirmative answer.

Keith pursed his lips, then, after a thoughtful pause, shrugged and sighed. "I suppose inquiring as to how the wench got out of a locked room would be trifling at this point, eh? Obviously, she had a cohort."

"Obviously," Alasdair snarled.

The temptation to grin was strong, but Keith suppressed it. His brother would no doubt backhand him off his mount were Alasdair to discover that Keith found even a tiny sliver of amusement in this situation. And, truly, the sliver was tiny. Not to mention a bit ironic. It still amazed Keith that, after centuries of trying, the ones who'd ultimately breached the unbreachable Cavnearal were a girl, and a boy not yet old enough to sprout his first whisker, let alone shave it off! 'Twas doubly amazing that one of them — the *girl,* no less! — had also accomplished the singularly exclusive feat of *escaping* the keep in the same mysterious way.

Similar thoughts were going through Alasdair's head — though, truth be known, his terminology was crasser than his brother's.

He'd *wanted* Vanessa to escape; Alasdair kept reminding himself of that over and over, like a silent

269

chant. Yet, oddly enough, he still found himself vexed. Aye, he'd wanted her to escape, but since he was duty-bound to *try* to thwart her, he'd hoped at the same time to, at the very least, be rewarded for his effort by learning how she'd gotten into Cavnearal originally.

That was going to be difficult to do if he couldn't find her. And, as Keith had already pointed out, the woman appeared to have vanished.

Where had she gone?!

Alasdair didn't know, but he was going to find out. His glare shifted to Keith. "Take these men and search the village. *Thoroughly.*"

Keith was perplexed. He sat back in the saddle, and regarded his brother shrewdly. "Might I ask what you intend to do while I'm searching?"

"Isn't it obvious?"

"Nay, 'tis not."

Alasdair's grin was as frigid as his gaze. With a flick of his wrist, he turned his mount around, and nudged the large black stallion into motion with his knees. From over his shoulder, he informed his brother curtly, "I intend to find out once and for all where this blasted second entrance is . . . and there's but one who can tell me. Mark my words, Keith, Duncan Forster is going to rue the day he ever set foot on Cavnearal soil!"

With that, Alasdair urged his horse to a trot. Without once glancing back, he swiftly retraced the narrow, steep, moonswept path back to Cavnearal.

The south tower room had an excellent view of the northwest side of Cavnearal, as well as the keep's entrance—a shaft of land that twisted down the side of the boulder, then opened gradually into a path that was well guarded from the gatehouse.

Marette Gray was excruciatingly aware of the land-

270

scape at this angle, for she'd spent many hours staring at it when she'd been locked inside this very room a mere week prior, waiting impatiently for her brother's anger to cool.

It was to this room that Marette went after parting company with that . . . that *heathen*. And 'twas at this room's long, narrow window that she now stood, her shrewd gaze trained on the figure three stories below that darted swiftly toward the fortress's seaward wall.

If the baggy clothes hadn't alerted her to the runner's identity, the short black hair that billowed out behind the slender figure would have.

Vanessa Forster.

The corners of Marette's lips curled upward in a crafty smile as she watched the chit stop at the thick stone curtain wall and glance up to the top, which was a good two feet above the girl's head. The wench's hesitation was brief. In no time, the girl scaled the jagged stone wall, and catapulted herself over the top, disappearing on the other side.

Marette's grin broadened. Ah, at long last, the wench was gone. 'Twas a most pleasing sight! Now, she'd but two more hated Forsters to rid herself of before Cavneareal was once again set to rights.

She doubted freeing Hugh Forster and that scrawny son of his would be much trouble. Especially since aiding Vanessa's escape had gone so smoothly. Nor did she harbor even a sliver of fear that she might be caught aiding them. Who would suspect The Devil's eldest sister to have her hand in any of their rival's escapes? Not a soul, that's who!

And even if someone *did* suspect, that was all they would do. Suspect. None would dare point an accusing finger at her . . . unless they'd concrete proof to reinforce their accusation. And Marette had taken care to assure herself no such proof existed. First, she'd feigned illness and skipped the evening meal. Claiming a headache, she'd taken to her bed at midafternoon . . . and at the appropriate time dispatched her apologies to Alasdair via her lady's maid, Mildred.

She'd even gone so far as to ask Mildred to drag a cot into her room and place it close to Marette's own bed. "In case I should worsen and need your assistance in the night," she'd told the old woman, who in turn had accepted the explanation without question.

As had been Marette's plan, Mildred had been snoring loudly by the time she'd sneaked out of the chamber. Barring a very noisy, unforeseen calamity, the near-deaf old woman would remain sleeping until dawn.

"Two more, and finally this keep will be free of all cursed Forsters," Marette whispered as, with one last glance at the stony spot where she'd seen that Forster chit disappear, she spun on her heel and left the cold, sparsely furnished room.

Marette was a diligent Presbyterian, as all good Englishmen these days were—and even if they were not, none was foolish enough to admit they clung to the Old Religion for fear of bringing the Queen's wrath down upon their heads. No matter what faith one practiced, murder was still an unpardonable sin.

Marette knew that. And 'twas for that reason alone she felt a twinge—a very *small* twinge—of gratitude that Alasdair had intruded upon her and Vanessa in the corridor outside the hall that afternoon. The finely honed dagger Marette had clutched in her fist, concealed in the folds of her skirt, had begged to find its way into hated Forster flesh.

Oh, nay, she knew not which Forster had claimed the life of her beloved Robert, not precisely, nor did she see any point in placing the blame on only one head. As far as she was concerned, *all* Forsters were to be held accountable for Robert's death. 'Twas they who'd taken her beloved away from her, cutting their time together so horribly short.

What had gone through her brother's mind to let a Forster into Cavnearal in the first place? Alasdair's logic was beyond her. And, as if admitting one was not bad enough, he'd admitted *three!*

That was not to be tolerated. And since no one else seemed up to purging the keep of those heathen Scots, Marette took the duty upon herself. Only that morning she'd decided it was past time to take matters into her own hands. Alasdair had been given the opportunity, but had wasted it. Marette would not be so compassionate. She would set things right. She would see her family's ancestral home swept free of Forsters before another half fortnight had passed, and she'd use any means at her disposal to do it. Even . . .

Aye, even murder, if it came to that. And it would, if, for whatever reason, the cursed Forster men would not leave as willingly as their woman had. Either way, they *would* be leaving.

Whatever it took, Marette vowed she would do. And not for a second would she allow herself to regret any of her actions.

Vanessa was tired. Nay, not just tired, she was *exhausted.*

The muscles in her legs still felt cramped from the two hours she'd spent patiently crouching on that infernal ledge, waiting for the search to either widen, or cease entirely.

It hadn't ceased. She was not surprised.

The instant she'd deemed it safe, she'd inched her way to solid ground. Since she hadn't a mount, she was forced to set out on foot, heading due north. Toward Dunnaclard. Toward home. Toward *help!*

She had appropriated a thin woolen blanket from the first house she'd passed in the village, picking it up from the ground, where it had been tossed carelessly beside the shack's doorstoop. A Scot would *never* be so wasteful! The covering offered little protection. The cold night air nipped at her cheeks, and penetrated the baggy, stolen tunic, biting into the tender skin beneath. It turned her breath into a misty gray vapor.

Though she was chilled to the bone, Vanessa let her anger heat her. It did an admirable job!

All the fury she'd pushed aside upon hearing of Alasdair's lies had flourished during her time on the ledge. With each step she took, she nurtured her anger until it burned. 'Twas bad enough The Devil had lied to her, but 'twas doubly bad that, because of his lies, she'd not been able to uphold her promise to her mother. That chaffed Vanessa raw, and fueled her ire until it smoldered like liquid heat pumping hot and fast through her veins.

As they'd done often during the last week, her thoughts focused on her mother. Had the babe come yet? And, if so, was he or she still alive? Vanessa didn't want to believe that the God she'd always held in such high esteem would take yet another of Hannah Forster's bairns, but the plain fact was, stillbirths happened all too often, and mothers losing sometimes a half dozen bairns at birth were not unheard of.

A tightness fisted in Vanessa's chest as she pushed onward, skirting past a patch of bramble, her direction unvaryingly north. Her booted feet crunched over the forest's moss- and leaf-strewn floor. The whisper of a frosty breeze rustled through the ceiling of near-bare branches above her.

So intent was Vanessa on her thoughts that she didn't at first notice the raindrops filtering through the branches above, and splattering coldly atop her raven head. Soon, however, she could not help but notice them.

Sweet Lord, were the fates conspiring against her? Mayhap she was not destined to return home?!

It was not raining hard, just a sprinkle, yet there need not be a severe storm for the result to be the same. The thin woolen blanket she hugged around her shoulders would not stay dry for long. If the rain worsened—aye, even if it did not, but merely kept on falling!—the covering would be soaked through in no time. Her hair already felt damp where it curled against her brow and neck, and her lashes felt wet and cold against her cheek whenever she blinked. The tip of her nose was numb and, had she a looking glass to see her reflection, she thought it would appear red as well.

She shivered, hugged the blanket closer, and trudged on. In no time she noticed that the leaves and moss no longer crackled dryly beneath her boots. The forest floor was moistening.

She was going to have to search out shelter, and do it soon. Not only did the continuing drizzle tell her that, but the muscles in her legs ached, and her eyelids felt gritty with exhaustion. Cold as she was, there was no trapping a yawn in her throat. If there was an inch of her body that was not weak from tiredness, she did not feel it. The last decent sleep she'd had was the night before, and even that had not been restful. She'd foolishly spent most of it staring at a sleeping Alasdair Gray. And then tonight . . .

Ooch! She was *not* going to think about *that!*

With a sigh, Vanessa glanced at her surroundings. Trees. Bramble. Underbrush. Moss. Everything was wet, and nothing looked even remotely like a shelter.

Water-heavy storm clouds were gathering in the sky, making the light dimmer than when she'd started out and casting the dense forest in murky shadows. Somewhere in the distance, she heard a yowl that might belong to either dog or wolf. She hoped it was the former.

How long she walked, she was uncertain. It felt like hours, but in reality could have been only a few minutes. All Vanessa knew was that one moment she was forcing her bone-weary body to keep moving, and the next she was standing in front of what appeared to be a deserted hunting shack.

She closed her eyes and counted to ten, positive that when she looked again she would discover the thatched-roof shack was naught but a figment of her exhausted mind. It was not, for when she opened her eyes, the shack was still there.

Her heart skipped a beat, and her grin, though weary, was steeped with relief.

As she'd surmised, the blanket had become soaked in no time; the dampness penetrating the wool, seeping into the tunic, which now lay cold and clammy against her skin. Her hair fell in saturated black waves around her face. Her stomach grumbled, but right now, hunger was the least of her complaints.

As though in answer to her prayers, she spotted a stack of wood piled up beside the shack's left outer wall. The thatched roof overhung the wall on this side, and even from such a distance, the wood looked enviably dry.

The thought of a roof over her head and a blazing fire to warm her was too great a temptation to resist. A small measure of her energy returned. In no time, Vanessa had gathered an armful of twigs and branches, and was shouldering open the shack's door.

Chapter Fourteen

If there was a fraction of his body that wasn't wet, Alasdair didn't know where it was.

The storm that had started out as an annoying drizzle quickly gained momentum. Within an hour—at approximately the same time he'd set out from Cavnearal for the second time after talking to Duncan Forster—the wind was howling through the marshes and valleys, whipping at autumn-bare tree branches and scattering what few wilted leaves still clung to them.

His padded leather jack offered some protection from the elements, but not a lot. His trews were saturated, as was his hair. Icy trickles of rain sneaked beneath his collar and dripped down his chest and spine. The stallion beneath him fared no better; its black sides glistened, and every time the horse shook its head, Alasdair was treated to a bath of fat, cold droplets.

The rain streaking down from the sky made visibility poor. 'Twas for that reason he almost rode past the shack that blended so smoothly with a dense patch of the trees to his right.

The scent of charred wood mingled with the acidy tang of rain, snagging his attention. Shielding his eyes with his cupped hand, he squinted through the rain and saw the outline of the hunting shack that his father had built years ago, and which Alasdair had never used. Indeed, he'd forgotten the place existed.

Besides two narrow windows, the only other openings in the decrepit wooden shack were the door and a hole cut into the thatched roof that served as a crude sort of chimney.

Curling tendrils of smoke wafted up from the latter. Despite his chilled, wet state, Alasdair grinned. It had taken him the better part of two hours to hunt the foolish wench down, but by God, he *had* found her! Only now did he admit that he'd harbored doubts of ever seeing Vanessa again. Truly, a girl who'd so easily tumbled him to a hard stone floor and marked the back of his hand with her teeth was capable of anything . . . including disappearing into thin air, were that her desire.

With a click of his tongue and nudge of his knees, Alasdair guided his mount toward the shack. The stallion's steps were quick and impatient, as though he, too, sensed the beckoning heat and warmth, and was eager to reach it.

Alasdair dismounted, gathered the reins in his fist, and led the horse toward the door. He scowled when he noticed the door was open a crack. Obviously, the wind had been the culprit . . . but why had Vanessa not immediately closed it against the damp wind and rain?

A trickle of unease prickled the dark hair at his nape, and skittered down his spine. The stallion, as though sensing his master's mood, whickered softly. Alasdair ran a soothing palm down the horse's nose, even as he used his free hand to push open the door.

The first thing he noticed upon entering the shack was that the hole in the thatched roof was woefully inadequate for good ventilation; a dense cloud of smoke hovered in the air, stinging Alasdair's eyes and clogging in his nostrils. His gaze strayed to the hearth, and his scowl deepened. The fire was in need of stoking; the flames were low to the hearth's stone floor, a mere flicker of orangey warmth emitted from what was now mostly glowing cinders.

His steely gaze narrowed, straying lower still, to the figure that lay on its side, curled on the dirt floor in front of the hearth.

The woman's short, thick black hair told him who she was, as did the familiar, slender figure hinted at beneath the folds of the damp blanket she was huddled deeply within.

She was shivering.

Alasdair heard a faint sneeze, but the sound was for the most part muffled by the woolen blanket.

"Ooch! mon, close the door before I catch me death. And"—another sneeze was followed by a pair of watery sniffles "—leave that infernal horse without. 'Tis no stable we be in, but a . . . a . . ."—*aaaachoooo!*—"shack that will be smelling like one come dawn if that beastie spends the night in here." Softer, Vanessa added, "Not that I'd be able to"—*sniffle, cough*—"smell it, mind ye, with me nose so stuffy and all."

"You're sick," Alasdair said, and he was annoyed to find that, even to his own ears, the words sounded horribly stilted and foolish.

"Aye, and ye be truly brilliant to have figured it out so quickly," she chided, then sniffled loudly. "Tell me, Devil, what"—*aaaachoooo!*—"was yer first clue?"

"Your sunny disposition," he replied dryly.

Tugging on the rain-damped reins, Alasdair guided the stallion inside the tiny, unfurnished, one-room shack. An icy gust rattled the frost-smeared windows, and he had to fight the cold wind to get the door shut. By then, the dirt floor directly in front of it was slick and muddy.

"How sick?" he asked as he halted his mount beside the far wall, and quickly unstrapped and removed its saddle and blanket.

"Dinna fash yeself. 'Tis naught but a fever and

279

chills. Nothing serious. I've a watery nose and eyes. Oh, and a cough that seems to be worsening. Periods of sneezing, and a wee bit of difficulty breathing. Indeed, me chest feels as though yer horse has been prancing on it all morn! Other than that, I be fine." Her words ended in an abrupt fit of coughing.

Alasdair stifled a groan. It had been his experience that the only thing worse than an angry woman was a sick one. Bloody hell! Now what was he going to do?

The question had no more entered his mind than the answer swiftly followed. What else could he do? It was a two-hour ride on horseback back to Cavneal. Not that he would have retraced his path at this point. If the weather was good, mayhap he would have considered it. But, unfortunately, the fact remained that the weather was not good. Nay, not bloody good at all! Bringing Vanessa out in the cold, damp air would do naught to improve her condition. Most likely it would worsen it.

A fever was nothing to take lightly, Alasdair knew; every year, fevers claimed the lives of a good many people on either side of the Border. So what choice did he have, really? Truly, he had none.

He was here.

She was sick.

He'd no alternative but to nurse her . . . at least until the weather cleared and they could make the journey back to his keep with little risk to her health.

If there is a God, Alasdair thought, and there were times in the last fortnight when he'd doubted there was, *then the sky will clear, the rain will stop, and the sun will commence to shining. Right now. Right this very second!*

Another burst of wind rattled the door and windows. Needles of rain drilled into the glass. 'Twas obvious the storm had no plans of abating in the near future.

Alasdair sighed as he finished tending his horse. So much for divine intervention.

Vanessa heard the crunch of his boot heels on the bare earth floor as Alasdair moved about behind her. She also heard the whickers of the horse he'd brought in. Were she not so tired, and her body not so sore, she would have rolled onto her other side and demand he bring the beastie outside. Unfortunately, she lacked the energy. Besides, her throat was sore, and it burned whenever she spoke.

Wiping her nose on the blanket, she huddled deeper within the damp woolen folds and decided her best course of action would be to simply ignore him. And if she could manage to fall asleep, even though she felt sick and achy and miserable . . . so much the better!

She almost did exactly that. Almost. The fringe of sleep had no more blurred the corners of her mind when she felt the blanket being rudely lifted. Her fingers protectively fisted the damp material, but she was too weak, and after a humiliatingly short struggle, the covering was wrenched from her body.

She shivered. Her eyes narrowed, the green depths spitting unconcealed fury. Now what was the hateful Sassenach doing?!

Vanessa's body screamed a protest as she flipped onto her back and glared up at her tormenter. Her anger thickened her accent. "Ooch! mon, but ye try me patience! Canna ye see I be sick, or are ye blind as well as stubborn?!" Her attention shifted to the blanket that Alasdair negligently tossed into a shadowy corner of the room. "I'll thank ye tae fetch that and give it back . . . and I'll be thanking ye tae do it *now!*"

"And I'll be thanking *you* to stop acting like a spoiled, disobedient child, and start treating yourself like the sick woman you claim to be!" he replied just as hotly. "Bloody hell, wench, think about it! Wrapping yourself up in a cold, wet scrap of wool is not the way to rid yourself of a fever. I'd think that, even

281

being a Scot, and a . . . *woman*"—he snarled the word as though it was an even greater insult than the former—"you'd have enough common sense to recognize that."

She hesitated long enough to trap a sneeze in her throat and nostrils. When the urge passed, she snapped an insult in Gaelic that questioned not only Alasdair Gray's parentage, but his distant ancestor's as well.

His steely gaze sharpened on her. Alasdair was not fluent in Gaelic, but he knew enough of the guttural language to understand that his lineage had just been challenged. The remark did not sit well.

While the words had felt very good in the saying, the way The Devil's glare pierced her made Vanessa question her own logic. In that beat of hesitation, she also noticed something else. Something much too disturbing. In order to return his gaze, she was forced to look up the entire length of Alasdair Gray's virile body. Up his heavily muscled thighs. His lean hips and flat stomach. His impressively wide chest and shoulders. His strong, hard jaw and sharply chiseled cheeks. Then, finally, deeply into his anger-darkened eyes.

Her heart stammered a few beats, then smoothed itself out in an erratic, thundering rhythm. Her head spun, but she attributed the malady to her fever. It was difficult to breathe when one's chest was congested. Aye, that was her problem. At least she desperately *hoped* the source of her discomfort could be traced to her illness. The pity of it was, Vanessa was not entirely certain that was true.

"Stand up, Vanessa. Now."

She swallowed hard, and winced when her throat felt as though it had been seared by one of the glowing coals in the hearth. Mayhap defying this man had not been the smartest thing she'd ever done? Ooch! well, smart or no, 'twas too late to change her mind

now! To do so would make her look weak, and a Forster was *never* that—especially in front of a cursed Sassenach!

Her chin inched up a proud notch. She let her defiant gaze speak for itself, and was smugly pleased to
see by the way the muscle in Alasdair's cheek ticked
that the gesture had its desired effect.

His voice came low and harsh. "I'll warn you but
once, wench. Either you get to your feet under your
own power, or you'll do it under mine. I care not
which."

"And I care not to stand at all—Eeek! Put me
down this second, ye thick-skulled Sassenach! I said I
dinna want to stand!"

Alasdair pretended not to hear her angry outburst
as he bent at the waist and, his fingers shackling her
slender upper arms, hauled her roughly to her feet.
Vanessa swayed, and he swore under his breath when
he was forced to brace her. Without his support, he
feared she would tumble right back down to the floor.
Not that Alasdair would mind having this woman
groveling at his feet, of course—especially after all the
trouble she'd given him this past week!—he simply
preferred her faculties be intact when she did it!

When she'd stopped swaying, he released her and
fisted the hem of her tunic. He'd managed to tug the
garment up past her stomach by the time she realized
what he was doing, and tried to slap his hands away.

Alasdair would be damned if he'd allow the stupid
wench to remain in those wet garments—*his* garments, he realized only now!—and let her get sicker
than she already was. He would tend her even if it
meant having to force his ministrations down her
stubborn Scots throat!

His eyes darkened to a murderous shade of blue,
and lowered.

Hers shimmered an angry fever-and-fury-induced
green, and lifted.

Their gazes met and warred.

"The clothes come off, Vanessa."

"Over me dead body, they do."

His smile was pure ice. "Aye, and that's exactly what it will be shortly if you don't get out of those wet clothes and into something warm. You've a fever, remember?"

"I dinna forget. But, in case ye've not noticed, Devil, there be naught warm for me tae wear."

No, now that she mentioned it, Alasdair hadn't noticed. He did now, though. And his mind and body burned at the thought of spending even a moment around this woman when she was naked. Her nose wrinkled — he thought she looked almost cute when she did that — and she sneezed, reminding him briefly of her illness. Unfortunately, his mind chose that precise moment to remind him of how wonderful her naked body felt moving hungrily beneath his . . . which somehow managed to counter the state of her health.

With a scowl, Alasdair forced his thoughts back to the matter at hand. Though it grated on his pride, 'twould seem a compromise was definitely in order.

He spun on his heel and collected the damp blanket from where he'd tossed it in a heap in the far corner of the room, near the door. Retracing his steps, he spread the covering over the dirt floor in front of the hearth, then knelt and stoked the fire, adding enough of the wood stacked beside it for the flames to blaze.

Only when he was done did he again turn back to her. She was standing precisely where he'd left her, her stance a little wobbly, glaring at him.

With a toss of her head, Vanessa flicked her cold, wet hair back from her cheeks and brow. It was an impulse she immediately regretted, for it set her temples to pounding. "I could have done that."

Alasdair's jaw hardened. "Now you don't have to." He nodded at the blanket. "The second that's dry, I

284

want you to undress and wrap up in it."

The glare he sent her made Vanessa think better of arguing with him. He would find out when the time came that she had no intention of obeying his dictates . . . even if he was right about them. "And what will ye be doing whilst I undress?"

"Why, standing outside in the rain waiting for you to finish, of course," he replied dryly, not to mention very insincerely.

" 'Tis good to know," she replied with feigned innocence, while purposely ignoring his sarcasm. "After all, 'twould be most improper for ye to—"

"Vanessa . . ." Alasdair began impatiently, only to have her cut him short.

"—stay and watch. Dinna ye think the March Wardens would agree?"

Alasdair gritted his teeth and counted to ten. Thrice. It didn't help. "You try my patience, wench."

She smiled as though he'd just bestowed upon her the most flattering compliment. He supposed that, in her mind, he had. Alasdair sighed and shook his head. He'd a difficult enough time understanding English women; these Scots women were even more baffling!

Vanessa shivered. While the blanket had indeed been damp—blast it, but Alasdair had been quite right about that!—it had at least provided a wee bit of warmth. Without it, the chilly night air, and her equally wet clothes, prickled coldly at her skin. Wrapping her arms about her waist for warmth, she stepped around Alasdair and sat as gracefully as her sore, aching body would allow upon the dirt floor beside the hearth, her spine and the back of her head braced against the roughly timbered wall.

The horse whickered, and she heard its hooves stamp the earth floor before the animal quieted. The air was filled with the sound of wind and rain pummeling the windows and the flames that snapped in

285

the hearth.

Again, she closed her eyes with the intent to sleep.

Again, The Devil, insolent man that he was, intruded upon her peace. She heard his approach a brief second before she felt his virile heat seep into her left side. She sighed, and found her senses filled with the sharp earth-and-rain smell of him. Why the scent wasn't disturbing was a wonder to her.

Oddly enough, she found his scent, indeed his very nearness, reassuring in a way she couldn't fathom. Vanessa didn't want to know the reason why. As her da had often instructed, there were some questions in life 'twas best left unanswered. And this, she had an uneasy feeling, was one of them.

"Your teeth are chattering," Alasdair remarked with a bluntness that made her want to smack him.

Pride forced Vanessa to lie, even though the truth was apparent to them both. "They are not."

"Are, too."

"Not."

"And your lips are blue."

Well, she could hardly argue with that. She had no way of knowing what color her lips were. All she knew was that they felt cold and slightly numb against her chattering teeth. She sneezed, sniffled loudly, then shrugged.

Alasdair swore. "Damn it, Vanessa, is it so bloody hard for you to admit that you're cold? There's naught to be ashamed of about it. You are, after all, sick."

"I am *not* ashamed," she snapped, "and as for being cold, I've already told you that I am no—Eeek! Not again!" Before she could blink, Alasdair had twisted to the side, slipped his right arm beneath hers and his left under her knees, and with a lithe movement, settled back against the wall . . . with her on his lap!

"Yes, 'again'," he growled. "Now, be quiet and stop squirming. Whether you care to admit it or not,

286

you're chilled to the bone and in need of warmth."

She could deny it no longer. After all, with her body pressed against his, the proof of her chilly state was apparent in the shivers that continuously skated down her spine and through her limbs. Surely he had to feel them, too. "I can sit nearer to the fire for heat," she said, and her voice sounded shaky, for her lips trembled around the words.

"Aye, you could. Were I to let you go. Unfortunately for you, I've no intention of doing that until the blanket dries."

"That could take hours!"

"I know," Alasdair growled, and inwardly prayed it wouldn't take nearly that long. Holding this woman in his arms, no matter how innocently, was a torture unlike anything he'd ever endured.

Her fevered heat seeped through her damp clothes, through his, and soaked into his skin. Into his very blood! The smell of rainwater and pine needles clung to her hair and clothes, surrounding them in what felt like a soft, fragrant cocoon. He cupped her cheek in his palm and tucked her head beneath his chin. Oddly enough, she did not fight him. In his wildest dreams, Alasdair had never imagined that the feel of cool, wet hair against his skin could have such an overpowering effect on him.

She shifted to find a more comfortable spot, and it was all Alasdair could do to not sandwich her hips in his hands and hold her still. While his mind registered the fact that she was sick, his body did not. Indeed, his body was too busy remembering how wonderful it felt to be one with this woman. And his body wanted to feel that unique oneness yet again. Now. He craved it.

He gritted his teeth and sucked in a sharp breath. Damn it! He should never have set out after her. The smart thing to do would have been to send one of his vassals.

Quick upon the heels of that thought followed a sensation that Alasdair was totally unfamiliar with. It tightened in his chest, clawed like a fist in his gut. Foreign though it was, he recognized his reaction immediately for what it was. Jealousy. White-hot and sharp.

The thought of someone else holding Vanessa the way he was, of threatening to disrobe her as he'd done only moments before . . .

Vanessa sneezed, coughed, then sniffled in a most unladylike manner. A frown pinched her brow. She was starting to question just how sick she was. Obviously, sicker than she'd thought; it was the only thing she could think of to explain the strange, contented feeling that had stolen over her.

Alasdair's chin atop her head was an oddly wonderful pressure. His damp shirt felt cool and moist against her cheek. Nice. Soothing. Even though she was feverish, the rhythmic puffs of his breath warmed her scalp and made it tingle. His heartbeat echoed in her ear, the rhythm strong and lulling.

Vanessa's mind tried to warn her against the soft feelings cluttering her mind, filling her senses. This man was not only her enemy, but he'd lied to her. Common sense told her that she should be trying to slap his arrogant face, not cuddle in his arms like this.

Unfortunately, anger, she soon discovered, was an emotion that was beyond her at the moment. While she would have liked to trace the cause back to her illness, she wasn't sure that was it. Odd, but the sharp stab of betrayal she'd felt when Marette had told her of Alasdair's deception had scattered like dry leaves in an autumn wind the second he'd dragged her into his lap, the second the heat of his body had enfolded her and eased her chill.

It felt good to be in this man's arms; she was simply too tired and achy to question why.

She sneezed again, and wiped her nose on her damp sleeve.

Alasdair glanced down, then, trapping a groan in his throat, closed his eyes and rested his head back against the timbered wall. He tried not to notice the childlike way she'd done that, yet he could no more not notice that than he could ignore the way she snuggled so nicely in his arms. As though she belonged here. The fit was perfect.

Something between them had changed. He could deny it no longer. His dislike of all things Forster — a feeling that had been drilled into him from the cradle — was unsalvageable. Hate though he did to admit it, he no longer disliked all Forsters, only the majority of them. And while he couldn't deny that he still mistrusted the woman he held in his arms, he could also no longer lie to himself and say he didn't like her. He did. He liked her too much.

When he thought about it objectively, Alasdair found much to respect and admire in this particular Forster. She was small, yet powerful enough, determined enough, to have knocked him to the floor of the vault on their first meeting and bite his hand. He'd frightened her when he'd related her duties as a pledge, yet she'd proudly stripped and lay upon his bed like a sacrificial lamb. When the chance to escape had presented itself, she'd taken it without question.

'Twas no more than he would have done were the situation reversed. But the fact that she — a *woman* . . . a *Scots* woman, no less! — had shown such courage and fortitude . . . well, he could do naught but admire her for it.

Another emotion churned inside Alasdair, but unlike the previous one, this was not so easily labeled. Perchance because he had no desire to discover its meaning? Aye, 'twas a distinct possibility. Yet, familiar or not, the emotion coursed through him like a wave of white heat, and it was strong. Staggeringly so. A surge of protectiveness and concern for the sick woman he held in his arms, oh so near to his chest and heart, was the closest he dared come to naming it.

The definition was lacking, and he knew it.

Chapter Fifteen

Alasdair awoke in lazy degrees. A scowl furrowed his brow as he tried to clear the fog of sleep from his mind.

Sleep. When had he fallen asleep? He didn't know. Didn't remember. Didn't really even care. All he knew was that he *had* fallen asleep and something, somewhere, had awakened him.

But what? A noise? A movement? A person?

The dark hairs at his nape prickled. That was his first indication that he wasn't alone. Odd, but he felt no threat of danger.

His frown deepened when his second indication of another presence intruded upon him, banishing what was left of the layer of sleep that clouded his mind in one fell swoop.

He shivered when something warm and soft and moist feathered the side of his neck, then the line of his jaw, the crest of his chin. A groan slipped past his throat, past his suddenly parched lips. The noise echoed in his ears, vaguely resembling the growl of a hungry animal.

There was a light pressure in his lap, hot and firm. A body.

A *woman's* body.

His frown eased, and his groan melted into a sigh. The barest trace of a satisfied grin slanted one corner of his mouth upward. Waking up to a woman was always pleasurable, especially when that woman was nibbling seductively at his lower lip, the way this one was.

He shivered again when her tongue — so hot and wet and soft — darted inside his mouth and stroked the inside of his upper lip. She dragged the tip over his teeth, retreated and sipped at his lower lip, then commenced those teasingly wonderful nibbles again. If he died right now, he would die happily.

He would also die unappeased, for he was quick to recognize another, more insistent pressure — nay, *urge* — in the region where the side of her hips met the front of his.

Her mouth sipped its way over the line of his jaw, her lips settling finally on the sensitive lobe of his ear.

Alasdair pried his eyes open, and blinked the sleep from his gaze. His attention focused on the back of his own hand; it was open, his palm and splayed fingers cradling the woman's stomach. He sucked in a sharp breath, and found his senses filled with the muted scent of rainwater and pine needles.

Vanessa.

He wasn't surprised. Somehow, deep down, he'd known even while he slept that Vanessa Forster was the woman he was holding. The woman whose sweet, sweet mouth and tongue was even now busy driving him to bittersweet distraction. What Alasdair didn't know, couldn't begin to comprehend, was why it felt so good and natural to wake up with her scent in his nostrils, her body in his arms.

He marveled at how large his hand looked against the backdrop of her narrow, firm stomach. Bloody hell, the woman was no bigger than a slightly over-sized child!

Mayhap he wasn't as awake as he'd originally given himself credit for, for quick on the heels of that thought came the realization that even now, so soon after they'd first made love, there could well be a child quickening in the abdomen upon which his hand rested. *His* child.

The realization was staggering and . . . well, aye, he had to admit, if only to himself, that the idea of Vanessa carrying his babe inside her womb was also pleasing. Very much so. The passion they'd shared so briefly might well have created a new life. Alasdair was experienced enough in the ways of lust to know that, yet also naive enough still to feel a strong, protective surge of amazement and awe. That, and a surge of something else, something stronger, something all-consuming.

That surge was desire, fiery and sharp. It washed over him like a tidal wave, so intense it threatened to drown him in its violent undertow. Never in his life had he wanted a woman the way he wanted this one. Here. Now. Dear God, he *craved* to be one with her again!

He knew the second Vanessa awakened. It was when she stiffened in his arms, and her mouth stopped working its all too sweet magic on his flesh. Her sigh felt fever-hot against his skin, and the sneeze she showered upon him slightly moist. He couldn't help but grin.

Vanessa glanced up just in time to see the corners of Alasdair's lips quirk upward. She completely dismissed the unladylike sniffle she was in the middle of. Indeed, she could not have completed the sniffle anyway, so distracted was she by the sight of a genuine smile on The Devil's face.

All the Border knew about Jenny McLeod. Had he smiled at his wife that way? Vanessa wondered? And if he did, was it any wonder Jenny had fallen in love with him? Vanessa frowned, and instantly chastised herself for the thought. What did it matter to her what type of relationship Alasdair had had with his wife? Why, it didn't matter at all. At least, it shouldn't.

But it did.

Like a dog worrying a bone, no matter how she tried to push the thoughts from her mind, they refused to go. Questions plagued her. And while she knew the answers were certainly none of her affair, her curiosity was overpowering.

"God bless you," Alasdair murmured, in response to the sneeze that finally came from Vanessa.

Vanessa opened her mouth to thank him. No more, no less. It came as quite a surprise to hear that those were *not* the words that stammered off her tongue. "Tell me about her," she said, then promptly wished she could bite the words back.

At some point he'd draped his right arm around her shoulder, and her breasts were now pressed firmly to the side of his chest; the wall of muscle hardened against her as he asked, "Who?"

Well, it was too late to turn back now, wasn't it? Aye. "Yer wife," she prodded, though she had a feeling he knew perfectly well the "who" she'd been referring to. Still, her curiosity was so acute, she decided to humor him by adding, "Jennifer McLeod Gray. Tell me about her . . . please?" That last slipped awkwardly off her tongue.

"What do you want to know?" Alasdair asked after a long, tense pause had slipped past.

"Everything."

"Everything?"

"Aye," she replied readily. "Well, er, only that which ye wish to tell me, of course."

He thought on that for a moment. "And if I wish to tell you naught?"

She sneezed again and, as she wiped her nose on her almost dry sleeve, frowned and said, "Never mind. Forget I asked ye. 'Tis none of my affair."

"True."

She'd tucked her head back against his shoulder— truly, he made the most wonderful pillow—and therefore felt rather than saw him nod. "And yet . . ." she prodded when he said no more.

"You still want to know," he finished for her, then sighed when she nodded against his shoulder.

"Aye, I do."

Alasdair drew in a long, deep breath and released it slowly through his teeth. From the corner of his eyes, he saw his stallion's ears perk at the sound.

Jenny. Somehow, it felt wrong, almost sacrilegious in fact, to have her name cross his mind while he was holding Vanessa's fevered body in his arms. Yet, he'd agreed to appease this woman's curiosity — reluctantly, aye, but agreed all the same — and appease it he would.

"All right," he said finally, and at the same time rested his head back against the wall once more. His lashes flickered down, and he could feel the muscle in his cheek tick as his mind churned to find the proper words. It took only a second for him to decide on blunt honesty. "I killed her," he said flatly. "Is that what you wanted to know?"

No, actually, it wasn't. Vanessa frowned. Many rumors circulated on both sides of the Border about The Devil — his cunning raids and usually victorious trods, his almost inhuman supply of strength and fortitude, his fierce Gray temper and dark good looks — but that he'd killed his wife had never been one of them.

Her curiosity piqued. Why would he think such a thing? she wondered. It never crossed Vanessa's mind to wonder also if he had a *reason* to think his assessment sound. That perchance there was indeed a scrap of truth to his claim that he'd killed Jenny Gray?

" 'Tis not what I heard," she murmured finally, and her frown deepened.

"Nay? And what did you hear? Or do I not want to know?"

She shrugged. "That Jennifer Gray stumbled whilst walking and fell off that massive boulder ye call yer home. The jagged rocks and crashing waves of the Firth claimed her life, not ye."

"Then you've heard but half of the story, wench."

"There be more to it?"

"Aye."

Vanessa fingered the laces of his tunic as she waited for him to elaborate. When he didn't, she prodded. "Weeeell?"

"Jenny fell to her death, that much is true," Alasdair agreed tightly. "What the tale you heard didn't say, but that is also true, is that she was running away from me at the time. Were it not so dark, and were she not so frightened, I've no doubt she would still be alive."

A shiver of unease iced down Vanessa's spine, prickling at the short, dark hairs curling at her nape. A part of her did not want to voice the question that sprang immediately to mind. But a larger part of her insisted that she do exactly that. She had to know. Cautiously, she asked, "What was she frightened of?"

"Me."

"You?"

"Aye."

She shook her head, trying to absorb this information, and failing miserably. It was true that The Devil's temper could be quite fierce when it was aroused. Yet even though it had occasionally pricked her own fear, Vanessa had never been so frightened of the man that she would blindly flee him to the point of stumbling over a cliff.

Nay, what he was telling her made no sense. Surely there was more to the story? "Why was she frightened of ye? Were ye trying to kill her?"

His laughter was short and sharp, totally devoid of humor. "Nay. But methinks she was probably wishing that was the case."

"Well then? If ye werena trying to kill her, then what reason did she have to fear ye?"

"I was trying to do something worse than murder, and that frightened her."

The man was talking in riddles. "Worse than murder?"

"In Jenny's mind, aye. Much worse."

She was going to regret asking this, Vanessa knew it, but ask she most certainly did. Her curiosity would not let her do otherwise. "Ooch! mon, will ye just spit it out?! What were ye trying to do to her that could possibly be worse?"

"Bed her."

"Oh." Vanessa's heartbeat stammered, and her breath caught in her throat when she repeated the word with an entirely new inflection. "Oh!" Did her cheeks look as red and as hot as they felt? She hoped not! "But ye were married for *two* years before she died!"

"Aye."

"That makes no sense, mon. Unless . . . Ooch! are ye saying that in all that time, ye never, er, I mean that the twa of ye dinna . . . ?" Vanessa was supremely grateful for the sneeze that cut her query short. Sweet Saint Andrews, she thought as she sniffled into her sleeve, if she could not *think* the words, how on earth could she *say* them?!

Vanessa was not the only one having trouble speaking. Alasdair was having trouble in that area as well. Mayhap because his wife was a subject he didn't allow even his own family to broach? Perhaps. And yet, oddly enough, where he forbade Keith and Marette and Kirsta to mention Jenny, even in passing, Alasdair found himself suddenly overwhelmed with the urge to share the story with Vanessa. The desire to do that was as frightening as it was strong.

"Well," she said, her voice nasal from her stuffed nose, "methinks that would answer the question about why ye never had any bairns, eh?"

The words brought back much too vividly his earlier thought. That this woman could have conceived his child. That was not a matter Alasdair wanted to think upon just now. He swiftly changed the subject. "Jenny was but a child when she became my bride, Vanessa. She was but scarcely fourteen summers old."

"That is not so young."

"Mayhap not for you, or the women you are familiar with, but it was young for her." He sighed, reluctant to remember, yet unable to stop. "Jenny was . . . I don't know how to describe her. To say she was small and fragile sounds, well, inadequate. She was more than that. She was . . ." He shrugged when words failed him.

Vanessa stiffened when a sharp pang of dislike for Jennifer Gray arrowed hotly through her. It was an unreasonably strong reaction, and yet one she couldn't seem to control. While she'd heard talk about the woman, she'd never actually met The Devil's wife. Therefore, she had no good reason to dislike her.

Yet she did. She disliked Jennifer Gray intensely. How very peculiar!

It was Vanessa's turn to change the subject, for she'd suddenly become uncomfortable with the discussion. She refused to ask herself why; truly, she did not want to know. "Is the blanket dry yet, do ye think?"

Alasdair shrugged absently, and not for the first time did Vanessa berate herself for broaching the subject of the man's wife. Ooch! but would she never learn to control her curiosity and keep her mouth shut?!

She sighed and, as reluctant as she was to draw away from the warmth and strength that Alasdair's body offered her, she squirmed off his lap and stood.

A shiver coursed down her spine. She'd not slept long; the fire was still blazing. And yet she felt suddenly cold, suddenly . . . aye, she felt empty. The achiness inside her stemmed from an entirely different source than her fever. An entirely *alarming* source. It could be traced back to the lack of Alasdair's closeness, and the liquid-heat of being wrapped in his strong arms.

She must be sicker than she'd thought for such thoughts to take up so much of her concentration.

She was not, and never had been, a girl given to fancy.

Until she'd crossed paths with The Devil.

Lately, however, 'twould seem she spent a goodly amount of time indulging in fantasies—hot, wild fantasies—about *him!* More than would be considered safe. And surely more than were appropriate, considering their situation.

Their situation. Ah, now that was something else Vanessa didn't dare contemplate too closely, for fear of what she'd discover.

She cast the stallion a brief, critical glance, then crossed to the fire. The cramped muscles in her legs and back ached a protest when she bent and retrieved the blanket. Straightening, her eyes lifted, and locked with contemplative silver-gray ones.

She felt a bolt of nervousness, as was evident in the way her accent thickened and her voice cracked a wee bit when she reminded him of his promise to go outside while she disrobed. "Now, dinna be telling me ye've changed ye mind," she warned when he frowned at her. "The *only* admirable rumor I've heard tell about any Gray is that they be men of their word."

Alasdair's gaze volleyed between the window—which rattled with the cold, wet rain and wind that pelted it from without—and Vanessa, whose expression said she was stubbornly determined to send him outside in such foul weather.

"My 'word,'" he replied evenly, "was given in jest."

Her stare remained level, as did her tone. "Mayhap, but 'twas *not* taken as such. Ye promised me privacy, Devil, and I'll see ye uphold that promise."

His scowl deepened. "'Tis raining quite fiercely."

She smiled.

He tried again. "'Tis bitter cold, too. And windy."

"Aye," she agreed with a shrug. The effect was ruined by a sneeze and sniffle, but Vanessa cared not. She had the man by his pride, and sick or no, she was enjoying herself. For once, she had the upper hand, and she'd not relinquish it easily! Her gaze strayed to the window. "Methinks 'twould have been better had you thought on that *before* ye made ye promise. 'Tis too late now, though. Do ye not agree?"

"Promise or no, I'll not go outside in this storm," Alasdair growled, "and that's that. Don't look at me in such a way, Vanessa. I mean it. I'll *not* be going outside in such foul weather without a *very* good reason."

Vanessa's smile broadened.

It was no longer merely raining. The storm had arrived in full force, and the rain poured from the sky like a sheet of wet ice.

The drops pounded on Alasdair's already saturated head, and actually stung when they hit his face. His thick leather jack repelled only a portion of the moisture. A very *small* portion. Rain still slipped beneath the collar, and dripped icy paths down his chest and spine.

His trews were plastered wetly to his legs, and his feet squished inside his boots from all the rain that had tunneled down his legs and crept inside of them. If he had to guess, he would say a good inch of water now resided in the bottom of each boot.

With an impatient sigh, he leaned back against the timbered wall of the shack, inside of which Vanessa was now undressing. Or at least that's what she was supposed to be doing. He didn't dare spy on her through the window to find out. She was taking her bloody sweet time about it, too! He'd been outside in this devilish weather for no less than ten minutes, waiting for her to signal that she was done. The signal had yet to be given, and with each moment he waited, the muscles in Alasdair's jaw bunched a little harder.

The wind whipped at his wet hair, and he squinted when the wet ends stung his eyes and slapped wetly against his cheek and forehead. Another minute. That was all the time she had left. After that, he was going in there, damn it, and to hell with the consequences! If he stayed out here much longer, she was not the only one who would be sick!

One minute stretched into two.

Two minutes stretched into four.

A shiver rippled over Alasdair's shoulders, and shuddered like a drop of melting snow down his spine. What on earth was she doing in there?!

He didn't know, but he was going to find out. He hadn't wanted to leave the dryness of the shack in the first place, but her repeated digs at the value of a Gray's word had finally made him feel honor-bound to do so—with great reluctance.

Still, enough was enough. She'd only to strip out of her wet clothes and wrap herself in that—gulp—enviably warm, dry blanket. Surely she'd completed the task by now. How long could it take, after all?!

Unless . . .

The rain blurred his vision when his gaze narrowed. He wouldn't be surprised if she'd finished undressing at least five minutes ago, and was probably now wrapped comfortably in front of the fire, chuckling at his stupidity at staying outside so long. A woman who would tumble him to the floor and bite him . . . aye, he would not be surprised to discover that was exactly what she was doing. The impudent scamp!

Swearing beneath his breath, Alasdair pushed away from the wall and took a step toward the door. The feel of his feet squishing wetly in his boots made him curse more vehemently.

Another step brought him up parallel with the window. In another few seconds he would sorely regret not surrendering to his curiosity and glancing inside.

He cleared the last three steps to the door and, without a thought to knocking, unlatched it and pushed it open. The wind gusted, wrenching the

301

latch from his cold, wet fingers. The door swung inward, and banged loudly against the timbered wall. The stallion snorted in surprise. A startled gasp dragged Alasdair's attention toward the hearth. Rather, to the woman standing in front of it. The very lovely, very *naked* woman!

Like an animal trapped by a sudden, bright light, the way he'd burst into the room froze her in the process of bending to retrieve the blanket spread out over the floor near her feet.

Alasdair's breath whooshed from his lungs, and his heartbeat doubled, throbbing against the cage of his ribs. The firelight played over her bare flesh like liquid gold, making her skin look soft and creamy and oh so inviting and touchable. His hands curled into fists at his sides.

Cold air gushed through the open door, washing over Vanessa and prickling the skin on her arms and legs. She shivered, and felt her nipples pucker. Alasdair's gaze dropped there. And narrowed. His breathing went shallow and ragged.

Swallowing hard, and blushing to the roots of her hair, Vanessa snatched up the blanket and tossed it over her shoulders. The toasty warmth of the covering enveloped her; the heat was minor compared to the hot warmth of Alasdair's gaze.

She felt better now that she was covered somewhat; not as vulnerable, not as weak and feminine.

A toss of her head scattered her dark curls around her face and shoulders as her gaze lifted and meshed with passion-dark blue. "Well? Dinna just stand there." She sighed impatiently when he did just that. "Ooch! mon, *close the door*," she prodded.

He did so by absently hooking his toe around the edge of the door and jerking. The stallion whickered, then fell silent when the door slammed shut. Vanessa did not hear the sound; the beat of her heart, hammering in her ears, blotted it out.

Alasdair's eyes never left hers as he took a stride

forward. His size and strength dwarfed the small abode, made it seem tiny and much too crowded. And warm. Of a sudden, Vanessa felt very, *very* warm. She only *wished* her reaction was from the fire blazing in the hearth, but she knew it wasn't.

He took another step forward. Another. His advance toward her was not threatening. At least, not in the sense of physical danger. It was sensuously threatening, though. Vanessa had seen that look in his eyes enough times to be able to recognize it for what it was. Lust. Passion. Need.

The dark glint in Alasdair Gray's eyes, the muscle that ticked erratically in his cheek, the way his attention kept straying to the folds of the blanket that concealed her breasts from view . . . Aye, Vanessa thought 'twas a very good thing she was standing directly in front of the hearth, for she might have been tempted to take a reciprocal step backward. And that would have been a blow to her pride that she wasn't entirely sure she could sustain at the moment.

"Ye be wet," she said abruptly, submitting to the urge to say something, *anything*, that would break the tension that hung between them like a thick, velvety cloud. Now that she'd said the words, however, she noticed just how true they were. In fact, they'd been a grave understatement.

Alasdair was not merely wet, he was soaked to the skin. She noticed the way his trews clung to his heavily muscled legs like a second skin. Rain rivered down his leather jack, plunking in fat drops to the muddy puddle that was swiftly accumulating on the hard-packed dirt floor around his feet. The wind had whipped at his wet hair, tousling it around his head. Rain-dampened strands curled appealingly against his neck, against his wet brow and cheeks.

Vanessa's fingers curled into a white-knuckled fist around the blanket. The temptation to reach out and smooth back those wet curls was almost too strong to resist. Almost. With effort, she restrained the urge,

303

and wondered at the stab of disappointment that arrowed through her.

Alasdair, on the other hand, felt no need to practice the same self-restraint. The firelight and shadow played over Vanessa's face, making the curve of her cheek look oh so touchable and inviting.

He didn't think twice, but simply reached out and cupped her cheek in the palm of his hand. Her skin was smoother than the most expensive silk, such a sharp contrast to his own roughened flesh. Her fevered heat seeped into his very blood, setting a fire in his veins.

Never had a simple touch affected him so drastically. Never had the rainwater-fresh scent of a woman sent his senses into such a deliriously wonderful tailspin.

Until now.

Until Vanessa Forster.

His gaze dipped to her mouth, and he swallowed hard as he watched the tip of her tongue dart out to moisten her gently parted lips.

Alasdair groaned low and deep in the back of his throat. Before he could give his body the command to do so, he'd angled his head and slanted his mouth over hers, greedy for a taste. Just one, he promised himself, to appease his thirst for her.

Damn, but he should have known better.

The second he felt her lips shiver under his, Alasdair knew he would never be satisfied with one kiss, one taste. Not with this woman. Not now, mayhap not ever.

His appetite for Vanessa Forster was ravenous; he would be appeased by nothing less than total surrender of . . . aye, of her body *and* her soul!

Chapter Sixteen

His lips felt delightfully cool against Vanessa's fever-warmed ones, his arms hard and strong as he wrapped her in his embrace, pulling her closer. Then closer still.

They met thigh to thigh, hip to hip, mouth to mouth.

When his tongue stroked hungrily at her lips, Vanessa did not hesitate, but flowered open for him. The sensuous thrusts and parries of his tongue mating with hers was thrilling, his taste more intoxicating than the most potent Scots whiskey.

Her chills, aches, fatigue — aye, even the knowledge of his betrayal, which had pricked her like a knife — all of it melted away, forgotten to the magic of his kiss, to the feel of his body pressing, *straining*, against her.

Her fists loosened, releasing the blanket; Alasdair's strong arms encircled her; his chest, pressed against hers, kept the covering in place.

Her hands opened, and her palms ran up over the wet leather of his jack. Higher. With the tips of her fingers, she worshipped the impressive broadness of his shoulders, her open palms sandwiched the planes of his face. The ends of his hair were heavy with rain, wetting her fingers as she tunneled them through the moist, silky strands. She cupped his head and rose on tiptoe, returning his kiss with a hunger that matched if not exceeded his own.

The whicker of the stallion and the sound of flames snapping in the hearth were but vague whispers compared to the soughing of their equally swift, equally ragged breaths.

Only hours before, this man had taught her the true meaning of passion and desire. The knowledge was lethal, for it meant Vanessa now knew exactly what wondrous sensations he could furnish with just a gaze, a touch, a kiss. And oh, how she yearned to feel those heady sensations again!

She was hot, burning up, but this time her condition did not emanate from her ill health. Oh, no, 'twas not that. It was desire, pure and raw, that pumped through her veins and made her heart stammer, that caused her spine to arch until her breasts were crushed against the solid wall of his chest.

She needed to feel more of him, *all* of him. Now! Her body cried out for his touch, for his possession, with a strength that was too strong to ignore or deny. Truth be known, she wished to do neither. The need to feel his naked flesh against hers, to become one with him again, to have him take her to heights that only he could, raged inside her.

She fisted his wet hair and pulled him closer still, strained toward him, intensified the kiss. Her knees had liquefied when his lips had first claimed hers; only the strength of his embrace kept her erect.

But not for long.

Vanessa was unaware of the instant he bent and lowered them both to the floor. One moment she was standing, then the next thing she knew, the hard-packed dirt floor was pressing against her back. And Alasdair's luxuriously muscled body was blanketing the front of her. Ooch! but it was a heady combination.

He eased the intimacy of the kiss to taste her full lower lip, even as he shifted so most of his weight was supported by the floor. His left leg draped her thighs, his knee dimpling the ground next to her hip.

At some point, the folds of the blanket had parted; the cloth now puddled around the sides of Vanessa's body, leaving her naked and exposed. His leather jack felt incredibly cool and wet against the burning flesh of her breasts and stomach.

Her hands slipped down, over his shoulders, down his back. Her chin tipped up when he sipped his way over her jaw.

"I want you," he whispered huskily, then nibbled the sensitive curl of her earlobe until she shivered.

"Aye," she agreed, and hoped the way her body arched up into his, the way her fingers fisted his jack and her arms tightened, pulling him closer, as though she wanted to melt right through his wet clothes, right into his skin, showed how much she also wanted him.

It did. But Alasdair required more. He wanted, *needed*, to hear the words. "Tell me," he urged, his voice harsh and ragged. "Tell me you want me, Vanessa. All of me."

She sneezed, sniffled, then nodded. "Aye, I do. Can ye not tell? I want ye. I need ye. I—Make love to me, Alasdair. Now. Please, mon. Afore I . . ."

"Before you . . . what?"

Her sigh was long and tortured. "Afore I remember that which I dinna want to think upon right now."

It wasn't the answer Alasdair wanted—it hinted at a dark meaning that he couldn't begin to understand—yet he decided he would settle for it. At least for now. What mattered was that she'd said she wanted him, needed him; the knowledge cut through Alasdair like a knife, sharpening his desire until it was a physical ache inside him.

Her body was a perfect cushion beneath him. The heat of her melted away his chill, and sparked his passion until it burned like wildfire inside of him.

With a groan, Alasdair levered himself up and away from her. He stripped off the jack and tossed it aside, then tugged the wet tunic up and over his head. The garment soon followed in the jack's wake; both were forgotten long before they fell into a wrinkled pile upon the floor.

He kneeled on the dirt floor beside her, his gaze drinking in the sight of her naked body. Lord, she was beautiful! So perfectly formed. Her breasts were firm and the rosy nipples temptingly pearled. His hands clamped into fists as his attention trailed over the narrow tightness of her stomach. Lower. Setting finally on the nest of dark, springy curls between her legs.

She moaned, and reached to snatch up the blanket.

"Nay, do not hide from me, wench," Alasdair growled. He reached out and shackled her wrists in his hands, pinning them to the floor on either side of her head. The movement caused him to arch over her, and the dark hairs pelting his chest grazed her sensitive nipples.

She moaned.

He shivered, shifted, and coaxed her legs open with his knee. She offered no resistance. With a sigh, he settled his hips between her thighs. Even through his rain-dampened trews he could feel the moist, inviting heat of her pressing hungrily against the long, hard core of his need.

Her legs lifted, wrapping around his hips, locking him in place, and Alasdair suddenly found it impossible to remember that she was the same imp who'd invaded his keep, who'd knocked him to the floor of the vault and bitten his hand, who'd stubbornly defied him at every turn.

Desire burned away caution, until the fact that she was a Forster, his enemy, mattered to Alasdair not at all. She wanted him equally as badly as he wanted her. The way her spine arched and she strained against him told Alasdair that. For now, her desire was more than enough. Lord knew, it was much more than he'd bargained for!

His gaze lifted, and he saw that she'd shut her eyes. Her thick black lashes flickered against her cheek. Her color was high. From passion, fever, or both? He didn't know, and when his gaze dipped, he found he didn't care.

Her breasts rose and fell with her every ragged breath. Her nipples were temptingly rigid, glistening a mouth-watering shade of rosy pink in the flickering firelight. Alasdair swallowed hard, even as he arched over her, angled his head, and suckled one into his mouth.

The sensation that bolted through Vanessa was so intense that her back arched up off the floor. A moan echoed in her ears; it was too low and harsh to be recognizable as her own.

Alasdair levered himself up on one elbow. His free hand skimmed her stomach — her flesh trembled under his touch — and rose. Slowly. Higher. He hesitated for a beat, then gently cupped her breast in his palm. The combination of the firm, round feel of her nestled in his palm and the sharp, rainwater-sweet taste of her on his tongue was enough to make him dizzy with desire.

He sighed, and his warm breath poured over her skin like a hot summer breeze. Vanessa's chin tipped up, and she arched her back, moaning when he suckled even more of her breast into the hot, moist recess of his mouth. Her palms cupped his head, holding him to her.

His tongue laved her nipple, circling, making it so rigid it ached. His teeth nibbled, causing a sharp sensation to shoot through her. The sensation spiraled downward, tugging in that secret place between her legs.

She wanted to say something, anything, wanted to tell Alasdair how very wonderful he was making her feel. But she couldn't. Mere words seemed inadequate to describe the sensations raging inside her. Then, too, she would have needed a voice for that, and hers had abruptly deserted her. All she could manage was a watery sniffle.

It wasn't possible to think beyond the way Alasdair's mouth felt on her breasts, or the way she would gladly die to keep him this way, doing this, forever if she could.

Alasdair swallowed hard, trapping a groan in his throat. She tasted so good. Wonderful. The way she arched up beneath him, the way her hands held his head so his mouth couldn't leave her breast . . . dear Lord, her passionate response to him was driving him wild!

He needed to feel more of her. Needed to *taste* more of her. Right now.

She whimpered softly when his mouth left her breast. Her fingers tightened in his hair, making the roots of it burn against his scalp when she tried to coax him back.

It took all of Alasdair's willpower not to capitulate. His tongue stroked the line of her ribs. Downward.

She trembled and, as though she sensed his destination, her fingers relaxed and her hands slipped down to his shoulders. Her fingers curled inward, her nails biting into his skin as he sipped his way over her flat, tight stomach.

Lower.

Her womanly scent filled his nostrils, made his head spin. It was Alasdair's turn to tremble, and tremble he did as his mouth skimmed the nest of dark, tight curls.

Her legs were closed to him. He tried nudging them apart with his chin. When they did not open, but instead stiffened beneath him, he hesitated and glanced upward.

Vanessa's eyes snapped open, and she glanced down.

"Wh-what are ye doing?" Oh, but the crack in her voice was humiliating. Yet she couldn't help it. She levered herself up on her elbows, and her breath

310

clogged in her throat when she saw the way she needed to look down the slender length of her naked body in order to meet his gaze.

Seeing Alasdair there, his handsome face so close to . . . Well, the pose was truly arousing!

Oh, aye, she found the unspoken threat of what he was about to do very, *very* exciting.

"I'm making love to you," he said finally, and the heat of his breath poured over her, melting what little resistance she'd clung to. "If you'd rather I not, just say the word and I will stop."

"Nay!" She felt her cheeks heat when she heard the vehemence in her reply.

Vanessa's embarrassment faded a wee bit when Alasdair smiled up at her. Her heart stammered beneath her breasts. Ooch! but what a smile the man had! More special in that it was so infrequent. In a thousand years, she would never grow weary of seeing it.

Of its own volition, her hand reached down and cupped his cheek. The dark whiskers shadowing his jaw and chin scratched at her palm and the sensitive inner flesh of her wrist. 'Twas not the unpleasant sensation it should have been. She sniffled, cleared her throat, and repeated much more calmly, "Nay, dinna stop. Please."

His smile melted as his expression grew serious. His eyes sparkled a lusty shade of blue in the firelight. "Then open your legs for me, Vanessa. Let me love you."

She shook her head. "That isna the way a man l-loves a woman," she said; yet her voice lacked conviction. "Is it?"

"Aye. 'Tis one of the ways. If . . ."

"If what?" she prodded when he hesitated.

Judging by the way his jaw hardened, the words he settled on were not the ones his mind had originally chosen. "If he wants to. And *if* the lady consents. Do you consent, Vanessa?"

311

"I—I dinna know if I do or not."

"Nay?" One corner of his lips tugged up in a grin that melted her heart. "Then mayhap the lady needs convincing?"

Her breath shivered into her lungs when he stroked the curve of his chin over her pelvis. If she'd thought the sensations that raged through her when he'd suckled her breast were strong, they were naught compared to the bolt of desire that thundered through her now!

Her eyelids thickened and her chin notched up. The tips of her hair swayed against her shoulder blades. As though from a distance, she noticed the scratchy pressure of her elbows digging into the hard dirt floor. The core of her concentration remained rooted on Alasdair, on the place where his chin rested so sensuously on her.

Her eyes shimmered a deep shade of passion-darkened green, her gaze never leaving his as, huskily, she replied, "Aye, mayhap she does."

The ends of his hair fell over his shoulders, tickling the tops of her thighs when he gave her the barest of nods. The gesture was almost courtly. Almost. For there was nothing at all mannerly about the way he shifted his weight to his knees, until they flanked either side of her own, then rested his palms atop the floor on either side of her hip and . . .

In her entire life, Vanessa had never whimpered. Although Dugald would no doubt argue the fact, she was sure she'd never made a sound even similar when she was bairn. In her mind 'twas a simpering, undignified noise reserved solely for very weak women— like those of the Sassenach ilk. Therefore, it came as a shock when she felt a whimper bubble up in her throat, heard it pour from her lips. Even worse than having made the sound was knowing that she couldn't have stopped herself from doing it if she'd tried.

And she could not have tried. She would have needed a logical thought to accomplish such a tremendous feat, and she abruptly had none. As it was, thoughts of any nature scattered like snow in a fierce Highland blizzard when she felt the heat of Alasdair's breath wash over her, down there . . . only a second before his chin again nudged the creamy ridge where her thighs met.

This time, Vanessa offered no opposition. Indeed, she had none *to* offer. Her legs, her knees most especially, felt watery, as did any need she may have felt to resist. His intention was clear, and she had to admit, he'd sparked her curiosity. She'd no idea a man could love a woman this way. She'd not even heard *whispers* of such an intimacy! Yet, now that she knew it existed, she had to admit something else as well; that she wanted to experience it. Now. With Alasdair.

He nuzzled his head between her legs, and Vanessa's breath caught when his whiskers scraped the tender insides of her thighs. Her skin burned, but it wasn't an unpleasant feeling. Oh, nay, not at all! 'Twas quite exciting, in fact. Quite —

Oh dear Lord!

Vanessa's mind went blank when she felt him drape her legs over his shoulders. He repositioned himself and . . .

The first stroke of his tongue shivered through her like a bolt of lightning. Her elbows buckled, and she collapsed breathlessly back to the floor. The blood pumping hot and fast through her veins felt like fire. The fever had made her hot. Alasdair Gray's mouth made her hotter still.

Sweet Saint Andrews, why had no one ever told her about *this?!* While she'd known the basics of what happened between a man and a woman — such information could not be avoided when one had older brothers — she'd never known, never *imagined* that a man's mouth, his tongue, could . . .

Ooch! but 'twas not just his tongue causing her such sweet pleasure, was it? Nay, 'twas not! For, even as the thought had drifted through her mind, she felt the hot, intimate intrusion of his finger as well.

He stroked her until she burned and, aye, humiliating though it was to admit, she whimpered now as well. And just when the pressure built, threatened to peak, until she thought she could not stand it another second of it, he stopped.

Waited until she'd caught her breath and her passion cooled just a sliver.

Then started anew.

Her fingers entwined in his hair, fisting handfuls of the silky black strands in her moist palms. Beads of sweat that were formed by nothing so simple as the breaking of her fever dotted her brow and upper lip. Indeed, it felt as though her fever—the one this man's mouth and hands had sparked inside her—was blazing out of control.

Was he trying to drive her insane?! 'Twould seem so! For surely no one could ache as badly as she did—*for him, now!*—and live through it.

And yet Alasdair proved to her time and again that such blissful madness was indeed possible. He brought her to the brink of pleasure time and again, but always stopped just shy of letting her soar.

Vanessa twisted her head back and forth, and moaned her frustration. She felt him smile against her. 'Twas a most exciting feeling! Her voice sounded rough and scratchy, even to her own ears, when she whispered breathlessly, "Please. Ooch! mon, ye torture me so."

"Nay, m'lady, I torture us both," he replied as he shifted and slowly, slowly, sipped sensuously up her body. Over her stomach. Over the indentations of her ribs. Higher.

He paused at her breasts, lavishing each achingly erect nipple with moist, hot strokes of his tongue. Vanessa writhed beneath him and, her hands still cupping his scalp, urged him higher still.

He kissed his way up her neck, nibbled his way over the delicate line of her jaw, the crest of her chin, the curve of her cheek, down the pert length of her nose.

Then, finally, when she thought she could stand the wanting no more, he slanted his lips over hers. His kiss was hard and deep and draining.

Vanessa groaned, and returned his kiss with an unbridled passion that astounded her. His earthy scent filled her nostrils even as the taste of him stung her tongue and made her dizzy — for, combined with his own, thoroughly unique flavor was the taste of herself.

"Now," she rasped against his mouth. "Please, mon, *now*. I canna take much more of this!" Her arms wrapped about his neck, holding him close as she arched her hips beseechingly beneath him, accentuating the demand.

How Alasdair had held his passion in check this long was beyond him. The taste of her was still sharp on his tongue. Her womanly scent still filled his senses, made his head spin, made the part of him that was intricately male harden and throb with a need that would have staggered him had he been standing.

The second he felt her wrap her firm, silky legs around his hips, felt her arch up into him, grinding against the very core of his need until he had to bite back a groan, Alasdair knew he was lost.

The very tip of him pressed against her, and he could feel her beckoning heat. Damn it, he simply *could not* wait a second longer. He had to have her, *all* of her, and he had to have her *now!*

His tongue swirled inside her mouth, mating with hers. He reached down and pulled himself free of his trews. His hips thrust forward. In one breathtakingly sure stroke he buried himself fully inside her. She was hot and wet and so damn tight! Never, *never*, had perfection felt so good.

For the length of one throbbing heartbeat, neither of them moved a muscle. Indeed, for a fraction of a second, the sensations that pounded through Alasdair made movement impossible. Then, just when he could stand it no longer, he began to move inside her. Slowly at first—his strokes long and deep and filling—and then more quickly as the pressure within him, within her, began to build.

Vanessa met him thrust for passion-hungry thrust. Her legs tightened around his hips, and her own hips arched as she greedily pulled him in more deeply still.

He filled her, almost withdrew, then filled her again. And again. And again. Until Vanessa's heart was pounding and her breathing was ragged. Her hands were splayed on his shoulders, and her fingers curled inward, her nails digging into him when she felt the first spark of the most exquisite sort of fire begin to throb and burn in the region where their bodies became one.

She didn't want this pleasure to stop, and yet she couldn't tell him that without relinquishing the magic of his kiss. And she would not, *could not*, do that. Not now, perhaps not ever. There was a part of her that never wanted this pleasure to end, yet she was powerless to hold back. His thrusts were driving her wild, and before she knew it, she felt her inner muscles convulse and spasm around the long, achingly hard length of him.

His name whispered past her lips as she felt the first delicious wave of sensation wash over her. Ecstasy, white-hot and sharp, hammered through her veins, burned like liquid fire in her blood, flooded her senses. She clung blindly to Alasdair as she writhed beneath him and rode out a blinding tidal wave of pleasure so exquisite she wished to God it would never end!

Alasdair was but a step behind her. Though he would have liked to hold back, would have liked to be able to bring this woman to climax again and again, he knew the instant she rasped his name that such was not going to be the case. That, and the sweet, sweet throbbing of her body, milked the very life out of him. He was powerless to do aught but ravish her mouth with his own, and wrap his arms around her, holding her closer than he'd ever in his life held a woman, as the violent spasms of his own completion rocked through him.

Chapter Seventeen

Alasdair sighed. He was sitting on the floor, his back braced against the wall. He wore only his trews, yet his chest and brow were beaded with sweat.

His gaze shifted to the fire. Vanessa had fallen asleep almost immediately after they'd made love, curled in the crook of his arm, her head pillowed atop his shoulder. For the longest time, he'd simply lain there enjoying the feel of her. Necessity was the only thing that could make him relinquish such a tiny slice of heaven.

Her sniffling and sneezing, combined with the unnatural heat of her body, had prompted Alasdair to reluctantly brave the horrid weather and go outside to gather more wood. He'd fed the flames until they blazed.

The small room was now bright with the flickering glow of firelight . . . and it was also hotter than hell!

His attention shifted to the woman who lay on the floor, curled up in front of the hearth. The woolen blanket cloaked her from chin to toes, and yet, despite the heat, she lay there shivering pitifully.

An hour ago, she'd begun to cough. Loudly. It was a dry, hacking sound that made the hairs at his nape prickle in alarm.

Bloody hell, he was going to have to do something. *But what?!*

While the storm outside had lessened in severity, a thin film of drizzle continued to fall, and the air had a

318

crisp snap of cold to it. The late-morning sky was a cloud-heavy shade of dreary gray. Were it not for that, Alasdair would have simply gathered Vanessa into his arms like so much firewood and rode hellbent back to Cavnearal. And help.

As it was, he was afraid to bring her out in this weather for fear of worsening her condition. And in the last few hours, her condition had already deteriorated at a disturbing rate.

Alasdair knew he'd made many mistakes in his life, but none of them seemed graver than the mistake he'd made today. *How could he have been so stupid?!*

Oh, aye, making love to her had felt good—Lord, had it ever!—yet at the same time, it had also sapped what little strength she had. He'd an uneasy feeling Vanessa could have used that energy now to fight the fever that was raging through her body.

Alasdair dragged his fingers through his hair and shook his head. Wearily, he pushed to his feet and crossed over to kneel beside her. He stroked her brow with the back of his knuckles. Her skin felt furnace-hot and dry.

Her fever had risen.

Damn it! What was he going to do? What *could* he do?!

He'd soaked her tunic—nay, *his* tunic, since she'd stolen it from his wardrobe—outside in the rain, and every ten minutes or so he'd swabbed her brow with the cold, wet cloth. It hadn't helped.

Unfortunately, he knew not what else he could do. The Grays were a hardy lot, and Alasdair couldn't even remember the last time he'd fallen ill. Nor Keith or Marette. Kirsta was the sickly one in the family, but Alasdair had never had cause to nurse her. One of the servants did that. Lord help him, but he didn't even know *which* servant!

Alasdair's hand lingered on her brow. Vanessa moaned and tipped her chin, unknowingly turning her face up to his touch. The gesture suggested a simple trust in him that Alasdair wasn't at all convinced he'd earned or deserved.

His choice, if there'd ever really been one, was made in that instant—to the feel of Vanessa's too-hot breath pouring over the back of his hand.

He had to get help; he was smart enough to know that his powers stopped shy of knowing how to tend someone as sick as Vanessa had become.

Despite the gruesome weather, he had to bring her home to Cavnearal.

"Gone? Both of them? *Still?!*" Keith glared at his older sister. "When? Where?"

The rain and wind rattling the study windows meshed with the sound of flames snapping in the hearth; both sounds filled the tense silence that stretched between brother and sister.

Marette leisurely smoothed her dark-blue skirt over her lap, rearranging the material so that it draped in elegant folds over the edge of the divan upon which she primly sat. "I've no idea," she said with a shrug. "Nor do I care. I'm sure Alasdair will return shortly. And as for the heathen"—she grinned coldly, secretively—"we're well rid of her, I'd say."

Crossing his arms over his chest, Keith leaned a shoulder against the hard stone wall of the study, his gaze raking his sister from dark head to hem-hidden toe.

As far as he was concerned, Marette looked entirely too pleased with herself. What the devil had she been up to? And did he really need to ask? No, unfortunately, he did not. He knew his sister well; he knew she was gloating right now, preening like a contented cat whose belly was filled with stolen cream.

Keith hoped for Marette's sake that she'd nothing to do with the Forster woman's disappearance. And if she did, that their brother never discovered her duplicity. If Marette had thought being locked in the tower room for a few days was bad, 'twas nothing compared to what Alasdair would do if he ever found out it was his own sister who'd been the one to aid in Vanessa Forster's escape.

"Aye, I've no doubt you'd be happy to see the last of her," Keith replied slowly, evenly. "I've a thought Alasdair would not agree with you, however."

"So? I don't see where that matters now, brother. She's already gone. Like it or not, *agree* with it or not, there's naught Alasdair can do about it."

"Ah, but there is. He can find Vanessa and haul her back here," Keith suggested. His keen gaze did not miss the way his sister stiffened at his answer.

"To what end? We've no need for her."

"Don't we?" He lifted the tankard he'd temporarily forgotten he held to his mouth, regarding his sister from over the dented pewter rim as he swallowed back a goodly portion of ale. He wiped his mouth on the back of his sleeve, before adding, "Have you forgotten so soon about the sizable fine the woman will fetch us?"

Marette's grin returned with feline intensity. "No."

"Then mayhap you've forgotten that Cavnearal is in desperate need of provisions to weather the coming winter? Provisions, I might add, that we'd planned to buy once the Forster settled his debt." Or so Alasdair had told him, and so Keith believed. For himself, Keith never troubled over such trivial matters. He'd no need to; 'twas Alasdair's job.

Marette shook her dark head, and regarded her brother gravely. "You can cease the pretense with me, Keith. The game is over. I know your secret."

It was Keith's turn to stiffen. "Do you?" he asked cautiously. "And, pray tell, what secret is that, sister dear?"

Marette leaned forward ever so slightly and, in a conspiratorial whisper, confided, "The one you and our brother have taken great pains to keep hidden away in the dungeon beneath the vault. In fact, there are *two* such secrets. Aren't there . . . *brother dear?*"

Keith bit back a groan. He didn't need a mirror to

tell him that his face had just drained of color; he could feel the icy pallor of his skin, and knew if he touched his cheek, it would feel as cold as the pane of glass that the wind rattled in its window casing. "How did you — ?"

"That doesn't matter. The fact is, I *do* know that Hugh and Duncan Forster were never released the way Alasdair promised the heathen they would be. And I'm not the only one who knows."

He knew he would regret asking, but he *had* to know. "Who else?"

"Who do you think?" Marette replied cryptically.

The glint of delight in his sister's narrow, blue-gray eyes told Keith all he needed to know. This time he didn't even try to suppress his groan. "You've done some rotten things in your time, Marette, but I don't think Alasdair will ever forgive you for this one. He's going to be furious when he finds out."

"*If* he finds out." She shrugged. "I've no plans to tell him. Do you?"

Keith glared at his sister, horrified. In a proper booming-Gray voice, he bellowed, "Do I *look* daft?!" The second his sister's lips parted to answer, Keith glared her to silence. "He'll not find out from me. But he *will* find out."

"You think it? How so?"

"The . . . er, *heathen,* as you call her. Mark my words, Vanessa will tell him the first chance she gets. At the same time she tries to kill him, most likely."

"Ah, but Alasdair would need catch her first, would he not? Tell me, Keith, what do you think his chance is of doing that?" She held up a slender, long-fingered hand to delay his answer. "Keep in mind that we are talking about the same disreputable heathen who somehow managed to steal into Cavnearal in the dead of night, when men more clever than she have been trying to accomplish the same feat for centuries . . . without a scrap of success, I might add. I wouldn't be at all surprised if the girl was already safely ensconced in Dunnaclard, as we speak. In which case Alasdair would have to go though her entire clan to get to her and, quite frankly, Brother, I can't imagine why he'd trouble himself to do so."

Keith was swiftly losing what little patience he had with his sister. "Marette . . ." he started, his tone low and biting. Before he could finish the thought, however, a guard burst into the study.

"Riders," the burly man said as he hesitated in the doorway.

Keith pushed away from the wall, his gaze locking with the guard's as he asked hopefully, "Alasdair?"

The guard shook his head, and both men ignored Marette's loud sigh of irritation. His gaze never wavered from Keith's as he said the words Keith wanted least to hear. "The Douglas from the east."

"Oh, Lord," Keith said, his words floating on a shakily released breath.

"And," he added, "the Forster from the north. The Forster being the larger of the two forces."

" 'Oh, Lord' indeed," Marette agreed stiffly.

The tone of his sister's voice did not help fortify Keith's resolve. If Marette was concerned, that surely meant there was just cause for concern. Such did not bode well. "Where's Henrick?" he asked weakly, while inwardly hoping and praying that Alasdair's second-in-command was within shouting distance.

He should have known better . . . and did, when the guard shook his head and said, "He's out searching for the wench. As are most of the men. 'Twas m'lord's order."

"Well?" Marette asked after a long, tense moment had slipped past. "What are you going to do, Brother?"

"Me?" Keith squeaked.

Marette nodded. "Aye, Keith, *you*. Who else? Alasdair and Henrick are out searching for the heathen. Indeed, 'twould seem almost *all* of the men are out searching for her. The responsibility of action now rests with you."

"But I've never —"

"Mayhap not, but you are about to," she said, cutting him short. The look she sent him indicated it was time Keith assumed control of the situation. "Aren't you?"

Keith's gaze volleyed between his sister and the guard. Both were staring at him, waiting for him to make a decision, give a command. Yet his mind went blank. In all his twenty-two years, he'd never been in charge of Cavnearal. Not even for a minute. That was Alasdair's duty, and Alasdair had always done his duty admirably well.

Alasdair. Keith's churning mind latched onto his brother's name as though it was a sliver of driftwood and he a drowning man. Of course! Why hadn't he thought of it sooner? All he need do was ask himself what Alasdair would do in this situation, and then do it. It was so simple! He felt better already. Well, relatively so, considering the circumstances.

"Gather what men are left," Keith ordered, his strides uncharacteristically long and confident as he crossed the room. "Leave half to guard the keep; the rest come with us."

His gaze locked with the bigger man's, and after but a second of shock, the guard smiled. "We ride?"

Keith nodded briskly. "Aye!"

Alasdair knew something was wrong even before he turned his mount up the steep, twisting dirt path that led to Cavnearal. It was Fenn, who met Alasdair at the gatehouse, that confirmed his suspicions.

Since Alasdair refused to stop, Fenn was forced to jog next to the stallion to impart his news. The old man's knees ached at the jostling pace, and his watery gaze kept straying to the woman his lord held tightly to his chest. That his lord had arrived at the keep bare-chested was shocking enough. That Alasdair's tunic and jack had been surrendered to the wench he cradled in his arms—*a Scots wench!*—was scandalous. Wisely, Fenn made no comment on it.

"Douglas *and* Forster, you say?" Alasdair asked as he

guided his mount toward the quadrangle. His tone was distracted, for Vanessa had moaned and squirmed uncomfortably in his arms. While the air against his bare back was frigid, the unnatural heat Vanessa's body emanated had kept him warm during the journey. Alasdair supposed he should be grateful that, while the sky was still overcast and threatening, at least the icy drizzle had stopped a scant hour before. After he'd already become soaked again, of course.

With his free hand, Alasdair stroked Vanessa's hot, dry brow until she stilled. When they reached the quadrangle, he held her close to his chest, then dismounted and ascended the stone steps leading into the keep two at a time.

Somehow Fenn managed to keep pace with him. He regarded his lord oddly as they burst into the foyer. Alasdair seemed surprisingly unconcerned at the news of two rival clans riding toward Cavnearal. Mayhap Fenn had not made himself clear? He tried again. "The messenger said that, from the look, the whole of Clan Forster is riding this way."

"All right," Alasdair said, and nodded. He ascended the stairs to the upper chambers in the same manner he'd climbed the ones into the keep; two at a time.

Fenn fell back a bit, his knees finally refusing to let him enjoy such a brisk pace. He caught up with Alasdair at the door to his lord's bedchamber.

The door was closed. With the woman in his arms, Fenn realized it would take a bit of fancy maneuvering for his lord to open the door and not drop the wench. He moved to open the door for Alasdair, but before he could take a step, Alasdair had applied the bottom of his booted foot to the thick panel of oak.

It took two solid kicks for the latch to give, and the chamber door to swing open. Before the door even had a chance to smash into the stone wall behind it, Alasdair was inside the chamber and gently placing Vanessa, who whimpered a protest, atop his bed.

Alasdair's attention turned to Fenn.

The old man took a shocked step backward. He'd known Alasdair Gray since The Devil was but a child, yet never had he seen such concern glisten in the young man's steely eyes. Nay, not even when he was facing another, fiercer Border reiver over drawn swords had The Devil ever shown so much as a sliver of concern.

Until now.

"Fetch . . ." Alasdair's jaw bunched hard and his tone grew husky. "Oh, I don't know, someone, *anyone,* who can help this woman. She is deathly ill. Then, I want you to fetch Marette."

"Your sister's not been seen for hours, m'lord."

Alasdair's gaze narrowed furiously, and he bellowed, *"Find her!"*

"A-aye, m' lord," Fenn stammered as he backed clumsily toward the door. Though in his current mood, he had a feeling his lord would welcome the news unfondly, he felt duty bound to add, "What about the Forster? And the Douglas? They—"

Alasdair had already turned his attention back to Vanessa. She was moaning in her sleep, thrashing about. He shook his head and said distractedly, "I care not. Let Keith manage it. I've more important matters to attend right now."

Fenn stared at his lord, his mouth gaping open in shock. Had he heard Alasdair correctly? Surely not! "More important matters than seeing to the safety of Cavnearal?"

Alasdair's answer was spoken through impatiently gritted teeth. "Do you have any idea what will happen to Cavnearal if this woman dies? The Forsters' wrath will spread far and wide, and it will not stop at Carey and Humes's door. Nay, if satisfaction is not immediately forthcoming, they'll take the matter straight to their king, and young Jamie will be forced to act. He and Elizabeth have been wanting to settle these Borders for a while now, and this will give them a prime excuse to do exactly that. By means of a letter of fire and sword."

'Twas that last statement that propelled Fenn to action, for he knew that a letter of fire and sword issued on them would cast them all as outlaws, to be hunted down like dogs and executed by their own countrymen. And all over the life of a small, stubborn Scots woman who'd meant naught but trouble for them from the first!

"I'll get Mildred, m'lord. She'll know how to tend the, er, *lady*," Fenn offered, even as he turned to leave.

"And Marette," Alasdair reminded the old man. "And the boy."

"The boy?"

"Donald, I think his name is."

"Donald?"

"Her brother," Alasdair explained sharply. "Get him before finding Marette. Vanessa's been crying out for him. Maybe his presence can soothe her where mine could not."

"Aye, as you wish, m'lord."

Alasdair watched the old man shake his head, then round the corner before his attention again shifted back to Vanessa.

She looked so small lying atop his bed. So . . . fragile. Her short, wind-tousled dark hair made a sharp contrast to the whiteness of the pillow her head rested atop. The bleached linen matched the shade of her skin: pale with an alarming undertone of sickly gray.

Alasdair sat on the edge of the bed. Even unconscious, she must have sensed his presence, because she tossed onto her right side facing him.

After coughing hard for what felt like an eternity, she called out, her voice hoarse and scratchy from coughing. "Duncan?"

Ah, *Duncan*. That was the boy's name! Alasdair shook his head and, trying to soothe her, stroked her dark hair back from her brow with his palm. Her fever, he noticed, had not risen. Unfortunately, it didn't appear to have come down so much as a degree, either.

"Nay, Vanessa, 'tis not Duncan," Alasdair said softly,

soothingly. Whether she was reacting to the gentleness of his tone, the comfort of his touch, or both, he did not know. For whatever reason, she did quiet a bit.

She opened her eyes and looked at him. Or so Alasdair thought, but could not be entirely sure. Her eyes were a fever-dazed shade of green. Her gaze seemed to stare straight through him, and Alasdair questioned whether or not she actually saw him at all.

"I want" — *cough, cough, sniffle!* — "Duncan. Please."

"Aye, I know you do." A stab of jealousy that she should want Duncan, and not himself, cut through Alasdair. It took great effort to push the unreasonable reaction aside. "He'll be here soon. I promise."

"Nay, Alasdair, I want him now." Her tone was too weak to be demanding, even though he was sure that was the tone she strived for. "Please, go get Duncan. I" — *cough, cough* — "want to see my brother."

Ah, so she *did* know who he was. Alasdair had wondered. "Nay, wench, I'll do no such thing. I've sent someone to fetch him for you. You'll have to be patient and wait, for I'll not leave you alone."

Vanessa frowned, then nodded, closed her eyes, and with a weary sigh, relaxed back against the pillow once more. Truly, she felt too awful to argue. The pounding in her head simply would not abide loud voices, even her own. And she knew that if she were to surrender to temptation and say that which she most wanted to, she *would* say it loudly. Very. She'd a feeling that unladylike bellowing was the only tone of voice a Gray responded well to.

Vanessa was just drifting off to sleep when she heard a soft young voice come from the direction of the doorway. She recognized the speaker immediately. Kirsta. Pity she was too weary to open her eyes and offer the girl a proper greeting.

"What's wrong with her?" Kirsta asked as she hesitated in the doorway.

Alasdair did not bother glancing toward the door, for he also recognized his sister's voice. "Fever."

"Oh. Is she going to die?"

"I don't know."

"I see. Well, 'twould be best if she did, though, wouldn't it?"

That question brought Alasdair's chin up. His steely gaze narrowed, and he glared at his sister from over his shoulder.

Kirsta's blue eyes widened, and her cheeks paled as she took an instinctive step backward, into the sconce-lit corridor.

Alasdair felt a pang of regret. Too often, he saw fear in his young sister's eyes whenever she looked at him. Mayhap he should be used to it by now, but he wasn't. To the best of his knowledge, he'd never given the girl a *reason* to fear him. Yet, fear him she did, and had almost since she was cradling. It confused and annoyed him.

He forced his voice to soften as he turned his gaze back to Vanessa. "You're too young to be wishing death upon another, Kirsta."

"You're wrong about that," Kirsta said, and her voice came a scant distance closer, suggesting to Alasdair that she was once again standing framed in the doorway. "I'm not so young. Why, Jenna Ferguson is but one summer older than me, and 'twould seem her age has not stopped Keith from setting his sights on her."

Alasdair resisted the temptation to bellow his reply on that matter. First, he did not want to awaken Vanessa. Who knew how long her sleep would remain this peaceful? Also, he'd no desire to scare his sister off again. He did that much too frequently as it was. "Keith is too young to know what he wants," Alasdair said evenly. "He is infatuated with the Ferguson girl for now, but 'twill pass."

Kirsta sighed. "Keith is not so young, either, Alasdair," she said, her tone only slightly impatient. "Besides, were you and Jenny not already married when you were his age?"

The last thing Alasdair needed at that moment was to be reminded of his wife. It brought back an image that had been plaguing him for the last few hours, as he'd ridden as fast as he dared with Vanessa's fever-hot body cradled protectively to his bare chest. The image was that of Jenny, running away from him and blindly falling to her death. As if that didn't prick his conscience badly enough, it was intensified by the knowledge that Vanessa, too, had run from him. Now, she also hovered at death's door. If she died, 'twould be his fault. Alasdair knew it, *felt* it. He would have killed her the same way he'd killed Jenny; indirectly, mayhap, but dead was dead, no matter what the cause.

Alasdair wasn't at all sure he could live with that kind of guilt—compounded by two. Surely appeasing his conscience was the *only* reason he was so concerned about Vanessa's welfare. Wasn't it?

Vanessa shivered.

Alasdair scowled, and only now realized there was no fire blazing in the hearth. Bloody hell, how could he be so insensitive?

Cursing beneath his breath, he pushed off the bed and in three angry strides, reached the hearth. Kirsta was talking about Jenna Ferguson, and Alasdair simply did not have the heart to tell his young sister that he wasn't the slightest bit interested in the subject. His mind was having a most difficult time straying away from the very sick woman laying atop his bed.

He'd no more coaxed the wood to flame when a commotion sounded in the hall. Alasdair straightened and turned in one fluid motion. His attention fixed on the door just in time to see Donald—er, *Duncan* Forster—barge into the room.

In his haste to rush to his sister's side, he carelessly brushed Kirsta out of the way. Alasdair's wasn't the only glare that narrowed on the boy; Kirsta's did as well, and if looks could kill, Duncan Forster would be lying on the floor in a pool of his own blood.

Mayhap Kirsta was not the gentle creature she wanted everyone in Cavnearal to believe she was? The thought flickered through Alasdair's mind, but he was never given the chance to form an opinion. Before he could draw another breath, he found himself standing toe to toe with a furious Duncan Forster.

Alasdair had to glance down a goodly distance to meet the boy's glare. He noticed that one of Duncan's eyes was swollen and bruised. That particular wound had come from Alasdair's own hand when he'd questioned the boy about the second entrance to Cavnearal; Duncan had refused to tell him. There was a good-sized knot on the left side of his jaw where one of the guards had punched him. His hair was tousled around his young face, the dark fringe across his forehead almost obscuring the two-inch cut that had already dried to a brownish-red crust on his forehead.

One dark brow slanted high as Alasdair returned Duncan's stare levelly.

"What have ye done to me sister, mon?!" Duncan demanded, his green eyes spitting fire. His cheeks were flushed, and his hands flexed and released fists beside his boyishly lean hips. "So help me, if she dies, ye'll have *me* to deal with, Devil!"

Alasdair declined stating his opinion of the boy's threat. He answered evenly, with more patience than he would ever have given himself credit for possessing, "Vanessa is sick."

"T've no doubt she is . . . sick of being a Gray's prisoner!" Duncan replied hotly.

Kirsta stepped into the chamber, and entered the conversation before Alasdair could say something he would regret come dusk. Her soft voice sounded strained and impatient. " 'Tis no fault of Alasdair's that your sister is sick. She took a chill and has a fever."

"No thanks to any of ye." Duncan shot only a sparing glance at the girl from over his narrow shoulder. His gaze swiftly returned to Alasdair. "Tell me, Devil, were ye trying to kill her, or did ye just get lucky?"

331

The words pricked much too close to the guilt Alasdair was already nursing. His eyes narrowed, and shimmered a cold shade of gray in the glow of firelight. "If you cannot control your emotions, Scot, you will be escorted back to the dungeon. The last thing Vanessa needs right now is to awaken to your shouting. I won't have you upsetting her."

"You won't have?" Duncan's laughter was short and harsh, devoid of humor. "*You* won't have?! I've got news for ye, mon . . . I don't give a fig what ye will or willna have! In fact—"

"That's enough," Kirsta said and, in a show of bravado Alasdair would never have given her credit for possessing, she stepped between him and Duncan, forcing them apart. She was facing the boy, and Alasdair scowled down at the top of her head as she planted her fists on her slender hips and returned Duncan Forster's glare measure for icy measure. "You are upset. That's understandable; the wench is your sister, after all. However, that is no reason for you to barge in here flinging accusations. Lest you forget, with the snap of his fingers"—she snapped her own for emphasis, right under Duncan's nose—"my brother can have his guards drag you forcibly back to the dungeon, and keep you there for the rest of your miserable Scots life. The way I see it, Alasdair is being most generous to let you into this room to begin with."

The sweet smile that curled at the very corners of her mouth took a bit of the sting out of her words. But only a bit.

Kirsta nodded toward the bed, and added sharply, "If you care for your sister at all, and want to help see her through this ordeal, then I suggest you stop ranting at my brother and set about doing something constructive. Yelling will not help Vanessa recover, Duncan. Upsetting her, however, may well have the exact opposite effect. In which case, the blame for her death would then rest solely atop your"—she wrinkled her nose and shrugged as her pale blue gaze raked him—

"unappealingly boyish shoulders."

That Kirsta had wounded the boy's fledgling self-esteem was evident in the blush that warmed Duncan's cheeks, as well as the glare he bestowed upon her. That he saw a large measure of reason in her words was also apparent, for, after a mere beat of hesitation, Duncan cursed in Gaelic and spun on his heel, striding angrily toward the bed.

Alasdair glanced impatiently toward the door. Where was Fenn? He should have found Mildred and brought her here by now. What the devil could be keeping them? Mayhap he should go find the servant himself?

Alasdair took a step toward the door, but stopped when he felt Kirsta's hand on his forearm. It shocked him to realize that this was the first time he could remember Kirsta ever touching him.

"Where are you going?" she asked softly enough so the scrawny Scots boy could not hear her.

He frowned. "To find Mildred. Where else?"

"Where else indeed," Kirsta murmured, regarding him oddly. "Truth to tell, Alasdair, I was thinking 'tis after Keith you should be heading. Mildred will see to the woman. She's nursed me through bouts of fever much worse than this, which makes her more than qualified for the task. Your place is not here."

What Kirsta hadn't said, but what her tone implied, was that Alasdair's place was out in the countryside looking after Cavnearal and its people. As he'd never thought twice about in the past, but had always simply *done.*

Alasdair's thoughts spiraled. Why did the safety of Cavnearal suddenly seem unimportant to him? Such indifference was not like him! Why couldn't he summon up so much as a scrap of concern about the two rival families that were even now riding against his keep? Why did he delude himself by thinking that Keith could handle the situation, when he knew in his heart that his brother could not? And why, *why* did the core of his concentration refuse to budge from the sick woman laying atop his bed?

Alasdair scowled darkly. His thoughts were churning too violently for him to notice the way Kirsta's eyes widened, or the way her fingers trembled before she quickly snatched her hand back.

"If Vanessa dies . . ." Alasdair began huskily, yet for a reason he could not fathom, his mind refused to complete the thought, and his voice trailed off. He wanted to tell Kirsta the same thing he'd told Fenn a few short minutes ago. That if Vanessa died, 'twould mean disaster for Cavnearal, for the Grays.

But he couldn't say that.

Because, deep down, Alasdair recognized the words for what they were: a convenient excuse . . . a lie.

Chapter Eighteen

Vanessa felt as though she'd been trampled by an army of horses. Her head throbbed mightily, and her throat stung whenever she swallowed—though she tried not to swallow too often. The muscles in her arms and legs burned when she so much as *thought* about moving them. Her lungs were congested, which made her rapid, shallow breaths sound raspy and harsh.

Hushed whispers buzzed in her ears, but she was unsure if the sound was a product of her fever-induced imagination, or if people around her were talking.

Where was she? Where was . . . ?

Alasdair.

Oh, God.

Vanessa groaned, the sound low and hoarse and scratchy, when memories of their lovemaking washed over her like a wave of liquid heat. She remembered . . .

Everything. Vividly.

Yet, oddly enough, that was *all* she remembered.

Were they still in the hunting shack? Was Alasdair—and the dratted horse she had *told him* to leave outside—still here with her? Or had The Devil realized his mistake in making love to her again and left just as soon as she'd drifted off?

The barest hint of a frown creased her brow. She recalled having fallen asleep. Vaguely. More, she remembered the way Alasdair had rolled onto his back, his strong arms wrapped around her naked waist as he'd effortlessly hauled her relaxed and oh so satiated body with him. She'd ended up with her front cushioned against his. His chest and hips had made the hardest, warmest, most wonderful mattress she'd ever had the pleasure of sleeping upon.

And sleep she had. Deeply. Dreamlessly. Unnaturally so, she realized with a start.

Her lashes flickered against her cheek when she tried to open her eyes. What should have been a bairnishly simple task took an inordinate amount of concentration. The insides of her eyelids felt as though they'd been scrubbed with sand; they stung and watered as she managed to pry them open just a crack.

The room was awash with firelight. Vanessa moaned when the flickering orange glow pierced her eyes and, like a sharply honed dagger, cut straight through to the base of her aching skull. She closed her eyes and was in the midst of sending up a prayer begging to be released from this agony when she felt something cool stroke over her forehead, her cheek, her jaw, then, finally, her fever-parched lips.

Another moan slipped past her lips; unlike the last, this one was edged with gratitude. Truly, she'd never felt anything as splendid as the cold, wet cloth that was being dragged slowly, slowly over the crest of her chin, down her throat, over her collarbone.

Lower.

She arched into the soothing caress, only to frown — aye, all right, truth be known, she *pouted* — when it hesitated on the upper swell of her breast, then melted away. The muscles in her arms screamed as she instinctively reached out to bring the soothing touch back.

Vanessa realized her mistake in opening her eyes wide only after she'd felt a reciprocal bolt of pain thunder through her head and shiver down her spine. By then it was too late to correct, for the deed was done.

"Duncan?" she asked weakly as she struggled to pull into focus the shape that hovered on the edge of the bed beside her.

"Nay, 'tis not he," a hauntingly familiar, oddly husky voice whispered.

Alasdair, Vanessa thought with a mental sigh, and her eyes drifted shut once more. For some reason, knowing Alasdair was near, knowing 'twas he who swabbed her feverish skin with the wonderfully cool cloth, made her feel a wee bit less miserable. "I saw the dark hair, and"— she winced; even the sound of her own hushed voice made her head pound—"ooch! but me head hurts. I canna see or think straight, mon."

"That's not surprising, since you've been quite sick."

"I've been slightly ill," she corrected weakly.

Alasdair shook his head. Even sick as she was, she still sought to oppose him. Was there no winning with a stubborn-as-all-hell Scot—even if the Scot in question was a *wench?!* His voice lifted a decibel, and his tone sharpened. "If you consider almost dying 'slightly ill,' then, aye, you were slightly ill."

"I did *no*—"

"Aye, kitten, you did. Almost."

Something in his tone—*concern? relief?* . . . *what?*— made Vanessa force her eyes open again. Squinting against the stabbing pain, she dragged Alasdair into focus. He was sitting in one of the short, wide chairs that usually flanked the hearth, but which he had instead pulled up close beside the bed.

It was nighttime, or so the darkness outside the windows at Alasdair's back suggested. The room—his bedchamber, she realized, not the shack she remembered falling asleep in—was lit only by the fire that blazed strongly in the hearth.

Vanessa's first thought was that Alasdair looked ghastly. His inky hair was tousled around his brow and cheeks and neck, as though it had been combed through many times with his fingers. Dark smudges bruised circles under his eyes, beneath his chiseled cheekbones; the shadows of both were accentuated by his unusually pale complexion.

The simple act of a frown made her head pound, as

did the way she forced her gaze to dip. The saffron-yellow material of the tunic that fell from Alasdair's broad shoulders and over his wide chest looked as though he had spent the better part of a fortnight wearing it. How odd, she thought, since the man had always seemed to take care that his appearance was, at the very least, *neat*.

"What happened to ye?" she asked weakly. "Ye look . . . well, truth be known, ye look like the devil."

That comment brought a faint smile to his lips. Though the gesture barely reached his steely gaze. "And well I should, wench, since 'tis precisely who I am."

She rolled her eyes and sighed, inwardly wondering how a faint smile on this man's lips could make her feel a wee bit less miserable. Ooch! but 'twas confusing. "I dinna mean it that way, mon." Her gaze narrowed, again raking him. "Methinks that, looking as ye do, ye'd live up to at least a handful of the rumors I grew up hearing about you." Her voice lowered conspiratorially. " 'Tis said ye eat bairns, ye know."

"Aye, I do." When her green eyes widened, Alasdair chuckled and added, "*Know,* that is. About the rumor."

"Oh," she said, and her horrified expression melted.

They lapsed into an uncomfortable silence, during which Vanessa's gaze strayed wearily over the room. She started in grateful surprise when she saw that another chair had also been dragged over to the bed, this one positioned on the opposite side of Alasdair's. Her heart stammered out a joyful beat when she saw that the second chair was not empty.

"Duncan?" she whispered as her gaze shifted back to Alasdair.

"Shhh," he said. "The boy's exhausted. Let him sleep."

"Aye, but . . . but . . ." Vanessa shook her head, then winced when the pain in her skull throbbed to renewed life. "We need to talk, mon."

"Aye," Alasdair said, his tone and expression sud-

338

denly serious, "we do. But not now. You need to rest, build up your strength. We'll talk in the morning."

Her green eyes narrowed and, despite the pain, she shook her head again. "Nay, we'll talk now."

"Vanessa . . ." Alasdair sighed. It was clear from her tight expression and angry gaze that she was not going to do as he requested. Lord, but the woman was stubborn!

"Ye lied to me," she said, and her matter-of-fact tone invited no denial.

Alasdair, on the other hand, did not intend to deny the accusation. Much as he would rather have postponed this conversation until tomorrow, Vanessa was not going to be denied. He nodded, deciding it was time she knew the truth. "I suppose in your eyes, 'twould seem so."

Out of respect for her aching head, Vanessa did not shout the way she wanted to. Her voice did deepen angrily, though. "Ye told me that me da and brother had been released half a fortnight ago, Devil. They were not. If ye dinna call that a lie, then I dinna know what is!"

"I didn't say that."

"Aye, ye did!"

Alasdair dragged his fingers through his hair, and shook his head. "If you think back, kitten, you will recall that my exact words were: 'Your father and brother took leave of the vault at dawn'."

Without taking her eyes off Alasdair, she nodded at Duncan. "Me brother be right there, Devil. 'Tis obvious they did not do as ye promised."

"Ah, but that's just it, Vanessa. They did." Alasdair sighed. She was not going to like hearing what he had to say, but he felt a need to say it anyway. The deception had, oddly enough, nagged at him greatly this last week, and he found he was actually looking forward to putting an end to it. "When I told you they'd left the vault, I wasn't lying, for leave the vault they most cer-

339

tainly did. What I . . . er, neglected to mention was that their new destination was the dungeon."

"The dungeon?" Vanessa hissed through gritted teeth. She would have loved to bellow her anger at this man, if only her head could stand it. Instead, she let her furious gaze and the angry thickening of her accent do the job for her. "Ooch! but would Carey and Humes not be equally as appalled as I am tae be hearing aboot that! 'Twas bad enough tae know ye lied tae me aboot their leaving, Devil. 'Tis doubly bad to hear where ye've been hiding me kin. Ye should be ashamed of yeself."

The hell of it was, Alasdair *was* feeling ashamed. Just a tad, of course, but ashamed all the same. He scowled darkly. His plan had seemed sound enough at the time of its conception. Bloody hell, it *still* seemed sound! After all, he could hardly have let the two male Forsters go—especially when this female one was so adept at slipping in and out of his keep! What guarantee had he that she wouldn't have escaped the second she was able? That she hadn't was not the point. He'd no way of knowing that at the time. Needless to say, if she'd done that, Alasdair would never have been able to collect the sizable fine owed him. Nay, keeping Hugh and Duncan Forster had been a sound plan. Given the same circumstances, Alasdair knew he would do the same again.

His mistake had been in lying to Vanessa about it. Alasdair realized that only now, as he looked into her fury-darkened green eyes. The kitten he'd likened her to was spitting mad now, and he'd a feeling that, were she stronger, he would even be feeling the sting of her razor-sharp claws.

Alasdair tried to appease his guilt by reminding himself that he hadn't *really* lied to her. Well, not exactly. He'd just not told her the complete truth. It didn't work; her expression still made him feel like a puddle of mud.

After casting him one last, demeaning glare, she forced herself to sit up on the bed, the pillow cushioning her back, and turned her attention to her sleeping brother. Duncan's gangly body was sprawled over the chair. His head was cocked to one side, his cheek cushioned atop his narrow shoulder. His lips were slightly parted, and his breath snored softly in and out of his lungs.

"Vanessa . . ." Alasdair began, only to have the words wilt when she turned the full force of her glare upon him.

"Where is me da?" she snapped. "Still in the dungeon?"

Alasdair nodded. In all his life, he couldn't recall ever feeling as wretched as this woman was making him feel right now. It didn't seem to matter that he felt justified in what he'd done; that Vanessa did not share that opinion wounded him more than he cared to admit. Especially since he knew that . . . bloody hell, she had a right to feel the way she did!

Vanessa sighed. There was a tightness in her throat that did not stem from her illness. Nor did her fever explain why her eyes stung and watered.

"Then this last week . . . offering meself up as yer pledge . . . even when ye—" She'd been about to say "even when ye made love to me," but she found she simply could not push the words past the bitter lump in her throat. She could not think on that now. 'Twould be her undoing.

Her dispirited tone gnawed at Alasdair. He didn't like the way she was making him feel, and yet, try though he did, he couldn't stop feeling as though he'd just kicked her favorite puppy. Indeed, he knew that in her eyes, he'd done worse.

" 'Twas all for naught," she said softly, her voice a harsh whisper. She sniffled, and wiped her nose on the sleeve of the white linen nightrail that she only now realized she was wearing. She hoped Alasdair would attribute her watering eyes and runny nose as part of her illness. She would rather die than have him guess the truth.

341

And the truth was, Vanessa was appallingly close to tears. Oh, the shame! She hurt incredibly, as though someone had just stuck a dagger in her heart and given the blade a vicious twist. It was difficult to tell which hurt worse; the humiliation of having The Devil play her for a fool — *oh, how he and the rest of his family must have laughed over that!* — or the bitter-tasting guilt of knowing she'd not upheld her promise to her mother.

Both cut equally as deeply.

I will not cry, I will not cry, I-will-not-cry! Vanessa chanted the words over and over in her mind, even as she felt the first humiliating tear slip warmly down her cheek.

Alasdair's gaze tracked the full, salty drop as it rounded the delicate curve of her cheek, trailed over her chin, hesitated for a beat, then splashed onto the back of the hands she clasped tightly in her lap.

He'd always had little patience with sobbing women, always found them annoying. And yet, for some reason Vanessa's tears had a completely opposite effect on him. Mayhap that was because she was not sobbing hysterically, the way Marette was wont to do. Nay, Vanessa cried quietly, with silent dignity. And oh, how that made him feel even worse!

Another tear slipped down her cheek. Another. She was quick to wipe them all away on her sleeve, but not so quick that Alasdair didn't see them. And react to them. The sight of her tears tightened the muscles in his gut, spread higher, wrapped around his heart like a steely fist that squeezed unmercifully tight. For the first time in his life, Alasdair found himself ready to give a woman — *this* woman . . . this *Scots* woman! — anything, if only she would stop crying. Her admirably dignified tears were shredding him up on the inside. "Vanessa . . ."

Vanessa sneezed, sniffled, then wiped her nose on her sleeve. Despite the thundering pain in her head, she shook her head briskly. Alasdair's tone was riddled with compassion, and that was the last thing Vanessa wanted from him right now. 'Twould only make her cry all the harder . . . and the fact was, she did not want to be crying at all!

"Ye've disgraced me, Devil," she said softly, and her voice humiliated her even further by cracking pitifully. She swallowed hard and tried to control her tears, but she just didn't have the energy for it. One by one, they fell, splashing on the back of her tightly clenched hands until her skin was moist and warm from them. "I dinna think I can ever forgive ye for that."

"I did only that which I felt had to be done at the time. For the good of Cavnearal."

Vanessa gave an unladylike snort. "So, ye feel yer lies were justified. Is that the way of it?"

"Aye."

"Lies are never justified, mon. Even we 'heathen' Scots ken that. And they be especially *un*justified when they be stealing a person's honor." She turned the full force of her watery gaze on him, and felt a small sliver of satisfaction to see a faint red undertone beneath the bronze of his cheeks.

"If you're referring to me bedding you—"

"Ooch! that isna what I be talking about," she said, quick to cut him short. Making love to this man was not a matter Vanessa felt ready to think on yet, never mind discuss. Nay, not at all! "What I be referring to is me honor. The honor ye stole from me with"—*aaachooo! sniffle, sniffle*—"with yer lies."

"I stole nothing that was not freely given, kitten."

Wish though she could, Vanessa could not deny that. The truth, after all, was apparent to them both. But, while Alasdair was talking about intimacies shared, Vanessa was talking about something else entirely. She coughed, then shook her head. "Ye dinna understand what I be referring to, do ye, Devil?"

Alasdair sighed impatiently. If he'd learned nothing about this woman in the last week, he'd learned that it was futile to push her. Vanessa was stubborn beyond reason; she would explain herself in her own sweet time, in her own sweet way, and nothing he could do or say would speed up the process.

She regarded him levelly. "Did ye know me mother is expecting another bairn shortly?"

"Aye, of course," he said, and frowned. What did Hannah Forster's condition have to do with Vanessa's honor? Drawing in a deep breath, Alasdair sat back in the chair, confident that Vanessa would connect the two vastly — at least in *his* mind — different topics. Eventually. He'd only to wait. Bloody hell, but he hated waiting almost as much as he hated a woman's tears!

"Me mother's lying-in is next week, Devil," she said impatiently. "Unless, of course, she's already had the bairn." Her glare narrowed and pierced him. "If I were ye, I'd be sincerely hoping that she hasna."

Her tone suggested that she'd supplied enough information for Alasdair to make the connection himself now. Alasdair's frown deepened into a scowl. What was the woman talking about?!

Vanessa saw his vague expression, and sighed in frustration. Ooch! but the man could be thick-skulled when he was of a mind to be. Even for a cursed Sassenach! With her fist, she wiped away another tear before it had a chance to fall. "In the past three years, me mother has lost two bairns at birth. 'Tis only natural she'd be concerned about losing this one, too, aye?"

Alasdair regarded her quizzically, his steely gaze suggesting she get to the point.

Vanessa rolled her eyes. It was a pity she was feeling so weak, for if she'd an ounce of energy left in her, she might have surrendered to the urge to smack Alasdair for being so obtuse. Truly, 'twas hard to believe sometimes that this man — who was legended on either side of the Border to be the best strategist both England and Scotland had ever seen, a reiver to be feared! — could not seem to link two extremely obvious thoughts together!

"I think," Alasdair said as he sat forward once more, his elbows cushioned atop his rock-solid thighs, his expression intent, "that you'll need explain yourself a bit more, wench. What does your mother's"—he stumbled upon the word, for such terms were not usually discussed so freely—"lying-in have to do with aught?"

"Me word means a lot to me," she said, and wiped another tear from her eye before it had a chance to fall. "The word of a Forster—*any* Forster—has always been reliable. Until now. Ye've broken a time-honored tradition of trust by lying to me about releasing me da and brother. Me word no longer is good, and that pains me sorely."

Good Lord, she was back to *that* again? As much as Alasdair did not want to bellow, he was finding it extraordinarily difficult to restrain the urge. He wanted to reach down her throat and pull the words out. Why, *why?!* couldn't this woman just state what was on her mind and be done with it? Why did she insist upon talking in riddles that he simply did not understand?! And why did he not, in turn, simply come right out and ask her to clarify her concerns?

That last question prompted Alasdair to ask, after taking two very long, very deep, steadying breaths, "Have I somehow caused you to break a promise to"— he scowled in confusion—"your mother?"

Vanessa's accent thickened with the emotion she was trying so hard to keep locked inside. "Ooch! but ye are a quick one, Devil, tae make the connection so quickly. Aye," she said, and her voice cracked just a wee bit as another tear slipped down her cheek, "I gave me mother a promise. Ye see, Devil, she dinna take the last two losses well, and was understandably scared that she would lose this bairn as well. She wanted me da by her side for the birth, which is only natural, and 'twas promising her I was that he would be. I swore on me sister's grave tae have him home to Dunnaclard in time, and I dinna do it. I failed. Thanks to ye. It pains me sorely tae admit that 'tis the only promise I've ever broken in me life!"

Alasdair took the news like an iron fist connecting

solidly with his midsection. The air whooshed from his lungs as he sat back hard in the chair, his thoughts racing.

If he'd had to say why the two rascals had sneaked into his keep, he would have guessed their reason was naught but to create mischief. Truth be known, in the last week he'd given the matter little thought, preferring instead to simply deal with the results, not the circumstances which had caused it.

Her tearful confession now forced Alasdair to give the matter thought, and he didn't like the conclusions he reached. "Did you never think to tell me that from the start?" he asked and, only out of respect to the sleeping Duncan and Vanessa's illness did he manage to keep his tone to a low, tight timbre.

"Of course not," Vanessa answered instantly. She coughed, then sneezed.

Alasdair sat forward and held out a handkerchief, but she ignored the offer and wiped her nose on her sleeve. He sighed and, dropping the handkerchief to his lap, sat back once more.

Vanessa gazed at him levelly, her green eyes still shiny with unshed tears. "What good would that have done?"

It was getting more difficult by the second not to yell and release some of the anger that was building inside him. He managed to control himself. Somehow.

"Vanessa," he said, and his voice was husky, the angry edge to it tightly leashed, "had I known your reasons, I would have released Hugh immediately. And you and Donald as well."

"Donald?" She frowned in confusion.

Alasdair nodded to the boy who slept on in the chair flanking the opposite side of the bed.

"Duncan," she corrected impatiently.

"Whatever." He shrugged. "The boy's name is not important at the moment. What is, is that you were not honest with me from the outset."

Her gaze narrowed on him. "Methinks ye've got

nerve to be chastising *me* for dishonesty, Devil. Especially after the lies *ye* have told me! Besides, I'm of a mind that had I told ye the truth that first night, ye'd not have believed a word of it."

Alasdair was of a mind that she was probably right about that. He was not, however, of a mind to admit as much. "Ah, but we'll never know, will we? For you did not tell me the truth."

"I did! I told ye I'd come to free me da, and 'twas true. I simply . . ." she sniffled loudly, and grinned just a wee bit, "er, *neglected* to mention me reason, in much the same way ye neglected to mention not freeing him." Sick though she was, there was something very satisfying about being able to throw Alasdair's own words back in his face. Her grin broadened."

"Point acknowledged," he said as, dragging his fingers through his inky hair, he sighed and shook his head. He should have learned by now that, at least where this woman was concerned, there was no winning. Lord, but she could talk circles around him, making him question his normally sound logic and motives. Alasdair didn't like that, not at all. At the same time, he had to admit he admired her for it. 'Twas a rare ability, that. Few could boast of being able to make Alasdair Gray question himself. Yet this woman did exactly that. Constantly.

Vanessa rested back against the pillow. She was starting to feel tired again, and achy. That annoyed her. She'd never had much patience for sickness in others, and she had even less when it came to herself. Unfortunately, her bone-weary body was telling her there was naught that could be done about it.

"This has to stop," Alasdair said and, when she sneezed, then glanced at him quizzically, clarified, "This blasted feud. It has got to stop. Don't look at me that way, Vanessa. I'm quite serious."

"I know. 'Tis *why* I'm looking at ye this way." She shook her head. "Ye be daft to be thinking ye can stop a feud just like that." She snapped her fingers for effect, of which there seemed to be none. Alasdair's eyes glistened, and his expression remained dead serious. "They dinna call them blood feuds for naught, don't ye know?!"

Duncan snored loudly, snagging Alasdair's attention for just a second. When his gaze turned back to Vanessa, his expression was dark and thoughtful. "Why?"

Vanessa waited a beat, and when he did not continue, frowned and asked, "Why . . . what?"

It was Alasdair's turn to look at her as though she should be able to figure out his meaning without explanation. When she didn't, he explained evenly, "Why do our two families feud?"

" 'Tis the way of it." She shrugged, wondering what he was getting at. " 'Tis *always* been the way of it."

"Nay, Vanessa, I'm afraid that's not good enough anymore." Alasdair sat forward, and absently picked up the washcloth from the basin, wringing out the excess water. After a fraction of hesitation, he stroke the cold, wet cloth over her feverish brow. "This feud of ours had to start somewhere. I want to know where. Why."

"It started with a horse," she said matter-of-factly, and at the same time prayed he would not ask her to be more specific.

He didn't. Instead, Alasdair frowned down at her and, equally firmly, said, "I'd heard it was a sword. One that your great-great-grandfather stole from mine."

She winced when she shook her head, the pain in her temples throbbing to life. "Then ye heard only partly right, mon, for 'twas *your* great-great-grandfather who stole a *horse* from mine."

"Why?"

"Why what?"

"Vanessa, think about it. Why would Ian Gray go to the trouble of stealing a horse from Garrick Forster when horses are plentiful?"

"Why would Garrick Forster go to the trouble of stealing a sword from Ian Gray when swords are, and

348

have always been, equally as plentiful?" she countered oh so sweetly.

Alasdair's grin was quick and sure; indeed, it bordered on being arrogantly patronizing. "Simple. He wouldn't."

"Ooch! but he *did*."

"Nay, Vanessa, he did not."

"I beg to differ with ye, Devil."

"Then don't."

"I have to, since ye be wrong."

Their gazes narrowed and warred, their voices tripping over each other.

"Truly, Devil, ye've got the tale all wrong—"

" 'Tis just like a Forster to not know what they are talking about—"

A third voice overrode them both. "Ye both be wrong. The feud started over a blasted woman . . . as feuds are wont to do."

Simultaneously, Alasdair and Vanessa turned the brunt of their anger-darkened gazes on Duncan.

"How do ye know?" Vanessa asked tightly.

Duncan shrugged and sat up straighter in the chair. " 'Tis a well-known rumor, Vanessa."

"So is the one about him"—she nodded at Alasdair—"eating bairns, but we both know there's not a scrap of truth to it."

"We do?" Duncan asked, surprised.

"Aye," Vanessa answered, with more force than she should have, or so said the renewed pounding in her head. "The mon's bark be worse than his bite, Duncan. Ye should know that by now."

"Now wait just a moment—" Alasdair said, only to be cut short by the glare Vanessa leveled upon him.

"Oh, shush, Devil. I be speaking to me brother, not ye. And I'll be thanking ye to stay out of this." Her attention turned back to Duncan. "The mon growls something fierce, Duncan. Oh, aye, I'd be the first to admit that. But 'tis all he does. Why, he's not once hurt me." She frowned, then amended, "Except for the bath, where he near drowned me." She saw her brother's expression cloud with fury, and rushed to add, " 'Twas not his fault, mind ye."

"It wasn't?" both Duncan and Alasdair said in unison.

Vanessa smiled weakly when she found the brunt of both a steely and inquisitive gray gaze drill into her. She shrugged. "Mayhap I pushed ye a wee bit too far, Devil."

"A wee bit?" Alasdair asked, and his tone was low and mocking.

Vanessa's cheeks heated. 'Twas a strange sensation, so seldom did she blush. "Aye, a wee bit," she agreed, unwilling to concede any more than that. As it was, she'd surprised even herself by having admitted that much! 'Twas rare for a Forster to acknowledge making a mistake, no matter how minor.

Alasdair pushed to his feet and crossed to one of the long, rectangular windows carved into the far wall. His gaze was narrow and brooding as he gazed at the Firth. There was no wind today; the water was as calm as a sheet of glass. The mirrorlike surface hugged the side of the boulder, and from this vantage point, he could see a small portion of where the boulder curved sharply, the jagged cliff melting gradually into the narrow dirt road that traced the edge of the coast and, a bit farther, the dense green forest.

The road was not deserted.

As far as the eye could see, the twisting, turning dirt road was littered with men. Forsters, the lot of them. The smoke from their campfire wafted up through the tree branches from a spot cloaked by the forest.

They'd arrived at dusk the previous day, a mere two hours after he and Vanessa had reached Cavneal. The amount of them was staggering; it looked as though the entire clan had ridden against Alasdair's keep, men and women alike, and were even now stationed without. Waiting.

While they'd made no attempt to breach Cavnearal — yet — neither had they given any indication they intended to leave.

Alasdair pinched the bridge of his nose between his middle finger and thumb, trying to rub away the tension he could feel building there. He sighed. Unfortunately, the Forsters gathered outside were only a portion of his current problems. Word had reached him only that morning that Keith and more than half of the men who'd ridden with him were now the reluctant guests of the Douglas.

Also, Alasdair had yet to deal with Marette for her part in Vanessa's escape. At the moment, his sister was again locked in the tower room. This time, Alasdair had put her there for her own safety, rather than as punishment. He'd wanted to thrash the girl within an inch of her miserable life for what she'd done to Vanessa; if not for Marette's interference, Vanessa would never have been able to sneak out of Cavnearal to begin with!

Could things get worse?

Alasdair had an uneasy feeling that, aye, not only *could* they get worse, but they were going to. Soon.

The Forsters would not sit quietly outside Cavnearal forever. Sooner or later, they were going to make a move against the keep and its occupants. The hell of it was, Alasdair had only a skeletal army with which to mount a defense; the rest of his men were with Keith, the lot of whom he'd no doubt were even now warming a cell in the Douglas's dungeon.

His thoughts took an abrupt turn, and a frown creased his brow as he turned his back to the window, his gaze sharpening on Vanessa. "As I said, this feud has to stop."

Duncan looked confused, for the boy had slept through that part of the conversation.

Vanessa, on the other hand, knew exactly what Alasdair referred to. "And how do ye intend to do that?"

"Gradually," Alasdair replied, and one corner of his mouth curved up in a self-assured grin. "Very gradually. Methinks 'twould be best to begin small . . . with the two of us."

Vanessa didn't like the sound of that. She liked even less the roguish glint that sparkled in The Devil's eyes.

Chapter Nineteen

The ground was still wet from yesterday's rain, the road littered with muddy puddles that slurped at the black stallion's hooves as Alasdair guided his mount over the narrow dirt path leading away from Cavnearal. Glancing down and to the right, his gaze settled atop Hugh Forster's dark head.

The Scot's carriage was, as always, ramrod straight and proud. His shoulders were uncompromisingly squared, his chin tipped rebelliously high, his hazel-green eyes aloof, his expression stony and unreadable. 'Twas a stance that Alasdair had seen often . . . in the man's daughter.

Since leaving the keep ten minutes before, Hugh had been mumbling a stream of Gaelic curses beneath his breath. Alasdair knew his mother's legitimacy, or lack thereof, had been assaulted . . . as had his own. Speculating on a Gray's ancestry seemed to be a favorite Forster pastime.

It wasn't until they reached a sharp curve in the road that Alasdair reined in his mount and, resting his wrists atop the saddle pummel, frowned down on Hugh Forster. The Forsters had set up camp a few hundred yards past the bend; Alasdair's ears detected the grumble of dozens of male voices, and the faint whicker of horses.

Hugh must have sensed Alasdair's attention on him, for he seemed oblivious to the fact that he'd just stopped ankle-deep in a cold, muddy puddle as he glanced upward. Hugh's gaze had a goodly distance to travel, too, for both horse and rider were of impressive strength and size.

Their eyes met and locked.

"Ye be a cocky one, aren't ye, Devil?" Hugh said, and there was a glint of admiration in his eyes, a trace of respect in the grin that tugged at one corner of his lips. "Ye know, don't ye, that I've but to yell to bring the full force of me men down upon yer arrogant head." The Scot nodded meaningfully toward the tree-shadowed path they'd just traversed; a path that was glaringly empty.

Alasdair shrugged. He'd a very good reason for being Hugh Forster's sole escort, but it wasn't a reason he cared to share at this time. "You won't," Alasdair said simply.

"Ye think so?" Hugh's laughter was short and harsh; the husky sound seemed to scratch its way out of his barrel chest, and up past his throat.

Alasdair met the Scot's gaze with a level one of his own. "Nay, sir, I *know* so."

The respectful address gave Hugh pause. His eyes narrowed suspiciously. "Then ye dinna know much about a Forster, mon."

"Ah, there you are wrong." A wry grin tugged at Alasdair's lips as he shook his head and sighed. "In the last week, I daresay I've learned more about you Forsters than I ever cared to know."

Hugh smiled with paternal pride. 'Twas obvious he took the words as a compliment. Alasdair was quick to assure the man that they were not. He leaned to the side, his gaze sharpening on Hugh. "Did you know your daughter bit me?"

"Did she now?" Hugh's grin broadened.

"Aye. Right after she toppled me to the floor."

"She did that, too?" Hugh's eyes widened in surprise.

Alasdair nodded.

"Well, I maun admit, the lass has always been a wee bit impulsive. Rash. Headstrong." Hugh sighed and scratched the underside of his darkly bearded chin. "She's a bit . . . er, lad-ish, I guess ye would say."

Alasdair frowned when he was abruptly assailed with a flash image of Vanessa, lying flat on her back on the dirt floor of his hunting shack, her warm, soft, naked body straining into his. The recollection came and went with lightning speed, leaving him breathless, his heart racing. While there was a time when he would have been the first to agree with Hugh, that time had come and gone. Now, *boyish* was the very *last* word Alasdair would have chosen to describe Vanessa Forster!

Sitting up straight in the saddle, Alasdair nodded toward the bend in the road. "Go home, Hugh."

"I'll be going nowhere until ye tell me why ye be releasing me. And after that, I'll be wanting to know why ye are *not* freeing me daughter and son as well."

"Duncan was given the choice of accompanying you back to Dunnaclard. He chose to stay with Vanessa."

Hugh glanced at the younger man shrewdly. "And me stubborn, impulsive, irresponsible . . . er, daughter. Was she given the same choice?"

"Vanessa is sick." Alasdair sighed. "I told you that before we left Cavnearal. While her health is improving, she's still too weak to travel yet."

"And if she was feeling better? Would ye be letting her go then, Devil?"

"No."

Hugh opened his mouth to say something, but Alasdair did not give him the chance. "Vanessa stays at Cavnearal until the fine is paid."

"And when it is, ye shall release her?"

Alasdair's hesitation was telling. He didn't question the odd, stabbing pain he felt in his chest when he nodded and said, "Aye, but only then."

"How do I know ye'll not be changing yer mind when the time comes?"

"A Gray's word is as good as a Forster's."

Something in the way Alasdair's expression hardened, and his steely gaze narrowed, glinting with sincerity in the pinkish-gray, early-morning sunlight, suggested to Hugh that the young man's words were double-edged. The hidden meaning they inflected, however, was not discernible.

The two men stared at each other for a long moment, then Hugh gave a brisk nod.

Feud though the two families had, for over a pair of centuries, both Gray and Forster had always harbored a deep and abiding regard for the other. Mutual respect between feuding families on either side of the Border was not as uncommon as one would expect, considering the violent times.

"Ye take good care of me daughter until I return, Devil," Hugh said, his gaze straight and direct, not the least bit humbled, even though he'd to glance up a good distance to return The Devil's gaze. "If I find out ye've hurt her in any way—"

"I won't."

"Aye, I believe ye won't." Hugh frowned. Hate though he did to admit it, even to himself, he found he really did take Alasdair's word in this matter. The young man would not hurt Vanessa. Hugh felt positive of it. And relieved. Oh, aye, he felt vastly relieved!

"I will return with the fine money posthaste," Hugh said, then spun on his heel. The big man's booted feet squished through mud and puddles as, his carriage proud and straight, he walked toward the bend in the road as though he'd been doing nothing more important than taking an afternoon stroll.

Hugh Forster did not glance back.

Alasdair did not expect him to. It simply wasn't in the man's nature.

The head-to-toe glare the man had given Alasdair the instant before he'd turned and left was also out of character for Hugh. Hugh's eyes had been narrow, his gaze intense as it raked Alasdair. His expression had been hard, uncompromising, as though . . . aye, as though Hugh had known of the intimacies that had transpired between Alasdair and his daughter.

Hugh could guess, but he'd have no way of knowing that, of course. Or would he?

Scowling thoughtfully, Alasdair turned his mount around and began retracing the path back to Cavnearal.

'Twas not uncommon for women captured in a raid to be used in the most elementary fashion. Indeed, 'twas the way of things on this tumultuous Border. But the fact was, Vanessa Forster had *not* been captured in a raid. The wench had freely offered herself as a pledge in her father's place, and therefore would be expected by the March Wardens—who would decide the matter if it were to ever come before them at a Day of Truce—to be treated fairly and with the utmost respect.

His scowl deepened. Alasdair did not think her seduction and subsequent loss of virtue would be considered either.

"If you do not stand aside, I swear to God I'll upend this pitcher of water over your stubborn Scots head."

"A wee lass like yeself? Methinks I'd like to see ye try."

"Is that so? Well, *methinks* I'll do more than *try,* you arrogant little—Step aside, and step aside *now!*"

Alasdair heard the angrily raised voices before he'd breached the stair landing and turned down the corridor leading to his bedchamber. He reached the threshold just in time to see Kirsta toss the entire contents of a pitcher of icy mountain water in Duncan Forster's face.

The boy sputtered in surprise, shaking his saturated head and splattering droplets of water everywhere. "Why ye—!"

"Eeek!" Kirsta stepped lithely out of reach when Duncan made to grab her upper arms. She was, of course, careful not to move too fast, for the wet stone floor was slippery.

A giggle, followed by a cough, followed by a sneeze, followed by a sniffle, followed by yet another giggle drew Alasdair's attention to the bed.

Despite himself, Alasdair had to smile at the sight that greeted him.

Vanessa was lying atop the bed—*his* bed, and God, how that moved Alasdair!—with the covers drawn up to the bridge of her nose, obscuring the lower half of her face. She was peeking over the sheet, her green eyes shining with amusement, her attention fixed upon her thoroughly saturated, thoroughly infuriated brother. "Ooch! Duncan," she said, her tone light, "did I not tell ye to never dare a Gray? These cursed Sassenaches be a maun stubborn lot, don't ye know? They'll always take ye up on it. And do ye one better, if they can."

"Aye, I think I've just learned as much," Duncan said as, with another brisk shake of his head, he caused a spray of more droplets to rain down upon the wet stone floor. His beige tunic clung to his boyishly lean chest and shoulders. His dark hair was plastered wetly to his skull, and his cheeks, forehead, and the very tips of his eyelashes glistened with moisture.

All told, the boy made a most comical sight. Apparently Alasdair was not the only one to think so, for, now that she'd removed herself from harm's reach, Kirsta was indulging in her own fit of giggles.

The sound of his young sister's laughter tickled Alasdair's ears; light, melodic, delightful. It gave him pause. God's truth, he couldn't remember ever hearing Kirsta laugh like that. Or, mayhap he'd simply never taken the time to notice?

Kirsta was usually a gentle, subdued child. Certainly not the sort given to flights of fancy, nor anger so lightning quick and intense that it would prompt her to throw a pitcher of water at someone, then stand back and laugh at her handiwork.

Yet, with his own two eyes, Alasdair had just witnessed his sister do both. It was with great relief that he realized he was not alone in his reaction to a Forster's stubbornness. 'Twould seem Kirsta suffered from the same malady herself.

Vanessa was the first of the trio to spy Alasdair framed in the doorway. Her heart skipped a beat, and the dark hairs that curled at her nape prickled with hot awareness an instant before her eyes drifted past her brother, seeking out Alasdair's.

His smile was heart-stopping. Even more heart-stopping was the way it broadened when their eyes met and held. She couldn't have stopped herself from grinning back if she'd tried . . . and trying was never a consideration.

She lowered the blanket, then nodded to her brother and Kirsta — who had, after sparing Alasdair a brief, curious glance, again commenced glaring hotly at each other.

"Methinks it be in a Forster's and Gray's blood to fight," Vanessa said, her tone amused and . . . oh, aye, mayhap a bit breathless from the sight of Alasdair Gray.

"Nay," Alasdair said as he stepped into the room, " 'tis an acquired skill. One taught from the cradle."

"Ah, but one we've both"—her gaze drifted to Kirsta and Duncan, then back to Alasdair—"er, *all* seem to have mastered well. Would ye not agree, Devil?"

Alasdair's shrug was too light to be casual. "Like any skill, kitten, it can be forgotten if not put into daily practice." His attention shifted to his sister, and he nodded to the puddle that had formed on the cold stone floor circling Duncan Forster's feet. "You do intend to mop that mess up, do you not?"

Instead of blushing and stammering the way she was wont to do in his presence, Kirsta surprised Alasdair by leveling the brunt of her gaze on him and saying tersely, "Nay, why should I? 'Twas the arrogant boy's stubbornness that prompted me throw the water in the first place. I gave him fair warning, Alasdair, but he chose to ignore it. Therefore, it seems only fair that *he* be the one to clean it."

"Yer logic be lacking, wench," Duncan said through gritted, and slightly chattering, teeth. "Of course, 'tis no more than I would expect from a thick-skulled Gray."

Kirsta's chin tipped haughtily high. "And your manners are atrocious. Which, of course, is no more than *I'd* expect from a heathen *Forster.*"

"That does it!" His hands clenching and unclenching at his sides, Duncan took a threatening step toward Kirsta.

Kirsta, in turn, took two instinctive steps to the side and, in yet another move that left Alasdair stunned and confused, she slipped behind him. Using Alasdair's broad back and shoulders as a shield, she peeked out from behind her brother and glared at the advancing Duncan.

Duncan was smart enough to stop in his tracks. Angry though he was, he wasn't so foolish that he would try dodging the infamous Devil to get his hands on the insulting little chit.

Alasdair's attention fixed on Vanessa, who was

360

cautiously watching the events before her. "Do you see what I mean, Vanessa?"

Vanessa had an uneasy feeling she knew exactly what Alasdair was referring to, but she wanted to hear the words all the same. She shook her head. "Nay, Devil. Why don't ye explain it to me?"

"All right. My sister and your brother are, at this very moment, at each other's throats," he said, his tone low and uncharacteristically patient. "Why? For no other reason than a centuries-old blood feud that no one can seem to remember the true origin of."

"Don't be silly, Alasdair," Kirsta said from behind him, her eyes never leaving Duncan. "Everyone knows the feud was started when an arrogant Forster demolished the original Cavnearal—the very first fortress to ever sit atop this boulder."

"Nay, lass," Duncan scoffed. "Ye be wrong. The feud started over a woman."

"Ye both be wrong," Vanessa chimed in from the bed. " 'Twas started over a horse."

"A sword," Alasdair corrected as he reached behind his back and, gently grabbing his sister by the upper arm, hauled Kirsta out from behind him. "Take the boy below and sit him in front of the fire in the hall until he's dried. Fetch him a pair of Keith's trews and a tunic." He examined the saturated Duncan from head to toe. "They'll be a bit big on you, aye, but warm and dry all the same."

"Well?" Alasdair prompted when neither moved.

Kirsta's jaw set in a hard line that was undeniably Gray as she nodded at her brother and, chin held high, spine set rigidly straight, shoulders proudly squared, she marched out of the room. Not once did she glance back to see if Duncan was following her.

'Twas obvious from the boy's expression that he did not want to leave his sister alone with Alasdair. 'Twas equally obvious from Alasdair's that Duncan had no choice in the matter. If the boy did not leave

361

willingly, the glint in Alasdair's steely eyes said he would not hesitate but to pick the boy up, toss him over his shoulder like a sack of oats, and forcibly carry Duncan down to the hall.

In the end, to salvage what little pride he had left after Kirsta's humiliating dousing, Duncan left. He closed the door behind him with a teeth-jarring slam.

Her fever had broken during the night. And yet, Vanessa wondered if she wasn't having a relapse when she felt a wave of heat wash over her as her eyes lifted and connected with Alasdair's.

He took a step toward the bed. Another.

Vanessa's heartbeat doubled, and her throat felt suddenly dry and tight. The spicy male scent of him carried to her even before he reached the side of the bed, and sat on the edge.

His weight made the mattress dip.

Their hips brushed.

Vanessa swallowed hard, and quickly changed position, putting some much-needed distance between them. Ooch, but 'twas simply not possible to think straight when this man was touching her in even the most innocent way!

Alasdair lifted his hand and brushed her forehead with the back of his knuckles. Her skin felt cool and dry. The gesture was intended only to see if the warm red color in her cheeks had been brought about by a recurrence of her fever . . . and yet, even though he ordered himself to do so, he couldn't seem to find the strength to pull his hand away. "This has to stop, kitten."

"Aye," she agreed, and her voice sounded suddenly hoarse and gritty even to her own ears. Was he referring to the feud again, she wondered, or something more basic? More intimate? "H-how do ye suggest we go about that, mon?"

"Simple," he said as, leaning over and toward her,

he rested the open palm of his free hand on the mattress beside her hip. "One of us must swallow our infernal pride, and take the first step toward peace between our families."

"Ye dinna ask for much, do ye?" she said. Though Vanessa tried to make her tone sound sarcastic, she failed; it simply wasn't possible when Alasdair's battle-roughened fingertips were stroking soothing circles against her right temple.

"From you?" he asked, as he leaned toward her a bit more, until their bodies threatened to brush. "I ask for naught."

"But ye just said—"

He halted her words with a kiss, quick and fleeting, then pulled back just far enough for his lips to move warmly against hers when he spoke. "I know what I just said, Vanessa. Now, if you'd be quiet and give me a chance to explain, I can tell you what I have already done to achieve that end."

"Ye?" she asked breathlessly.

"Aye," he answered, equally as breathlessly. "I've released your father. He should be riding toward Dunnaclard as we speak."

His breath felt hot and moist against her face—such a wonderful distraction that it took almost a full minute for the magnitude of his words to sink into her passion-fogged mind. "I . . . ye . . . why . . . ?" She frowned suspiciously up at him. "If ye be lying to me again, Devil, I swear upon me sister's grave that—"

"I'm not."

Vanessa looked at Alasdair, stunned. Heaven help her, she believed him. How could she not? His eyes were sincere, his husky tone low and convincing.

A surge of elation shivered through her. There was a chance—a wee one, aye, but a chance all the same—that her promise to her mother would be upheld yet, and that Hugh Forster would indeed be at his wife's side during the birthing.

Thanks to Alasdair Gray.

Vanessa's reaction was so blindingly intense that she wasn't aware she was going to throw her arms about Alasdair's neck and drag him down atop her for a tight, deep hug until she'd already done it. Even then, she did not regret such impulsiveness.

She turned her head and lavished joyful kisses on his temple, the corner of his eye, his cheek, the bridge of his nose, then, finally, his mouth. 'Twas on the latter that she lingered, for she found herself suddenly unable to draw away from the beckoning warmth of his lips.

"Thank ye," she whispered softly, huskily against his mouth. Unbidden, a tear slipped down her cheek.

Alasdair shifted, and sipped the tear away. It tasted warm and salty on his tongue. "Why are you crying, kitten?"

She slapped him lightly on the side of his head. He had to ask?! "Ooch, mon, because I be happy. Why else?"

"I've pleased you, then?"

Another tear slipped down her cheek. Vanessa's heart pounded when Alasdair also sipped that one away. And the next. "Aye," she said, her voice cracking with emotion as she tightened her arms around his neck, "ye've pleased me greatly, Alasdair."

Her heartfelt admission warmed Alasdair to the core. Dear God, he wondered, when had this happened? When had her joy become his joy? Her pain, his pain? Alasdair didn't know. All he could be certain of was that it made him feel oh so warm and wonderful to make this woman happy. And natural. God help him, it felt so very natural 'twas almost frightening.

His breath felt hot and misty against Vanessa's cheek, his chest delightfully hard and heavy, cushioned atop her own. Against her breasts, she felt each beat of his heart. The rhythm was fast, erratic. It matched her own to bittersweet perfection.

Her senses spiraled. How could this man bring her infinite joy, and yet at the same time, infinite confusion? Why, *why* did she feel a sudden, urgent need to repay in kind Alasdair's generosity in releasing her father?

This feud of ours had to start somewhere, Vanessa. I want to know where. Why.

His words of yesterday echoed in Vanessa's mind, forging questions where, before, there had been none. The blood feud between Forster and Gray simply was — had always been. Why, hating all things Gray had been a tradition in her family for near on two centuries. She'd never thought to examine it.

Until now.

Until Alasdair Gray's kindness had made her open her eyes, and caused a sliver of doubt to creep into her very soul.

Ooch! but 'twas confusing! Alasdair insisted the feud was started over a sword, where she'd always believed 'twas over a horse. Duncan, on the other hand, said 'twas for the love of a woman, while Kirsta insisted it began over the destruction of the first keep to ever sit upon this massive boulder.

Vanessa frowned. If she were to question her parents, her other brothers and sisters, Keith and Marette Gray . . . would she discover as many *other* causes? Her frown deepened. She'd an uneasy feeling that she would.

Indeed, it seemed that the only motive both families could agree upon was that it had started at the hands of the other. Which, of course, could not be true. One of their ancestors had to have started this mess. But which one? Why? And did it really matter at this late date? Nay, it most assuredly did *not!*

Vanessa loosened her arms around Alasdair's

neck. She moistened her suddenly parched lips. The words clogged in her throat, for 'twas against a Forster's nature to say what she was about to say, but Vanessa swallowed hard and forced her lips to form the words. They came out stiffly, but none the less sincerely. "Ye be right, Devil. This fighting has got to stop."

Alasdair blinked hard. Had he heard her correctly? It took almost a minute for him to decide that he had. A drop of hope trickled into his body. "I'm glad you agree, Vanessa."

"I do." She stroked his dark hair back from his brow with her palm. "Ye've taken the first step in freeing me da. I shall take the second."

"You shall?"

She nodded thoughtfully. "Ye asked me once how Duncan and I came to be in yer keep, and I'd not answer ye. I shall answer ye now, and I shall tell ye the truth."

"Vanessa, I did not release Hugh as a ploy to get that information," Alasdair said tightly. In fact, he was insulted she would even think that! "When you told me about your mother, and your promise to her, my conscience would let me do naught else."

"I know," she said softly, breathlessly . . . sincerely. With the pad of her thumb, she smoothed away the scowl that had furrowed between his thick, dark brows. "But when a blood feud goes on so long that neither side can recall its exact origin, then 'tis time the feud should end." Her hand stroked over his brow, opened and cupped the hard, high line of his cheek. "Ye've released me da, Devil, and now, to show me gratitude, I will tell ye the secret way into yer keep."

It was wrong, somehow, in a way Alasdair couldn't begin to understand. "Nay, wench," he said, and shook his head. "There was a time not so long ago when I would have used any means at my disposal to coerce that information from you. That time is no longer." He turned his head and feathered his lips over the sensitive inner flesh of her wrist. Her pulse throbbed strong and steady against his mouth as he whispered hoarsely, "Tell me only that which you want to tell me, Vanessa, and no more."

And that, Vanessa thought, was precisely the problem. She wanted, *needed*, to tell Alasdair . . . well, everything. She wanted there to be no more lies between them, wanted to somehow set the turbulence and violence of the last two centuries to rest at long last, so they could look toward a peaceful future—for both their families.

Vanessa's gaze shifted, focusing on the puddle in the middle of the stone floor, and the way the firelight glinted off the slick wetness.

She was silent for a long, tense moment as she weighed the magnitude of what she was about to divulge against the magnitude of what Alasdair had already done. Trust needed to be forged somewhere, and she'd a feeling Alasdair had been right yesterday when he'd said it must start with the two of them. Absently fingering the laces of his tunic, Vanessa confessed softly, "There be a ladder of grooves cut crudely into the seaward side of this rock. 'Twas those Duncan and I used to invade yer keep."

Alasdair frowned down upon her. Was she serious? Indeed, her tone and expression—both reluctant, but undeniably sincere—suggested that she was. And yet . . ."Vanessa," he said cautiously, "were that true, I'm sure a Gray would have found these . . . er, grooves decades . . . mayhap even centuries ago."

While neither her expression nor her gaze changed, even minutely, both became as stony as her voice. "Are ye calling me a liar?"

Alasdair wisely declined answering that. Instead, he countered her question with a question of his

367

own. "How did you come to hear about these . . . grooves, you say they are?"

"I dinna hear about them."

He waited for her to continue. When she didn't, he prodded her along. "Then how do you know they are there?"

She frowned, and leveled the full force of her gaze on him. "I be here, am I not? What more proof do ye need?"

Alasdair gritted his teeth and resisted the urge to yell, but just barely. "All right, Vanessa, let me phrase this another way. When did you first hear about these grooves?"

"Are ye deaf, mon? I could have sworn I just told ye that I dinna *hear* about them anywhere."

He sucked in a deep, steadying breath, followed quickly by three more. It didn't help. Very calmly, he said through gritted teeth, "Where did you, er, *learn* about them, then?"

"In the Bible."

"The Bible?" he echoed dryly.

"Aye." She frowned, then quickly amended, "Well, nay. Not *in* the Bible, precisely, but on a sheet of parchment tucked into it. 'Twas me great-grand-mother's Bible, ye see, passed down through genera-tions of Forsters, always to the youngest daughter. The eldest daughter," she confided, "received me great-grandmother's cherished brooch — 'tis a price-less heirloom, from what I'm told — whilst the middle daughters received naught."

Alasdair sighed. "Vanessa, what does this have to do with grooves being discovered in Cavnearal's rock?"

"Ooch, mon, have a care. I be getting to that part! Now, where was I? Oh, aye, I remember. Ye see, not so long ago, when Catholicism was banished from me homeland, me mother insisted upon me burning the Bible. 'Twould not go well for us, she

368

said, if the book was discovered, and 'twere determined the Clan Forster still practiced the Old Religion."

"But you didn't do it?"

She sighed heavily. "Alas, I found I could not. Instead, I hid it beneath a loose stone in the hearth in me bedchamber and, well, quite honestly, forgot for the longest time 'twas even there. So it remained . . . until just over a fortnight ago."

"When you resurrected it?"

She grinned at his choice of words, for they seemed most appropriate. "I'd hoped to carry on the family tradition and present the book to Kayla or, should me mother give birth to a lass, of course, and" — her tone grew husky with emotion — "were the child to live."

" 'Tis a noble desire, Vanessa. But, tell me, do you not think your mother would have had a thing or two to say about it when she discovered you'd not carried out her orders in burning the book?"

Judging by the look on her face, 'twas obvious Vanessa had not once considered that. Alasdair chuckled softly. Now why wasn't he surprised? But, of course, he already knew the answer to that. After spending the last nine days in this woman's company, he'd come to realize that, while Vanessa had a plan for seemingly any occasion, those plans were, more times than not, impulsive, with ensuing repercussions rarely given anything more than the barest consideration . . . if that.

Vanessa sneezed, sniffled, then glanced up. Alasdair's face was close enough to hers that the tips of their noses grazed.

She groaned inwardly. Dear Lord, the man was smiling again. Didn't he know how dangerous such a seemingly innocent gesture could be? Hadn't he guessed her thoughts became muddled whenever his eyes twinkled that devilish shade of blue-grey, and

369

when the weathered creases in his tanned face deepened into lines of laughter rather than frowns? Apparently he did not, for as she watched, Alasdair's
smile broadened and, before she could guess his intent, he'd angled his head and his lips slanted over
hers.

His kiss was short and hard and demanding.
When it ended—and, much to her chagrin, Vanessa
devoutly wished it never would!—she was left feeling
breathless and drained and . . . wantonly aching for
more!

At some point, he'd shifted position, and now lay
stretched out on the mattress beside her.

Vanessa was surprised to find that the weight of
him was not burdensome at all. Nay, just the opposite; 'twas unbearably pleasant.

She shifted her gaze to the stone-and-timbered
ceiling—truly, the sight of this man's smile was entirely too distracting. "Kirsta said yer brother's being
held for ransom by the Douglas, and that yer other
sister be locked in the tower room again. Is that
true, Devil?"

"Aye, 'tis."

"Why?"

"Methinks Keith's arrogance once again precluded
his good sense. He was, no doubt, easily picked up
by the Douglas."

"Nay, I was referring to Marette. What hideous
crime did she commit this time, that ye felt a need
to lock her away?"

"She helped you escape. 'Tis crime enough, don't
you agree?"

Vanessa grinned, just a wee bit, despite her resolve not to. "Of course I dinna agree. I was maun
pleased to have her assistance, don't ye know?"

Alasdair stiffened. "Marette's 'assistance' almost
got you killed, wench. You'd do well to remember
that."

Vanessa frowned at the ceiling. If she didn't know better, she'd have sworn she detected a hard edge of concern in Alasdair's voice. She shook her head, deciding she must be mistaken. Why should he care if she lived or died?— Unless, of course, 'twas for the fine her family still owed his—a fine that, now that Hugh Forster had been freed, could only be collected by way of Duncan and herself.

The thought did not sit well with Vanessa. And yet, try though she might, she couldn't banish the idea from her mind. Was the unpaid fine Alasdair's sole cause of concern for her safety? And did it matter so very much if it was?

Aye, it did. For reasons Vanessa was afraid to contemplate too closely, it mattered a great deal.

Alasdair wondered what thoughts had caused that thoughtful frown to pucker between her dark, delicately arched brows. Was the wench planning yet another way to escape him? Had she not figured out yet that he'd no intention of letting her go? Not, he quickly amended, until the fine—which must now go to freeing his brother—was paid in full.

He'd an uneasy feeling, however, that the fine had at some unknown point become nothing more than a subterfuge, a convenient excuse to mask his real reason for wanting to keep this woman in Cavnearal. In his bedchamber. In his *bed*.

"Vanessa," he started, only to have the thought abruptly terminated by a sharp rapping upon his bedchamber door.

Cursing under his breath, Alasdair pushed himself up and off the bed, and crossed to the door. In the time it took him to do that, three more pounding knocks had been delivered upon the thick oak panel.

Since Vanessa had been too ill to worry about preventing her escape, and since Alasdair had spent the better part of two days at her bedside, his presence undoubtedly deterring her from any attempt she might make in that direction, should she find the energy to try, the door had not been barred from without. It opened easily under Alasdair's hand.

Alasdair's steely gaze narrowed on the young guard who stood in the hallway. The guard, in turn, froze in the act of lifting his hand to knock again.

"Y-you've visitors, m'lord," the guard—Harrington, if Vanessa remembered correctly—said, and lowered his arm to his side.

"I wish to see no one." Alasdair made to close the door.

The young guard cleared his throat, and added quickly, "Methinks you'll want to see these two, m'lord. 'Tis Hugh and Dugald Forster. They're waiting in the hall, and say they'll not leave until they've spoken with you."

"Did either say what he wants to speak to me about?"

The young guard shook his head. "I didn't think it was my place to ask."

Alasdair's eyes strayed over his shoulder. Vanessa looked genuinely surprised to hear of his guests' identity. But no more so than Alasdair was himself. Had he not freed Hugh scarcely an hour before? He had. Truly, Alasdair had not expected to see his rival again for at least a fortnight—'twould take no less than that long to gather the coins needed to pay the fine, and free his son and daughter.

So what did Hugh and Dugald Forster want? There was only one way to find out. His attention returned to Harrington, who was regarding him cautiously. Nodding abruptly to Vanessa, Alasdair ordered Harrington to stay with Vanessa until he returned. "Do not, I repeat, do *not* let her out of your sight."

Harrington nodded, but did not move. In the end, Alasdair had to place his palm between the young man's shoulder blades and literally push him into the bedchamber; and even then, the man went reluctantly.

Alasdair slammed the door shut, then, in after-thought, lowered the plank that barred the door into place. It wasn't that he didn't trust Harrington; he did. Vanessa was another matter entirely. If there was a way to escape in the short time he'd not be by her side, she would find it.

And, the simple fact of the matter was, Alasdair was not ready to let the wench go.

Not yet.

Mayhap not ever.

Chapter Twenty

Something was very, very wrong.

Alasdair scowled as his attention shifted from the sporran Hugh Forster had plunked down atop the table with a hearty laugh, to Hugh Forster himself. Then he focused all his attention on Dugald Forster, a man who was Alasdair's junior by a mere two years.

Dugald's size was comparable to his father's. Also like Hugh, the son's dark, shaggy hair was shot with strands of silver, although not to the extent of his sire's. The length, Alasdair noticed, was only slightly shorter than Vanessa's—the ends just long enough to whisk the man's broad shoulders when he shrugged. Dugald's chin was clean-shaven, and his entire face sported a variety of scars in a variety of shapes and sizes. The largest was the one that cut through three others in a crescent just below his left cheekbone.

Apparently all the Forster offspring had inherited Hugh's piercing green eyes, and Dugald was no exception. Right now, those eyes were narrowed shrewdly, glinting with amusement as they met Alasdair's.

" 'Tis all there. Count it if ye dinna believe me." Dugald, who stood on the opposite side of the table, next to his father, pushed the coin-heavy sporran toward Alasdair. "Go on, now. Do it and be done with. We'd like to leave this wretched keep and be home in time for the evening meal."

Alasdair reached forward and picked up the sporran. The muscles in his forearms and biceps bulged with the heaviness of the thing. Either it was filled with coins or with rocks, he decided, for nothing else could have added this much weight to a mid-sized leather purse. His eyes didn't leave Dugald's until he'd unfastened the flap and lifted it.

Alasdair's jaw tightened when he looked down, assessed the shadowy contents at a glance, then closed the flap. He tossed the sporran back on the table with enough force to jostle the two empty pewter mugs sitting atop it.

Hugh appeared to be trying, and failing, to hide his grin. "I believe we had a deal, Devil, did we not? As soon as the fine be paid, Vanessa and Duncan would be released." He nodded his dark head to the sporran, although his attention never left Alasdair. "The fine be paid, Devil. In full."

Aye, Alasdair thought, something was wrong here, and he'd an uneasy feeling he knew exactly what that something was. The fine had been raised too quickly to have been "raised" at all. Obviously, the Forster had enough coin from the start, but, for his own reasons, was turning it over to Alasdair only now.

It was galling to think he'd been played for a fool, but the evidence was indisputable. Hugh Forster had pledged himself instead of paying the fine. But why?

Why else?

Alasdair's scowl deepened when he wondered if Vanessa had been in on her father's plan from the start. He'd like to think she hadn't, and yet . . . "Did you see what you came here to see, Hugh?"

"Aye, Devil, I did," the elder Scot said, his grin widening. "And then some."

375

"Did ye think we Forsters be such paupers that we couldna pay such a measly sum?" Dugald asked.

Alasdair's shrug was too casual to be genuine. "Cavnearal's had a bad year. I'd no reason to think Dunnaclard's was any better."

"And no reason to think we'd not," Hugh added, and his cheerful tone scratched against Alasdair's raw nerves. "Ooch! but Dunnaclard has had a fine year, mon. Our herd be fat with beasties we've . . . er, cultivated from the Gray, the Douglas, and the Graham. Our sheep have yielded more wool this year than that in the last half score combined, and our cows be nice and plump."

"Sounds impressive," Alasdair said dryly. From the corner of his eye, he saw a plump, redheaded serving wench hovering in the doorway.

Alasdair nodded curtly at the two mugs on the table, and his expression suggested she add another while refilling those. She did so quickly, if not a bit nervously, and when she was done, Alasdair directed her to find Oric and tell the guard his presence was requested in the hall. The girl looked relieved to hurry to do her lord's bidding.

"Sit," Alasdair said, gesturing to the bench that flanked the opposite side of the table. He didn't wait for his offer to be carried out, but lifted first one, then the other, heavily muscled leg over the bench and sat down himself. His steely gaze left no room for compromise; that, combined with his stony expression, suggested that nothing would be done until both men did as they'd been directed.

Hugh was the first to comply. After a tension-filled moment had passed, his son followed suit.

"Ye be wasting our time, mon," Dugald grumbled, then lifted his tankard and drank deeply of its foamy contents.

Alasdair wrapped his hands around the pewter

mug, his palms absorbing its metallic coolness. His right elbow brushed the sporran; the contact was an unneeded reminder of its presence. He lifted the tankard to his mouth, but only swallowed a scant mouthful of the yeasty-tasting ale before he lowered the mug back to the scratched tabletop. "Did you know Vanessa has been sick, Hugh?"

"Aye," the man said, and nodded. His piercing green gaze perused Alasdair warily. "She's had the fever, you said, but is improving."

"She is. Slowly."

Dugald's eyes glinted with suspicious green fire. "Ooch, Devil, dinna be telling me tha—"

The glare Hugh sent his son terminated Dugald's tirade in mid-word. The younger Scot stared broodingly down at the foamy contents of his mug. It was obvious from the red undertone in his tanned cheeks that he took exception to being chastised in front of a Gray. 'Twas also clear he would not speak of the embarrassment for the same reason.

"Are ye suggesting we leave that irresponsible, pigheaded, reckless . . . er, daughter of mine here, Devil?"

Alasdair nodded. "Until she's well enough to travel, aye. When that time comes, I will escort her back to Dunnaclard myself."

"Will ye now?" Hugh said. He lifted his tankard, but did not drink. The mug made a perfect shield for his grin. When he again felt his expression was suitably controlled, he set the mug back on the table. "And how long are ye thinking that will take? A fortnight? Twa?"

"Mayhap."

"Longer?" Hugh prodded.

Alasdair shrugged and averted his gaze to the fire that crackled in the huge stone hearth. "Mayhap."

"Hmm." The older Scot tapped his fingers

thoughtfully against the side of his mug. "I dinna like the idea of leaving me daughter here with ye, Devil. Why, that ye've not disgraced her yet is a miracle unto itself, don't ye know? Methinks it best not to tempt fate any longer than is necessary."

It was a good thing Alasdair was not given to blushes or embarrassment, or he might have blanched at the man's words. Had Hugh not yet guessed that he was too late to save his daughter's innocence? Or was he simply trying to make Alasdair squirm by bringing the subject out into the open? Mayhap the man truly *did* think his daughter had spent a fortnight in her rival's castle and come away unravished?

Nay, Hugh Forster was not that naive. The man belonged to these turbulent Borders, just as Alasdair himself did. They both knew the way of things, the traditions, which meant Hugh *had* to know his daughter was no longer a maiden.

Hugh lifted the pewter mug to his lips and glanced toward the fire, but not before Alasdair saw the knowing glint in the Forster's shrewd green eyes.

In that instant, Alasdair knew that Hugh had correctly ascertained what had transpired between himself and the man's daughter. Why Hugh was not demanding restitution, however, was not so clear.

The sound of a throat being cleared snagged Alasdair's attention, and drew it back and to the left, toward the doorway.

Oric's burly form seemed to crowd the arched stone entrance. The man's expression was hateful, his gaze mean — but that was nothing new; 'twas Oric's usual countenance.

Alasdair nodded Oric into the hall. The guard scowled fiercely at the two Forsters, who were seated in Cavneareal's hall as though they belonged there, even as he complied. 'Twas a most galling sight! When Alasdair lifted the sporran and handed it to him, Oric hesitated, then reluctantly hoisted the leather strap over his shoulder.

Alasdair sighed and, thinking about the herds of sheep and cattle that, unlike Dunnaclard, Cavnearal did not have, he said reluctantly, "Bring it to the Douglas, and come back with my brother and whatever men are being held with him."

Oric nodded briskly, awaiting further instructions. When none were forthcoming, he sent a hateful glare at the two Forsters, then spun on his heel and stalked from the room.

The man's heavy footsteps could be heard retreating down the corridor; to Alasdair's ears, they sounded like the gusts of a very cold winter wind pounding at Cavnearal's ice-frosted windows.

"And now, Devil," Dugald said, drawing Alasdair's gaze back to him, "about me sister . . ."

Vanessa tucked her hair behind her ears and shook her head. "Nay, Avery, that makes no sense." She pointed to the elaborately carved marble chess board centered atop the mattress between herself and the young guard, Avery Harrington. More accurately, she pointed to the playing piece that had been exquisitely carved in the shape of a horse and rider in full battle gear. The former was rearing up on its hind quarters, the latter positioned atop the horse, petering in his saddle. Both looked like they'd been frozen in time. "One forward and two to the side. Ooch, mon, but how come only that piece be able to move in such an odd way, when the rest canna?"

Avery gave a long-suffering sigh. "I've already explained, 'tis the rule of the game. Knights move one and to the side. Bishops move diagonally. Castles move in a straight line, vertically or horizontally *only*. Pawns may move ahead one square or two on the first move, and only one on every subsequent move."

"And this one?" Vanessa asked, tapping the tip of her index finger atop the crowned head of the largest piece.

"The king may move only one square at a time, in any direction he chooses. Unless, of course, he castles."

"Castles?"

Avery shook his head. "I'll explain it if this game ever proceeds to that point, and at this rate, I sincerely doubt it will."

"All right." Vanessa shrugged. "What about this one? What does it do?"

"That's the queen. She can move anywhere she bloody well pleases."

Vanessa regarded the young guard thoughtfully. "While the king can still only move one?"

"Aye."

She smiled. "Methinks I like that rule, Avery."

Avery, on the other hand, liked her smile. Truly, 'twas so captivating that, for just a moment, he completely forgot about the chess board and pieces that he'd fetched out of his lord's wardrobe.

He shook his head to clear it, and looked back down at the board. The pieces were neatly set atop their proper black-and-white marble squares, though none had yet been moved. "N-now," he stammered, "should we commence playing the game?"

"Aye. After ye've explained to me why the . . . knight?" She glanced at him quizzically. "Why the knight moves in such an inane fashion."

"I've already told you, 'tis the rule."

" 'Tis an absurd rule. Methinks it should be changed to one that makes more sense."

"And I think that if anyone could do that, kitten, 'twould be you."

That voice did not belong to Avery Harrington!

Vanessa's eyes snapped upward, and met Alasdair's, in the same instant Avery snapped to his feet from where he'd perched himself on the edge of the bed. His movement was too quick, and it jostled the board, toppling some of the pieces over onto the mattress.

"Ooch, Devil, now look what ye've done!" Vanessa gathered up the fallen pieces—they looked like tiny, black-and-white marble soldiers strewn out atop the battlefield of a mattress—and set them back on the board. She couldn't remember their proper order—darn, and Avery had explained it to her so patiently, too!—so instead she simply placed them on any conveniently vacant, black marble square.

The young guard's cheeks were hot with color as he glanced nervously from Alasdair, to the chessboard, to Vanessa, then back to Alasdair. "I—I was helping her pass the time," he explained feebly.

Vanessa's tone, on the other hand, was not cowered. "Dinna look at him so fiercely, Alasdair. Canna ye see he be nervous enough as 'tis'? And who could blame the lad, since ye look ready to bite his head off."

"I gave Harrington orders to—"

"Aye, to not let me out of his sight," Vanessa agreed, and nodded. "I know. And he dinna."

Alasdair drew in a deep, long, steadying breath. Followed quickly by two more. It didn't help. "I did not give him orders to teach you how to play chess."

Vanessa grinned. 'Twas not a wise thing to do, mayhap, but she couldn't resist. "Nor did I hear ye give him orders that he could not."

Alasdair glared at her.

Vanessa glared back, though she continued to grin.

Avery must have sensed this was the perfect moment to retreat, for he glanced at the door and said timidly, "If I'm no longer needed, m'lord . . . ?"

Alasdair did not answer. Avery must have considered that an assent, for he nodded and took his leave of the bedchamber posthaste. He was careful to close the door quietly behind him.

"I see you've acquired an ally," Alasdair said, nodding to the door.

"Avery be a sweet lad," Vanessa admitted, then quickly added, "for a thick-skulled Sassenach."

Although it went against his nature to do so, Alasdair couldn't resist returning her grin. "Be careful, wench, for that is starting to sound like an endearment."

Aye, more so than he could imagine! Vanessa realized that, at some point, the words had stopped tasting like an insult on her tongue. She picked up the queen and absently ran the pad of her index finger over the delicate grooves that comprised the piece's crown. The marble felt cool and smooth beneath her fingertips. "Is me da gone?"

"Nay," he answered, his tone and expression suddenly sober.

"Dinna tell me ye've taken him prisoner again. And me brother Dugald as well."

"All right, I won't."

She glanced up, surprised. While neither Alasdair's expression nor his gaze changed so much as a fraction, Vanessa somehow knew that he hadn't. With a frown, she wondered when she'd come to know this man so well?! "When does Duncan leave?"

"Immediately."

She nodded, knowing she would sorely miss her

382

brother's company, but knowing also that it was time the lad went home. Vanessa refused to ask herself why she felt so relieved to know 'twould be Duncan returning home this day, not herself. "May I see him before he leaves?"

"Nay, you may not."

"Ye be a cruel man, Devil."

"Aye, so legend says. But even *I* am not that cruel, Vanessa."

If he'd wanted her full attention, he had it now. She stared at him, puzzled, "But ye just said—"

"Only that you could not see Duncan now. I'm sure there will be plenty of occasions for you do exactly that in less than an hour's time."

"Meaning?" Vanessa asked cautiously. The hair at her nape prickled, and she'd an uneasy feeling she did not want an answer.

Want it or not, however, Alasdair gave her one. "Meaning," he said dryly, as he turned and strode toward his wardrobe, "that Duncan will not be the only Forster leaving Cavnearal."

"I know that. Me da and Dugald will be leaving as well."

Alasdair opened the wardrobe door with more force than was necessary; the door slammed twice against the hard stone wall beside it before it finally just sagged open.

It took three drawers of searching to find what he sought. When he did, Alasdair slammed the drawers closed, then the wardrobe door, and crossed to the bed. He tossed a pair of chocolate-brown trews and a wheat-colored tunic on the mattress beside the chessboard.

Vanessa's fingers curled tightly around the chess piece. The hem of the queen's delicately carved gown bit into the heel of her palm. "I'm leaving," she said flatly, and a cold, empty ache settled deep inside her.

Alasdair nodded. "Within the hour. Your father has given me that much time to prepare you for the trip, and not a second longer."

"But the fine—?"

"Has been paid." And when she opened her mouth to ask the next obvious question, Alasdair answered her before she had the chance. "In full."

She shook her head, confused. After a full minute had passed, she muttered, "I dinna understand."

"Don't you?" he countered dispassionately.

"Nay!"

"I think you do."

"Then ye think wrong," she argued, and although she wasn't positive, Vanessa would have sworn she'd detected an icy edge of accusation in his tone.

Alasdair nodded to the trews and tunic. The former was strewn over the mattress, the latter over the chessboard. "Get dressed, Vanessa. I'll give you a quarter hour. If, at the end of that time, I come back only to find you still in that nightrail, I'll remove it for you and get you dressed myself. Forcibly, if need be."

Vanessa knew Alasdair Gray well enough to know he did not make idle threats. The glint in his steely eyes told her he *would* carry out the promise. With naught else to do but as she was ordered, Vanessa nodded, and waited for Alasdair to leave.

She did not have a long wait. After one penetrating glance, Alasdair spun on his heel and vacated the chamber.

Unlike the man who'd left before him, the door was not closed quietly.

A damp breeze whispered into the tower room through a few hairline cracks between the window and casing. Marette shivered, but did not step back. For nearly a fortnight she'd waited to see the scene now playing itself out in the courtyard, four stories beneath her. 'Twas too delicious a sight to deny herself.

Whoever said victory is sweet . . . they were right.

Marette found this particular victory sweeter than most. How many nights had she lain awake imagining various ways to rid Cavnearal of those hated Forsters? Too many. Yet she didn't begrudge a second of it, even though the one plan she had put into motion had been far from successful.

Regardless of that botched scheme, however, the result had, thankfully, been the same. All things heathen and Scot were leaving Cavnearal.

And Marette couldn't have been happier.

In fact, she thought it was probably a good thing her brother had locked her in this dreadful room again; she doubted she would have been able to hide her catlike satisfaction from Alasdair, just as she doubted he would appreciate seeing it.

That little heathen had bewitched her brother, but all would soon be back to normal. Because the wench was leaving.

Even now, Marette could see the girl—the chit looked so small from this distance, like an ant that could easily be trod upon—descending the stone stairs. The cool autumn breeze tossed her disgustingly short black hair around her face and shoulders as she huddled in—aye, Marette had a feeling that was Keith's jack!—and approached the two men and one boy who sat patiently on horseback, awaiting her.

Marette grinned when she saw that no horse waited for the heathen. Were they going to make her walk all the way back to Dunnaclard? Oh, but that would be priceless! Not to mention well deserved!

Unfortunately, the thought had no more crossed her mind when she saw the chit's brother — the youngest, the one Kirsta insisted was more stubborn than his sister — lean low in the saddle and help Vanessa up on the horse behind him.

Alasdair stood on the bottom step. From this angle, Marette saw no more than the top of her brother's inky head, and the broad shelf of his shoulders. Words were exchanged between Alasdair and Hugh, but Marette was too far away to hear them. Hugh Forster must have found whatever was said amusing, however, for he tilted his head back and roared with laughter.

That sound did reach Marette, though it was muffled and faint from the window and the distance. It was, however, distracting enough for her not to notice the slight grinding of wood against wood as her door was unbarred and opened. If she had, Marette might have glanced behind her and seen Kirsta hovering in the doorway, her blue eyes wide, her cheeks unnaturally pale.

"Go," Marette urged, and rested her forehead against the cold, smooth glass. Her breath came quick and fast; it fogged the window when she repeated, "Go and never come back. Do not *dare* come back here." Her eyes sharpened on Vanessa Forster's dark head. "Next time, I will not settle for temporarily ridding my keep of Forsters. Nay, next time I will kill the first one who dares to set foot in Cavnearal. This I swear."

Very quietly, Kirsta pulled the door closed, and lowered the bar back into place. Alasdair had said to release their sister from the tower room as soon as the Forsters were gone, but she would find someone else to do the chore.

The hatred she'd heard in Marette's voice frightened her; Kirsta had no wish to look into her sister's eyes and see how deeply that hatred and anger ran. In the few days she'd nursed Vanessa, she'd come to respect the woman, and even like her.

She hoped that if a Forster must return to Cavnearal—and she sincerely hoped none would—that that Forster would not be Vanessa. For there wasn't a doubt in Kirsta's mind that Marette had meant every word.

Chapter Twenty-one

Vanessa was deeply troubled.

Arriving home to Dunnaclard to find that her mother's time had not yet come had been wonderful. Thanks to Alasdair, she'd not dishonored her promise after all! And yet . . .

When one week turned into two, two into three, and the bairn still showed no signs of wanting to be born, she became worried. This delay wasn't natural . . . was it?

Truly, Vanessa had no idea. While she knew how bairns were conceived — had known that for years — aside from the most elementary basics, the way they came into the world was still mostly a mystery. Even her mother, who'd over a fortnight ago seemed in good spirits to have her two children and husband home, was no longer so cheerful.

Hannah Forster was resting now, as she was wont to do in the afternoons. Vanessa doubted she was asleep, though, since the woman rarely slept these days. The bairn's twisting and turning and kicking, she said, would not allow it.

Indeed, Vanessa felt certain that, if she were to leave her bedchamber and creep down the hall and into her mother's, she would find that Hannah Forster's brow was creased with the frown that had been her constant companion of late. Vanessa had almost grown accustomed to seeing dark smudges beneath her mother's eyes, where before there'd been none;

her rimmed and red lids bespoke of sleepless nights spent crying.

Hugh Forster was the only person capable of bringing a smile to his wife's lips these days . . . although even that 'twas rare.

Whenever she saw her parents together, Vanessa knew in her heart she'd acted wisely by sneaking into Cavnearal that night so many weeks ago and, in a manner of speaking, selling herself to the legendary Devil. If it brought so much as a quick, fleeting smile to her mother's lips at this trying time, then the price had been well worth the paying.

The price had been a steep one; steeper than Vanessa had ever expected to pay; steeper — much, much steeper — than the paltry sum of coins Dugald had surrendered to Alasdair upon her and Duncan's release.

The fine Vanessa had personally paid had not been monetary. Oh, nay, it had been far worse. It had been physical. The price she'd paid for her father's freedom, she paid for with her heart. And she paid it silently.

Vanessa sucked in a shaky breath, and leaned back in the chair she'd dragged up to the window. It was snowing outside, just a flurry really. She watched airy snowflakes flutter against the window; some clung to the glass for an instant before the heat of the room melted them away.

Cold and empty. Aye, 'twas how she felt. And had for the last fortnight and a half . . . ever since leaving Cavnearal.

Vanessa sighed. Oh, who was she trying to fool? 'Twas leaving *Alasdair Gray* that had been the difficult part, not leaving his keep. When was she going to summon up the courage to simply admit it, if only to herself? To admit that . . .

Ooch! to admit she missed the arrogant, thick-skulled Sassenach more than she'd ever missed anyone in her life! She couldn't get him off her mind. In fact, it seemed that the less she wanted to think about Alasdair, the more she *did* think about him.

During the day she wondered what he was doing. Had he ridden out on a raid or a trod, and if he had, had he returned safely? A week ago, the Douglas had raided both Dunnaclard and Cavnearal. The arrogant reiver had ridden off with a few dozen head of beasties from both keeps.

Hugh Forster had been furious, but refused to set out after the thief for fear of leaving his wife when her time was so near. 'Twas rumored that Alasdair, on the other hand, had immediately instigated a hot trod, and had set out in hot pursuit. Whether he'd been successful or not, no one knew yet.

Nor did Vanessa care. That the Douglas had not orchestrated one of his legendary ambushes, and in the process either wounded or killed Alasdair, mattered to her a great deal.

She thought of the scars that marred her eldest brother's cheek and brow and jaw, scars that Dugald was often given to boasting about, and she knew she would rather feel the blade herself than to let such marks mar Alasdair Gray's handsome face.

"How long?"

The words, and the sound of the door closing, were Vanessa's first indications that she was no longer alone.

Duncan crossed the room, and perched on the stone window ledge, his booted foot dangling against the stone wall. His gaze was dark and contemplative as he stared at his sister. "How long, Vanessa?" he asked again.

Vanessa sighed. "I'm in no mood for riddles, Duncan. Please, tell me what ye be talking about and be done with."

He did, and Vanessa instantly regretted asking him to be so abrupt.

"How long have ye been in love with The Devil, lass?" he asked softly.

"I am *not* — *!*"

Vanessa was halfway out of the chair before Duncan sprung to his feet and pushed her back down again.

"Aye, ye are. Ye just won't admit it."

"That's because there's naught to admit," she said, and felt a blush heat her cheeks. With others she could lie easily, but never with Duncan. A quick glance told Vanessa this time was no exception. " 'Tis a simple attraction," she said finally, and added a shrug for good measure. " 'Twill pass in time. I be sure of it."

"Are ye? Well, I for one am not."

Her eyes narrowed as she glanced up, piercing him with her fiery green gaze. "Dinna make more out of this than there is, Duncan."

"Dinna make *less* out of it than there is, Vanessa." He glared back, equally as firmly.

"Ye dinna understand. I dinna . . ." She shook her head, cleared her throat, and tried again. "I *canna* possibly . . . Ooch! Never mind!"

"Ye canna lie to me, lass. To the others, mayhap, but not to me. Ye never could."

"Oh, Duncan," she said tiredly, as she felt the fight drain out of her. Resting her head against the back of her chair, she sighed and closed her eyes. "What am I to do? I canna . . ." Vanessa let her shrug finish the sentence for her, for her tongue refused.

"I'll grant ye, lass, that ye *shouldna* love him. Gray and Forster have feuded too long for either side to stop doing it now. Unfortunately, I've a feeling that hearts know not the way of can's and should's, nor honor the ways of blood feuds."

Vanessa opened one eye to peer at him. "Then what do they know?"

"What they want," Duncan said so matter-of-factly

391

that she could have sworn for a second that he was the older of the two. "There's no rhyme or reason to love, lass. The heart knows what it wants, and aches when it canna have it. 'Tis the way of things."

"Aye," Vanessa agreed, and nodded her head miserably. "Ye've got that right. What ye've yet to tell me, however, is what can be done about it."

Duncan's answer, if it could truly be considered one, was vague. "As I said, lass, Gray and Forster have feuded too long for either side to stop now."

His words made a wispy memory tickle the back of Vanessa's mind. "Alasdair said much the same thing once, although with an entirely different inflection." She opened her eyes and looked at her brother. "He said the feud *could* stop, if both sides tried hard enough. 'Tis a thought worth considering."

Duncan regarded her oddly. "What else did The Devil say?"

"That 'twould need to stop with someone." She shook her head, her gaze straying to the window and the flakes of melting snow that clung to the glass. "Nay with *two* someones. Him and myself."

"Sweet Saint Andrews, don't tell me he was suggesting ye marry him!"

The force of her brother's words startled Vanessa, but only momentarily. She chuckled. "Nay, Duncan, nothing so rash, I assure ye. He meant a gesture, nothing more. Indeed, he even made the first gesture himself."

"He did?"

"Aye," she said. "He released our da."

Duncan's tone grew patronizing. "He'd no choice about that, lass, once Dugald arrived at his door with the fine."

"But Dugald dinna arrive until *after* Da had been released."

"That's not the way I heard the story told, lass."

"I know." Vanessa peered meaningfully at her

392

brother. "Tell me, Duncan, do ye believe everything ye hear?"

"I — well," he stammered, and the way he swiftly diverted his eyes told Vanessa that her brother was also thinking of the many rumors they'd heard about Alasdair; rumors that 'twere simply impossible to put much faith in after one had met The Devil in the flesh. "Mayhap not everything, but . . ."

"But . . . ?" she prodded.

Duncan shook his head, and quickly changed the subject. "Ye said he made the *first* gesture. Was there another? Mayhap more than one?"

"Aye," Vanessa said noncommittally, and it was her turn to glance guiltily away.

She could feel the brunt of her brother's gaze burning into her, and were she one to squirm, she would have been doing so most heartily at that moment. Vanessa knew her brother well, knew the exact second he struck upon the one bargaining tool she could have held over Alasdair.

"Ye dinna," he said flatly. And, when she said nothing, he insisted, "Please, tell me ye dinna tell him about the grooves in the stone, lass. Anything but that. Vanessa? Vanessa!"

"Ooch! Duncan, stop yer yelling," she snapped. " 'Tis not as though I had a choice."

"I dinna believe it! Good Lord, lass, do ye mean he *tortured* the information out of ye?"

"Nay, of course not!"

"Then he maun of had a weapon to threaten ye with. A sword, perchance? Or, worse, a threat against Da or me?"

"Nay, 'tis not The Devil's way."

Duncan pushed himself away from the window ledge, and crouched down beside his sister's chair. Vanessa was not looking at him. He did not think that an encouraging sign. "Ye defend him most staunchly, Vanessa. Have ye noticed?"

Nay, she hadn't. Her words echoed in her ears, as did the harshness of her tone when she'd . . . oh, aye, when she'd leapt to Alasdair's defense. There was no sense denying it; the truth was plain—embarrassingly so. To both of them.

Duncan placed his hand over his sister's, which was loosely splayed atop her thigh. "He dinna force the information from ye at all, did he, Vanessa?" he asked gently. "Ye offered it freely."

Vanessa nodded, hung her head, and released a long-suffering sigh. "Ooch! the shame. Da would have me head if he were to know the truth. As would Dugald, and Angus, and our sisters, too, methinks. And our mother. I dinna know how I can ever look them all in the eye again, Duncan, I really dinna."

A drop of moisture splashed onto the back of Duncan's hand. He was so surprised that at first the magnitude of it escaped him. Another teardrop followed. Another. He stared at the back of his rapidly moistening hand in mute shock. Her tears felt warm, and looked like shiny crystals against his tanned skin. He'd never seen anything like them before, quite possibly because he'd never seen Vanessa cry before.

Well, aye, there was that one time whilst clinging to The Devil's infernally narrow ledge, but that didn't count. Vanessa had confessed 'twas naught but the stinging sea spray that made her eyes water then, and he had believed her. Duncan realized only now that he'd believed Vanessa then only because he'd *wanted* to, not because she'd convinced him. He'd not thought to question the episode before because, quite frankly, he hadn't thought his sister capable of tears.

Duncan lifted his gaze, and stared at his sister in wonder. In his ten and four summers, he'd seen all three of his other sisters cry—indeed, Kayla was often given to bouts of unwarranted sobbing; 'twas due to her tender age, or so their mother claimed. And yet . . .

While he'd seen Vanessa dressed like a boy, and riding astride more times than not better than one, while he'd seen her sneak into a Day of Truce that traditionally forbade her sex admittance, seen her enter Cavnearal's supposedly unenterable walls, and even seen her yell directly back at their father in a way not even Hugh Forster's sons would dare—she'd been most displeased to learn of their da's plan, and that Hugh Forster had not needed rescuing after all—there was one thing Duncan had never seen Vanessa do. He'd never seen her cry.

When the shock finally wore off—and it took a few minutes for it to do so—he reached out and awkwardly pulled her close.

Vanessa wrapped her arms about her brother and, nestling her face in the curve of his neck between his shoulder and chin, sobbed heartily.

Duncan stroked her back and murmured nonsense words in her ear, soothing her as best he could. Truly, he'd no experience with sobbing women on which to draw from!

It seemed to take forever for her tears to dry, and her crying to diminish to pitiful little hiccups. By then, the back of Duncan's tunic was wet, and plastered warmly to the top of his lean shoulder and a goodly portion of his back.

Finally, Vanessa pushed herself up and wiped her nose and eyes on the sleeve of her white linen blouse. "I've a p-plan," she said, and even her voice sounded watery.

"I'm not surprised." When she opened her mouth to speak, Duncan slanted his index finger across her lips to stop her. With his free hand, he wiped the tears on her cheek away with his knuckles. "I've a plan as well." His hand turned inward, and he hooked his index finger beneath her chin, then gently drew her gaze up to his. "This time, lass, we do things my way."

She sniffled loudly. "And if I say nay?"

"Then we dinna do anything at all."

He was serious. Vanessa could tell by the determined glint in her brother's eyes, and the tight set of his jaw. At that moment, Duncan looked quite a bit like their father. She almost told him so, then thought better of it. He would not take such words as a compliment.

"Well?" Duncan prompted when two full minutes had silently passed, and still she said naught.

Vanessa nibbled her lower lip thoughtfully, then sighed, shrugged, and lifted her chin from his grasp. "Ye drive a hard bargain, Brother."

"I learned from the best. Do ye not agree?"

"That ye learned from the best? Ye know I do." She sent him a watery grin. His patient glance said that wasn't at all what he was referring to. And, of course, Vanessa knew that. She nodded. "Aye, Duncan, I agree to abide by yer plan, whatever 'tis, since ye've abided by so many of me own . . . er, somewhat impulsive ones in the past. I just hope and pray ye wisdom proves more sound than mine."

His grin did not belie his misgivings. "Aye, lass, so do I." Then, under his breath, much less assuredly, Duncan added, "So do I."

The last one and one half fortnights had been the worst Alasdair could remember. Nothing had gone as he'd wanted it to.

First, coins he'd collected from the Forster, funds he'd intended to use to prepare Cavnearal and its people for the long, harsh winter ahead, need instead be squandered on freeing his hotheaded brother from the Douglas's reiving hands.

Things had gone downhill from there.

Quick upon the heels of that fiasco had come his brother's announcement that he planned to ask for

Jenna Ferguson's hand in marriage. Alasdair was of a mind that the girl's father would have quite a bit to say on the matter — none of which would be the least bit congratulatory.

As for what Alasdair had had to say about it . . .

Bloody hell, he didn't want to think about that right now. The shouting match he and Keith had engaged in a mere week prior still seemed to echo off the cold stone walls of the vacant hall in which Alasdair now sat.

Keith hadn't spoken a word to Alasdair since. Instead, he'd sent missives through a very reluctant Kirsta and, occasionally, through a gloating Marette. Alasdair didn't bother to inform his brother of how childish he was acting, mostly because he wasn't at all certain he'd be able to control his temper the next time the two met. Therefore, he was putting off speaking to Keith for as long as he could.

That approach was equally as childish as Keith's instigation of it. Alasdair might have realized that, had he taken the time to think on the matter. He didn't. In fact, he'd been having a good deal of trouble thinking about anything for the last few weeks.

Except Vanessa Forster.

Her, he thought about constantly, and in a variety of ways that would no doubt have made her blush crimson from hairline to toes, should he ever have occasion to share them with her.

During the day he remembered how she'd looked the first time he'd ever laid eyes on her; filthy and skinny, no bigger or shapelier than a scrawny lad. She'd been standing behind her brother, whilst peeking around at Alasdair, piercing him with those expressive green eyes of hers. While Duncan had obviously shoved her back for her own protection, the haughty set of her chin said she just as obviously thought she could protect herself, while her more than direct gaze dared any and all to argue the fact.

He also recalled his shock upon finding out that the "scrawny lad" was not only not a lad, nor scrawny or unappealing. Lord, no! If she had been, there was a good chance Alasdair would be upstairs in his bed-chamber, in his bed, fast asleep by now. Lord knows the rest of the house had retired hours ago.

Yet he couldn't sleep. At least, that was the reason he gave for spending as little time in his bedchamber as was humanly possible. Insomnia. Everyone was plagued with it now and again. It didn't matter that he'd never suffered from it before. These had been a few very trying weeks, especially since the Douglas seemed to be particularly fond of Gray cows and sheep of late.

Alasdair sighed, lifted the mug of ale he'd forgotten he held, and drained it in one, deep swallow. Hate though he did to admit it, he recognized his theory about insomnia, about arduous, time-consuming, and ultimately unrewarding raids and trods for exactly what they were. An excuse.

The truth of the matter was, Alasdair had no taste for his bed; it felt cold, empty, far too big and un-comfortable now. Unnaturally so. He'd a feeling he knew why; because Vanessa Forster was not in it . . . and he desperately wanted her to be.

The reason was that simple.

And that complex.

Shifting slightly, he lowered his arm over the side of the chair and dropped the pewter mug onto the floor. It tipped onto its side and rolled in a half-circle be-fore the handle clinked against the stone floor as it came to rest beneath the chair. The night distorted the sound, made it echo in the empty hall.

Alasdair barely noticed. His thoughts had turned dark and brooding. His thoughts had turned toward his wife. Jenny.

She'd been so sweet. So delicate. And so bloody young!

While he couldn't lay claim to sweet and delicate by any means, Alasdair knew he'd been horribly young himself when they'd wed. Young, and full of his own importance, and . . . aye, foolish enough to believe Jenny's maidenly blushes and obvious terror of him would melt as soon as she warmed to the stranger who was now her husband. She never had. Not, at least, in the way a wife was supposed to warm to a husband.

While most men would simply have taken what they considered to be their right by marriage, Alasdair's pride would not allow him to do that. Nor would his conscience. He would have her willing, or he would not have her at all.

Eventually, he grew to realize 'twould be the latter.

As time passed, the thought of bedding the small, fragile girl became not only harder to envision, but a bit repulsive.

And that, Alasdair thought as he reached to the side and felt around on the cold stone for his tankard, was the problem. He'd never once considered Jenny a woman; in his mind she'd always been, and always would be, naught more than a pretty girl.

His fingers grazed pewter. He frowned, then remembered. Ah, 'twas his mug! He grinned and, fumbling around a bit more, managed to snatch the tankard up and raise it to his lips . . . only to remember, once he'd tipped it back and naught more than a drop of liquid dribbled over his suddenly parched lips, that he'd drunk the last of the ale moments ago.

Alasdair pushed to his feet. He lurched to the left, and had to grab the arm of the chair to steady himself until the room stopped making those large, sweeping circles about him.

In less than two minutes, he'd slipped out into the corridor at the back of the hall and located the ale barrel. He thought it uncannily lucky that the barrel was in the exact spot in which he'd left it the last time he'd refilled his tankard.

Or was it the time before?

Mayhap 'twas the time before that?

Nay, it couldn't have been. He'd just had a fight with Marette, and, as he recalled, his mug had been full of whiskey then. He wasn't sure when he'd switched to ale.

With a shrug, Alasdair dismissed the matter and, lifting the tankard, drained half its foamy contents. He then refilled the mug and retraced his steps back to the chair — upon which he sat down quite heavily. Again, his clumsiness was blamed entirely on the revolving room; it never occurred to Alasdair that the cause might instead be the liquor he'd been consuming in quantity for the last four hours.

Not, that is, until he heard the keep's outer door squeak closed.

Alasdair frowned. Bloody hell, he couldn't recall hearing it open! But open it must have, for, if he listened carefully, he could detect the sound of muffled footsteps on the stone floor outside the hall.

He sat up straighter, a small bit of the liquor-induced fog evaporating from his mind.

There, he heard it again. And yet again. Aye, those were footsteps, all right. There wasn't a doubt of it in his mind. They sounded as though they were heading toward the stairs.

Alasdair was on his feet in a beat, and across the room in two. The second he stepped foot in the corridor, his mind was clear, his finely honed battle skills automatically rushing to the fore.

In afterthought, he glanced down at his empty hands, and grinned wryly. His sword was upstairs. Yet, while he might be weaponless, he was by no means defenseless.

His steely gaze sharpened on a minuscule shadow that flickered in the moonlight, midway up the stairs.

A shadow that, if studied closely, was not a shadow at all, but a person.

That the person was an intruder, he knew at a glance. Only people who had no business being where they were skulked and clung to shadows — and this person was doing both.

Therefore, Alasdair did that which came most naturally to a Gray. He bellowed. "Halt!"

The shadow did not halt. Rather, its surprise at hearing Alasdair's yell caused it to stumble, and topple head-first down five very hard, very cold stone stairs.

The grunt the intruder gave upon landing — on its shoulder, with its thin, trews-clad legs sprawled all akilter over the stairs above its hips — told Alasdair the person was still alive. The lean build; dark, shaggy hair; and the fact that the person had come this far without detection told him something else entirely: his unexpected *guest's* identity.

"Alasdair?" Kirsta called sleepily from the top stair landing. "Was that you?"

Alasdair glanced up, and squinted at the light of the candle Kirsta had lit and now carried closely in front of her. "Go back to bed, Kirsta. 'Tis naught to be alarmed about."

"But isn't that . . . ?"

"Aye," Alasdair growled, answering the question before she could fully voice it. "I said go back to bed, Kirsta."

She did. Or, at least, she went back to her room. Whether she actually went back to bed or not, Alasdair couldn't say. Nor did he care.

Shaking his head, Alasdair reached down and tightly shackled the intruder's arm with his fingers. With one yank, he'd hauled the "guest" up, and a second later was dragging his "catch" into the great hall.

It took effort for Alasdair to not surrender to temptation, and slam the person into the chair he'd so recently vacated. Oh, how he wanted to! Quite badly. But he didn't. Instead, he braced one hand on either chair arm, and leaned forward until his furious gray gaze was level and locked with wide, nervous green. Very slowly, his tone much too calm to be anything but furious, he said, "You'd better have a damn good reason for stealing into my keep again in the dead of night, Duncan Forster. Once was bad enough, but this time . . ."

Duncan swallowed hard, and pressed back as far as he could into the chair. It didn't help, for he could only retreat so far, after all. The size and strength of Alasdair Gray crowded him into the chair, even as the man's warm, ale-scented breath scorched over his cheeks and jaw. Duncan's heart was pounding out a fast, staccato beat against his ribs and, no matter how he tried, his breathing refused to regulate. His throat felt tight, his mouth dry. How could he be expected to speak now?

Alasdair's insistent gaze convinced Duncan that he should find a way, as did the husky, promising tone of his next words. "You've but five seconds to answer me, boy. And if you don't, I swear by all that's holy, I'll reach down your throat and pull the words out myself. This is your last chance, so I suggest you answer me this time, Duncan. Why-are-you-here?"

Duncan swallowed dryly. Given the choice, he was able to find his voice with unprecedented speed; though it came out in a shaky croak. "'Tis Vanessa. She be the reason I'm here."

"Vanessa?" Alasdair repeated, and his tone grew huskier still, this time with concern. If it was possible for the force of a mere gaze to pin a person in place, Alasdair's gaze now did that to Duncan. "Sweet Lord, what's happened?"

There was a wealth of emotion in those four, throatily uttered words. That, combined with the stricken look in The Devil's eyes, told Duncan that his plan was going to be more successful than all of Vanessa's past schemes combined. Ducking his gaze, for he felt sure Alasdair would be able to read the duplicity in it, he said softly, "Sit down, Devil. I'm afraid the news be not good."

Alasdair did exactly that. He sat. On the floor. Directly in front of the chair on which Duncan sat. Hard. Blindly, he reached for the newly filled tankard he'd set aside just moments before, and downed the contents. He'd a feeling he was going to need something stronger than ale after he heard what Vanessa's brother had come here in the dead of night to tell him.

The covers were thrown back, and Vanessa was unceremoniously dragged out of her warm bed by a wide-eyed, overly excited, redheaded servant.

"Come quick, lass. 'Tis time," Molly fairly chirped, even as she forced Vanessa's arms through the sleeves of a robe, then tied the sash tightly around Vanessa's waist.

"Time," Vanessa repeated, her words muffled by the yawn she stifled with the back of her fist. "Time for . . . what?"

"For the birth, of course," Molly answered—as patiently as her obvious excitement would allow. "What else?"

Vanessa, who was in the process of stretching her weary limbs, froze. Her eyelids, still gritty from sleep, snapped open. She had to blink twice before she was able to pull Molly into focus.

The girl was nearly a score and nine, yet the plumpness in her constantly blushing cheeks made her look much younger. Her blue eyes shined vivaciously as she said, "Yer mum's been calling for ye, lass. Ye'd best hurry."

Vanessa nodded and, now completely awake,

headed for the door. Molly hurried to keep up with her.

"And Da?" Vanessa asked as they walked quickly down the sconce-lit corridor. "Where is he?"

"At yer mum's side."

Vanessa nodded, pleased. She was barefoot, and the stone floor felt cold beneath the soles of her feet; the slight chill helped banish the last traces of sleep from both her body and mind. "And Dugald and Duncan and Kayla and . . . Ooch! Molly, where be me brothers and sisters?"

"The men are still abed. Yer mum dinna want to wake them."

"And Kayla?" Vanessa asked as she retied the sash of the robe around her waist. In her excitement, Molly had not tied it properly.

"Her, too. 'Tis only ye and yer da she wants with her now."

Vanessa nodded, and increased her speed. Whilst her parents' bedchamber was just down the corridor from her own, Dunnaclard was not a small keep, and the corridor in question was quite long. She used the time to question Molly. "How long has she been having the pains, Molly? How close are they? Is Gerttie with her, as well?" Then, last, as though she was afraid of the answer, Vanessa asked, "How is she faring?"

Molly, who was a bit breathless from trying to keep up with her mistress's pace, answered the questions in the order they were received. "Two days . . . she tells us now, although no one saw any indication of it. The pains be fierce, but too irregular to time. Gerttie arrived an hour and a quarter ago. Physically, yer mum be bearing up well."

"And her mind?"

"Not so good." From the corner of her eye, Vanessa saw Molly twisting worriedly at the hem of her apron. The servant's head was down, her focus on the stones that passed quickly beneath their feet. "She does seem better now that yer da be with her, though."

The words would have been encouraging, were it not for Molly's subdued tone. "What aren't ye telling me, Molly?"

"Well . . . The pains, as I said, are irregular but strong. Yer mum has yet to cry out, though. Indeed, she's shown little emotion at all. She stares at the ceiling, winces now and again, and squeezes yer da's hand when the pains be fierce, but naught else. I've had four children meself, lass, so I know of what I speak when I say that, well, 'tis just plain peculiar for yer mum to be so subdued at this stage of the birthing."

Vanessa agreed. While she'd not been in the room during the last two births, she'd paced the corridor outside her mother's door. She still remembered the way her mother had screamed when the pains started coming hard and fast.

" 'Tis not natural," Molly said breathlessly, as they stopped in front of the bedchamber door.

Not a single noise from inside filtered into the corridor. The hairs at Vanessa's nape prickled. 'Twas entirely too quiet inside the chamber. Eerily so. She glanced at Molly, who seemed to be trying to regulate her breathing, and failing. "Ye be sure she wants me inside?"

Molly bobbed her bright red head up and down. "Aye. I'd not have woken ye if 'twere otherwise."

There was no arguing such logic. Vanessa nodded and, sucking in a deep breath, reached out, lifted the latch, and slowly pushed open the bedchamber door.

Chapter Twenty-two

Tired.

The word couldn't begin to describe how Vanessa felt as she slowly retraced her steps to her own bedchamber. *Exhausted*, she thought, would be a better word. Jubilant and exhilarated would be more accurate still.

The servants were up. Vanessa could hear them on the floor below as they prepared the morning meal. Her stomach grumbled in response, but she ignored her hunger. Right now, all she wanted was to go to bed, pull the covers up over her head, and sleep. It would take at least a fortnight of constant rest to replenish the energy this night had drained from her.

Vanessa stumbled wearily into her bedchamber. The room was dim. Outside, the first wispy fingers of dawn lit the sky in faint blue and gray streaks. Two inches of pristine white snow covered Lowland hills and valleys alike.

Freshly fallen snow to greet a small, fresh new life.

She smiled. 'Twas a most appropriate combination, Vanessa thought as she closed the door behind her, and at the same time, with her free hand, untied the sash holding her robe closed. She shrugged the garment off her shoulders.

Yawning, she wearily pulled the thick curtains back from her bed and . . .

Her yawn transformed into a gasp.

The bed was not empty.

Indeed, her mattress, which she'd always considered large, seemed to have shrunk—dwarfed by the man who was negligently half sitting, half lying atop it. His hands were clasped loosely atop his chest, his wide shoulders cushioned by the pillow that, a mere six hours before, Vanessa's own head had rested upon.

She swallowed hard as a surge of adrenaline pumped hot and fast through her veins, bringing her instantly awake. She did the first thing that came to mind.

She snapped the curtains shut.

Alasdair grinned. "Good morning, love." His steely gaze raked Vanessa from darkly tousled head to bare toes, and his grin broadened. "You look terrible."

Vanessa splayed her palm over her breastbone, as though that simple contact could somehow stop her heart from racing. It didn't. Her fingers trembled against the cool white cloth of her nightrail. "Thank ye kindly, Devil," she replied, and winced. Even to her own ears, her voice sounded high and shaky. "Did ye travel all this way to insult me?"

"Nay. I came to claim what's mine."

"Aye, and what be that?"

"You, kitten. I came to bring you home."

Warily, she said, "I *am* home."

He shook his head. "As of tonight, Cavnearal will be your home." Alasdair regarded her levelly, his expression abruptly sober. "A wife's place is beside her husband."

"Y-ye arena me husband."

"Yet," he conceded with a nod of his devilishly dark head. "But from tomorrow onward, I shall be."

Vanessa closed her eyes and drew in a long, deep breath. This must be a dream. Oh, aye, that would explain it. Dreams weren't supposed to make any sense, and this one made even less sense than most!

She'd almost managed to convince herself she was

407

having a nightmare . . . until she opened her eyes, and saw that Alasdair was striding arrogantly around the bed toward her.

Her breath caught. Good Lord, this was no dream! Would that it were! She took a quick, instinctive step back, and Alasdair halted.

"I . . . ye . . ." She shook her head to clear it, then at a near shout, demanded, "Have ye gone daft, mon?! I willna marry ye. Not tonight. Not tomorrow. Not *ever!*"

"I don't recall giving you a choice."

"I dinna care if ye *gave* me one or not, for a choice has already been made. I'll not marry ye."

Vanessa's heart raced when Alasdair simply grinned, took a step forward, and said oh, so confidently, "Aye, you will."

"Nay, I'll not."

He took another step toward her. Another. "Aye, you *will.*"

"Nay, I'll *not.*" She took two steps back, only to find she'd retreated as far as she could. The wall pressed up hard against her back, and she could feel the rough, cold stone grinding into her shoulder blades and hips. Belatedly, she realized she should have spared less attention to Alasdair, and more to where she was going. Heading toward the door, not the wall, would have been the smart thing to do.

A foot of space separated his body from hers. Alasdair was quick to close even that small distance.

The heat of his body was the first thing to envelop her, followed closely by the intoxicating scent of him. A groan clogged in her throat when the hardness of his chest lightly grazed the rounded firmness of her own.

Was the contact, while brief and fleeting, also accidental? Vanessa thought not. "T-truly, mon, ye've gone daft."

"Aye, Vanessa, I'm of a mind to agree. Why else

would I have stolen into your keep—a nice change of pace, that," he added with a grin "—and threatened to whisk you back to Cavnearal with me? As my wife?"

As he spoke, Alasdair had splayed his palms over the stone flanking either side of her shoulders. Leaning forward, he now crowded her against the wall.

"I—I dinna know, but surely there be another reason ye arena telling me of. Yes?" Her breathing had suddenly gone rapid and shallow; her head spun.

"Aye, kitten, there *is* another reason." He was on eye level with her now, so when he angled his head and moved a hair's breadth closer, his lips grazed hers as he added, "I know your secret, kitten."

"Ye do?" she asked flatly. Ooch! but 'twas simply not possible to think straight with this man's breath warming her face, while his mouth deftly sipped at hers.

"I do," he replied, then nibbled at her lower lip.

A shock of raw, hot sensation swept through Vanessa. She shivered, and asked breathlessly, "And what secret is that?"

"The one you'd rather not have me know about."

"Oh, *that* secret," she whispered shakily, even though she'd not a clue as to what he was talking about. She would need to ask him to clarify his remark . . . later. Right now, however, she could not think past the way his tongue was stroking slowly over first her lower lip, then the upper.

"Aye," he rasped hotly against her mouth, "*that* secret. Duncan told me about the babe, Vanessa."

"Did he?" she asked, even as she lifted her hands and stroked her palms over the hard shelf of his shoulders. He felt so very good. Hard and warm. Exactly as she remembered. Nay, *better.*

Had her senses not been so hungry to reacquaint themselves with the scent and feel and taste of this man—*Lord, how she'd missed him!*—Vanessa might have questioned how, since the bairn was a scant two hours old, her brother had had time to ride to Cavnearal, and how Alasdair had in turn had the time to ride all the way to Dunnaclard. She might also have wondered why Duncan would have bothered to do such a thing at all.

But she didn't; her mind and body were too drunk with Alasdair's nearness for her to waste time on such trivialities.

She remembered Alasdair telling her once that the feud had to end somewhere, and that with the two of them would be as good a place as any for peace to start. At the time, she'd though he meant releasing her father, and she'd reciprocated by telling him of the grooves in Cavnearal's rock. Now she knew otherwise.

What was happening finally began to penetrate her overworked senses. Alasdair Gray wanted to marry her, and in so doing, join their families in a way that would *force* peace to interfere on what had, until now, been two centuries of violence and bloodshed. The plan was ideal. Vanessa wished she'd thought of it herself.

"Tell me, Vanessa. Tell me you'll return to Cavnearal with me. Tell me you'll agree to be my wife."

"Aye," she answered readily — so readily, in fact, that she wondered if mayhap she'd made the decision weeks ago, and was only now realizing it. "I will."

Alasdair smiled.

Vanessa's heart somersaulted.

Angling his head, he kissed her deeply. She coiled her arms about his neck and returned the kiss with equal ardor. She was, after all, going to be this man's bride soon; surely a smattering of passion was allowed? Not, of course, that it really mattered; already she'd sampled desire at this man's skilled hands. Twice, in fact . . . both times outside the bonds of matrimony. 'Twas too late to worry about her honor now!

Alasdair groaned, low and deep in his throat, and deepened the kiss to a fervent pitch. Vanessa leaned weakly into him. Any reluctance she might have harbored melted to the white-hot desire this man sparked in her blood.

A moment slipped past, or maybe 'twas an hour. Vanessa was unsure. By the time Alasdair was done kissing her thoroughly, she'd lost all track of time. Only his arms, encircling her waist and holding her enticingly close, kept her erect, for her knees had gone weak and watery quite a while ago.

He pulled back slightly, and gazed down at her. His breath was coming hard and fast, and while he struggled to regulate it, the feat just wasn't possible. "Get dressed, kitten. Hurry."

She nodded, unable to speak, unable to even attempt ironing out her own uneven breaths. Her mouth felt full from his kiss. 'Twas an exhilarating feeling. More exhilarating still was the way she could still taste him when she flicked her tongue over her lips.

There were certain aspects of marrying Alasdair Gray that she looked forward to most eagerly. She grinned. 'Twas an odd reaction for a woman who'd said only moments before that she would never marry this man—not ever—not for any reason. But then, consistency had never been a strong point with her, and she sensed Alasdair already knew that. Of course, the declaration had also come before he'd kissed her breathless and reminded her of how good things could be between them.

And Vanessa knew from experience that things between them could be very, *very* good . . .

Sneaking out of the keep, Alasdair soon discovered, turned out to be a good deal simpler than sneaking *into* it had been. He needed only to follow Vanessa through the numerous passages that snaked beneath Dunnaclard. They'd still half a mile to walk before they reached the snow-strewn valley where he'd tethered his mount and left the men he'd brought with him, but all in all, their escape didn't take much time at all.

In less than an hour from when she'd walked into her bedchamber and discovered him lounging upon her bed, Alasdair found himself seated atop the stallion, with the warm, slender back of Vanessa Forster-soon-to-be-Gray blanketing his front. The back of her head was braced by his shoulder, and her dark hair tickled the sensitive skin beneath his jaw.

She'd fallen asleep before they'd put even a quarter hour's distance between themselves and her ancestral home. Alasdair let the stallion choose its own pace as they headed toward Cavnearal. Following the trail of men and beasties—his men, *Forster* beasties—Alasdair was glad he'd had the foresight to bring along some of his men. They not only served as added protection, but they were handy to have about when two hundred head of Forster sheep had appeared.

Twas a small favor, Vanessa falling asleep so quickly, but one Alasdair was infinitely grateful for.

At his suggestion, she'd donned a baggy tunic, a thick leather jack, and a pair of trews that, in his jaded opinion, were indecently snug. The latter allowed her to ride astride in front of him.

The attire had seemed a sound choice . . . when they were at Dunnaclard. Only now did he recognize the mistake of it. With Vanessa seated upon the saddle in front of him, Alasdair's inner thighs were forced to glove the outer side of hers. The curve of her bottom nested tightly between his legs, and there was a not part of him that didn't throb warmly at the intimate contact.

'Twas a pleasing distraction . . . entirely *too* pleasing.

He'd circled one arm about her waist, and the palm of that hand was splayed over her abdomen. It was a tender, protective gesture, he knew, but luckily the wench wasn't awake to either see or feel it. The thought that his child was growing inside her womb touched Alasdair deeply. More deeply than he wanted it to, far more deeply than it, by all rights, should have.

The instant Duncan had confessed that Vanessa was carrying his child, Alasdair knew what he had to do. And he'd done it. Still, he couldn't help feeling deep down that . . . well, that something was missing. Something important. He'd no idea, however, what that something could be.

Mayhap Alasdair didn't know, but Vanessa did.

She shifted on the saddle in front of him, and while her eyes were closed, her breathing purposely slow and even, she was not asleep, nor had she been for quite some time. She simply wanted Alasdair to think she was, so she'd have some time to work a few problems out in her mind.

It bothered her tremendously that she'd left Dunnaclard without telling a soul where she'd gone. 'Twas not like her. She felt a pang of guilt to know that her absence would be discovered before dusk, and that, in turn, would cause her family, especially her mother, undo worry. This first, however, was a problem that could be easily remedied. As soon as she reached Cavnearal, she would have Alasdair send one of his men to inform her family of where she went and why.

Vanessa felt a wee bit better now that that was settled.

And then her thoughts swerved again, and the scant peace of mind she'd found evaporated like the misty vapor that the chilly November air had turned their breaths into. It hadn't bothered her before leaving Dunnaclard, but now that she'd had time to think on it—nay, *dwell* on—the more it worried her.

Alasdair had not once said he loved her.

Of course, Vanessa did not expect him to. She'd much rather not hear the words if he did not feel the emotion in his heart.

And still . . .

She told herself it didn't matter. Love was not essential for a contented marriage, especially in a time when husbands and wives were joined for the mutual benefit of their families, not an untoward attraction to each other.

And still . . .

Was it asking for too much to hope that, in time, mayhap Alasdair would come to care for her? As Duncan was fond of saying, anything was possible, although, personally, Vanessa thought this was one matter that did not fit the theory.

Alasdair wanted to stop the feuding between their families, and Vanessa had, at some unknown point, come to want that, too.

A marriage between Alasdair and herself would unite Gray and Forster for the first time in centuries. The union would force two of the strongest riding families on both sides of the Border to learn to coexist in peace. It would take a good deal of adjustment—she did not expect peace to reign overnight—but it *could* happen. If she married Alasdair.

And still . . .

Her word had already been given, and a Forster was worth nothing if his word wasn't good. Vanessa had already proved that hers most definitely was. She'd no intention of backing out of the impending wedding now.

And still . . .

Sweet heavens, why could she not just face it and be done with?! 'Twas a most difficult thing to admit, even to herself, but what Vanessa wanted most of all—so badly that she ached for it—was to have Alasdair Gray return her love.

Her heart's desire was that simple.

Which meant it wasn't simple at all!

Vanessa's first indication that all was not as it appeared came four hours later, when Alasdair guided the stallion through Cavnearal's courtyard, toward the stairway leading into the quadrangle. He'd no more halted their mount when the keep's front door burst open, and Duncan came bounding down the stairs.

The stone was slippery from the coat of fluffy snow that covered it. Apparently, Duncan hadn't taken that into consideration, for his feet slipped out from under him and he wound up tripping down the last few steps, coming to a halt, finally, on the ground closely beside the stallion.

Frowning down upon her brother's dark head, Vanessa watched silently as he picked himself up, and, in brisk, agitated strokes, brushed off the snow that clung to the back and knees of his wheat-colored trews.

It wasn't Duncan's actions that baffled her so much as the bright red splotches she detected on his otherwise pale cheeks. Also, when he reached up to help her dismount, she noticed that he refused to look her directly in the eye. 'Twas not an encouraging sign.

"I can explain everything, lass," he said, and snatched his hands back from her waist as soon as her feet made contact with the snowy ground.

Alasdair had also dismounted. He stood between the two, and now it was only the breadth of his body that separated brother from sister. "I've already explained it to her, Duncan."

"You have?" Duncan asked, his surprised gaze shifting to Alasdair.

"Of course he has," Vanessa inserted, adding an encouraging smile for good measure. Now what, she wondered, had caused Duncan to look at her as though she'd just sprouted another head? "Methinks 'tis a good plan, Duncan. I'd not be here if I thought otherwise."

"Aye, you would," Alasdair said, and it was clear from his tone that he meant it. "I'd not traveled all that way to take no for an answer, wench. If you'd not come with me willingly, I'd have bound and gagged you, thrown you over my horse, and brought you forcibly. Either way, you would still be here."

Vanessa scowled at her husband-to-be. There was a time when such words, coming from the legendary Devil, would have scared her senseless, but that time was no longer. She knew Alasdair better now, and she'd not lied when she said his bark was worse than his bite. Or, rather, his bellow. "Ye realize how barbaric that sounds, do ye not, Alasdair?"

"Barbaric, mayhap." He shrugged. "But none the less true."

Her scowl deepened. "Admit it, mon, ye'd have done no such thing."

"Aye, I would have."

"Nay, ye would *not*—!"

"Aye, I *would*—!"

"Ooch! that's enough, the both of ye!" This time, it was Duncan who stepped between *them*. His gaze shifted accusingly between Vanessa and Alasdair. "Do ye always fight so?"

"Only when he is wrong," Vanessa snapped.

"Which would mean never," Alasdair added, his tone equally as brisk.

"Which would mean *constantly*," she corrected sharply.

Alasdair's eyes narrowed to steely slits, and he returned her imperious glare with a level one of his own.

It was clear from his patronizing expression that, as a woman, she could not be expected to keep her facts straight. Oh, but that was galling! Vanessa reacted on instinct; her hand lifted, and her open palm arched toward the man's arrogant cheek.

Alasdair caught her wrist before the blow could connect . . . but just barely. Her palm was close enough for his wind-chilled cheek to feel its angry, burning heat. "I warned you about slapping me, woman. I'll warn you only this once more."

Her jaw clenched, and her eyes were hot with furious green fire. "Is that so? Well then, Devil, let *me* warn *ye* that I'll be doing maun more than slapping if ye ever think to treat me as less than yer equal again."

"You are *not* my equal, Vanessa," he said, and the words came from between gritted teeth. "You are a woman."

"Why, ye arrogant — " She clamped her mouth shut before the last word could pass her lips, and at the same time wrenched her wrist from his warm, powerful grasp. Alasdair didn't release her immediately, but rather tightened his grasp for a beat, as though to prove that her wrist was freed only because he desired it to be so. "Aye," she snapped, her gaze raking him from dark head to snow-dusted, booted toe, "I'm not yer equal, Alasdair Gray. I be yer *better.*"

And with that, Vanessa spun on her heel and made ready to stomp up the stone stairs and into the keep.

She was not, however, allowed to get that far. She'd no more set foot on the landing when she felt familiar fingers encircle and bite into her tender upper arm, stopping her cold.

Her gaze dipped to the shackle of Alasdair's fingers, and the heat in her intensified. His grip was not tight. Yet. But it threatened to be. "Let go of me arm."

"Why?" Alasdair demanded. "So you can slip on the stairs the way your brother just did?"

"I'd rather do that than be helped like an invalid into yer home."

She watched the muscles in Alasdair's jaw bunch as

his gaze volleyed between her eyes and . . . her stomach? Now why was he looking there? she wondered.

"Vanessa," Alasdair said, his breath fogging the air, "if not yourself, then think of the babe."

Duncan, whose presence she'd forgotten in the heat of her anger, groaned. The sound attracted Vanessa's attention, but only briefly. Her confused gaze was quick to return, and lock in silent challenge, with Alasdair's brightly determined one.

"What are ye talking about?" she asked, and mentally commended herself on the calm, even tone she was able to maintain—odd, since calm and even was *not* how she felt. "Alasdair, the bairn has naught to do with any of this."

"The babe has *everything* to do with it." It was his turn to glare at Duncan, when the boy again groaned. Like Vanessa's, his attention refused to tarry on the boy for long. "If you were to slip down these stairs—"

"Then I would pick meself up and dust meself off the way ye just saw my brother do," she explained reasonably, her tone edged with confusion. She'd accused Alasdair of being daft before, but now she wondered if perhaps that description wasn't accurate after all. 'Twould certainly explain why he kept changing topics with lightning speed, never allowing her to grasp what he was talking about before swiftly moving on to the next. "Mayhap I should be asking ye what *ye* would do if *ye* fell down the stairs?"

"Do not patronize me, Vanessa."

"I am not patronizing ye, Alasdair, but simply trying to understand yer reasoning." She glanced down and to the side, and her heart stammered a beat when she saw that they were alone. Duncan had vanished, leaving only a trail of footsteps in the snow, footsteps that led toward the corner of the keep before disappearing from view.

"The babe, wench," Alasdair said and, for whatever

reason, when she tugged her arm, he let her go. "I ask only that you think of the babe."

"All right," Vanessa said stiffly. It had started to snow again—a mere flurry—and she swiped at the flakes clinging to the shoulders of her jack. "If ye want me to think of the bairn, I will think of the bairn."

Again, Vanessa spun on her heel.

This time when she headed toward the door, Alasdair made no attempt to stop her. That was because the words he heard her muttering softly beneath her breath as she crossed the threshold froze him in place.

"A wife is dutiful," she grumbled irritably. " 'Tis sure I am that, with a wee bit of practice, I can learn to be dutiful. I'll consider this me first lesson. This mon who is to be me husband wants me to think of the bairn. 'Tis a stupid request, but the mon be a Gray after all. So think of the bairn I shall. 'Tis not a difficult request to honor, I suppose, though I fail to see what me new baby sister has to do with aught . . ."

She was too far into the keep for him to hear the rest of what she said. He thought that was probably for the best.

"Duncan!" Alasdair bellowed as he turned and descended the stairs. He stopped at the bottom, his steely gaze scanning the area, only to discover what Vanessa herself had just seconds before. Unlike Vanessa, however, Alasdair stalked the snowy footprints leading toward the corner of his keep like a wolf hunting down his weak, defenseless prey.

Weak.

Defenseless.

He grinned. If Duncan Forster, that conniving little cur, wasn't already, he would be *both* once Alasdair Gray was done with him!

Chapter Twenty-three

Without a doubt, this time had to rank amongst the worst five minutes of Vanessa's life.

Being discovered by her father on the Day of Truce last year had been the first; Hugh Forster had seen fit to deliver instant punishment to his two miscreant children by walloping both her and Duncan's bottoms. Publicly. In front of five hundred of the fiercest reivers in both Scotland and England.

The second had been her humiliation at having been locked inside Alasdair Gray's vault all those weeks ago. The shame of that one, of being caught without so much as a harsh word passing — let alone a drawn sword! — still chaffed her pride.

This, however, surpassed those moments.

'Twas difficult enough to come back to Cavnearal in the first place, and more difficult still to come back as The Devil's imminent bride. Ooch, and an *agreeable* bride at that! 'Twas doubly hard to enter her intended's keep . . . alone . . . and come face-to-face with a hall filled almost to overflowing with Sassenaches — all of whom had stopped what they were doing to turn and gape at Vanessa as she stood paused in the stone archway.

She squared her shoulders, and through sheer force of will, kept her gaze even and steady. How, she did not know, but she did it. She was a Forster.

The pride in question was put to the test when one of

the guards stood, lavished a vivid curse on her impeccable Scot's ancestry, then stomped from the hall.

Alas, the man was not alone.

Vanessa's pride, as well as her resolve, was tested even further as, one by one, the majority of the guards who'd gathered in the hall for the midday meal cursed in a similar fashion shoved their trenchers aside, stood, and stalked not only outside of the hall, but outside of the keep.

One of them, she recognized as the man who'd first been appointed to guard her, back when she was Alasdair's pledge — or so she'd thought at the time. It was the silent one. Oric, she thought his name was. Vanessa might not have noticed him at all had he not gone out of his way to make sure his elbow whacked solidly against her left shoulder as he passed by.

Apparently cold wind and snow were more favorable company than a Scot, for at the end of five minutes, the only people left in the hall besides herself were a half dozen serving wenches who were trying their best to ignore her as they began clearing the tables of half-touched trenchers of food, and Avery Harrington, the young guard who'd patiently tried to teach her how to play chess.

Vanessa's attention fixed on the latter, but not harshly. Was it his fault that the rest of Alasdair's men had gone to such great lengths to make her feel unwelcome? Nay, 'twas not.

For whatever reason, Avery had remained, and for that she was grateful. She bestowed upon him her most charming smile as, her carriage still painfully straight and proud, she advanced into the hall with her chin high, and her shoulders set as though a fancy farthingale gown draped from them, instead of a baggy tunic and jack. In other words, as though nothing out the ordinary had occurred.

She sat herself on the bench across the chipped table-top from him. "The men will be having a most jolly

421

time laughing at yer expense this night, methinks."

Avery nodded graciously. "I don't doubt it. But my reputation is such that, in time, I think I can live the scandal down."

Vanessa curled her fingers around the handle of the nearest tankard, claiming it before the wench who was cleaning this particular table could whisk it away. Before Vanessa took her first sip, she knew from the scent that the brew was ale. And a good quality of it at that! It tasted rich and yeasty on her tongue. Quite good. Mayhap these thick-skulled Sassenaches could do something well after all?

"So, ye've a reputation, do ye?" she said as she set the mug down, and regarded the young man levelly. " 'Twould make us two of a kind then, methinks, for I've quite a reputation of me own."

"Aye, so I've noticed." With a tilt of his blond head, he indicated the virtually empty hall. "You can clear a room like no other, I'll wager."

Vanessa cringed on the inside, where her most recent humiliation, at the hands of Alasdair's men, was still raw. Her fingers tightened around the mug handle, and her green eyes narrowed warily.

Those were her only two outward signs of emotion, but the young man had obviously detected one of them. His cheeks pinkened with embarrassment. "I'm sorry, I meant no offense. Truly."

She hesitated, then, finally, nodded. The young man's words had been spoken so sincerely that she could do naught but believe him. As a distraction, she took another, longer sip of the flavorful ale. Ooch! but wasn't the brew tasty.

"Might I ask why you did it?"

Her gaze had wandered. It now snapped back to him. "Did what?"

"Tolerated their"—he nodded curtly to the doorway—"degradation. Why did you not simply turn and leave. No one would have been surprised if you had.

And 'twould have been a sore lot easier for you, aye?"

"Mayhap for the moment it would have, but eventually, such a reaction would serve only to make things maun harder." Vanessa shook her head, and took another sip of the oh so tasty ale before adding, "Think on it. How can I make me husband's men accept me if I keep turning and walking away from them?"

Exactly what reaction Vanessa expected, she was unsure. Certainly, it was not the one she got.

Avery had been in the process of taking a sip from his own tankard. Her words caused him to choke in mid-swallow.

Two tables down, a serving wench dropped her tray; it clattered noisily to the table. The wench stared at Vanessa, blinked hard, then hurried over to a girl who was cleaning another table and whispered excitedly in her ear. The second girl, after staring at the first in stunned amusement, dropped her tray and, in turn, hurried over to yet another table and another serving wench.

Vanessa watched this strange process unfold thrice in the time it took Avery to stop coughing long enough to speak.

The young man's voice came out as a strangled croak. "Your *husband,* did you say?"

"Aye," Vanessa replied in the low, patient tone she usually reserved for her youngest sister. Nay, that was her *second* youngest sister now, wasn't it? With the wee one's arrival this morn, Kayla was no longer the bairn of the family. "Why are ye looking at me that way, mon?"

"Y-you said *husband.*"

"I know what I said. What of it?"

He shook his head as though there was something important he should understand by now, but didn't. "And . . . wait. You were referring to The Devil, were you not?"

Even his men called him that? She was surprised.

423

Still, Vanessa nodded slowly, wondering what the man was getting at. She supposed he would tell her in due time. Meanwhile . . .

From the corner of her eye, she noticed that all six of the serving wenches had set to cleaning the table directly behind Avery. They were going about the chore silently, but with a vengeance.

Avery shifted position so that he was now leaning forward, with both elbows braced atop the table. "Mind you, mistress, I mean no offense, but I've a strong desire to ask you something."

"All right," Vanessa said warily, when it was apparent he was awaiting her consent before asking his question. Again, she looked briefly at the table behind him. The wenches were no longer cleaning, but instead seemed to be taking great pains in how they stacked each trencher upon their individual trays. How very strange.

"When did you ask The Devil to wed yo—?" Nay, that didn't sound right. Avery hesitated, pursed his lips, and swiftly reworded the question. "What I mean to say is, does m'lord know of your plans to . . . er, wed?"

The voice that answered did not come from Vanessa, but from behind her.

"Of course he does, you bloody dolt! How do you think she came by the idea in the first place?!"

Two of the serving girls dropped their trays—again—while a third caught hers barely in time to stop it from crashing to the floor. Eight pairs of eyes snapped toward the doorway, for, while that booming voice may have come from Vanessa's side of the hall, it had not come from Vanessa's side of the table.

A chord of familiarity warmed Vanessa's veins, even as did a surge of irritation. Must the man shout so loudly that those in the next country could hear him equally as clearly as she did?! She decided that as soon as they were wed, that was the first of his traits she would work to change. Gently, of course, but change it she most certainly would. If it killed her. She refused to live with a man whose normal tone of voice could be heard by deaf people, by God!

If it killed her. Vanessa regretted the thought the instant she turned around to see a furious Alasdair Gray framed in the arched stone doorway. With one hand, he was holding up a very nervous, and slightly bruised-looking Duncan.

Her brother's feet, she noticed, dangled a good six inches above the floor. And, as his eyes sought out and found hers, Duncan's cheeks turned an alarming shade of reddish-blue . . . whether from lack of air or acute fright, she couldn't say.

What Vanessa *could* say was something about her future husband's mistreatment of her brother. She'd quite a few, very choice words to say about *that!* She was not, however, going to lower herself to bellowing them at the top of her lungs like some ranting, thick-skulled Sassenach.

Vanessa took a long, deep drink from her tankard, then set the mug aside. Very calmly, she stood and lifted her legs over the bench. The click of her boot heels against stone as she approached Alasdair sounded unnaturally loud in the otherwise tension-filled silence.

She stopped only when the toes of her boots grazed the toes of his. Looking eye-level, her gaze came only to the hollow beneath Alasdair's shoulder. Vanessa was not intimidated. Slowly, her eyes traced their way up, over his neck, past the hard set of his whisker-shadowed jaw, past the pinched line of a mouth that had, only hours ago, kissed her breathless, then the regal bridge of his nose. Finally, her furious green gaze ensnared his eyes.

"Ye've ordered me never to slap ye," she said, and though her tone was calm, her accent was thick and each word was spat from between gritted teeth. "Because me mum taught me that a wife should please her husband in all ways, I'll abide by yer wishes and no' slap ye, the way I wish so badly tae do. Instead, I will issue ye a warning o' me own. If ye dinna release me brother *this instant,* I'll be forced tae wound ye in a way I was taught maun early could wound a mon's . . . er, *pride* the most."

Usually, a good loud shout relieved Alasdair's anger. But not this time. First it was the brother's lies, now the sister's threats. Truly, he'd stomached more than enough insolence from these arrogant Forsters. His patience was at an end!

Alasdair leaned menacingly forward. Then, in roar to end all roars, he bellowed, "Out! Both of you! I want Cavnearal rid of all things arrogant and Scot, and I want it rid of them *now!*"

If he was expecting a tirade, he was disappointed. The wench did not yell back at him. Instead, she met the intensity of his gaze head on, more boldly than any man would have dared, and very calmly, very *politely,* replied, "The pleasure will be all mine, ye thick-skulled Sassenach bastard. But first, ye maun let me brother go."

He did. Quite abruptly, in fact. His fingers simply uncurled from around the fistful he held of Duncan's tunic, and he let the boy drop.

Duncan hit the stone with a grunt and a curse.

In a beat, Vanessa was kneeling at his side, and glaring hotly up at Alasdair. He glared just as hotly back.

For the second time in almost as many minutes, yet another uninvited voice intruded upon the medley. This one was feline-sly and cold as ice.

"I suggest you take my brother's advice," Marette Gray said as she stepped to Alasdair's side, and glared haughtily down her nose at Vanessa and Duncan. "As you've no doubt learned by now, Gray men are not known for their patience. Nor," she added with an icy grin, "are their women. I'm of a mind that if Alasdair does not toss you out of this keep, I'll be forced to take it upon myself to do so. Somehow, I doubt either of you would like the way I went about it."

Ignoring the spiteful wench, as well as her words,

Vanessa directed her attention to Duncan. He winced as she gently fingered the fresh purple bruise swelling on his jaw. Another marred the boyish curve of his cheek, but the latter looked not to be quite so nasty.

She turned accusing eyes to Alasdair. "Ye hit me brother," she snapped, unmindful of the fact that the statement, because of Duncan's obvious bruises, was rhetorical. "I'll no' marry a mon who uses his fists to argue with a defenseless lad. Such a mon be no mon at all. Methinks 'tis right the Forsters have fought ye Grays for centuries, if yer ancestors behaved as barbarically as ye have this day, Devil."

Her attention returned to Duncan, and she helped the lad to his feet. While his stance was shaky, the boy nevertheless tilted his chin with Forster pride and brushed away her assistance once he was on his feet. "Come on, lass, we'll not stay another minute where our company be not wanted."

Vanessa nodded in agreement as she stood at her brother's side. Silent and proud, the two exited the hall.

"Vanessa."

She halted in the act of opening the thick oak door leading outside. She'd half a mind to pretend she'd not heard Alasdair call out her name. Oh, if only she could!

"What?" she said stiffly, and her heart raced when she wondered if Alasdair was going to call her back and apologize for his harshness to both her and Duncan. And if he did, how would she react? But she wasn't given the chance to find out, which was probably for the best; she wasn't at all sure her pride could withstand another of The Devil's trouncings.

"Go to the stables and take one of my horses," Alasdair said stiffly. "And before you return to Dunnaclard, remember to ask your brother about the babe."

'Twas a most strange request, but then, it had been issued by a Gray, and therefore wasn't supposed to make sense. What made even less sense was the way

Duncan blanched. She would query her brother about that later, but first . . .

She turned around slowly, her angry green eyes burning right into Alasdair. "I shall leave this keep the way I originally entered it," she replied, her chin high, her voice edged with pride. "With naught but the clothes on me back . . . and me sword."

Alasdair nodded to Avery, who stood abruptly and rushed from the hall. Vanessa paid the young guard no mind. Alasdair was staring at her and staring at her hard, and she was returning his gaze with equal force. 'Twas about time the man discovered the true grit of a Forster; she steadfastly refused to be the first to look away.

Avery returned posthaste, and pressed the small, light broadsword that Alasdair had absconded from her weeks ago into her hands.

Vanessa's fingers curled around the leather-wrapped hilt, the muscles in her arms automatically conforming to the weapon's familiar weight. The nod of thanks she bestowed upon Alasdair was cold and condescending in the extreme. She waited until she was sure he knew that, then turned, slipped her hand into the crook of her brother's arm, and together the two Forsters walked with silent dignity out of Cavnearal.

The sound of the door closing behind them cut through Alasdair like a sharply honed dagger. His first instinct was to call Vanessa back. He didn't, of course, but he found the urge hard to stifle.

It made no sense. Ever since Hugh Forster had pledged himself instead of pay the fine, Alasdair had wanted naught but for his keep to be free of annoying Forsters. It seemed like the more devoutly he'd wanted that, the more Forsters he'd ended up housing.

Now, finally, he had his wish. Not a single Forster remained within Cavnearal's walls. He should be happy

428

about that. Ecstatic. So why wasn't he? Why, now that he had what he wanted most, did he not seem to want it anymore?

He was damned if he knew. Dragging his fingers through his hair, his gaze fixed on one of the long windows carved into the far end of the hall. The snow was coming down hard, and the grayness of the sky promised it would come down harder still before this, the first good snowfall of winter, was finished.

Damn it! Why had he let Vanessa and Duncan anger him to the point where he'd ordered both out into such dreadful weather?! Truly, Vanessa could arouse his ire like no other. To the point where all logical thought abandoned him. It wasn't at all like him to allow a woman to get under his skin so, but the fact remained, she did.

"Alasdair . . ." Marette said cautiously, correctly interpreting the emotion that etched her brother's expression. "Don't do it. Let them go, and consider yourself well rid of them."

While he didn't acknowledge his sister's words, they gnawed at Alasdair on the inside. She was right. He should let them go. Truly, he should not even care if the pair made it back to Dunnaclard alive, or if the storm took its toll by taking their lives. He should *not* care.

But he *did*.

"Alasdair . . ." Marette repeated, and this time a tinge of selfish concern crept into her voice.

Alasdair silenced his sister with a quick, piercing glare. "Shut up, Marette. For once in your life, just . . . shut . . . up!"

He took a step forward, toward the door, and hesitated when he felt his sister's hand on his upper arm. Her grip was desperate, her fingers biting through the thickly padded jack and the sleeve of the tunic beneath, biting into his skin.

He shook her clinging hand off with such force that Marette felt the vibration all the way up to her shoulder. She gasped in surprise, but the sound was muffled by Alasdair's steps as he strode determinedly toward the front door.

Marette's eyes narrowed to catlike slits, and her lips thinned with fury. The bloody fool was actually going after them! She couldn't believe it! She shook her head, her nostrils flaring with anger. This would not do. Something was going to have to be done if her brother brought those heathens back into this keep.

Something desperate.

Something permanent.

'Twould seem she was the only one left in Cavnearal with the good sense and nerve to correct this most *in*-correct situation. And do it, she would. Without hesitation.

Marette Gray had not entered the hall unprepared. Her gaze riveted to the door that her brother had just slammed out of, she casually slipped her hand into the pocket on the side of her skirt.

A sinister grin curled over her lips when her fingertips brushed a cold metal blade that was as hard and as sharp as her resolve.

Chapter Twenty-four

Duncan stopped on the bottom step, and glanced down at his sister. The snow was falling hard now; already her short, dark hair was dusted with flakes. More beaded her thick lashes, and her brow and cheeks were wet from the fluffy white flakes that had clung to her skin and melted almost on contact. Her cheeks were red from cold, yet they'd been outside less than a minute.

It would take at least six hours, with luck, to walk back to Dunnaclard. While he knew his sister's pride was as strong as her slender but firm body, the fact was, the weather wasn't going to improve anytime soon, and he was about to lead her into the brunt of what promised to be a punishing storm. And for what purpose? To save his own pride? Somehow, the expense did not justify the cause.

"There's something I maun tell ye, Vanessa," he said finally, reluctantly.

"Tell me later."

"Nay, I'll tell ye now."

She sighed impatiently. "Duncan, in case ye've not noticed, 'tis snowing fiercely. We've a good distance to cover this day if we're to reach Dunnaclard by—"

"We aren't going to reach Dunnaclard, Sister. Indeed, we are not going to leave Cavneareal at all. Not in this weather, and certainly not for this reason."

She was sure she'd misheard the lad. Hadn't she? His resigned expression told her that, nay, she had not.

"I . . ." Duncan sighed, and shuffled his booted feet in

431

the snow that was swiftly accumulating upon the stair on which they stood. "I've a confession to make."

"Duncan, dinna fash yeself over it. Whatever it is, surely it can wait until — ?"

"Nay, Vanessa, it canna."

She'd a sneaking suspicion that the red blotches staining her brother's cheeks had not been put there by the bitter cold wind that was stinging her own cheeks and tossing her dark curls about her face. "Make yer confession and be done with, then. I be getting cold."

Duncan nodded, and his gaze dipped to the toe of his boots, which he studied with unnatural concentration. His voice took on a shaky, self-deprecating timbre. "I've lied."

"Ye have?"

"Aye."

"To me?"

He hesitated, then shook his head. Flakes of snow rained from his dark hair, dusting his lean, jack-clad shoulders. "To The Devil."

"Ye dinna not need me to tell ye that be not a safe thing to do, Brother."

"Nay," Duncan agreed, and winced when he absently fingered first the bruise that swelled on his jaw, then the smaller one that marred his cheekbone. "I discovered that on me own."

"I can see that. Now, if that be all . . . ?"

Again, he shook his head.

Vanessa struggled to swallow an impatient sigh. She only partially succeeded. Why did the lad feel confessions need be made now, when she was half covered in snow, and chilled to the bone despite the thickness of her attire?!

Then a most disturbing idea struck her, and she frowned as Alasdair's parting words sliced through her memory. Vanessa wasn't sure *how* she knew what her brother had done, the lie he had told, she just did. Why hadn't she figured it out before, when it seemed so obvious to her now?!

She glared at Duncan, and then, when she saw movement from the corner of her eye, glared at Alasdair. He was standing on the top step, staring down at them. He was without benefit of a jack to protect him from the storm, she noticed, yet he seemed not the least bit cold, even when the brisk wind whipped at his tunic and hair, and tossed snow all about him.

Slowly, she ascended the stairs, stopping one from the top. Angling her chin, she swiped back from her eyes the hair that the wind insisted upon tossing there. This time, knowing what she did, Vanessa found it a wee bit difficult to return his gaze as directly as before. Ignoring the pain the words caused, she said flatly, "Ye wished only to marry me because ye thought I was carrying yer bairn. Is that not correct, Devil?"

"Yes . . . no. *Damn it!*" Alasdair sucked in a deep lungful of the crisp, cold air. He released the breath slowly through his teeth; it poured into the air in a thick, vaporous stream. " 'Twas my initial reason, I confess. 'Tis not, however, my reason now."

Vanessa's heart skipped a beat, but she staunchly doused the spark of hope his words kindled inside her. "Meaning?"

Her heart ached with every tension-thick second it took for him to answer. And there were quite a few.

"Meaning," he said finally, sincerely, "that I'm still of a mind that a union between us would be mutually beneficial."

"To end the feud," she said, supplying the reason that he, for whatever reason, had not.

She was offering him a perfect, logical excuse. Alasdair knew he'd be a fool not to take it. And yet, that was all it was, an excuse, and he knew it. "Nay, Vanessa," he sighed. "Although, as I've told you often, I'd like nothing better than to see peace between our families, that has naught to do with why I want to . . . why I think we should . . ."

"Wed?"

"Aye," he agreed, obviously thankful she had supplied

the word, which saved him from having to say it.

Her lashes were wet from melted snow. Vanessa dried them with the heels of her hand, then glanced up at Alasdair. "Why?"

"Why what?"

"Why do ye wish to wed me, if not to stop the feud?"

His answer was a long time in coming.

While she waited for it, Alasdair nodded to Duncan, who ascended the stairs and disappeared into the warm, dry keep. He did not close the door behind him, and in the ensuing silence, Vanessa thought she heard Kirsta Gray's raised voice, followed quickly by her brother's, coming from the direction of the hall. She paid the argument—which, from the sounds, was quickly escalating—no mind. Grays and Forsters seemed destined to fight in one form or another!

Alasdair heard the racket as well, but he also chose to ignore it, having reached the same conclusion as Vanessa.

Why did he wish to wed this woman? Lord, but that was a good question. And a scary one! The answer touched upon emotions Alasdair did not want to feel for *any* woman. Emotions he nevertheless felt, down to the very core of his soul, for *this* woman, and this woman *alone*.

His gaze dipped as his mind struggled to form the words his tongue was reluctant to utter. His attention fixed on Vanessa's softly parted lips. A delicate flake of snow clung to the shell-pink flesh; the muscles in his stomach convulsed as he watched it melt, until it was naught more than an enticing drop of moisture.

Alasdair groaned low and deep in his throat. While he knew he should not, there were some things that a man simply could not resist. For him, kissing Vanessa Forster—right here, right now, hard—was one of them. Mayhap he could not tell her with words, but his body was adept at speaking the feelings he harbored for this wench. Indeed, his body ached to express them most fully!

Vanessa knew what Alasdair was going to do. She could have stopped him; there was ample time before his lips slanted over hers. She did not . . . for the simple reason that she did not *want* to.

The kiss was long and deep and draining. For both of them. When it ended, it was unclear which of them was supporting the other, for both were left weak-kneed and panting, their bodies clinging to each other for support.

Alasdair took a few seconds to catch his breath. Then he drew back and cupped Vanessa's cheeks in his palms. Her skin felt both hot and cold against his . . . and so very soft, so very wonderful. He pressed his forehead lightly to hers, and his eyes darkened to a shade of smoldering midnight blue.

"I love you, Vanessa," he said, and was not a little surprised to discover that the words he'd had so much difficulty expressing moments before now slipped off his tongue with ease. "While I may not have known it at the time, I think I fell in love with you when"—he grinned devilishly—"aye, when you tumbled me to the floor of my own vault and bit my hand."

Vanessa froze. She was afraid to blink, afraid to breathe, afraid to move. She did not want to do anything that would shatter the frail intimacy of this moment. Her lips still burned from his kiss, while at the same time her mind burned from his confession.

Alasdair Gray loved her!

His words warmed her, deep down, in a way a fire blazing in a hearth could never do. They heated her soul, making the chilly wind feel suddenly not so chilly, the snow that had moistened her hair and dampened her face and blurred her gaze naught but a mere inconvenience.

"Vanessa?" he said when she continued to stare, glassy-eyed, up at him. Not a single emotion could be read in either her gaze or her expression. That troubled Alasdair. Mayhap he'd misjudged the wench? Mayhap his ardor was not returned? He gulped. The idea was wounding in the extreme, but could not be dismissed.

"Say something, Vanessa," he urged. "Please."

She didn't. Couldn't. She would need a voice for that, and hers was trapped along with the wedge of emotion that had clogged in her throat. Instead, she smiled. Only a wee bit at first, and a bit hesitantly . . . then, when she saw a vast measure of relief flicker in his beautiful eyes, her smile broadened until she was fairly beaming.

At first Vanessa blamed the sting of moisture blurring her gaze on the wind aggravating her eyes, but she quickly recognized it for the lie it was. She was crying and, oddly enough, she found she didn't really care this time.

Standing on tiptoe, she threw her arms about Alasdair's neck and dragged his mouth down to hers. This time it was *she* who kissed *him*, and kissed him most soundly indeed!

"Devil! Look out behind ye!"

So lost were they in the passionate kiss that, had Duncan not shouted the warning, neither would have had any indication of impending danger until it was too late.

Vanessa's eyes snapped open. Since she was the one facing the door, it was she who saw Marette Gray advancing behind Alasdair. The woman's arm was raised, and a streak of muted sunlight glinted off the long, deadly blade of the dagger she clenched tightly in her fist.

There was no time to think, only to react. Bunching her hands into white-knuckled fists, Vanessa braced each against Alasdair's suddenly stiff shoulders, and shoved with all her might. He staggered back a single, surprised step. It was enough.

Marette cried out her fury, even as the dagger arched downward with lightning speed.

Duncan rushed from the doorway, intent on stopping Marette, with Kirsta close on his heels. It was clear from the distance, however, that he'd be unable to reach Marette in time; it was also clear from his expression that he was going to try to anyway.

Alasdair spun on his heel, just in time to see the steely blade pass whisper-close to his shoulder. Trained for battle, his arm came up automatically, delivering a bone-shattering blow to his sister's forearm, which effectively unbalanced her aim.

Unfortunately, he did not unbalance it enough.

Marette grunted in pain, but she was not to be stopped. Using momentum to her advantage, she diverted the blade back on target. Almost.

Instead of sinking it into the filthy little heathen's heart, the way she wanted so badly to do, the dagger was instead buried to the hilt two inches beneath Vanessa's left shoulder.

"No!" The word tore from Alasdair, as though it was his flesh the knife had penetrated, not Vanessa's. Indeed, the pain that cut through him made it seem as though it had been. His arm came up for a backhanded blow, and the back of his fist connected solidly with Marette's jaw. He heard bone snap and, heaven help him, Alasdair hoped to God he'd somehow managed to kill the bitch.

Marette was sent flying backward down the stairs. Her wrist slammed against a corner of the stone stair, and the knife went flying from her hand, landing in the snow far out of harm's reach. Her back made a teeth-jarring collision with the hard, snow-covered ground.

She was still conscious, staring hatefully up at him. Alasdair sneered, and descended one step, his murderous gaze fixed on his sister, his intent to remedy that situation.

Two things stopped him. The first was the fingers that Duncan Forster coiled with surprising strength around Alasdair's upper arm. The second was Vanessa's moan, low and husky and heartrending.

His gaze shifted, scanning the faces of the men who'd been drawn toward the keep's entrance by the commotion. Their expressions seemed to echo the sentiment that, Gray or no, there was naught to be proud of in attacking an adversary's back. Alasdair guessed there to be six or seven score, with still more drifting over to see what the fuss was about. Their expressions were sober, their gazes harshly accusing as more men than not glared at the crumpled form of the now-sobbing Marette.

Alasdair addressed the biggest and strongest of the lot. That man was Oric. "I want this"—his lips pinched over the word—"*woman* removed from Cavnearal, and I want it done now," he growled at Oric.

Oric nodded, straightened his big body . . . and answered with a soft lisp. "Aye, m'lord. Where do ye withsh for me to thend her?"

"I care not, nor do I care what you do to her on the way. I want only to never set eyes on her again."

"Ath ye thay, m'lord,"

"Alasdair, nay!" Marette cried out, her voice garbled and barely discernible from her fractured jaw. "Y-ye cannot do this to me. I am your sister!"

"Nay," he sneered furiously, "you are not. No sister of mine would do what you just did." His eyes raked her crumpled form dispassionately. "Consider yourself lucky I'm allowing you to leave Cavnearal with your life, Marette, for my first inclination was not so generous."

He gestured for Oric to take the woman way, and was glad when the guard did so posthaste. Truly, if he had to look at Marette for one more minute, he wasn't entirely sure he could refrain from strangling her with his bare hands.

Alasdair spun on his heel, and his breath caught painfully in his throat at the sight that greeted him.

Vanessa was lying upon the snowswept landing, her dark head cushioned atop her brother's lap. Tears streamed down Duncan's face as he stroked her brow with shaking fingers and whispered soothingly to her in Gaelic. Kirsta knelt beside the boy, and Alasdair was shocked to see that his frail little sister was pressing her palm hard against Vanessa's wounded shoulder in a feeble attempt to staunch the flow of blood.

In his life, Alasdair had seen much bloodshed. Indeed, he'd even spilled quite a bit of it himself. Reiving was, and always had been, dangerous business. Men were often killed or wounded in either a raid or a reciprocal hot or cold trod.

Yet never had the sight of crimson-streaked snow brought a watery sting to his eyes the way it did now. Nor had it ever caused fear to claw coldly at his heart, as it did when his gaze shifted to Vanessa's pale face. His voice husky beyond belief, he said, "Is she . . . ?"

Duncan shook his head. "Nay."

"Thank God," Alasdair sighed, and only then did his feet obey his command to move. His steps felt leaden as he approached the trio, and hunkered down next to Vanessa. He reached out to touch her—but at the last moment, found he could not. He lowered his hand, pillowing his palm atop the rock-hard shelf of his thigh, and stared in mute shock at the drop of moisture that splashed onto the back of it.

It was a tear. *His* tear.

"We need to get her inside," Kirsta said, and while the words were most sensible, Alasdair couldn't help but notice the way his sister's soft voice trembled over them.

He nodded and, leaning forward, slipped one arm beneath Vanessa's knees, the other beneath her back. She groaned when he lifted her. Alasdair winced, swearing again that he could feel her pain as if it was his own.

She opened her eyes as he was crossing the threshold, and he glanced down into green eyes that were glazed from pain.

"Alasdair?" she said weakly.

"Aye, kitten?" His voice cracked with emotion; he didn't try to hide that. Why bother, when the tear that streamed down his cheek, and splashed warmly onto hers, spoke for itself?

Her wounded shoulder was next to his chest, and a goodly portion of his tunic was already warm and sticky with her blood.

He inhaled sharply when she reached up with the other hand, and wiped the salty path of his tear away with the pad of her index finger. "Why are ye crying?"

They were halfway up the steps; he was taking them two at a time, but at a slow enough pace to cause her the least amount of pain. Concentrating on putting one booted foot in front of the other, he said throatily, "I've lost one wife already, Vanessa. I won't lose another."

"Ah, ye be a cocky one." Though she tried to keep her tone light, it was evident she was in a good deal of pain. "In case ye've not noticed, I've not agreed to marry ye."

"Yet. But you will." He reached the landing, and turned down the corridor leading toward his bedchamber. Many nights he'd dreamed of seeing this woman in his bed again, but not even in his worst nightmare had imagined the reason would be *this*. And then another thought struck him, and he glanced worriedly down at her. "Won't you?"

"What do ye think, Devil?"

"When you're around? I think of you. When you're not around . . . I think of you." He applied the sole of his boot to the door of his bedchamber, and in that manner sent it crashing open. "You consume my thoughts, wench. Have you not figured that out by now?"

"Aye."

"Aye?" he asked as he laid her gently on the bed. Alasdair was aware of Kirsta and Duncan's presence in the room, but only vaguely. "Aye, you've figured it out?"

She shook her head, and gasped at the pain that shot like lightning through her shoulder. "Nay," she said, once the burning edge to the pain had dulled a wee bit. "Even though ye be a cursed Gray, not to mention the most thick-skulled Sassenach I've ever had the misfortune to meet, I'll forgive ye on both counts and . . . aye, I'll marry ye anyway."

He was afraid to sit atop the bed for fear of jarring her. Instead, he arched over it, cupped her pale cheek in his palm, and brushed his lips against hers. "If you live, I'll hold you to that promise, wench," he rasped against her mouth.

"I'd expect nothing less. Just remember . . . a Forster's word *always* be good." He opened his mouth, but Vanessa silenced his reply with the finger she slanted over his lips. "Remember, too, that I love ye, Devil."

Alasdair absorbed those softly uttered words right into his soul. It took a full minute before he felt composed enough to speak, and even then, his voice was still shaky with emotion as, against her lips, he whispered, "If it takes a near mortal wound for you to tell me you love me, wench, then I think I can live happily having heard the words but once."

"Begging your pardon, m'lord, but the wound is not mortal," a gritty voice inserted from behind Alasdair. " 'Twould need to be down a good three inches for that. The wench will heal."

Alasdair straightened, and turned toward the speaker.

Peering around him, Vanessa's gaze met and held the older man's. "Ye be Fenn of the bagpipes, are ye not?"

"In the flesh."

Vanessa grinned. Well, as much as she could when it felt as though the upper left side of her body was on fire. "Mayhap I'll convince ye to play a decent Scots melody, instead of those weak Sassenach tunes ye favor, eh?"

"As soon as you're well, mistress, I'd welcome you to try." The man bowed his wispy gray head respectfully, though not before Vanessa saw a shimmer of amusement in his dark-brown eyes. "I'd set about tending your shoulder," he added meaningfully, addressing Alasdair, who stood between him and his patient, "if I could find a way to get to you."

"Wait! Afore ye shoo me future husband away, Fenn, I've a question I'd like for him to be answering."

Alasdair glanced at her from over his shoulder. "Aye?"

Vanessa tried to deliver a stern gaze upon Alasdair, and failed. Between the pain in her shoulder, and the joy in her heart which overshadowed it, 'twas simply not possible. "I'll be knowing why ye dinna tell me exactly *how many* beasties ye stole from me clan. Thanks to ye, there'll be a fine muckle of Forsters who go hungry this winter. Why, ye greedy, thick-skulled Sassenach oaf! How dare ye . . ."

Alasdair smiled. He'd ceased to hear what she said, while instead he simply enjoyed letting the soft timbre of her voice pour over him. Nothing had ever sounded so good! It meant she was alive.

His grin broadened, and never slipped so much as once . . . even when, as it turned out, Vanessa's lecture carried all the way through Fenn's tending of her wound — though she did pause to gasp every now and again — and the bandaging thereof.

Epilogue

Tynesdale, English East March, on the Border
October 1585

"Last, you are charged with . . ." Robert Carey frowned as, thrice, he read and *re*read the final entry in what had amounted to an astonishingly long list of charges filed against Alasdair Gray. "It says here you're charged with *returning* two hundred sheep to their rightful owner, Hugh Forster of the Clan Forster. Of course, that can't be right."

" 'Tis right," Alasdair said.

" 'Tis'?" Robert queried.

" 'Tis," Hugh Forster insisted.

Robert wasn't precisely sure how to handle a situation like this, since in all his years as East English March Warden no one had every lodged a bill complaining about beasties being *returned*. In the end, he decided to handle it the only way he knew how. He put the required question to Alasdair Gray. "This is the charge that has been filed against you. How say you?"

For the first time all day, a hint of a grin tugged at one corner of Alasdair's mouth. "I say that any man who complains of having goods returned does not deserve to have said goods in the first place."

That comment created a stir in both English and Scot. The violence that had been suppressed all day behind tight glances and even tighter words was threatening to come to a head. Robert could feel it and, at the same time, sought to divert it. His attention shifted to

443

Hugh, whose furious green eyes indicated the man was less than pleased to have The Devil cheat him out of the satisfaction he'd come to the Day of Truce to attain.

In a voice that was too calm to be anything but practiced, Robert said, "In this one matter, I find in favor of Alasdair Gray. Since he's fouled the rest of the bills by confession, however, I've no choice but to find in favor of Hugh Forster to all prior." A tension-riddled silence fell over the gathering as Robert's attention turned back to Alasdair. "Have you any idea how great is the fine you now owe to the Clan Forster?"

"I know not the exact sum," Alasdair replied evenly, and his casual shrug made Hugh's gaze sharpen on him. "I imagine 'tis more than Cavnearal could pay in at least half a score . . . mayhap more."

"Then you are offering a pledge?"

While Alasdair's nod was meant to answer Carey's question, his challenging gaze never once left Hugh Forster's. "I am."

"Though I'm sure I'll regret this," Robert said on a bone-weary sigh, " 'tis my job to ask. What is the name of the pledge you are offering?"

Alasdair declined answering. Instead, he glanced to the left . . . and smiled at his wife.

Vanessa stood at the foot of the crowd, an equal distance between the two camps. Both English and Scot were so accustomed to her now that neither found her presence odd or intrusive. Perhaps traditions were finally changing on these violent, tumultuous Borders?

Her chin tipped proudly, she walked slowly toward her father. Except for his hair being streaked with yet more gray, she thought Hugh Forster looked much the same as he had when she'd last seen him, almost a year prior.

Vanessa stopped directly in front of her father, and her gaze strayed from him to the squirming, blanket-wrapped bundle in her arms. "The pledge being offered," she said calmly, evenly, "is Jonathan Forster Gray, the accuser's grandson."

While she spoke softly but firmly, the silence was so great that even those sitting in the rear heard every word.

Robert Carey had expected almost anything . . . but this. He eyed Hugh Forster, gauging the man's reaction. 'Twas a most amusing sight, one he was sure no other Day of Truce — past, present, or future — would ever equal.

First the Scot's cheeks, above his dark beard, went a ghastly shade of grayish-white. Then, when his gaze dipped to the babe in his daughter's arms, they flooded with color. Twice, Hugh opened his mouth to speak; twice, naught came out.

Vanessa knew the second Alasdair stepped into place behind her. As always happened when he touched her, even innocently, she felt a warm shiver skate down her spine as her husband draped his arm possessively over her shoulder.

Jonathan cooed and gurgled and grinned up at his father, proudly displaying the tiny pearl-white tooth that had broken through his bottom gum just yesterday morn. Vanessa didn't need to glance at Alasdair to know he was grinning back at the bairn. He always did. She didn't doubt her son would soon be spoiled from all the attention Alasdair was wont to lavish upon him.

"Well?" Vanessa said, when her father seemed powerless to do aught but stare down at the smiling bairn in stunned amazement. "What say *ye*, Hugh Forster? Do ye accept this pledge, or do ye demand another?"

"I . . . I — I accept him," Hugh said finally, hoarsely, and Vanessa gently placed her son in her father's extended arms. "But not as a pledge. Nay, lass, I accept the lad as me grandson, and as naught less."

Vanessa released a shaky breath, and felt Alasdair tenderly squeeze her shoulder. The wound there had healed well, as Fenn had promised it would. While she'd a scar, she'd also gained a most cherished husband out of the ordeal. And an equally cherished son.

If the way Hugh Forster was beaming proudly down

at his grandson — whilst murmuring nonsensical words to the babe in Gaelic — was anything to judge by, then 'twould seem the child was destined to succeed in the only matter either of his parents had ever failed at.

With naught more than a single-toothed smile and a few bairnish coos, the wee half-year-old Jonathan Forster Gray brought peace to two families who, for as many centuries, had known none.

FEEL THE FIRE IN CAROL FINCH'S ROMANCES!

BELOVED BETRAYAL (2346, $3.95)

Sabrina Spencer donned a gray wig and veiled hat before blackmailing rugged Ridge Tanner into guiding her to Fort Canby. But the costume soon became her prison—the beauty had fallen head over heels in love!

LOVE'S HIDDEN TREASURE (2980, $4.50)

Shandra d'Evereux felt her heart throb beneath the stolen map she'd hidden in her bodice when Nolan Elliot swept her out onto the veranda. It was hard to concentrate on her mission with that wily rogue around!

MONTANA MOONFIRE (3263, $4.95)

Just as debutante Victoria Flemming-Cassidy was about to marry an oh-so-suitable mate, the towering preacher, Dru Sullivan flung her over his shoulder and headed West! Suddenly, Tori realized she had been given the best present for a bride: a night of passion with a real man!

THUNDER'S TENDER TOUCH (2809, $4.50)

Refined Piper Malone needed bounty-hunter, Vince Logan to recover her swindled inheritance. She thought she could coolly dismiss him after he did the job, but she never counted on the hot flood of desire she felt whenever he was near!